L ᴇɢᴇɴᴅ

Also By Tom Stacey

FICTION
The Brothers M
The Living and the Dying
The Pandemonium
The Twelfth Night of Ramadan
(first published under *nom de plume* Kendal J Peel)
The Worm in the Rose
The Man Who Knew Everything (*first published as*
Deadline)

COLLECTED LONG SHORT STORIES
Bodies and Souls

INDIVIDUALLY PUBLISHED LONG
SHORT STORIES/NOVELLAS
The Same Old Story/The Tether of the Flesh/
Golden Rain/Grief/The Swap/Boredom, Or, The
Yellow Trousers/Mary's Visit/ A Kelpie from Rhum

TRAVEL AND ETHNOLOGY
The Hostile Sun
Summons to Ruwenzori
Peoples of the Earth (20 vols. Deviser and
supervisory editor)
Tribe, The Hidden History of the Mountains
of the Moon

BIOGRAPHY
Thomas Brassey, The Greatest Railway Builder in the
World

CURRENT AFFAIRS
Today's World (Editor)
The Book of the World (deviser and supervisor)
Immigration and Enoch Powell

FOR CHILDREN
The First Dog to be Somebody's Best Friend

SCREENPLAY
Deadline

DECLINE

TOM STACEY

THISTLE
PUBLISHING

For SFAS and DHS
who scarcely knew one another

And he opened his mouth and taught them,
    saying,
'Blessed are the poor in spirit: for theirs is the
    kingdom of...
'Blessed are the meek: for they shall inherit
    the earth.'

PART I

CHAPTER ONE

I write of father and of son.
Here is the son.

He was seventeen, and at Eton, the famous school in England. He was at chapel, which on Sunday mornings was compulsory, unless you were Roman Catholic or Jewish or born into one of the outlandish religions they went in for farther east.

He, Jamie Mainwaring, pronounced M*annering*, had been set an essay entitled 'Does Man Have a Soul?' This troubled him at various levels. First, he was meant to have it in by four p.m. that afternoon when he had an extra tutorial for history specialists with his Modern Tutor, F B Block. It was F B Block who had set the essay. Jamie hadn't yet written a line, and he had no chance of filling five or six sides, the acceptable minimum, by four p.m. if he were to row up the Thames to Queen's Eyot with Anthony and lunch there. It was a two-hour scull each way and already 10.30.

Secondly, it was a ridiculous question still to be asking two thousand years after the birth of Jesus

Christ, and four thousand or so after Abraham. If the answer hadn't yet been established one way or the other by now, it wasn't going to be settled all at once in AD 1984. It was a typical exercise in schoolmastery, getting the boys to show their paces, show *off*, really. The truth of the matter, the conclusion you reached, was neither here nor there. Such a state of affairs seemed to Jamie typical of the civilization in its current decadent phase and nullified it. If the question deserved asking, it deserved answering. He had a good notion to call F B Block's bluff and put down a single word. Yes, or No. For sure enough there *was* an answer, and in the end it could only be Yes, or No.

Now there was a hymn to sing, or if not sing, bellow. *Holy, holy, holy, Lord God Almighty.* If they were still asking a question like that, how did they have the nerve to be herding seven hundred and fifty boys into this enormous mediaeval edifice for compulsory worship?

The tremendous organ swelled and roared. *'Early in the morning, our song shall rise to Thee-ee'.* It was a hymn of hymns, to a God who they knew very well might not exist, or if he did, have no power or willingness to involve himself in his own creation, intrude into sequence of cause and effect, hear the rising song of humankind, let alone their yelps and gasps. It was a con.

Nevertheless Jamie gave it his all, in a howling falsetto, reading the alto line from his hymnbook. A good distance past, three years, three-and-a-half, his treble voice had faltered and then vanished. He could still miss it, the gift of soaring, that sheer sea-mew gift, the embodied joy *soaring*, early in the morning, our song rising to Thee. He was a child then, and half believed, Something, he couldn't tell what exactly. He couldn't soar any longer. Or believe.

How many soul-hours had he spent falling for the con, or pretending to? How could it be that they were still at it, conning the young, the conned conning, all these years, all these centuries? And here was F B Block giving the game away, asking *him*, Have I a soul? – exposing, moreover, the chicanery of the entire system by the fact that although statistically he, Block, was a lot closer to needing to know the answer, he had no sense of urgency about finding out what it was, *Yes*, or No. At fifty, or whatever, and already turning grey, crumbling into wrinkles and discolorations of the skin, Block ought to be lying awake at night screaming, if there was anything in it. If the question was serious.

Yet wasn't it?

Holy holy holy, Lord God Almighty. Any more of the alto would do him a mischief. He took the tenor. He really wapped the tenor.

Pa was a regular churchgoer. It was odd, that. A creature of habit, of course, but a thinking man in his way. Was this soul-delusion a hangover from ages past, like a voice that had never completely broken? Pa, as it were, having acquired in childhood a soul, run up for him by his Victorian nanny, still had it hanging there in his wardrobe. Pa was a more interesting case than F B Block, who in any case would be written out of the story by the end of the year when Jamie would have left the school.

Holy holy holy! All the saints adore Thee/Casting down their golden crowns around the glassy sea-ee. A likely story. And glassy? Would it be glassy? With this tenor part, bang in the middle of his compass, it was like plunging in with the organ naked, and riding with it. If he couldn't soar, he would surge, coming in on the combers in the swell and sea-surge of the organ. He'd not yet had a girl, to his chagrin, but he was sure this singing, this letting go, this massing and letting go into harmony, was some sort of analogy for sex. Surging and overwhelming and triumphant. Maybe if he had a girl on hand, available and willing, preferably Tibby, he wouldn't be inclined to give these hymns such a full treatment.

Tibby had failed to show for tea the day before. It had been one of those half-plans, 'I'll-come-if-I-can', dependent on some expedition of her mother's. Not seeing her had left him with a hollow yearning, and he had dreamed of her – not, in fact, a surging, overwhelming and triumphant dream, but a secret, narrow, exquisite one.

The boys gushed forth from the doors of the great Gothic edifice into the summer sunlight, spilling down the ancient steps and flooding out across School Yard, gouts of boys like blood from a wound.

Descending the worn flags, Jamie's feet slowed. The floor of the Chapel was pitched high – twenty feet or so from the ground – since Henry VI their founder, four and a half centuries ago, intended it as the chancel of a vast cathedral. Did not these mediaeval school buildings and boys' and masters' houses beyond, and even the pavilions and playing fields and squash courts and fives courts, the immemorial Wall and Jordan Brook wending to the Thames, did not the entire community of it hunch and cower about the great Chapel for fear of being snatched away by unbelief? Were they not all myth-bound, ringed by awe and reverence such as the English congenitally must fabricate? This Henry was hopeless as a king: even F B Block would not dissent from that; yet here he was in greeny bronze in the middle of School Yard obscured beneath awe-and-reverence as an old wreck beneath its barnacles.

CHAPTER TWO

Jamie said, 'You just give me four sides' worth of *why*, and I'll then do one side demolishing it. Five sides is plenty. More than enough.'

The willow leaves played above them against the sunlight as little black flames would.

'It's the definition of man,' Anthony replied. 'Soul. What distinguishes him.' Jamie and Anthony, best of friends, were lying back in the grass after a good lunch of cold sausages and cherries and light ale. The old river was right there beyond the willows, scarcely moving. They had pulled their riggers up among the rushes. Anthony added, 'Neanderthal man used to dye the bones of his dead with red ochre.'

'They weren't noted for their intelligence, the Neanderthals. Half ape. It's no recommendation.'

'What?'

'If it was Neanderthal man invented the immortal soul.'

'Listen,' Anthony said. He lifted his headphones off his ears and the first movement of Brahms's violin concerto reached Jamie tinnily across the grasses, strings heaping upon strings and then tumbling, strings over strings. It was midsummer. There were already skylarks. 'That's the soul of man.'

'Music.'

'That he can conceive beauty, the idea of beauty.' Anthony's familiar enthusiasms. 'Transcendent beauty. Love, truth, beauty. "He fathers-forth whose beauty is past change. Praise him."'

Anthony daren't have a thought without a clutter of quotations. 'Quoting treacle doesn't help. I need solid arguments I can get to grips with and pull apart. You suffer from the same disease as my father.'

'Meaning?'

The Brahms tape had clicked to a finish; the larks remained.

'Tags and symbols,' Jamie said. 'Pa takes refuge in tags and symbols. He trots out a line from Saint Augustine. A piece of Latin.'

'Yes?'

'It goes, roughly: If nobody asks me, I know what it's all about. If someone actually insists I explain, the mind's a blank.'

'Quote it. In Latin, preferably. Start off with it. Tie it in with Paul's "Behold, I show you a mystery". That's the beginning of wisdom: the acceptance of the mystery, your cloud of unknowing. The will to pierce that cloud is the activity of the soul, old man.'

On the row downstream, the boys pulled in parallel, stroke for stroke, the running up of their slides as their shoulders met their knees and the click of sculls against their riggers as the blades dipped and rose all in lazy rhythm against the lazy drift of this upper Thames and the negligible clouds in their English watercolour firmament. Both fluent oarsmen, Jamie was the more naturally athletic, Anthony being lank and skinny, and owlish in his circular specs.

This soul business was a grind. Jamie knew he would be late with his essay and F B Block would look at him in his stupid pitying way from under his brows as if to say What-are-we-to-do-about-you-Mainwaring? Anthony had been signally inadequate in briefing him. Love, beauty, mystery – what did poor Anthony know about love? He had yet to be seriously attracted by a nubile – still stuck on his own sex, a dead-end and not at all what nature intended. And this very Anthony had tried to put *him* down. 'The whole subject is beneath you, old man. Yours is not to reason why – not over souls. Your entire life has been mapped out for you already. You're heir apparent.'

'Heir apparent my arse. The Mainwaring Group is a public company, for God's sake, it's not a family sinecure.'

'Come, come, come, Jamie.' (Anthony could sound so *mamby.*) 'Your family's by far the biggest shareholder. You've got no choice in the matter, no choice at all.'

Anthony in a certain light was unendurable. Then so too was life.

Jamie let go of his oars to feather the water, and reaching behind him for his earphones blanked out all thoughts and larks with The Damned. He abandoned his being to the Dionysian frenzy of rock and upped his rate of stroke, duly disconcerting his friend.

'Conventional wisdom,' F B Block was telling his half dozen or so History specialists an hour or two later, 'has it that nineteenth-century industrial Britain was a chronicle of ruthless exploitation and moral irresponsibility. Only on the back of slave labour did this country become the greatest power on earth for three or four generations of man.' He paused to highlight the challenge. 'We go along with that?'

The murmur of dissent gratified F B Block. The dialectic approach always worked with bright boys at university entrance stage. They were gathered in easy chairs in his drawing room, the french windows flung open on the garden. Most of the boys were in their informal clothes – Jamie Mainwaring characteristically still in his crumpled rowing shorts and a jacket thrown over his tee-shirt.

F B Block resumed, 'Every manufacturer is seen as a Josiah Bounderby of Coketown. I suppose someone knows to whom I refer?'

The character was familiar, perhaps from a television serial glimpsed during the holidays. Someone said, 'Wasn't he the odious mill-owner in Dickens's *Hard Times?*'

'Precisely,' F B Block agreed. 'Such men existed in the forties and fifties, undoubtedly. Among mine owners and mill owners especially. But Dickens cheated, of course, like all good novelists. All his life he drew on the industrial murk of his youth. It wasn't his business to give credit to the emerging industrialists of quite another cut –men, I submit, with a genuine belief in the dignity of labour who attempted to create working and living conditions, and educational opportunities too, that lifted living standards and transformed expectations. A new Jerusalem by courtesy of the infernal machine. This was especially true of the newer industries. Carpets, paper, glass, soap, confectionery. Sophisticated steel products. Mainwaring?'

'Yes?'

Jamie Mainwaring's mind, as F B Block guessed, was not fully present. The boy was aware of getting quizzical pity from under F B Block's brows, intended to suggest that if by chance he were admitted to any university of quality, it would only be by a ridiculous misjudgment on the part of the examiners.

'Would I be correct in supposing that you spring from the Victorian industrialist of that name?'

'What name? Oh! Yes.'

F B Block's brows lifted. 'Great-grandfather?'

'Great-great, actually.'

It was Jamie to frown now. Here it was again. How they loved to slot him, they couldn't help themselves, not even Anthony. It was like a third name: James Mainwaring *Group*.

'You have no cause to be ashamed of your forbear, Mainwaring,' F B Block said.

Jamie felt like retorting, 'Who ever might? Who the hell cares who their great-great-grandfather was?' But he daren't rile F B Block, with his essay unwritten and already technically late (he'd rush it off after tea and shove it in his letterbox on the way to the Political Society meeting). Block represented the system: the trick was to get out from under, not to defy.

CHAPTER THREE

Yet it wasn't to be so easy – not so far as the essay was concerned. For when he got back to his room, there was Tibby. One or other of them had confused the day and he wasn't ready for darling Tibby. He had to wind himself down for Tibby: down or up, he couldn't be sure. When he was hectic and angry he frightened her, he knew. Sometimes it seemed to him there was only one kind of person she allowed him to be.

'It's horrible,' she said.

'What?'

'Everything. The music – everything.' Tiny crinkles had gathered on her child's forehead.

Jamie crossed the little room and flicked off The Damned. She didn't share his taste in rock. He snatched up his trumpet from the ottoman and gave a rapid chromatic scale. The girl winced.

'What else?' he demanded.

'The place stinks.'

'What of?'

'You.'

He was still in the tee-shirt he had rowed in. He flapped his elbows in mock distribution of armpit odours. He was in that frame of mind, he couldn't help himself. But he did move to the window and push it wider. Then he turned to lean over the seated girl and give her a tiny kiss on the lips that could be taken as entirely innocent. At this her eyes sparkled and her lips formed the pout she had practised in the mirror. She was wearing a long linen jacket, made for a man, several sizes too big for her, and blue jeans. And a brown trilby hat.

'I shouldn't have come,' she said taking her hat off.

'Yesterday,' he repeated. 'That was your day. You were actually expected then. I got you a beautiful cake. I've still got it, as a matter of fact.'

'And I've bought some brandy-snaps. In that bag.'

The mass of her brown hair was firmly held by a sprung Alice band across the crown of her head, as her school demanded. 'I couldn't have come yesterday anyway,' she said. 'It was a tennis tournament, us versus Heathfield.'

He began to straighten the room, which was a clutter of books, records, tapes, exhausted socks, the rowing blazer, rackets for tennis and squash. Half a wall was occupied by a cloth-covered board filled with photographs and pictures clipped from magazines without discernible rhyme or reason. A Rastafarian with hair like black serpents dominated. On the bureau in the corner lay several sheets of ruled paper on the topmost of which he had written his name and the title of the essay about souls. He gave a tug to the rowing scarf draped across the chair where the girl was sitting. She rolled sideways to let the scarf pull free. Moving behind her he drew the scarf across her body in a sinuous manner like a snake. The scarf proved unexpectedly long.

'What d'you suppose you are doing?' she snapped.

'Tidying the scarf.'

The snake-scarf continued its slithering.

'Tidy's makes as tidy's keeps' he said, 'as the saying goes.'

She glowered at him. 'There's no such saying.'

'Of course there is.'

'There isn't.'

'There is.'

'Isn't.'

She grabbed the tail of the scarf and leapt up. Each tugged fiercely, the scarf stretched and suffered, but she would not let go.

'My very best scarf!' he protested.

Suddenly he twisted, twining himself in the scarf, which imprisoned one arm and with surprising speed brought him right up close to her in the corner, where (she still holding her scarf-end) he made as to kiss her. She dodged him.

Anthony came in, with a cake on a plate, exclaimed 'Oh, sorry,' and turned to withdraw.

Jamie held him. 'Don't go. Tibby has enslaved me. Only you can rescue me.'

Anthony set the cake on the table and put bread slices in the toaster. Jamie, bound, slumped on to the ottoman, declaiming, 'This maiden torments me. She hath stied me in this hard rock. She will not let me kiss her, let alone shaft her.'

'I'll fetch the kettle, then,' said Anthony and left.

'I hate that horrid talk, Jamie,' the girl said. 'If you talk about that sort of thing, I'm going to stop seeing you.'

'I will . . . crumble away to nothing.'

'I don't care.'

The swift change in tone caught him. *I don't care.*

'Darling little Tibby.'

What could he do? She was fifteen, a child. All but a woman in the form of her but within, a child. Whatever he was, he was no child, and hairy. He felt a terrible power over her, a power to defile and destroy only. He was some sort of hero to her – he had learned of this from her slightly awful mother who had let drop with her archly chiding confidentiality, 'You're quite the little hero to Tibby, Jamie, which gives you a responsibility.' Whether it was true or not, he objected to any such hero-role utterly, vehemently. He could not tolerate Tibby's love on such terms. What he needed her love for was the very opposite – to make him sure who he really was, what he was, whether he was anything except bits and pieces ready-made for fitting together, a parents' Upper Class Young Hero Set. With Tibby he wanted to dismantle all the expectations.

He wound the scarf round his head in a hopeless turban and put on a clown's grin. Then back came Anthony with the kettle and a chair and laid the table for three, choosing to notice nothing.

Tibby said, 'Where do I go?' perplexing Anthony, but Jamie answered her without looking up – 'Right out of the door, last door on the left.' And alone now with Anthony he demanded, 'Do you suppose Jesus Christ was a cock virgin?'

'Without a shadow of doubt,' Anthony told him.

'What were his wet dreams about?'

'Nubile angels.'

Jamie began to sing in a moody way, stretching the line of the appropriate hymn-tune, 'Rampant-nubile-angels-in-the-height adore him. Paradise a seething mass of them?'

'It's not recorded.'

'That's the sort of thing you're going to have to know, Anthony, if you're to be a parson.'

'Theologian.'

'It could be a life's work.'

Anthony sat down. His bony, bespectacled face was haloed by a nude on the cloth board with her bum and boobs flung out like rugger balls on the instant of being passed. He buttered toast.

Jamie still stayed at the window, draped by the scarf. He didn't want to be behaving like this, yet he couldn't help himself.

'Seething and writhing belong to the other place,' Anthony said with a full mouth.

'How do I apply?'

From beyond the window the school clock tolled the quarter, and the essay still unwritten. The given world lay beyond the window – the walls of mediaeval brick, the solemn roofs, the megalith of the chapel, the clack of bat on ball and patter of applause. Someone practising on the great organ, an oozing melancholy. The antiquity and Englishness and given-ness boxed him and caged him.

'I'm so afraid . . .'

Anthony looked up.

Jamie had not meant to give utterance. His mouth had spoken on its own. Without turning, he added, 'Missing the point of it all.'

'Continue.'

He had to go on now.

'Don't you ever feel you have no substance? I mean, no substance of your own? You never feel that? You're what other people have programmed you to be. And they've been programmed to programme you. So it goes on. And it all amounts to nothing. Nuts. Zilch.'

From the tea-table Anthony said, 'Having nothing, yet possessing all things.'

Jamie turned to him viciously. 'You're buried in quoted shit, Anthony.'

'Two, Corinthians.' Anthony was unperturbed. 'You shouldn't look to substance in yourself – it's an illusion. "As in Adam, all die . . ." You should give ear in Chapel.'

Anthony winding him up. Why did he let him?

'Your Jesus,' Jamie sneered. 'You and your smug prelates. Wankers Anonymous.'

But here Tibby was back, wanting to know what they were gassing about.

'Bankers,' said Jamie.

'Jamie was talking about himself, his favourite subject.'

'Daddy says I should marry a banker,' said Tibby.

'I'd imagine he would,' Jamie told her. 'Feelthy bankers. You would see Vicky's current.' His sister, Vicky, five years his elder, shared her life with a young City man named Rowley.

'Taking money upon usury,' said Anthony.

'Disgusting,' Jamie endorsed. 'When your Jesus turned over the tables of the money-changers, he knew what he was doing.'

'I don't know if you know, Tibby,' Anthony complained, 'but this Jamie sings in College Chapel with more conviction than any man in the whole place.'

Tibby said she'd heard him in church at home, where they lived in neighbouring villages: it embarrassed her terribly.

'It splits the head,' Anthony said.

'A conditioned reflex,' Jamie explained, settling at last at the tea-table. 'Once the organ starts playing my soul starts dribbling. I can't help it.'

'There you are – soul,' Anthony pointed out.

'I tried to give up God for Lent. It was bloody tough.'

'I wish you wouldn't talk like that,' Tibby said sharply.

And Anthony added, 'I've warned you, Jamie. Christianity won't go away at the wave of a wand. Not once you're body positive.'

'Who ever said I was body positive?'

Leaning over the back of his chair, Jamie reached for a switch. The Damned burst on them loud enough to deafen until his fingers found the volume knob.

'Do you have to?' Tibby said. But he had to. It was such a day.

'Jamie decided he was an atheist the moment the bishop blessed him at his confirmation,' Anthony told her. 'In April.'

'How could I know any better?' protested Jamie. 'Up to then I was only a child.'

'Do turn it off,' Tibby said; and he forced himself to extinguish The Damned once more. 'Why can't you be normal?' she complained. 'You're only doing it all to bait your father.'

'Doing what?'

'Being an atheist.'

'That's not doing anything. The dear fossils have nothing to do with my becoming an atheist. I'm just getting rid of things.'

'Things they provided you, is Tibby's point,' Anthony said.

'If you insist.' Jamie refilled the teacups. 'My father has to have his regular religious fix like his brandy-and-soda. You know, when I caught that burglar he thought it was divine intervention the bloke wasn't carrying a knife. He thinks the Lord's got his eye on the Mainwarings. Same way he made sure the British won the War.' He adopted a frown of noble endurance and pretended to put his father in his voice. '"Good will triumph, James." The trouble with that is that the reverse must also be true. Anything that triumphs must be good. Including the syphilitic bacillus.'

'Monsieur Pangloss,' Anthony said, 'in a manner of speaking.'

'Exactly.'

Tibby was lost in all this clever talk. It was wonderful when Jamie caught the burglar in London the previous holidays. He was so modest about it all at the time, and she so proud – so proud of his ease and beauty and indifference to all the fuss. Why did he have to show off now? She declared, 'Your father's a very respected member of whatever.'

Jamie glanced blankly at Anthony, and Anthony said, 'Synod.' (How was it Anthony knew practically more about everyone's parents than they did themselves?)

'The Synod of the poor old C of E. Exactly!' Jamie exclaimed. 'Pa must be on the board of things. Great Britain Limited. He wants us to be shareholders, like British Gas.'

But Tibby was struggling to interrupt him. 'All you can do is sneer.' Their voices were rising together. 'Your parents are marvellous. You're spoilt, that's all. They've given you everything and you're too good for it!'

'Oh, heavens, you're so right.' Jamie was away now, fuelling his own vehemence. 'My sister Victoria and I are so loaded with privilege we can scarcely stand upright. Vicky will only sleep with beautiful commodity brokers pulling in fifty thousand upwards. The only trouble is' — he broke off into an unexpected silence; on the very point of entering Anthony's mouth, a piece of cake was poised — 'one of her tits sags!'

'Oh! Oh! How can you be . . . so *beastly!*'

Tears had started in her eyes and Jamie had swung to stare out of the window. He knew he had gone too far, but he had no choice. The school clock was chiming. Six at least. Time cornering him again.

'Anthony,' Tibby said. 'Will you please leave the room?' When he had done so, Jamie still did not turn. The sounds of the chapel organ reached him still, across the evening air, over the roofs. It touched him with a wild inchoate hopelessness. Was not life being lived for him? Were not all its discoveries already made for him, all its glories already annotated, glass-cased, the statues erected, the images graven, the plinths pre-lettered by the inviolable smug, by F B Block and his kind looking at him over their glasses? And in the world beyond the same conspiracy extended – the high and the mighty feeding on their delusions of lofty purpose? Nation, Government, Whitehall, Westminster, the Square Mile, the C of E, the seats of learning, history and God – the whole bang shoot in on the chicanery, *aware* the heart was dead in the body, the conviction so much mouth, the truth a fudge and formula, and all engaged in an elaborate cover-up as to the reality of it all, which was wretched, squalid, blind and lost?

Behind him Tibby had said, 'You think yourself something great. Special.'

He thought nothing of the kind; he had made no claims. Why should she say this? Great was precisely the word he would abolish.

'And you're really the opposite,' she told him. (Go on, he thought.) 'Listen. Are you listening?'

He did not turn. She went on.

'This is the last time I shall see you. You are absolutely horrible and unkind and priggish and sneery about everything and especially anyone who is stupid enough to care about you.' She stood and picked up her hat.

He did not move at all.

She came right behind him, and no longer caring whether the small face that she so longed to be taken as that of a woman had crumpled and puffed into that of a child, she resumed: 'I never want to see you or touch you or think of you again! I hate this room! I hate your smelly clothes! I hate you! You will never see me again! *I hope you are listening*!'

And he still did not move, nor betray anything even when, storming out, tear-wet, she slammed the door.

CHAPTER FOUR

And now the father.

That very evening? That very evening – boomed out in an enormous voice – 'Sah James and Lady Mainwaring!' The father and the mother.

Of the thousand or so guests at the State Banquet assembled in the Old Library of the Guildhall in the heart (the father would say heart) of the City of London, a few score were to be formally announced and presented to their host, the Lord Mayor. These were revered and usually titled captains of industry and commerce, to which category Jumbo Mainwaring – Sir James – belonged, and dignitaries whose eminence bore at least in part upon the territory of the evening's Guest of Honour and Head of State.

Gloved in white kid, Jane Mainwaring's hand and forearm slipped through the crook of her husband's arm as they advanced the length of the one-hundred-foot chamber built in the same perpendicular Gothic style in 1870 as the Guildhall itself, where they would dine, which was completed first in 1439, restored after the Great Fire of 1666 and again after the

German bombs of 1940. The gangway was lined with Councilmen in their gowns of mazarine blue (c. 1740). Behind them, the City flag with its red dagger alternated with the improbable national colours of the visiting Emir's diminutive state. The orchestra, so called, of the Grenadier Guards was doing the 'Belle of the Ball', a waltz (c. 1904), more or less inaudibly behind the general jabber. The mill of lesser male guests, likewise in white ties and tailcoats (mostly hired), together with their wives in long dresses variously combining high hopes and incautious judgment – several hundred in all – gave the Mainwarings a patter of applause equal to that for a useful drive past cover point on the cricket field. They performed their progress as if they were born to it, which they were.

They made a fine English couple. Jumbo was just on sixty now, but still with an aristocratic ease and vigour to his tall frame; and she, Jane, fifteen years his junior, beautiful still, of that cast of unassailable English beauty which women are the first to admire. Here and there a lady present, glimpsing them going up, required to know 'Who are those two?' The gentlemen, for the most part, recognized Jumbo from the financial pages of their newspapers –the natural command of eye, the confident cut of mouth and jaw: 'James Mainwaring – head of the Mainwaring Group,' they said. Oh, they were among the top people here all right.

The Mainwarings ascended the carpeted flagstones to the dais and made for the Lord Mayor in his chain of office and his jabot, ruffles, breeches and buckles, seated on his high-backed throne of scarlet plush. Pikemen, which is to say more City businessmen disguised as soldiers of King Charles II's Restoration army of 1660, guarded him from behind the throne.

'My dear Jumbo . . . Jane . . .'

The Lord Mayor welcomed the Mainwarings as if they were his dearest friends. They were nothing of the kind. The Mainwarings' acquaintance with the fellow was confined entirely to functions of City of London Corporation to which Jumbo was in line for election as Alderman the following year. They had never crossed the threshold of one another's houses, they shared no clubs, and the Lord Mayor's languid intimacy was a pastiche of what the outside world took to be the Old Boy net in operation. Every now and then certain diphthongs still sounded a shade unsure. Jumbo knew Sir Robert Neal was an Old Boy of nowhere anybody had heard of: he was a thrusting, smart-alec accountant who found himself head of one of the longer-established City receivers when the crash of '73–4 presented him with the opportunity of a lifetime. There are fashions in receivers no less than in art auctioneers, West End estate agents and couturiers. As Bobby Neal, already a young Alderman, grabbed for his partnership the lion's share of the bigger catastrophes of the period, and a rapid fortune with it, personal ambition waxed proportionately – in pace and grandeur. The Lord Mayoralty, a rich man's sinecure, all at once became imaginable, then with a bit of footwork attainable. Now it was in the bag, with the knighthood that went with it. The latest Dick Whittington.

'So very good to see you both here.'

Jumbo was suspicious of the fellow. Having arrived on the scene with a sort of charm that actors adopt to portray upper-class Englishmen, Neal had in recent years set about coating others' insolvency with a veneer of acceptability. He even wrote articles in the financial press that presented receivership as a legitimate manoeuvre of business strategy, citing the Americans' resort to 'Chapter Eleven' and Third World debt rescheduling as comparable parts of the 'armoury of self-preservation in the modern economy'. Such an attitude stank in Jumbo's nostrils. It undermined the morality of the City of London to which he had been bred. It positively encouraged irresponsible financial management. As far as Jumbo was concerned there were two types of insolvents – fools and knaves, sometimes combined in the same individual. Neal was in the habit of treating his clients as chosen friends: to be at the receiving end of Bobby Neal's charm was vaguely sinister. But he had no fears that his acquaintanceship would spill over into ordinary life.

As first Jane then Jumbo shook the offered hand, Neal was continuing in his acquired drawl, 'Good to have the CBI properly represented,' since he had reminded himself of Jumbo's membership of the

Confederation of British Industry's Council. Neal already sat, with Jumbo, on the Court of the Bank of England, the first receiver ever to fill such a seat. Oh, for sure, Bobby Neal had come up fast. His rise, Jumbo conceded, exemplified the fundamentally healthy flexibility at the top end of British society, which the Americans mistook and the Socialists pretended to be rigidly ossified. 'Two generations to come up, two to go down,' was what his father used to say, with its implied warning. This fellow Neal's offspring would be marrying establishment if they hadn't done so already.

'You must be sure to talk to our Guest of Honour,' Neal was adding now, with a warm collusion in his slow deceptive eyes, before turning, with readymade delight, to the next couple, a bemedalled geriatric and his tight-bellied dame, tottering gamely up the steps of the dais. Jumbo and Jane, directed by pikemen, took their seats to one side.

Strictly on time, minor royalty arrived – a ducal cousin of the Queen and his handsome, ambitious, foreign wife. And then the Guest of Honour, He was a tiny, dark brown, furtive man in an Arab headdress and filmy *mishlah* gown, to whom (so it appeared) the entire proceedings were ineffably tedious or meaningless. After pausing, reluctantly, to listen to an address of welcome from the Remembrancer, in his scarlet gown and full-buttoned eighteenth-century wig, and to receive the same verbiage in exquisitely illuminated script enclosed in a tubular casket wrought in florid silver, the potentate settled on the throne immediately beside the Lord Mayor to be greeted by selected grandees, conducted to greet him. He crouched there under his chequered headcloth like a cornered fugitive, giving each towering, toothy *khawaja* a narrow drifting glance as if to ensure they were not about to pull a dagger, then flicking forth from his lap a little soft brown hand.

This emir knew *they* all knew how narrow the line was between royalty and brigandry, and that as a little ruler on a shopping spree for a weapons system (to protect him from his neighbours) he was to be given the benefit of any doubt, Allah having hidden bountiful petroleum under his particular dune. He knew they were out to flatter him into buying more weaponry than he could possibly need. The mutual fawnings of these dignitaries was wasted on his desert air. A man got power by the gun and the dagger, and kept it by the gun, the dagger, the purse, the quality of his bodyguards, and watching his sons like a hawk. These English having forgotten such realities, fooled themselves with ridiculous pageantry. It didn't fool him. That afternoon he had taken tea with the Queen in Buckingham Palace. Tea. He had kept her waiting for twenty-five minutes: already he had picked up a hint from the supercilious diplomat the English had attached to his entourage that this had annoyed the royal *binte*. So what? All she ruled now was her household, while he ruled a sovereign state, albeit a sand-dune. The English themselves had lost the will to power. These days they were as good as their war-planes and their rocketry, no more, no less. He'd just as well buy it all from the Japanese or the Koreans, as soon as they were allowed to make it, from whom he bought most of everything else, without all this historical mummery.

As the run-of-the-mill guests now swarmed through to find their places for dinner in the Great Hall (the Guildhall itself) beyond, Jumbo and Jane mingled with the Sheriffs and Aldermen and other guests of special distinction in the adjoining Print Room to be eased with aperitifs in anticipation of taking their places at the top table. Jumbo had no desire to occupy himself with this Gulf sheikh. The Mainwaring Group had nothing specific to sell him. During the war one of the Mainwaring factories had made Sten guns, but Stens had been long superseded. It had been his father's decision to leave armaments to others and stick to the general run of steel manufactures. The profits were less spectacular, but the market steadier. That was the theory, anyway. Being so big, Mainwarings had usually been able to buy up the competition. But not abroad. The Mainwaring share of the world export market was falling all the time, though not by much more than the rest of British manufacturing. And of course the home market was constantly encroached on. The root of the problem was not in doubt: it was the per-formance of the British worker, undermined by three or four decades of the so-called Welfare State and wage-bargaining by the unions. Both, of course, had made it ever harder to compete in price and quality, and achieved the exact opposite of the declared intentions, so that the British were now way down the league in overall prosperity – including welfare and all the rest – among the civilized countries. Now at last other nations were experiencing the grievance-mongering and state intervention that had long plagued Britain, and the home government had curbed the unions and tried to boost enterprise.

Jumbo had stubborn faith in his country. Perhaps it was not so much stubborn as obligatory. He couldn't see himself without it. True enough, there were moments when he wondered what 'Britain' was. From time to time he and his chauffeur pulled in at one of the 'services' on the M1 route north to the Yorkshire and Durham Mainwaring factories, for a quick meal. The people who surrounded him were surely no part of him – innumerable Indians, of course, usually trailing several children; and the Englishmen themselves with their footballers' hair-dos, flabby bodies and complex gymshoes quite remote from the England he fought for in the last war. Though he wouldn't claim that music and poetry (apart from Jane's piano) had played much of a part in his life since he was a boy, he did wonder what Vaughan Williams or A E Housman would have made of this lot.

Be all that as it may, the conviction that somewhere still the old heart beat on was inseparable from the person he knew himself to be. The heart of a *country*, his country, the country that was *him*. England was not done for; it had been down; stained a bit, sullied; it was far from done for. He felt the old heart beating right here in the Guildhall, despite the ill-fitting hired tailcoats of the mob of guests, and a receiver for Lord Mayor. This great Guildhall and attendant panoply spanned five hundred years as a monument to English enterprise and trade. Its symbolism of durability would not be lost on this little emir from the Persian Gulf. Nor would his visit that afternoon to the Queen, who could trace her royal line through eleven hundred years.

Someone had provided him a drink. A voice beside him said,

'See you've got a Burma Star. Chindit?'

'Fifty-first,' Jumbo corrected.

'Little devils, those Japs,' the old man informed him, as if it were his personal discovery, and protected himself in retrospect with a gulp of whisky. If among the general mill of guests the tailcoats were hired, at least among these fellow distinguished guests they mostly fitted. Yet here Jumbo found himself cornered by the superannuated.

The rheumy eyes turned upon the orange ribbon around his neck, and Jumbo could see the fellow heading for a private obsession. 'Honours aren't what they were, eh? Take yer KCVOs. Always used to be the gift of Her Majesty. *Personal* gift: nobody's going to tell me HM approves of half the people getting her KCVO nowadays. When I got me letter offering a KBE, I said to meself, Lord Chamberlain's office has gone barmy. Near as dammit told 'em to keep it.'

'I'm glad you didn't,' Jane Mainwaring intervened with her humouring smile.

'It was for Lucille,' the fogey revealed. 'She wanted to be Lady Anstruther. Now she's gone. Lucille.'

Even Jane Mainwaring found the apt response elusive: his report of his wife's death had come unexpectedly, and so matter-of-fact. But the old man had his own momentum.

'You're Mainwaring, aren't you? That baronetcy of yours, that's worth passing down the line. Trust you've got a son-and-heir?'

'I have,' said Jumbo.

'He's seventeen,' Jane added.

'Oh, a young 'un.'

'In the holidays he caught a burglar,' Jane said, grateful to have something to tell him.

'Caught a burglar?'

'Raiding our London flat,' she confirmed.

'Spirited boy.'

'He brought him down with a rugger tackle,' said Jumbo, declining a second glass of sherry.

'Rugger tackle!' The fogey shook his head wistfully. 'Must be proud of a boy like that. Me own grandchildren are that age. Can't say what to make of 'em. Can't tell the boys from the girls. Can't see any of them bringing down a burglar with a rugger tackle.' There was sorrow everywhere. 'What the blighter get?'

'Six months,' Jumbo told him. 'Intent to commit a burglary.'

'Six months,' echoed the old man. 'Six months' rest at the taxpayer's expense. Thank God there are people like you in harness, Mainwaring, still a power in the land.' And he added, from the depths of him: 'Nothing's safe any more. Eh? Nothing's sacred.' He had reached a hand across his white waistcoat to grip Jumbo's arm. The glance Jane Mainwaring gave her husband was surprisingly protective.

Jumbo said lightly, 'Don't look to me to keep the world as it was.'

Fifteen or twenty thousand people (men, women and children) depended for their livelihood on companies in the Group which carried his name. He was the general on a field of perpetual battle. He was tired tonight, in his bones, though no one would know save Jane. For some reason he too felt sad. 'We've all got to move with the times,' he said.

'Move and not move,' said the fogey. Jumbo felt a momentary squeeze of his upper arm. 'Why should I worry? It's not my world, is it? I'm eighty.' He had served with distinction in the Sudan Civil Service when the place was England's, Jumbo knew, and then the Hadramaut before Aden was handed to the rabble by an ignorant government in Westminster. The old man was not ridiculous. History had stolen away the grain from his life: that was the explanation. Put another way, all that he had given the daytime of his life to build had perished, his tribesmen abandoned to barbarism, his feudal sheikhs to their cheapjack townee enemies. The vision was perished and the light with it. What was safe indeed? What sacred? Even the locusts move back once more. There was nothing left for Anstruther to do but die. 'Don't look to me . . .' Jumbo had said, and behind his own jocularity he caught a whiff of betrayal.

On his way to work every day a line of graffito, sprayed along the stonework of a church, caught his eye: WE ARE THE WRITING ON THE WALL. It teased him even now. What were they trying to tell him with their clever slogans? That his principles were rotten, his loyalties outdated, his unsleeping generalship futile? That he cared nothing for his employees, nothing for the quality of their product, nothing for the wealth of the nation? That after four generations of Mainwaring industrial eminence he was some sort of Belshazzar, ripe for nemesis? . . . One of the Mainwaring companies made cans for paint sprays.

Why should he let a thing like that nag at him? So ridiculous a thing. And he, as Anstruther reasonably said, a 'power in the land'? Anyone might think he was losing his grip. And yet it did vex him that the vicar hadn't troubled to remove it. He and Jane were always in the country on a Sunday, on the Sabbath, otherwise he'd have confronted the fellow after mattins and taken him up on it. There were vicars today – he knew well enough from Synod – so soggy in their vows as to suppose that others had a kind of right to deface churches. To such people the function of a Christian was to claim the right to nothing whatever: conviction was the prerogative of the under-privileged, and those brought up in the conviction of Christ crucified and God incarnate were by dint of that upbringing privileged. People who thought like that achieved the absurd: the token of belief was having no right to believe. A 'believer' was obliged to protest 'Who am I to claim "a monopoly" of the truth? That I am right and you are wrong?' And so on. So much for the blood of martyrs. No one died for the King of the Wets.

The martyrs' Saviour: in that same sermon in which he blessed the meek, he reminded his disciples they were *the light of the world.* That a city set on a hill *cannot be hid.*

Jumbo put down his glass and drew himself up.

There was something reassuring about a well-cut tailcoat and tight white waistcoat that no other garments could provide. The gothic walls soared above the hubbub of voices and music, declaring their sanctity, their five centuries of hallowed witness of worthy men whose Christian craft and thrift and honour had made the nation rich and just and noble, setting standards for the world, permitting lawbringing light. Pennants of immemorial guilds hung from the clerestory. The Guildhall did give him reassurance. More so here than Synod; more so than Parliament itself.

'I'm a good-deal older than you,' the fogey was confiding, as a prelude to some further incomprehension. He was peering through the mist of his eyes at the great levee of the *haute,* and not so *haute, bourgeoisie.* 'Can't make out who all these people are supposed to be,' he worried. 'And this little fellow from the Pirate Coast. Never thought much of the family. More than he deserves, all this.' Letting go of Jumbo's arm he flicked his hand at the vast chamber.

Just then trumpets sounded. The rest of the assembly was being summoned to their places at dinner in the Great Hall.

'He's an important customer,' Jumbo told him.

'Customer?'

'For Britain.'

It seemed to Jumbo he had the choice of feeling for the old man or not. As an industrialist he took pride in his hard-headedness, his realism, his firm sense of priorities. Living in the past was a manifestation of the English sickness. But this old man had nowhere else to live, and Jumbo allowed himself that thought – tonight especially, so it seemed – as he watched him groping for justification for his grief at the world turning out so different from the one he was formed for. Might not the same bewilderment be his too, but for his own son, to whom the living inheritance would pass? Was it not Jamie that kept the flame of his faith in what the country still was at core and could be seen to be again, young Jamie who gave life and blood to the pageant and ritual of its ancient institutions? Ever since the Sixties, when Jamie was born, he had heard his contemporaries (not infrequently over the brandy and cigars) disparaging the younger generation for their self-indulgence/fecklessness/promiscuity/ ignorance/godlessness, and so on. He would voice the opposite view. Declaring his faith in the nation's young had become an item of his stock-in-trade. He would speak of today's youth's 'search for solutions in a world where the issues were no longer clear-cut' as they were when he was young. When he spoke thus in public he would usually hear a murmur of assent from the thoughtful ones, perhaps from people like himself with families still young enough to respond to parents' faith if it was there.

Always behind these little speeches and fragments of conversation hovered the image of his growing Jamie, a boyish grace and grit, clarity of eye, a truth and chivalry from ancient inheritance, and an invisible bond, a blood guild, a *love* equal in strength to any inheritance.

From his place at the top table Jumbo Mainwaring joined the slow handclap accompanying the procession that wound into the Great Hall where the twelve hundred guests now waited at their places. Flanked by pikemen, it advanced by way of the ambulatory beneath effigies of Chatham, Wellington and Churchill – the Royal Duke and his Duchess, the nine-hundred-and-somethingth Lord Mayor and his dame, the diminutive Emir from his instantly rich dune, the City Marshal, the Swordbearer with his vertical weapon, the Common Crier and his mace, the Remembrancer.

Once again the trumpeters of the Household Cavalry in gold State uniform sounded from the high galleries, fit for King Henry the Fifth. But the grace said by the Lord Mayor's Chaplain was such that the God of any old faith could hear.

The assembly settled into a dinner of seven courses and three wines. The little Muslim potentate risked none of these, restricting himself to a plate of boiled rice and fish mousse and later a caramel custard, prepared by his own cook. His dusky attendant brought his own bottled water.

Jane Mainwaring's neighbour at table, Albert Scrimgeour MP, likewise denied himself at least part of the glories of the feast. He was attending in his role of the Opposition's spokesman on trade and industry, and during the *entrée* he produced a plastic box into which he shovelled the remaining half of his helping of *Tournedos Lucullus, pommes parisiennes,* and *haricots verts,* commenting that he could not bear to see so much good grub going to waste, he wasn't brought up that way. This manoeuvre was executed mock-furtively; when neither the manoeuvre nor his muttered comment appeared to arouse the attention of his neighbour, it became necessary to say more, in his marked Yorkshire.

'I can assure you, Lady Mainwaring, there are soom unemployed in my constituency would be glad of a few leftovers from the tables of the rich.' He stuffed his plastic box into an inside pocket. 'I wouldn't be surprised if soom of them 'aven't worked for your 'usband's Group in past times. Made redundant.'

'I can't see that little piece of meat going very far among Bradford's unemployed, Mr Scrimgeour,' Jane Mainwaring opined.

'It's the principle,' returned Scrimgeour. 'Isn't that so? The symbolic factor. If I'm to 'old oop my 'ead as spokesperson on industry in Parliament, speaking for ordinairy people, that is, I can't 'ave it said I spend my life wining and dining without a consideration.'

Jane Mainwaring regarded Mr Scrimgeour as if he were another mother's difficult child. 'You don't have to feel guilty eating a good dinner, Mr Scrimgeour. After all, its purpose is to persuade our guest of honour to spend his money on British manufactures. That could mean jobs for your constituents.'

'Profits for the Mainwaring Group, anyroad,' Albert Scrimgeour came back.

In Wandsworth prison a warder with a rather piglike face was leaning on a balustrade of B block, one of the spider wings radiating from the centre. He was looking down on a group of prison inmates slopping out with their plastic buckets on the landing below, across from where he stood. Three prison cleaners,

also inmates, had paused alongside the porcine
warder, also watching the prisoners slopping out in
the latrines on the landing below. One of the cleaners was a powerfully built man with a cropped head,
who seemed to take pride in the sly ugliness of his
appearance. He was happy to be known as Spike.

''E's new,' Spike said. 'The poxy little square
one.' He was referring to an inmate about to enter
the latrine.

'Came in last night, d'in he,' the porcine warder
said. 'Allocated from Pentonville.'

Spike leaned lazily on his mop handle.

'What's 'e in for then?'.

The warder did not reply at once.

'Eh?' Spike prompted. *'Sir?'*

'Dunno. Dope. Nonce, maybe. Dunno.'

'Fuckin' 'ell.' Spike turned to his fellow cleaners.
''Ear that? Fuckin' nonce. Little girls?'

'Dunno,' the warder said.

'Not on the Rule, then?'

'So it seems.'

''Ear that then?' Spike offered his companions.

'Don't like nonces,' one of them said.

'Little girls,' echoed the other.

By now the prisoner they had been referring to,
Ray Green, had disappeared into the latrine, which
various other prisoners from that lower landing were
also entering. The warder began to move away. With
a gesture of his head, Spike led his two companions
across the bridge and down the metal steps to the

entrance of the latrine. When Ray came to leave, Spike blocked him.

'Nonce.'

'Nonce? Me?'

As Ray Green tried to step round Spike, one of the other cleaners drove his mop handle into his stomach. Ray, a short, thick-set man, doubled up, winded. Spike kicked him full in the face. Ray fell, seemingly unable to get his breath. The three cleaners got to work on him at once with boots and mop handles, their victim with too little breath in him to make a sound.

CHAPTER FIVE

'You can be perfectly sensible, darling, when you want to be. Then all at once you say things it's quite impossible to understand.'

Her eyes narrowing, and mallet rocking, Jane Mainwaring lined up a shot and drove her black ball through the hoop unerringly.

'That's your problem, Ma, if you can't understand.'

Jamie, barefoot, in jeans ritually faded and ripped, and calico shirt made in Bombay, with strings at the neck in preference to buttons, watched his mother prove once again that croquet was her game.

'Don't try and tell me Tibby understands.' She glanced at her son. 'We're not seeing Tibby this weekend because you've quarrelled, haven't you?'

Jamie, weighted by the entire world, including croquet, pointedly refrained from replying.

'You expect too much from Tibby. She's only a child.'

His mother completed her break by dismissing his ball to beyond the great cedar. Dribble the labrador woke up. He regarded the excessively large yellow object at his nose with the tolerant disdain appropriate to humankind's obsessive requirement to fill time.

'Another thing,' she resumed. 'You can't take anything your father says on trust, can you? Not any more. I've noticed. Vicky's noticed.'

She always did this. Jamie had observed that if she had one complaint, she appended another . . . Half of him wanted to stay silent, half wanted to retort that that was exactly what *she* had done – taken everything his father said 'on trust' from the moment they met, he at thirty-eight, she at twenty-three, signing away her autonomy for life. 'Honour and obey': *finis.*

He stayed silent. What was the point of arguing? The very proof of his argument would be that she wouldn't know what he was talking about. There was no communication with Mama: it was best to start from that presumption. He even knew what she would say next, that his father was so proud of him, and would do anything for him. Then he would want to answer, Yes, he knew that: he knew it was true provided he accepted his father's premisses as to what life was all about.

What she actually said was slightly different.

'You've got every right to be happy, Jamie.' 'I know.'

Now it came.

'It's all he cares about,' she said. 'That's *why.*'

The french windows of the long drawing room known to four generations of Mainwarings gave on to the lawn with its great cedar. This southward-facing façade of the house, buried deep in Virginia creeper, had been entirely rebuilt by Josiah for Jumbo's grandfather as a young man in 1887. (Josiah himself always chose to live in rented houses.) Only a small portion of the original seventeenth-century manor, much smaller than the present house but of the same Cotswold stone, had visibly survived, in the front of the house on the other side: the front was always kept free of creeper.

Beyond the cedar the lawn dipped gently to the rose garden, and beyond the rose garden, lower still, lay the orchard. Then fields spread. Further, the land rolled upwards and ruckled into the line of the Cotswolds three or four miles away. The hills caught the evening sun. Certain cottages and houses of exquisite ochre surfaces were chosen by the sun and gleamed like gems against their coppices in the folds of the hills.

Nestling to the right in the middle distance lay the village of Upton, of which the Mainwarings' house was the manor. The square tower of its Norman church stood back, beyond the cottage itself, and its ochrous yellow stone gave back all the colour it received, and more, from the descending sun. Only England could declare its beauty thus.

Jamie appeared in the doorway wearing his Walkman. In a smaller adjoining room his father was engrossed in the final over of the day's cricket televised from the Oval. In the drawing room itself his sister Vicky was draped across an easy chair with her legs over the arm and her bare feet dangling, turning the pages of *Harper's*. Ash from her cigarette had dropped on her tent frock. Across from her, Rowley St. George, with whom she shared her life, was stretched diagonally on a sofa, engrossed in a copy of *Euromoney*. In contrast to his slovenly young lady, Rowley was dressed with planned elegance from his narrow handmade shoes upwards. He was a long, lean, sleek man of thirty, sleek as a cat, with soft hair falling across his forehead in a way he approved of. The sleeves of his sportively striped shirt were held with monogrammed cufflinks.

Jamie surveyed them silently, then announced, 'A major convulsion is taking place in the Milky Way. It involves hundreds, perhaps thousands of stars.'

This intelligence evoked no acknowledgement of any kind from either of those present.

'Every star,' Jamie resumed, 'represents an entire solar system. Debris is shooting out at millions of miles an hour. The whole constellation of Sagittarius could disappear.'

Vicky turned a page. 'Rowley's Sagittarius,' she said. At which Rowley glanced up with a frown.

Jamie continued from the door, 'It could involve the entire universe.' No response.

He crossed to his sister and looked up into her face from a crouching position. 'Do you know what it means to be a black hole?' He brought his face closer. 'Complete and total annihilation. Including time.'

'Oh Jamie, do go away.' Vicky flicked the ash from her dress on to the rug.

Jamie turned to Rowley. 'Your lover-girl sits there reading about a lot of layabouts and tax-dodgers in the *Tatler* and bloody *Bystander* and she's about to become a black hole. Make her look to her soul.'

'She lost it at the convent,' Rowley said.

Vicky read aloud from her magazine: '"Venus in conjunction with Pluto is bad news for Sagittarians planning on extending their love life. Your talent for arousing passion in others will largely desert you. But career and money-making will prosper and bring comfort to those who believe wealth or power lead to romantic success."'

Lady Mainwaring came in, having bathed and changed.

'Jamie, you know your father's expecting Mr Carstairs,' she said. 'You don't want to look like a hippy.'

'He's trying to look like a meths drinker,' Vicky put in.

Jamie said, 'Who cares about Mr Upstairs Downstairs when the universe is about to be quasared?'

'Take no notice,' Vicky told her mother. 'He's just showing off his physics A-level.'

'I do mean it, Jamie,' Lady Mainwaring said. 'One day you'll be working with Mr Carstairs.' When she added, 'He'll be forming his impressions,' she heard her daughter saying it with her in mockery.

'Make him put some shoes on, Mum,' Vicky added.

'God almighty,' Jamie exploded. 'From someone *flaunting* her horrible tortured chipolatas.'

'You both need shoes,' their mother told them.

'May Mr Carstairs not look upon my feet?' said Jamie. 'My aristocratic toes confirm our ancient commitment to the public weal. Mainwarings dishing out work for the workers to work at . . .'

'You're not in the least funny,' Vicky told him.

The prospect of working with Mr Carstairs 'one day' touched Jamie with a remote incredulous dread not unlike the prospect of passing away. (Mr Carstairs's ponderous manner of speech did carry a sepulchral timbre.) Moreover, there was something about the way Mr Carstairs's head fitted on to his neck which in the last resort was intolerable. The back of the neck went straight on up into the high head in such a way that the front of the head, namely the face, seemed to have insufficient reason for being as far forward as it always was. Meanwhile the ears were set too low and were rather large. It was the head of a man who was waiting to tell you what was what just as soon as he had finished not listening to whatever you might have had to say. Jamie had a theory that you could tell if a man was fundamentally stupid with greater certainty from the back of his head than from the front. According to that theory Mr Carstairs was

classifiably thick, and quite apart from his own prospective involvement with him it troubled Jamie that
his father seemed to put such trust is so anthropo-
metrically deprived a type.

Mr Carstairs had taken to *confiding* in Jamie how
greatly his father was respected in industrial circles.
Jamie found himself an unwilling recipient of confi-
dences about his own family from Mr Carstairs, however complimentary. Not long ago, when the three
of them were travelling together in the back of the
Daimler, Jumbo – as was his practice – drew from his
pocket his gold-cornered note-pad to inscribe himself an aide-memoire at the moment that Jamie was
starting to say something. Mr Carstairs chose to raise
a forefinger to his lips to restrain Jamie from interrupting the captain of industry's inner train of price-
less thought.

By the time Mr Carstairs arrived, half an hour
later, Jamie was in a pair of trousers, a clean shirt and
polished shoes, and the conversation was earnest.
Such was the effect of Jeremy Carstairs on this household, he being finance director of the Group over
which Jumbo presided by dint of mystic inheritance,
vowed commitment, and voting shares.

Carstairs, promoted by mere meritorious dog-
gedness, was invariably affected in the collective
Mainwaring presence by his own brand of awe-laden
gratitude. He was marginally too attentive to Lady
Mainwaring, and too aware of Jamie, whom he immediately asked in the name of wit if he had caught any

more burglars lately. Jamie in turn was invariably aware of the intrusiveness of Mr Carstairs, ignorant as Carstairs was that (on this occasion as on others) he was responsible for him having made a change of clothes. Carstairs was turning up more and more lately.

Then, naturally, in a matter of seconds, as soon as they had filled their glasses, he heard Mr Carstairs and his father talking about his (Jamie's) 'next move'. Jamie pretended to be deep in his magazine – it was the *Euromoney* that Rowley had brought as his weekend reading. His father was telling Carstairs, 'We'd like him to go to King's – King's, Cambridge. Cambridge anyway, if they're fool enough to have him.' (Father would be glancing at him now with chaffing pride.) 'Been a Mainwaring at King's for three generations.' (Over a century, he would say next.) 'Over a century,' came his father's voice.

Oh god of the godless heaven, the predictability of it, not only of their speech but of what they were presuming to determine for him.

Now Carstairs. 'To read? English?' (A glance towards him on his sofa, surely.) 'Poetry he fancies, so I heard . . .'

Not poetry in my eyes now, longnose, thought Jamie, but *Euromoney*.

'Economics and philosophy, we think. Don't we, Jamie?'

At his name, Jamie's head had to come up as if on a string. 'Why not?' he heard himself say.

'He's thought of history,' his father was resuming. 'But one picks up so much recent history through economics. Certainly since the period Mainwarings came to prominence, so to speak, with his great-great-grandfather.'

Carstairs said, 'He wants to come into the family business, then?' To which his father gave the standard answer, 'Family in name only, of course. No nepotism as a publicly quoted stock. But there should be something in the group to interest him. Eh, Jamie?'

This time he did not look up but settled for repeating, 'Why not?'

Pa would draw Rowley into the talk now, pretend to seek his advice. It came slap on cue.

'I suspect Rowley here doesn't regard this country as a place where money can be made any more.'

'Money can be made virtually anywhere,' Rowley opined, 'if one can suss out the market, get the timing right. But I think not really manufacturing, not easily. Not this place.'

His father told Carstairs, 'You hear the voice of a master of commodity futures.'

'Parasites,' Jamie muttered, though quite amiably.

Vicky overheard. 'You've no idea what you're talking about.'

'I didn't speak,' Jamie retorted.

'These financial market men like young Rowley,' their father was saying, 'your bankers and your brokers, can't afford to think in terms of Britain. Patriotism's a luxury for the few.'

'Multinationalism's the name of the game these days. Agreed.' Jamie could hear the fruity complacency in Carstairs's voice. He disgusted him. There was nothing his father could say that Carstairs wouldn't echo, fruitily.

Now it was Rowley, 'It's been a rather ridiculous anachronism for years, I'm afraid.'

'What?' queried Jumbo.

'British insularity. Britain as an entity. Patriotism.'

Now it was his mother telling Rowley that the cocktail bits came from Fortnum's, they were called Chinese something-or-other, made in California the packet said, and Vicky ought to use them at the City lunches she organised the cooking for. Was this intended as an instance of multinationalism? Ma wasn't a stupid woman, so why did she make herself out to be hen-brained? Vicky heard 'Californian' and annouced that Rowley was to visit California (Vicky *was* hen-brained). Rowley, showing off, put in that he was only going for a day, and Vicky protested, Why go to California *for a day?* 'I want to be back for the Twelfth,' Rowley replied, showing off again: the suburban upbringing which he failed to disguise by dressing at conspicuous cost surely included no ritual killing on the opening day of the grouse season. 'So what about Rowley's villa in the Bahamas?' Ma wondered, 'I thought you were off there.' But the roof wasn't even on yet, whined Vicky, and Rowley grandly added that August probably wasn't the best time of year for the Bahamas.

The *predictability* of this blather, and Mr Carstairs too, had a suffocating effect on Jamie that was almost physical. He raised his eyes from the fuzzy print of *Euromoney* and looked around the room in a swoon. He had known the room from infancy, but having been confined to the nursery wing until the age of eight, except on special occasions, he still could not quite rid himself of a veneration – its racks of porcelain maids and their swains which one was forbidden to touch, its sticks of Sheraton, his mother's walnut escritoire given her by her parents on her wedding day, the oil of his famously beautiful Mainwaring great-grandmother by Sargent, Munnings's steeplechasers commissioned by her racing son, the Tiepolo drawings, the tall Chinese vases stocked with tall flowers, the bits of gleaming Victorian silver on which the family crest had grown faint from the polishing, the plumped armchairs and long sofas, the *Harper's Bazaar* and Christie's catalogues, *Euromoney* and the pink *FT*. They swirled in his head, like Little Black Sambo and the tiger chasing round their tree and, mixed with the voices, became a mush of dead wood and pulp and pigment and ore and clay and clobber and gabble and goo and ghee in which he was destined, by immutable preordination, to be drowned.

He raised his eyes to the early evening distances beyond the garden, through the open french windows. There were the soft folds of the Cotswolds, and the trim walled fields and pastures that lay between. Behind some wall a mile away a figure moved, the upper body and the head alone visible, as if drawn slowly across the landscape on an invisible wire – such a clean pure movement of human intrusion, an exquisite intrusion of perfect regularity of pace and direction, though sometimes it disappeared behind dark coppices or where the ground dipped. Suddenly Jamie was alerted; his eyes focused; his breath held.

Carefully, he laid aside the magazine, rose, and crossing to the french windows, slipped unnoticed into the garden.

CHAPTER SIX

Skirting the lawn to be out of sight of the drawing room, he broke into a run, and moments later was streaking along familiar paths which took him past the rose garden and the two ponds and down through the orchard. He vaulted the gate into the first paddock, scuffing his polished shoes, burst through the hedge and into the next field, his pressed flannels picking up burrs and brambles, and still at a hurtling pace sped on past a copse where pheasants ran for safety. His direction was calculated so as to cut off on its selected route the figure he had seen from the drawing-room sofa.

Leaping a stone wall, he landed in a dense mass of willowherb on the bank of a ditch. Thus he reached a bridle-path that crossed from left to right. His arrival at this point induced an instant change of speed. Glancing left, to where the path emerged from the trees, but where the approach of no figure was discernible, he at once began to saunter along the bridleway to his right; that is, in the same direction as that in which he had seen the figure moving.

As he went, he pulled a stalk of grass and held its succulent end between his teeth.

Quite shortly he heard behind him the approach of a horse at a slow trot. He did not turn or respond in any way, but continued at his sauntering pace. He heard the horse reduce from trot to walk: he knew he had been sighted.

Tibby observed the crushed patch of willowherb against the ditch on her right. She reined back her hunter a little more, for she was already a mere thirty yards behind Jamie. He, however, seemed to reduce his pace accordingly, and she found that she had closed on him another ten yards or more. Thus they processed, at an even distance, though the pace was growing slower and slower. Then Jamie, at the edge of the coppice, paused entirely, and she saw him stoop to pick a stem of willowherb.

Half-turning as he straightened, he made it seem he caught sight involuntarily of horse and rider, now a mere ten paces behind him. He blinked exaggeratedly.

'Oh! You gave me quite a start.'

Tibby had stopped her horse.

'What are you doing?' she demanded coldly.

'Collecting wildflowers. This is a humble willowherb.'

'Since when have you been interested in wildflowers?'

'A countryman's natural companion,' said Jamie. 'Ah! and there's the humble meadowsweet.'

He advanced a step or two towards horse and rider to pick a stem of meadowsweet.

Tibby held tightly to her reins, so much so that Soldier-boy might have backed up. But he didn't.

'And there, ah! look, a great rarity.' Jamie had glanced across the ditch beside the path between them, where he now advanced, 'I scarcely dare to pluck one. But they are for my lady-love, so what the hell?'

He went halfway into the hollow where the ditch ran and came out with a dandelion, with which, making an ungainly posy with the willowherb and meadowsweet, he approached the girl on horseback.

Tibby made no move. Jamie lowered the flowers disconsolately.

'May I beg the fair maiden for her hat?'

They remained there in silence. The evening air was soft around them. No sound reached them but birds. Soldier-boy jerked his head to escape the gnats and shifted his feet.

'I'm nearly late for supper as it is,' she said.

Jamie stood with bared head. A pale ray of late sun caught his hair. Tibby took off her hard hat by its peak and handed it to him. She shook her hair. The same ray caught her hair and he saw how unspeakably pretty, how ethereally pure and faultlessly minted she was. He took the hat and fondled it as if it were the most precious object in the world to him. Then he began to tuck the wildflowers under the band across its peak. But the dandelion with its soft stalk could not be thrust in under, and he tossed it away impatiently. 'Bloody silly thing,' he said.

'Your tie's squiffy.'

'My *tie's* squiffy?' He had instantly whipped out an imaginary mirror to inspect himself, and had become himself a Third Avenue pansy. 'Oh my Gahd! Why didn't someone *tell* me?' He straightened his bow and in mock frenzy was powdering his face and applying lipstick.

'Do you know,' he resumed, 'Vicky's current, the young merchant wanker type, the very nastiest whizz-kid type need it be said, spends half of his life putting lip salve on his horrible flabby lips. Fancy sharing bed and board with that!'

'We're not waiting for Mr Jamie, Kate,' Jane Mainwaring told the white-haired maidservant, and set the others an example by proceding in to dinner. 'Do let's eat!' she called from the dining room.

Jumbo, as he came in, was telling his daughter grimly that he wasn't the least upset.

'You know Daddy hates people being late for meals,' came her mother's voice. The father (saying it for mother): 'It's just not fair on Kate, keeping her up.' Then mother (for father): 'Family meals *are* rather sacred.'

Vicky tried to catch Rowley's eye but her chosen consort was already busy for his hostess, tossing salad.

They helped themselves, the conversation now obscurely crippled, to cold beef and ham. In due course Jumbo had to say from his customary place, 'I can't conceive what he's doing.'

Nobody seemed to have any ideas worth giving utterance to.

Rowley divided a quite small, cold new potato. It was an odd but hitherto insufficiently recognised fact that in the consumption of cold viands and their accompaniments the racket of knives and forks on plates was far greater than in the consumption of hot.

'Did *nobody* see him go out?' demanded Jumbo.

'Oh Daddy – what does it matter?' At which Vicky's mother reminded her that her father was trying to persuade Jamie to be more responsible.

'Tame, Mummy. Like you,' retorted Vicky.

'Oh Victoria. How liberated we have become.'

A slight colouring at Jane Mainwaring's temples might be discernible.

Jumbo realized the other day that Vicky was very nearly the age her mother was when he proposed to her. What was it his daughter's face lacked against his wife's indisputable beauty then, and indeed, still? Sometimes Vicky resembled a botched portrait of her mother: Jane Mainwaring 'without the armature', meaning that component that held something together and made it effective.

'I just don't understand,' he found himself saying, 'how he can suddenly disappear.'

'You wouldn't be fussing if it was me.'

'Nobody's fussing, Vicky,' said Jane; and Jumbo felt his irritation justified now: it's time your brother learned to live in a world where other people exist.'

Rowley and Vicky both spoke together. Jumbo turned to Rowley. 'You said?'

'He's missing some excellent ham.'

'Ah.'

'And I was saying how pompous you sound, Daddy,' Vicky added.

Jumbo said nothing. Old Kate hobbled in with a pot of chutney and a long spoon. He'd done his best for Vicky, Jumbo thought. They both had. He couldn't say exactly where they had gone wrong. Did Vicky bear out what they said about the younger generation? One shouldn't generalize, and in any case it was hardly for girls to set the tone. She had plenty of friends, of a sort, and seemed to have a knack of taking life as it came; you could say that. He could only wish the child well.

'One day,' Jane told her daughter evenly, 'you'll discover what it is to be a parent.'

Jane was watching Jumbo going quiet. Why was Jeremy Carstairs coming so often? Jumbo had never shared his business affairs with her, not in any detail. He'd seldom have her visit him in the office and never brought her to the factories. He'd rather she keep 'clean of it', as he put it, here at Upton, at home, and running the London flat as an extension of Upton as best one might – that and her charitable work. Yet she knew when things were gnawing at him.

'Daddy would give everything and anything for you children.'

Passing behind her husband with her plate, Jane's fingertips trailed across his shoulders.

'"Children",' Vicky echoed.

Naturally Jane Mainwaring loved to have Vicky here at weekends, but it was thoughtless of her to come down and make little scenes.

Soldier-boy, tethered to a rowan on the edge of the coppice, is bored. It is the hour for gnats and there is more to life than shuddering your skin and swishing your tail.

A few yards within, under ash and oak and horn-beam, the ground banks up, and there in the gloaming the girl has lain on her back against the belly of the boy, with a disorder of wild-flowers in her soft brown curls. It is a chaste, serene tableau, such as might have been done in porcelain by the craftsmen of Derby for the whatnot of the Mainwaring drawing room. There is also a secrecy here, and the complicity of the cop-pice and its creatures. It is an ancient place where the first tillers of the adjacent land rolled and dragged the rocks and boulders they cleared of it; hence the bank-ing ground. Snipe and pigeons occupy the trees, and the boy can lead her to a badger's sett in this very place. He calls it Badger Wood and has known it from infancy.

Now the young swain's hand begins to stroke the girl-child's tummy, which is covered only by a shirt. When that hand strays to touch or nearly touch her young breasts, her own hand, inactive hitherto but sentinel, rises from the leaf mould and the wood-sorrel and takes his erring hand by the wrist gently, returning it to the permitted region, which is bounded elsewhere by the waistband of her riding breeches.

Now he shifts a little, so that he can begin to peck her with kisses, on her lips, her ear, the hairline there (for which he must raise part of the multitude of flowered curls), and so to her neck, and her chin, her lips again, her brow and her eyes. She flutters her eyelashes against his cheek. 'Butterfly kisses,' she whispers, and instantly – conjured by them, how else? – a butterfly, a tortoiseshell just beside their heads, is settling on a fern.

He feels within him a surge not in the first place of desire but of tremendous freedom, *libertas tremenda*, freedom and power, by which he can obtain anything he wishes. All the wonders of the world seem to be awaiting his discovery, all its delights and joys and mysteries ready to open to him. And more than this – that he in turn can give of himself totally, that on the instant he can reach down within and take command of that inner self, where the power of him lies, without fear or constraint but, instead, in whatever way he wills. It is as if this very wood, which all his life he had known, has kept for him all these years its Eden secret of liberation and power welling from the depths.

He looks at this girl-child now with this blaze in him, and heaves a mighty sigh. She sits up, puzzled by him, and he holds her away from him wondering if she could ever understand what is within him, what he has seen there. Could she grasp any such revelation? He would keep his love for her until she could so grasp him.

She tilts her head, and would draw towards him, escaping the blaze of his eyes; and he does let her close on him, opening his hands but not drawing her to him. He lets her body tilt towards him, and her face and her mouth to close upon his. But there is fear of him in her, and he knows of that fear. And at the last moment, the last fraction of time before her mouth ought to have closed with his totally, she pulls herself away and jumps up, her child's heart beating in furious purity for him and in fear of the power she glimpsed in him.

He does not insist or make any compulsion upon her. He helps her remount, locking his hands for a step, she still festooned with his flowers. She cannot see his face now, and all he requires of her is that he may nuzzle against her leg, saying nothing. Soldier-boy is patient and easy for their sakes. She finds a flower from her own hair, a wild orchid, and sticks it in his. For a moment longer he stays buried against her leg and saddle. She shakes her head, and the wildflowers scatter down. She fits on her hard hat, and he lets her go.

After Jamie watched her disappear at a trot beyond the coppice, he turned back the way he had come in wild thought. He had missed dinner already, and now he took a detour.

Upton church stood on its own, to the left, separated from the village itself by the width of a field and its own churchyard. Jamie reached it by leaping a stone wall and picking his way through the ancient stones and past the mausoleum where the bones of his grandfather and great-grandfather lay.

He knew it was the vicar's policy to leave it unlocked, and trying the studded arched oak door by its ring of twisted iron, he unlatched it with sudden clatter, and entered. The little church of bunched pews and choir screen of sombre heavy wood was unexpectedly dark and chilling. And in utter silence. A place on its own, biding its time. The coloured glass all but blocked the last of the daylight except for the west window, whose images glowed as if by their own low internal light and dropped slanted patches of amber, cobalt and purple on the rough flags of the narrow aisle. Skirting the ancient font where he had been christened, he moved up between the black pews. His townee shoes sounded loud. He passed the verger's rod in its brass clasp, and the Mainwaring pew with the hymnbook and bible bearing the initials of the grandmama he just remembered.

If accosted now, from the half-open door behind him, why he was here, could he have said? Was it to find some citadel of privacy in which to make confirmation of what had come upon him in Badger Wood? But why here, to a church? – a church which, like the coppice, he had known since childhood. (In the coppice it had seemed no religious afflatus.) In any case, he was no churchman, he was the very reverse: the church belonged to the antithesis of the freedom and the power he had glimpsed.

So was it for violation?

He sat where Mr Nicholls the parson sat, just beyond the choir screen. He sat there hunched, holding himself with his arms, as if against the chill – or to hold within what he had for a moment seen within and delved.

After a while he knew he must do something. Yet what? He could not bear now just to creep home, to face a scatter-shot of reprimand for his misdemeanour of absence, father's aloof disapproval, mother's puzzled regret, sister's shallow superiority . . .

The further panel of the west window triptych depicted the intended sacrifice of Isaac by Abraham. The hoary old man had already built his clumsy altar of faggots on a square rock and had trussed the boy, who in this mediaeval tableau had the appearance not of a child but a mature dwarf. The old man had his broad blade ready for the final deed.

An entangled ram was discernible on the left of the panel. Jamie had known the window and the story since his nursery days. It was a terrifying account, in what it implied for the innocent as victims of a blackmailing God.

Now he moved, in the near-dark, up the last steps to the altar. It was sanctified territory, where he had never trod before. He walked behind the altar. It was only a squared mass of stone or brick, nothing more. He was frightened now, but he had to act. No objects stood on the altar: crucifix and candles were kept locked away. Only a woven altar cloth lay across it.

Jamie drew off the cloth and put it around him. It was stiff and unyielding. He stood there behind the altar like a devil's bishop in his cope, staring down the length of the squat church that had known so much vowing and grieving, so much vain plea. The flame was still alive in him from what he had perceived in the coppice, but he was truly afraid now; and he knew that all these things had been sanctified by ritual and that what he was doing was an act of sacrilege upon many who had known him even before he was aware of them. He kicked off his shoes.

He clambered on to the marble of the altar top that he had laid bare. Upon this marble his feet found the shallow imprint of a cross. Now he was above everything. He was seeing the dark church as seldom a man had seen it. From up here he could view from a high point close to the ascended Jesus of the central panel; he could view himself in the brown tweed belted overcoat nanny put him into when he first entered here to worship as a child of six and was sat, with nanny, immediately behind the family pew below the lectern where his father stood reading loudly. He could view and review his own self from those primal days when they had started to tell him what he was to become – no, what he already was, what he believed and what he hoped for, what he must pass on, how he would die; he could look down on his own bowed head, on his gaped maw emitting worship, admitting faith, the entire cosmology of phoney certainties; he could hark and hear again that multitude of word and chant heaped on this altar from his own throat.

He felt a horror here, a vertigo; and swayed.

Still wrapped in altar cloth he sank down on the slab with its imprinted cross and lay like Isaac awaiting the broad-bladed knife and the flames' crackle. He would lie there and lie there, putting fear to the test. Fear compounded wildness, and wildness fear, but he lay there still, gripping the cloth. The marble was cold: it was a death slab, a catafalque. He would not budge. He heard the silence; beneath the silence he heard his heart, he heard wood creak in the body of the church outraged below. He lay still, he would defy, he would play it through. He saw the light of the glass above had dimmed. From where he lay, where no man or Mainwaring had lain and stared, the glass's images were indecipherable, its colours jumbled and mushed into one like the sounds of a humming-top. A strange calmness settled around him.

When the calm was in him, when he was quite sure he could stay there as long as he was so inclined, he rose, and slipped off the stone block. He spread the cloth as he had found it (though he could not quite rid it of the rumpling his tight grip had made at its edges). He put back on shoes.

Just below the steps from the french window that gave on the lawn, and to one side, Jumbo Mainwaring stood alone. He did not want to be seen there in silhouette, waiting.

It was a clear night, but with no moon a dark one, though the last light was still just extant, a whisper of it in the northwest, behind the house. He could still make out the line of the Cotswolds, but no intervening fields now. Here and there lights pricked. Sometimes at this hour he had seen roedeer flowing between the black copses in the middle distance, although not for some years now. He did not know if the deer were lately gone, or whether it was the weakening of his eyesight. There was a flock of birds, across the very last of the light far to the right: he could see those well enough. From the drawing-room he heard Jane beginning to play – Schumann, it must be. The *Kinderscenen.* She was hesitant. She re-started. She did not play now as often as she might, not as she did when they were first married. It was long since she had learned anything new or he had urged 'Play me something new,' and tied her to it with a promise of a certain time set aside to listen. He wondered why should she have chosen tonight to sit down at the piano.

It was absurd to worry about Jamie. What might befall him? He had not taken a gun out (Jumbo had made a surreptitious check of the gun room); a kidnap was too far-fetched to entertain. The boy had entered a contrary phase of late: it was a part of growing, the familiar strains of late adolescence. It was absurd to worry.

Mayn't he worry for him? – a father for a son, for all the son meant to a man? Mayn't a father's comfort, his comfort-and-joy, have its rightful corollary? Oh it was comfort to have him here, here at Upton, doing things about the place, rough shooting across the farm, going hacking with his mother, running down to the village on his bike. They all looked to him, did they not? – the cut of his head, the next Mainwaring. The 'young gentleman' – he had heard the phrase in old Will the cowman's mouth only the other day. Gentleman. The authority, power, the *precision* of that concept by which his own father, the boy's grandfather, had set such store; its antique provenance, Norman English, gentle man, gentil knyght, as ancient as the village church and that further antiquity that inspired it. A grail concept, handed down, never destructible, such as must return and return to Man willy-nilly by dint of its vesselship of truth, requiring recognition for as long as Man was this planet's scion.

He breathed the calm night air deeply. If there was no moon yet, the stars were bright. He remembered his mother saying of his father, that he 'always knew the right thing to do': the foremost of her praise of him, privately vouchsafed: 'the right thing' the sort of phrase in this age seen fit only for satire . . . as if the word *right* could shed its meaning and the soul and civilization of man survive! His son Jamie would know 'the right thing', instinctively: the assurance of that was in his face. Nicholls the vicar had spoken of Jamie the other day, chatting after mattins, 'He's a fine boy, that of yours, Sir James, even if I can't persuade him into church just now.' So he was; it was in his face; and so he may have sweet worry for him.

Jumbo scanned the darkness. Beyond the house, where the ground dipped, the highest of the climbing roses were visible – the great white ones, pure white, 'Iceberg', each with the ghostly candescence of their name. It was Jane's garden, the rose garden, yellows and whites. A christening gown, someone had called it, Jumbo remembered.

Jamie could look after himself. He had tackled that wretch of a housebreaker – got him by the knackers! Yesterday, Jamie had volunteered to trim back the Virginia creeper from the upper windows. Jane had objected, for the danger of it, preferring Adams to do it who was accustomed to ladders. But Jumbo had countered her: if Jamie wanted to, let him: he was old enough to assess his own dangers. And soon after, he, Jumbo, was in his writing-room upstairs when his eye was caught by the creeper twitching, sharply, at one side of the window. Then the boy's hand appeared, and he saw it grip the grille around the base of the window. (It must have been a hazardous manoeuvre, leaning sideways from the ladder-top.) He saw the manly strength of that hand, its rough power, the command of it, and on sight of that hand alone he felt pride and love in equal measure: pride in all that he had contributed (it was a muscular oarsman's hand the Thames at Eton produced), and love in all that the boy was to him by the natural right of his fatherhood.

Jumbo now began to make out an odd movement, past the cedar, towards where the church lay, in the paddock there. He strained to see. It was a circling, a twisting and dipping – a figure with arms made wings to imitate a bird. Every now and then as it approached the garden perimeter, it abruptly reversed its twirls and swoops. He could determine from its control and vigour that this was not drunkenness but the fantastical expression of . . . of energetic youth in joyful liberation. All the anxiety now dissolved from his face, and now he re-entered the house, closing the french windows behind him. Jane faltered in the *Träumerei* and looked up sheepishly, 'I'm rusty,' she said, but Jumbo told her, 'Don't stop, darling,' and settled on a sofa to do nothing but listen to her, disturbing himself only for a moment – a minute or two later – to return to the french windows and unlatch one half, leaving it ajar.

CHAPTER SEVEN

The Mainwaring flat in London was in Eaton Square.
It comprised a ground floor, slightly raised above
the level of the street and square outside, and a basement looking out on to a narrow area between it and
the street. It was in this area the previous holidays that
Jamie – interrupted by an odd sound at two o'clock in
the morning lying on his bed, when engrossed in a novel by Albert Camus – had looked out from his window.
There he saw a man whose intentions were apparently
to break into the premises. On the man taking flight,
Jamie, hastening out by the front doors of the flat and
the building itself, went in pursuit, and unimpeded by
any clothing beyond a shirt, underpants and one sock,
caught him some three hundred yards away (in Lyall
Street) where he held a part of him as ransom for the
whole, by an intimate grip learned at boarding school.
Police – summoned by a passer-by – soon arrived.

Looking back – not from this point, but later on –
Jamie would see this capture as a moment at which
things changed in him. He knew such an occurrence

to be symbolic: it did not make the change but marked it: there would have been a readiness for the change growing in secret. Nevertheless, that brief sequence of pursuit, seizure, surrender of his quarry and flurry of congratulations would come to fix it for him . . . and a few seconds of the sequence in particular. He would come to think of it in the way that is recalled by some vegetarians who, having been brought up meat-eaters like most of us, and being aware of no inclination to alter their diet, experience a doubt bordering upon disgust in a single mouthful of flesh, which by polite convention they must finish masticating and then swallow. From such a moment's awakening to their cannibalism, they date the beginning of their conversion.

For Jamie that moment occurred on the pavement in Lyall Street where he had brought down the would-be intruder on the pavement with a rugger-tackle at the knees. He was now holding him from the back with one arm clenched round the fellow's neck and with his other hand, threaded between the legs, in the unorthodox intimate clamp already referred to. Jamie was bigger built than his quarry, and fitter, too – with his rowing and rugby football he was as fit and fast and strong (not least in the hand) as he had ever been. His captive, though not much older than him, was overweight and, by the sound of him, at least a little asthmatic.

It wasn't mere sorrow for him that came over Jamie in those few seconds, nor flash of weird sexuality sparked by the vice of his fingers. It was an experience of a different order: this moment between the pursuit and the claiming of his quarry became the moment of pivot between all that rearing or training expected of him and the reward thereof in glory and fulfilment . . . and wild confusion assailed him. *Which was pursuer and which quarry?* There on the street they were wound around and among one another like an eight-limbed beast. His own face being thrust against the other's neck, he smelled his smell, breathed his breath, felt the thump of his heart, knew by strange transference the terror at his crotch –and not just bodies thus collided and clamped at this extraordinary juncture, but destinies also: each could have been either. So that, were it not for the little clutch of agitated onlookers now exhorting him and assuring him of the imminent arrival of the police, he would have defied chance, released him, let this doppelgänger gang awa' into the night, and himself dissolve all triumph, abandon any credit.

The fellow, Raymond Green, twenty-six, unemployed, already serving a suspended sentence, got six months in prison for attempted burglary on evidence given in the witness box by Jamie; and Jamie, fed congratulations by family and friends and written up in the *Kensington and Chelsea News,* as good as took it all as they expected of him, telling and re-telling the story as required, with modesty and easy wit as if it was nothing more than a winning try from some other player's well-timed pass.

On this night, five months later, in mid-September, events took a different turn.

The location was not far from the previous one – in Paulton's Square off the King's Road. Jamie was fully clothed, albeit in his 'distressed' jeans, sloganed tee-shirt and cotton jacket, as were his three friends, Anthony, Gus and Henry. The hour was close to midnight: they were already unstoppered, earlier that evening, by a rock concert at Hammersmith; and spirits, supported by liquor, were high. Comradeships formed over several years together at their famous school were deep and instinctive. Two of them had already left the school at the end of the previous term – and Henry to go up to Oxford, where their places were confirmed that very day by their A-level results. This provided the pretext for the friends' celebration, especially by Gus, the lesser scholar, whose A-level grading could only be the consequence, he modestly claimed, of a cock-up by his examiners. Anthony and Jamie had to go back to school, that same week, for one more term (or 'Half' in the jargon of the school) since both were to sit the November Cambridge examination.

Cars were parked head-to-tail along the length of the square, and Jamie was the first to leap on one of them. Long ago he had thought of car-leaping as a high-risk sport suitable for modern man, not dissimilar from the leaping of charging bulls engaged in by ancient Cretans. On this occasion the vehicles were stationary. Yet it was a start, and his footwear – rubber sneakers – were invitingly appropriate.

His idea immediately caught on, and in a twinkling he was at the head of a ragged procession, even a small stampede, each stampeder in raucous contest bent on reaching the very end of the square without a foot touching the ground. Anthony, owlish in his circular spectacles, brought up the rear with a curious prancing gait like a Viennese horse of the Spanish school. This elevated progress did no good to the bonnets and roofs of the BMWs, Volvos, Jaguars, Polos, Golfs, and Rovers taking their nocturnal rest there, but not much harm either, due to the surprising flexibility of the paint and bodywork of the modern motorcar. Several were fitted with anti-tamper alarms which a foot on roof or bonnet set off. These various electronic bleeps, wails, hoots and sirens mixing with the exhilarated whoops of the boys – Gus the drunkest and most voluble whooper – rapidly built to a rare cacophony, inflating the recklessness of its perpetrators. It rendered each of the first three either oblivious of or indifferent to the fact that fixed to the roof of one of the parked vehicles, about two thirds along the square in the direct path of their progress, was a blue light.

It was a common-or-garden police car, containing no less than two common policemen. A third constable visiting a household three or four doors away was in fact the first to respond to the caterwauling of the street and, rushing out, to register what was taking place.

If it had not been for Anthony bringing up the rear so laggardly with his bizarre prancing they might all have scattered and escaped. The others were over and beyond the police car (which was facing the wrong direction) before its astonished occupants popped forth like corks. The officer hurrying from the house arrested Anthony by merely intercepting his route; the other three boys, unable to abandon a comrade, surrendered with giggling readiness which had exactly the opposite impression they expected, namely that the British bobby should share their hilarity at the birth of a new international sport.

In the interview room at Chelsea Police Station all four were stripped to their underpants, and sat thus on a bench. At the desk a uniformed sergeant laboriously filled in charge sheets, while a plain-clothes policeman searched the pockets of their discarded gear, making four little heaps of loose change, keys, pens, wallets and wallets' contents. He took his time. In Anthony's jeans he came across a paper fold containing white powder. He focused its owner with supercilious immaturity.

'Where did you obtain this substance?'

'Substance?' echoed Gus. (The word struck him as infinitely comic.)

'I wasn't asking you.' The plainclothes man's narrow moustache seemed insecure on his soft white lip.

'Medicinal powders for the common cold,' Anthony assured him, sounding scholarly and suave.

'For the cobbod code,' chimed in Gus.

Then Henry, who had a long, sad, Plantagenet face and hair parted in the middle, furnished the fact that his friend had a very delicate constitution.

The plainclothes man regarded them both with his manufactured sneer, 'If I was you,' he said pausing there, 'I wouldn't push my luck.' He glanced at his colleague as an accomplice in the menace of capricious power. It was not only his experience but his training too that the insolence of hooligans evaporated swiftly under a quiet, persistent contempt, especially once they were stripped.

'My friend has a very delicate constitution, officer,' Henry repeated, oblivious.

Gus indicated the plainclothes man. 'That bloke planted it. Right, Jamie?' Jamie seemed preoccupied.

Henry said, 'Planted it. Exactly.'

'They're having you on, officer,' Anthony told him. 'Take no notice. I got it at the chemist. Look, it'll have Beechams written on it.'

'We're clever, aren't we.'

The plainclothes man's voice had gone almost inaudible.

'This could be very serious for you and your clever friends.'

The man at the desk produced a small plastic jar. The other decanted the powder into it, and turned back to Anthony. 'Do you have a cold?' Before he could answer, Gus had intervened blindly again. 'They can strike without warning. Very very suddenly.'

'It's Beecham's, officer,' Anthony pleaded. 'It's on the packet.'

'Father's got shares in Beecham's,' Henry informed the company, to which Gus added, 'Fine British company. None of your Swiss rubbish.'

The two policemen exchanged glances. The man at the desk produced from the drawer an implement like a pocket jemmy. It was a cobbler's tack-knife. He passed it to the plainclothes man, who picked up the first leather shoe to hand and began to prize off its heel.

The night in the cells was endured with negligible sleep, and with such discomfort and uncertainty as those minded to exercise their range of petty power will casually multiply. Their keepers, for instance, were distracted by other responsibilities until their requirements to be unlocked for a visit to the bog became desperate. There, deprived of shoes, the socked feet naturally got soggy with urine. No information was forthcoming as to their arraignment, or any other process concerning them. Anthony would not need his spectacles overnight, he was heavily assured: he might damage himself with their glass: they were best kept with his 'property'.

As to those others they found in the cells already, or who were crammed in after them during the night, they would acknowledge a commonality of species, certainly, as might for example the baboon with the chimpanzee; but in characteristics as broad as speech, response to threat, and bodily odours, they discovered their genetic differences to be surprisingly sharp.

Nevertheless, in the morning they were led out with the rest in the intended state of sullen dismay, and given stewed tea in large, scuffed plastic mugs, and three slices each of white loaf spread with margarine and Bovril. Gus started to tell the officer that Jamie's father was Sir James Mainwaring, 'head of the Mainwaring Group, cet'ra et cet'ra'. When the man in uniform appeared to be deaf, he persisted with the information that Jamie had caught a robber – 'We're all on your side, officer,' which likewise evoked no response. By this time they seemed to be the last ones left, their former cellmates having been called away in ones and twos, sometimes handcuffed – except for a single West Indian, newly arrived, on the end of their bench, groaning, with mauve lumps on his face and glistening patches in the fuzz of his head. A woman beyond the age of childbearing was led through the room carrying a poodle like a baby.

Then all at once their 'property' was brought in, each one's in a cardboard box, and without any further comment they were told they could go, dismissed as if too insignificant to waste more time over. The anti-climax was, if anything, more intolerable than all the rest.

They walked through the swing doors and down the steps of the police station in facetious silence. Two of them carried the heels of their shoes in their hands.

What now? Where to breakfast? Where to shave? The others had noticed nothing about Jamie yet, though perhaps they might have, if only from his silence. 'Claridges,' someone proposed. 'Claridges for breakfast.' 'They won't let us in.' 'Oh, *c'mon.*'

'Gus,' Jamie said.

His friend looked at him in surprise.

'I didn't appreciate your bringing up my father's name.'

'For God's sake, Jamie. I was only trying to persuade them not to bring charges.'

'I realize. I didn't appreciate it.'

It stunned them – this deadly tone, this coldness of eye.

Henry said, it helped get us off – your dad's name.'

'I think not,' Jamie replied. 'They had already decided. In any case, I'm afraid that isn't my point.'

It was a Friday morning. It was not yet eight a.m., but a low roar was already rising from mile on mile of city around them. It was a restless, overcast day, with a bite of autumn in the wind. Office workers in trim attire were walking briskly for bus routes and underground stations; cars and vans hurried past; all else possessed a preoccupation and purpose which seemed to make them out of place and futile.

'I'm going home,' Jamie said, and left them, moving off swiftly into the network of small streets towards Sloane Square.

At forty yards or so, they saw him pause. Anthony said, 'Gus – catch him up and tell him you're sorry.' And Gus did, at the double: Jamie had not moved by the time he caught up with him.

The two others waited for Gus to rejoin them.

'Guess what,' he reported.

Uncertain smiles crossed the faces of the other two.

'Jamie!' Gus prompted. 'Guess what?'

Anthony said, 'Well, what?'

'He was rolling a joint,' Gus told them.

'How the hell?' exclaimed Henry, giving voice to their amazement.

Jumbo was already well into his breakfast when a few mintues later Jamie let himself into the Eaton Square flat. He knew already Jamie had been out all night – he had knocked on his bedroom door at about half past seven and, getting no answer, had peeked in: the bed had not been slept in. When he had come in to breakfast he remarked to Jane, 'Jamie hasn't been home.' Nothing more. He caught his wife's eye, and in it was a scintilla of fear for whatever this absence might portend, and perhaps of guilt too. Whatever in a son was not of his father could be attributable to the mother. She glanced at the clock, 'I thought he was being very quiet,' she said.

Then a silence had fallen, except for Jumbo drinking his coffee and munching his toast and marmalade, and opening up and refolding his *Financial Times* each time he needed to turn a page. Sometimes

Jane felt deafened by the sound of Jumbo eating. Especially toast. Years ago Jumbo had taken to propping his morning paper on the metal stand especially made by one of the factory craftsmen for reading a newspaper while eating breakfast.

They both knew Jamie had been with his friends the night before, out on the town. If anything serious had happened they would have had a call by now. When each of them saw him pass the window and mount the steps, neither said anything.

Jamie made no attempt to enter quietly. He went straight down to the basement bathroom and ran a bath and shaved, and then to his room to change. When he came up to breakfast his father was just leaving the room with the *Financial Times*.

'The car will be here in five minutes,' was all he said as he passed, and Jamie said nothing. It was 8.20, and indeed at 8.25 Searle was there with the Daimler. At 8.30 they left, and nothing more had been exchanged beyond Jane saying, 'You didn't sleep here last night,' and Jamie responding, 'Oh? Nor I did,' as if with an effort of recollection.

More or less on the dot of a quarter to nine, Searle pulled in at the entrance of the Swallow Hotel in the Cromwell Road where Iseki and Ishikawa were of course waiting. They sat in the back with Jumbo, Jamie in front beside Searle. He had nothing to say to Searle: he mistrusted his obsequiousness and guessed his dislike was mutual. Jamie's own blue suit and boring tie felt like some kind of uniform, reducing him to a junior version of Searle who *was* of course in uniform, including a peaked cap which, Jamie knew, was greasy inside. Because his night had been so short – apart from everything else the cell had been cold – he fell asleep on the motorway north.

When he woke up and heard the two Japanese making conversation with his father he found that his original amusement at the bobbing ecstasy of their greeting, and their exclamatory awe at anything uttered by his father, had turned to disgust. His father had tried to brief Jamie about these Japanese – some plan to bring them into the Group on a 'joint venture' basis, by which they would provide 'fresh capital' and 'management skills' and 'open up new markets' and so on. It had sounded orderly and logical enough, yet now it seemed it wasn't so clear and positive after all; there was something in the sound of their voices and surely also in his father's bearing. It was coming out of sleep that he had become aware of this. An instinct. He had noticed a growing sombreness in his father's mood of late, a kind of beleagueredness. But now he felt he had detected an underlying agitation in him, a *suppliance* which was of course exactly the opposite of the appearance of things. The appearance was still infused with father's patrician condescension, his easy *de haut en bas,* unassailably secure as to the natural order. And the natural order in turn comprised the British right, if not to govern the rest of mankind, then to set its modes of conduct, not least for the parvenu Oriental. It was a right rooted in the Christian ethic, history, empire, victory in world wars and of course landed stability – an atavistic right encapsulated by the Mainwarings themselves.

Why did it now have for Jamie a quality of charade? . . . as if Pa were acting out the old formula as a cover for suppliance? He could not decide if his father was himself aware of this contradiction. He felt shafts of protectiveness for him, and half-wished to warn him, It is yourself you are deceiving, not them. These slight, sallow foreigners see through your patrician airs, they sniff the suppliant in you, they are stringing you along. The power is with them and they know it, and all their deference and awe and the gasps of grateful wonder at everything you tell them about the Mainwaring Group is as much a charade as your charade, in which I, your son and heir, who you don't even know spent last night in a police cell, have a supporting role.

Yes, there were seconds in which he would have broken in and warned him. But trapped there in front, beside the putrid Searle, he held his tongue.

It had begun to rain. He didn't want to have to pity his father.

It wasn't Jamie's first visit to Bradford, though he had not been here since he was twelve or thirteen. From the rain-streaked window of the Daimler the place looked even bleaker than he remembered. It seemed now a city of some former civilization that had met catastrophe, and then, later, another quite different race of men had migrated to the region and were making do with the crumbled remains they found. This impression, it occurred to him, was not so remote from the truth. All around were unoccupied factories or factory sites. Derelict open spaces separated clumps of vertical grey flats from squat patches of older, darker housing – new slums mushrooming out of old slums. Amid the old slums mean shops clustered in rows. GHULAM ELECTRONICS, Jamie read as the Daimler moved carefully through, CHAUDARI SUPER MARKET. Some shopkeepers had not bothered with Roman script at all and remained content with sign-written Bengali. Almost all those he saw in the grey streets were dark-skinned. Swathing them against the cold rain their clothes looked as if they had been picked from the dead of another race. A longish queue of people stood at a bus-stop; the car passed so close to the kerb here, and so slowly, that Jamie saw each face close-to, as if at an inspection of enemy prisoners: then all at once in the last place in the queue was a *white* face, or, rather, a grey one – an old man with pinched cheeks in a cap, who at the last moment looked up and into the car direct at Jamie with what seemed a fixed and hopeless plea for rescue. Beyond the bus stop stood a chapel with windows like a sermon on temperance, and across its entrance was erected a huge neon sign in some Eastern script made of green glass.

Several hundred yards ahead the vast Mainwaring chimney was already in view, and one of the Japanese – the smaller one, who bobbed and gasped more than the other – was asking Jumbo in his breathless exclamatory way what he knew the answer to perfectly well already, since Jumbo had only just finished explaining. 'Your oldest factory, Sir Jamess? Very old factory?'

Jumbo told him again, 'That's right, Iseki. The Bolt Factory. One hundred and twenty years old. The one from which the Group grew.' It was a loss-maker now, as they all knew, even Jamie.

The Bolt Factory was the only plant in the Group Jamie knew at all. He remembered the chimney from his childhood. He had been brought up here first for a memorial service for his grandfather, which all his Ryder cousins had attended too. There were early photographs of the factory in the old family albums. And a set of Edwardian picture postcards of it as well, with a floral design round the mount of the picture and in the sepia photographs themselves rows of workers in cloth caps with their wives in white bodices and broad hats. In the postcards the chimney bore the name MAINWARING in white bricks from top to bottom, and it still did.

'Making loss,' Iseki echoed, hot-potato.

'On its present product,' Jumbo said.

'You cannot change product?'

The Japs performed a double-act, Jamie could see, with this Iseki playing the simpleton. Iseki went in for most of the bobbing and gasping, and seemed to have more difficulty with his English than Ishikawa. The time it took Jumbo to respond suggested to

Jamie that his father was at least aware that Iseki's art-lessness was phoney.

'We've already discussed the Bolt Factory mak-ing drill-heads with yourselves,' Jumbo said at last. So they had. They had discussed it on this very car-ride. He added, The Bolt Factory remains part of the joint-venture package.'

'Ah. Par' of the package,' Iseki parroted. Parroting, with added surprise, what he knew per-fectly well already, was one of the tricks in Iseki's bag.

The great chimney was sometimes visible on the right of the car, sometimes ahead. This was the first of five of the Group's factories to be visited that day. Jumbo had tried to outline the strategy for Jamie. The Mainwaring Bolt Company was a separate corporate entity. It was tied to the Group by the forty-nine per cent stock owned by Mainwaring Group Holdings plc, the publicly quoted company; but the rest of the stock of the Mainwaring Bolt Co. was scattered among the family and in management terms it had stayed private. This anomaly stemmed from a generation or more ago when the overall business was expanding, mostly by acquisition, and the Group went public. The Bolt Company was still then very profitable, and the other half of the family shareholders – the Ryder cousins – decided to play cautious, seeing the expan-sion as speculative and declining to allow their Bolt Company stock to be watered down by outside inves-tors holding a majority of new shares. Subsequently the situation became reversed: the Bolt Company's profitability dwindled while the Mainwaring Group's factories relatively prospered. Today, the Group's overall profit margins had narrowed and its minority holding in the original Bolt Company was not helping the share price: indeed, the holding remained in place mostly because of the personal respect which the directors of the main board of Mainwaring Group Holdings plc had for their chairman. Jumbo, in his turn, refused to abandon faith in the Bolt Company. A single *specialized* new product line, nothing labour-intensive –drill-heads, for instance, for rock boring in mineral and oil exploration – capitalized and marketed by their prospective Group partners from Japan, could possibly turn it round and allow the Group to take full control of the Bolt company without the City analysts talking down the share price. Jumbo had assured – no, indicated to – his Ryder cousins that he didn't intend to bring joint venture partners into the Group without the Bolt Company coming with it. *'Sine qua non,'* Charlie Ryder had had the nerve to add at the last Bolt Company board meeting, trying to pin him down. Jumbo had to remind him that it was not within his authority as chairman of a public company to lay down such an absolute condition if it could adversely affect Group shareholders. Carstairs, who was also on both boards, put in a 'Hear, hear,' and Charlie, who knew nothing about business and whose only interests were his racing and his shooting, looked peeved. Yet it was Jumbo who really cared about the Bolt Company for its own sake, for the men who worked there, for what the original company meant to the Mainwaring name.

The chimney drew them like a shrine. The factory itself was sited atop a hummock of land.

'If no change of product, Sir Jamess,' Ishikawa said, 'Tokyo maybe will say this factory will be difficult for our agreement. Maybe.'

'The change of product could depend on you, Ishikawa. As far as we're concerned, the Bolt Company goes with the deal.'

'Ah so.'

'Oh. Goes with the deal,' echoed Iseki.

Jamie had heard the lapidary tone in his father's voice, and the transparent phoneyness of the Japanese's dismay. He also noted the pause Jumbo left before his response which skirted insult. 'It has been our position from the start, Iseki.'

Carstairs was waiting for them, with the works manager, a stocky man of forty in a freshly laundered overall with MBC in cursive script in red across the pocket. Jumbo greeted him by his first name. All five visitors were handed white plastic helmets also bearing the company logo. They entered the body of the factory at once. The racket of the place was overwhelming.

Even so it was soon obvious that a good part of it was lying idle. The works manager gave his spiel about the various steel components coming off the production lines and how the machines functioned, although none of the group could make out much of what he was saying, partly because of the racket, partly because of his Yorkshire speech. The information was in any case of little interest to any of them. Jamie gathered that the total workforce was eighteen hundred, and despite the factory not operating to capacity three shifts worked round the clock to save maintenance costs. The factory hands, he noticed, included few young men and, given the racial make-up of Bradford, relatively few Asians. Most were white men in their forties or older. Every now and then Jumbo himself explained more fully some technical aspect of the process referred to by the works manager. Jamie was surprised by the detail of his father's knowledge, and by the evident ease with which he comprehended the works manager's mode of speech.

The visitors caused a kind of forward wash of curiosity. The men – some reaching hastily for their helmets – would scrutinize the knot of visitors as they approached, but when the group actually reached them they seemed unable to be distracted from their tasks, which for the most part were fettling the cast products of the melting shop with machines that ground or polished. They busied themselves with a self-consciousness that acknowledged their presence but prevented any exchange of smile or nod or even a catching of the eye. The exception was the senior furnaceman of the foundry, which they reached last and where the heat was as formidable as the racket had been in the rest of the factory. Here the only sound was the low roar of rushing air that kept the furnace at maximum temperature. This foundry foreman, or 'sample passer' as it seemed he was called, had lifted his blue goggles on to his forehead. He was a bruiser of a fellow, half as big again as the works manager, a sweat-towel round his neck, with a fuzz of ginger hair covering his arms and chest above his grimy tee-shirt and his broad leather apron. The foundry was kept in half darkness for the heat of the metal at its various stages to be gauged by the eye, and so it was difficult to make him out under his hat and beneath the grime and sweat and ginger fur. Despite that, Jamie sensed the physical arrogance of the man and a kind of professional contempt in him towards them all, not excluding the works manager or Jumbo himself, who nodded to him in acknowledgement of long acquaintance. The works manager attempted to introduce him to the Japanese, and the furnaceman held out his wrist to be shaken, like a stump, to save them soiling their hands. Even that gesture was somehow performed with disdain, as if none of them was man enough to touch the hand of a real worker. And what a hand, Jamie saw – a massive meaty implement of a hand in which their own would be twigs. Only Jumbo took the thick stump in acknowledgement, between his thumb and forefinger; and as he did so Jamie caught the glint of cold restraint in the man's eyes behind their sandy lashes and beneath the blue goggles that he felt were raised only as a gesture of passing condescension.

CHAPTER EIGHT

All through his last 'Half' at Eton Jamie knew he was neither boy nor man, and suffered. Others did not suffer as he did: he could see that: Anthony, for instance, seemed scarcely scathed at all. That did not alleviate Jamie Mainwaring in any degree, but made him lonelier. He was now separated from the House whose community of forty or so boys he had been part of for the past five years, and was boarding out as an upstairs lodger in the home of a master, in a seventeeth-century courtyard alongside the heart of the original mediaeval cloisters and chapel. This gave him greater freedom from the petty restrictions on daily life. On the other hand, due to the situation of the master's house, the antiquity of the place, the veneration it obliged, the quarterly double bell-toll from the clock in the Tudor tower that governed a thousand lives, weighted him and shrouded him as with layers of impenetrable black. The factor of sex was a torment. So far from being, as some fool in Alternative Assembly had tried to tell them, a 'brilliant inspiration of the Maker by which mankind was caught up in perpetual commitment to life and its beauty', sex was the single most insidious obstacle between Jamie and the enjoyment of life. The splinters and shards of his desire, its squalid intrusions into dreams, its spasmodically induced release, had nothing to do with beauty and served to stiffen and weight the shroud more impenetrably still.

Even if she was ready for him, which he knew she was not, he doubted if he wanted to contaminate Tibby with this sex. He did continue to see her, and he grew that much more daring with her. Now and then, it is true, amid the splinters and shards, was a gleam of what might be joy, joy without fear. Perhaps he loved her – he couldn't tell, and feared he might only find out for sure when he had shattered or fouled that love. She could not be 'his' for as far as anyone could see – she was far too young: meanwhile he was afraid of contaminating her, and having done so of discarding her, while he himself swept on wherever life would carry him.

It was himself, of course, he feared. Meanwhile he resolved to honour her purity and preserve it. In contrast to only a few months previously, he treated her now with a courtly grace. He took it upon himself to provide a base to her education (which her expensive school had somehow overlooked), and led her through the *Oxford Book of English Verse* – skipping of course – and telling her about the history that seemed to go with it. Tibby herself had never guessed till then that poems and history went together: Jamie wove it all so cleverly. She wondered at the power of Jamie's reading, the power of the word in him. He fascinated her, but often seemed incomprehensible.

To read was indeed Jamie's surest solace, a sort of secret watering-hole. The books that drew him most strongly were the writings of Albert Camus (already mentioned), Hermann Hesse, Kleist, and most recently Isaac Babel. They included no English, though a few Americans (from the 'Beat Generation') were honoured. They were, in Anthony's phrase, 'peculiar not to say weird'; to Tibby, incomprehensible, and in the case of his latest discovery, Babel, alarmingly so. Alone in Jamie's room, she had begun to read one of Babel's stories, and increasingly horrified followed it to the end of its five pages. It was full of utterly casual bloodthirst and savagery at the height of some war. She dipped into another story and found it to be just the same. She was quite frightened, waiting for Jamie in the teacher's empty house. How could it be that this Jamie who when he was normal could be so wise and gentle and beautiful and limpid and wholly *hers,* was simultaneously so remote and strange and even dangerous, when glimpsed from another side? Remote and strange and dangerous as the Africa he was set on . . . Perhaps this was all part of the dare of loving Jamie. And what were books and written words against the surety she knew when he gazed at her in silence and she searched back into his strong lean dark face? Or when walking beside her, or in some other chance proximity, when his lean dark man's body should happen to touch hers at many points? Even Mummy was proud of Jamie for her.

The two of them were able to sneak a morning together that long St Andrew's Day weekend of this final term – Jamie typically *insouciant* at the approach of the examination for university entrance by which Tibby knew his father set such store. They had agreed upon a certain pledge, an act of der-ring-do on another plane than that of exam papers on economic history. A seal, Jamie called it, against his coming back from Africa. She wasn't quite sure what he meant.

At an address in King's Cross supplied by Gus, Tibby now lay face down on a hard couch covered with a white sheet. She was fully clothed except for the exposure of four or five inches of bare skin along the lower part of the back and the upper part of the buttocks – her shirt and trousers being drawn back accordingly. The white sheet, though recently laun-dered, was speckled with little brown spots. A cotton wool swab in short, thick, hairy fingers, deftly cleaned a patch of skin along the upper part of the buttock alongside the cleavage.

The girl's small hand wandered out from the couch until it found another – Jamie's. The two hands remained thus softly clasped. There was abso-lute silence.

On the swabbed area of maiden skin a plastic stencil was now placed and a coloured powder dusted across the stencil. When the same hairy fingers – from the other side of the couch – removed the stencil, there was the outline of a tiny butterfly in coloured powder, as if just that instant settled in the intimate hollow of her perfect back.

(The butterfly was the smallest item of all on the wall-chart of designs, except for the lucky ladybird. Even so she had to sign a form to say she was sixteen, which was only just true.)

Now a tattoo gun approached the region of prepared skin like the snout of a monstrous predator insect. Jamie hurriedly pulled a pair of earphones from his pocket, slipped them over the girl's head, and flicked the switch of his Walkman. His own shirt-sleeves were rolled back and part of the forearm was covered by paper tissue held by Scotch tape. On a chair beside him lay a leatherbound book opened at front endpapers: on the inside board a label was pasted on which was printed a family crest bearing the motto Amor *et fiducia*.

At the moment of first puncture, the clasped hands tightened and the girl's face bunched into a child's grimace. 'There, ducky,' said the man with hairy fingers, who was big and friendly and wore a spotty surgeon's smock. 'Not so bad, is it?' He breathed over her in concentration. 'All you've to do, keep quite-quite still. Like a good little girl.'

The tattooist worked away, breathing; in three or four minutes he was done. He drew back to review his handiwork, which was visible as lines of minute beads of blood. It was no bigger than half an inch, perhaps less.

'A treat,' he declared. 'Though I say it myself.'

'A tortoiseshell,' Jamie suggested.

'Nao,' said the tattooist, 'a butterfly.'

Just then the door opened carefully and a large lady came in who was young once and had overestimated her ability to remain so. She wore an angora jumper and no bra.

'Hallo, May,' said the tattooist.

'Lou,' she acknowledged.

'Quite still, little lady, just a jiffy longer,' Lou told Tibby.

May peered at Lou's latest achievement, grinned at Jamie, swung around and hitched up her angora jumper as far as her neck. Right across her fleshy puckered back was spread a tattoo of a gigantic butterfly.

'Biggest I ever did,' Lou declared proudly. 'Took a week.'

'And I was off work another,' May said.

Tibby never saw it. Jamie grinned and looked at his watch: it was still only eleven. The whopping butterfly primed his audacity and he knew just what he was going to fill the space with between now and lunch with father and the man from Unicef.

By twelve thirty, in the family flat in Eaton Square, Jumbo was edgy. Twelve thirty was their agreed time: he had extracted from Jamie – who had become so unpunctual lately – a special promise.

He poured two glasses from the sherry decanter and carried them through to the drawing room. He didn't want Carstairs to think Jamie kept him waiting.

Jeremy Carstairs half rose to take his glass, and subsided back among the balance sheets and profit-and-loss accounts.

Jumbo sat where he could see through to the darkened hall and the flat's front door. He said, 'I do consider that vital.'

Carstairs did not know exactly what it was that Jumbo considered vital. He looked appropriately grave. There was plenty to be grave about. He had depended on Jumbo to persuade the Japs and Jumbo had failed. Or, at least, he had not yet succeeded, and now it was impossible to pull back. It was only the prospect of the Japanese merger that had kept the Group's share price reasonably buoyant. If the City got any whiff of the Group pulling back from the merger now, the shares would plummet. And there would be nowhere to turn, except back to the Japs again, or possibly one of the Korean giants, or Krupp . . . and on even less satisfactory terms. They couldn't go back to the shareholders with yet another rights issue, not within four years of the last one. What for? they would say. Where's the new product? The revitalizing new acquisitions? The City analysts weren't fools.

Carstairs hadn't been alone in relying on Jumbo: the whole board had gone along too. To be fair to Jumbo, he had never promised, he had never been categorical, he had never said like Mr Ryder at the Bolt Company board meeting, *Sine qua non,* without the Bolt Company, no deal. But Jumbo had fought the Japs in the war; he went back so far; he knew the mentality. He had fought them in the war and the war was won after all, even if won in that nightmarish cataclysmic way when the British hadn't yet cleared them out of Burma, let alone all the rest of south-east Asia. Carstairs was only six when the war ended, but he knew enough. Perhaps it would have been different if we had fought them all the way, valley by valley, tree by tree, to the walls of the Sun-God's Tokyo palace. No tricks, no wizardry, just the ruthless pummelling and grinding into humiliation and abject surrender, soul-surrender, admission of ultimate compliance of where the power lay: in the West. Then they might never have dared to come creeping back to the walls of Bradford.

'Vital,' Jumbo repeated.

Carstairs remembered now what was vital. It was vital that the City analysts were not led to suppose that the door was firmly closed on Japanese involvement in the Bolt Company. Direct questions on that point must be side-stepped. Otherwise there would be people saying that the Group's forty-nine per cent of the Bolt Company should be written off as worthless. In actual fact, the Japanese in their negotiations had consistently refrained from either endorsing or questioning the value that the Group put on its Bolt Company holding in the last Group profit-and-loss account – perhaps out of tact, out of saving Jumbo's face. They must know it would have to be written off in the end. They had access to all the figures, which were not published: they knew it had made a loss four years in a row and that it had paid a dividend only by means of its bank borrowings. What they didn't know – Carstairs himself was probably the only outsider who knew – was that these borrowings were in turn guaranteed by the family's own shareholding in the Group. If the Bolt Company went, it would not only jolt the Group, it would knock quite a hole in the Mainwaring family finances. Charlie Ryder might have to sell his racehorses.

Carstairs glanced at Jumbo and thought he spotted fear. Seventeen years of service with the Group, six years on the Group board and five on the Bolt Company board, and he'd never spotted fear before. Up to now it had never more than fleetingly occurred to Carstairs that Jumbo could in the last resort be fallible, let alone afraid. Jumbo was the exemplification of the immutable in British industry. Bowater, Guest-Keen, Cadbury, Pilkington, Babcock & Wilcox, Mainwaring . . . the names were pillars of the temple, the blue chips. Mainwaring was there before the world began. In the beginning was a chimney. Now fear.

Jeremy Carstairs felt a sudden sense of betrayal. He was forty-eight, he had a wife and two children, yes, and a decent home, and was honorary vice-chairman of the golf club; but he had given his life to Mainwaring. There was no future for him elsewhere. He too felt the smearing of fear. He was protected up to a point – the Japs had promised to respect all existing contracts with the Bolt Company which guaranteed him a lump sum if — But what if the Bolt Company actually *failed?* He had already seen enough of the Japanese to realize how little he could expect from them. They treated Jumbo like some demi-god, the full kow-tow, but Carstairs, the Finance Director, might have been some sort of office boy, the way they gave him the run-around. Once Jumbo had entered the room he didn't exist. They'd had him working away till ten o'clock at night without a word of apology or consideration. After the merger – which wasn't a merger anyway, it was a take-over, and the PR people were going to have a job persuading the Press to call it anything else – he knew what he could expect from the Nips.

A crumb of dry biscuit which Jumbo had taken with his sherry had clung to the corner of his lower lip. Carstairs thought it odd that he'd never noticed the vulnerability of Jumbo's lower lip before. He wondered when Jumbo had last been afraid. In the war? In Burma, fighting the Japs? What had his lower lip looked like then?

Jumbo's fear had opened the gates of Carstairs's own fear. It outraged him.

He said smoothly, 'The popular Press might try to make something out of your having fought the Japs in the war, Jumbo.'

Jumbo said nothing. His face took on the square lines Carstairs now knew to be a front.

'I shall be ready for them if they try,' Jumbo said at last.

There was no fear in Jumbo. All Carstairs had seen was his own. Jumbo had had several of the same thoughts as Carstairs, but from much longer ago – months or years. He himself had never been afraid, just weighed down rather, darkened, regretful; but just now he had glimpsed the funk in Carstairs and knew Carstairs had been thinking, He isn't what I thought he was, he has let me down.

He looked at his watch again, and Carstairs said, 'Your boy's cutting it a bit fine.'

Jumbo was silent some more.

'He won't have gone straight to White's?'

'I think not.'

Then came the sound of a key in the lock. Jumbo looked up sharply.

Searle let himself in, carrying his grey cap. He came to the open door of the drawing room and said, it's after ten minutes to one, Sir James.'

'Mr Jamie will be here any minute,' Jumbo replied quickly, and at once turned to Carstairs. 'Now then, Jeremy. In any case there'll be redundancies at the Bolt Company. The vacancy rate at Bolton and Scunthorpe must be assessed as accurately as possible, at shopfloor and craft levels.'

Carstairs said, 'I've already got the preliminary assessments,' and was drawing out a document to pass to Jumbo when the front door latch was again heard, and Jamie came in wearing his leather jacket. He shut the door behind him. The light in the hall was dim, and when his father raised his eyes from the document he seemed not to recognize who he was, perhaps mistaking him for Searle. Jamie came to the drawing-room doorway as Searle had. 'I'll just change into a suit, Pa.'

Now Jumbo looked up properly and saw what Searle and Carstairs had already seen. Jamie's hair, cropped rectangular, was dyed a peroxide blond.

From the doorway Jamie knew by a son's instinct that the sight of him was like a blow to his father's stomach. A defensive scorn he couldn't help entered his face. He said, 'Okay? Only two minutes.' He began to move towards the stairs descending to his bedroom.

Then he heard his name. He turned and went back four paces to the drawing room entrance. His face wore a sheepish expectancy of trouble: he couldn't help that either.

'What is it?'

Jumbo felt sick – it was indeed in the stomach: not blinded but winded. Here was a person impossible to recognize. The son he had loved all his life, not recognizable. If his answer was not going to come of its own accord, he could not make it come.

'What's up, then?' Jamie said.

Jumbo could not quite look at him. His eyes were on the boy, but not actually regarding him, not interpreting him. A tallish peroxide blond young man shaved square up the sides and across the top, and dark eyebrows and an immature mouth. A freak. A robot. An oversized doll thing. A nothing.

Jamie came right into the room now and put the leatherbound book he was carrying into the bookshelf. It was one of a set. Jumbo saw the Walkman earphones round his neck and the lead dangling.

'How are you, Mr Carstairs?' Jamie said.

'Thank you, Jamie,' Carstairs replied.

'I' – Jumbo was locating his voice – 'can't take you to White's looking like that.' He completed the sentence quite quickly and evenly, if a little dry in the throat.

Jamie paused. Why did Mr Carstairs have to be there? His presence was restraining his father. Jamie felt primed for a real up-and-downer. He said,

'I'll put my suit on. You'll feel better.' The slight shift to aggressiveness made his face feel more normal, his mouth a little firmer.

'It's out of the question,' his father said between breaths. 'You are perfectly well aware of that yourself.'

From wherever all the blood from Jumbo's face had drained to, it now came rushing back.

'Why White's?' Jamie said airily. 'We could lunch with your friend anywhere.'

Then there was silence from both of them, as palpable as ice. 'You look half pansy,' Jumbo said.

'If I was gay you'd have nothing to do with me, would you?'

'But you're not a homo!'

'How d'you know?'

'I know you're not,' Jumbo came back very sharply, in thin, pure disgust now. He had had enough of this, though there was abyss below it on all sides.

Jamie said, 'You care about me just so far as I fit your expectations. Right?' (He regretted the 'Right?') 'My boyfriend likes me blond,' he mimicked.

His father ignored him now. He got up. 'I'll be off now, Jeremy. Can I give you a lift to the West End?'

'If you would, Jumbo.'

Carstairs followed Jumbo out, passing Jamie in the hall. Jumbo told Searle that Mr Jamie would not be coming. As the three left the flat in a troop, Carstairs was murmuring something about 'spirited'.

On the steps into the street they heard Jamie calling from the flat door. 'Look, I want to meet this fellow. I want to come with you.'

When Jumbo paused the other two did likewise.

'I hear what you say,' he called back in a narrow voice, 'I'll tell him . . . you're not well.'

From his room in the basement Jamie watched the wheels of the Daimler roll his father away. To Father's own preserve, his vivarium (dropping off Mr Carstairs, of course: no crossing of White's threshold for Mr Carstairs). Jamie had been in a frenzy of changing: now he stopped suddenly, half into his repulsive worsted blue suit trousers. He had supposed they might not actually go.

His father's over-reaction was laughable, pitiable. It was of course the prospect of violating White's Club that had appalled him. How pathetic. Jamie knew White's, the unrufflable complacence, the unassailable *hauteur*, the unendurable durability of the place. Pa had taken him there every now and then for lunch and once, indeed, for dinner. He pictured himself, beaconheaded, tagging along behind his father up the sweep of the staircase and into the Regency dining room, where Prinny hung in oils on the magenta plush. As they pause at the high desk to order luncheon, heads turn, frowns cross brows like titchy black clouds. Nothing would be actually said. *Jumbo's* boy? A *Mainwaring*? The senior steward taking their order, the queenly cashier upon her perch, would bat no eyelid. And on their descending afterwards, for coffee and a game of backgammon in the long inner room, sanctuary of sanctuaries, some reptilian duke in a corner leather armchair would raise his eyes and stare with laser incredulity.

On his chest-of-drawers his father stood beside his mother outside Buckingham Palace on receiving his CBE, in a frame of hammered silver. Had he known how to lay a curse on a man, he might have laid one now. Or might not, inasmuch as a person is also that which has gone into the making of him, and he would not yet curse himself.

CHAPTER NINE

After that it was not to be quite the same between Jumbo and his son. Jamie did indeed miss his lunch at White's with the senior official of Unicef whom his father had found for him (through an old friend at the Overseas Development Administration). Jumbo explained that young Jamie had had an accident that affected his head and he had been advised to stay at home, all of which was not immorally distant from the truth. As it was, Jumbo's guest provided a clear run-down of information on the various organizations dispensing aid in sub-Saharan Africa which his host, amid his obscure bereavement, supposed might prove of some purpose, somehow, some time.

It was not an easy time. Two days later Jamie had returned to school for the last time. Father and son had somehow avoided further encounter. That very next week the Japanese attended their first ever meeting of the Mainwaring Group Holdings company board. The meeting took place at the Group's Lombard Street headquarters. For Carstairs there

was an ominous finality about it, amid all the talk of
a beckoning future. The board had gathered for the
signing. Eleven of the fourteen directors were present – one banking knight, two industrial knights, a
Civil Service peer (a former Cabinet Secretary, no
less), a former Conservative politician who had been
a junior trade minister, Britain's last ambassador to
Brussels, three younger directors appointed from
within the Group and still in their forties (marketing, industrial management, and Carstairs himself as
Finance), a treasured Jewish QC with a reputation for
unrivalled knowledge of patent law, and Jumbo himself. A financial journalist had totted up that between
them the fourteen held sixty-one directorships. Their
experiences of business and industry and indeed the
world beyond was, one might say (and Carstairs often
heard Jumbo doing so), second-to-none. They constituted a balanced sample of the Great and the Good
of contemporary Britain, selling it out.

They were of course doing right by the shareholders, who had already approved overwhelmingly –
on a four per cent response and a show of hands
at the Extraordinary General Meeting – the terms
enshrined in the present complex document, where
a two-for-one share issue added nearly fifty per cent to
the value of their stock. They were doing right by the
company and its employees. They . . . 'We', Jumbo,
now on his feet at the head of the magificent polished
table, 'are truly glad to welcome our good friends Mr
Iseki and Mr Ishikawa' (Ishikawa made a quick bow

of infinite self-humiliation, from a seated position) 'back in our midst today, for the first time as our new partners, bringing as they do not only their capital investment but also their technical experience and management skills to a sector of British industry we have long considered ripe for stimulus from overseas.

'By signing these documents today, we are not only acknowledging the obvious merits of internationalism in the field of metallurgic industry. But by virtue of our Japanese friends' manifest willingness to bring us their money, their commercial energy, and their skills, we are performing a signal service to *Britain's* manufacturing sector and *Britain's* industrial future . . .'

This little speech had already been issued to the Press, embargoed until 3 p.m. that afternoon. It had been handed out that morning at the press conference which Jumbo had chaired. Carstairs had been impressed: the public relations people had insisted on fielding Jumbo, and they were shown to be right. Carstairs had been up there on the platform, seated just behind and to one side of Jumbo. Shortly before it had opened he had noticed a little twitch in Jumbo's cheek, just below the left eyelid, which he had not seen before, and it confirmed his suspicion that secretly Jumbo was afraid. Yet when the moment came, Carstairs was impressed. Jumbo at once took command of the proceedings with humour, grace and firmness. The City journalists seemed to accept the euphemisms at face value: 'co-venture' for the

creation of a management partnership to run factories which had been making things for the better
part of a century; 'convertible unsecured loan stock'
which would inevitably give the Japanese a voting
majority in a few years. When one bright spark asked
whether Sir James didn't feel the Japanese moving
into a traditionally home-based manufacturing sector like Mainwaring's to be a 'further surrender of
Britain's economic independence', Jumbo instantly
tossed it back expressing good-humoured surprise
that the questioner should not have noticed that the
'world was growing rather smaller'. In the moment
of pause Jumbo added, 'Would you prefer to have
British enterprise turn its back on commercial
opportunities offered by a buoyant Japan and its free-
market Pacific neighbours?' The fellow was silenced.
Nobody thought to ask why similar 'co-ventures' by
British companies in Japan were not considered necessary for Japanese products to enter British markets.
Nobody asked how it had come about that Japanese
managers could be counted upon to achieve a level
of productivity among English factory hands that
English managers manifestly couldn't. You had to
give it to Jumbo, Carstairs thought. He had been mas-
terly at the press conference.

Jumbo was a fallen idol, he had allowed the
Japanese to outface him over the Bolt Company;
but his performance throughout all the rest of the
so-called merger could hardly be faulted. It was
Jumbo throughout who had given the impression of

keeping the initiative, made the negative seem positive; Jumbo who had maintained the confidence not only of the Japanese themselves but the stock market. It would need only one major broker advising to sell to have undermined everything. That had never happened. The device they had settled for over the Bolt Company concealed the complete climb-down. Mainwarings' merchant bankers had come up with the idea, and nobody had rumbled it. What they had done was simply to leave the Group's holding in the Bolt Company out of the merger reckoning altogether: they had put no valuation on it at all. The implication was not, of course, that its value was nil, but that it could not be properly assessed until later when the rest of the integration was under way. The outsiders had swallowed it not least because of the assured glint in Jumbo's voice when handling the issue with the City analysts or the press: 'One thing at a time,' or 'We've decided to count our chickens in the part of the business where they're running about.'

There was a deception here, of course, although Jumbo had said nothing that could be laid at his door later. The board was fully aware that the Japanese were not going to put a single yen into the Bolt Company. The directors had avoided discussing it at their meetings, probably in order to spare Jumbo's feelings. It wouldn't be to spare Carstairs's feelings, that was for sure, even though the problem was sitting right there in all its ugliness on Carstairs's plate.

Carstairs felt not only anxious but aggrieved. Jumbo the patrician could play the lofty internationalist with these strange little yellow men. The Mainwaring family might have to write off a piece of their fortune. But the Japs would not dare to usurp Jumbo's position as eponymous chairman. They were for ever giving Jumbo their Shinto-shrine obeisance. Carstairs knew that he himself scarcely existed for them. And yet he, Carstairs, was the one who saw through Jumbo. He had caught the fear in him (or was it shame?). He could guess the stink that Charlie Ryder was going to make with his grand cousin who had the family baronetcy. He had witnessed the next Mainwaring baronet, who ever since this little heir was a small boy had somehow succeeded in making him feel like a family retainer, humiliating his father with a pot of blond dye. None of those present knew Jumbo Mainwaring as he did.

It was the photographer brought in by the PR advisers to record the signing who penetrated the façade, like the bit-part actor with two lines to say who screws up the entire scene. He was the creative type, naturally, announcing his giftedness the moment he entered the boardroom by his beard, his tielessness, and his volleyball footwear. He couldn't simply stand opposite Jumbo and Ishikawa as they sat at the table appending their signatures, press the tit on his Japanese camera and go away. He had to shoot them from three or four different angles while they repeatedly mimed the signing. Jumbo assumed his patrician mein each time and the Japanese filled the little intervals with their flatter-talk. The 'very-last' angle required by the photographer entailed his crouching at floor level from across the table. This was evidently in order to incorporate the portrait of Josiah Mainwaring in his frock-coat and side-whiskers on the panelled wall above. Ishikawa asked in mock awe, 'This gentooman the founder of your company, Sir Jamess?'

'Indeed, the founder,' Jumbo replied without expression.

'All our people' – *peepoo* was really what Ishikawa said – 'all our peepoo will be proud of founder, Sir Jamess. You may say the custom in Japan is to worship ancestors.'

If this was a Japanese joke, Jumbo doused it. 'To be precise,' he reminded him, 'he founded the Mainwaring Bolt Company.'

Carstairs heard the coldness all right. They all heard it, surely. The coldness . . . the disgust. The shame.

It was not shame, not yet anyway. Carstairs had again misread his master. It was, rather, a shaft of sorrow. Throughout this difficult time Jumbo had scarcely allowed himself sorrow. He was aware of its presence – in the next room, as it were, a dark place; but he was not going to allow it to possess him. In his twenty-six years at the top, since his father retired, he had built his reputation for facing facts and decisiveness. This merger, partnership, what-you-will, fitted his reputation. He knew that, and he knew his own confidence was paramount. He had learned that early: as a nineteen-year-old platoon commander he knew that not even a skirmish in the jungle could be carried through successfully without the leader's steady *confidence*. One did not countenance failure, one did not entertain regret. One faced facts; one held up one's head; one set an example; one led.

He had become aware, just lately, of some sort of muscular twitch beneath his left eyelid. It came on spontaneously at odd moments – this morning, for instance, at the press conference: a sort of momentary flickering like very distant lightning. He did not know if it was noticeable to others – he had no opportunity to check it in a looking-glass. It was of no consequence anyway. He was certainly not going to let himself believe in the fashionable ailment of 'stress'. What, one might ask, was ever achieved without stress?

In any case, the press conference had gone well.

Maybe it was, as some had suggested, a matter of congratulation that an industrial complex like Mainwarings was 'going Japanese' – an act of modern-mindedness, a discarding of shibboleths, a healthy coming-to-terms with a changing world. Hadn't the share price jumped? This was the City of London, feet on the ground, into the nitty-gritty. This was the way the English stayed with it. Of all her servants, had not Her Majesty the Queen bestowed her personal honours most fervently on the man sent out to turn the

British-settled colony of Rhodesia into a black republic? Jumbo had known the fellow. He was welcomed back like a conquering hero, and rightly so.

Three or four of his fellow directors were old friends, guests at each other's tables, fellow members of White's. They had made no demur on the merger. They had seen the virtue of it all, the virtue of necessity no doubt, but virtue none the less. They had plenty of opportunity to tell him otherwise, off the record, particularly Harry Fortescue, whom he saw at least twice a week at his club. Some wag had suggested that at the bar of White's there was no single item of information on himself offered by one member to another that could not be quite adequately and graciously fielded by one of three two-word responses: *Great fun, Rather fun,* or *Bad luck.* News of the Mainwaring Group's reconstruction as Mainwaring-Nippon would be perfectly entitled to *Rather fun* (plenty of torque in that middle one).

The Bolt Company – well, that was definitely *Bad luck* and didn't warrant discussion. It would have to be faced, by himself, more or less alone, with Carstairs alongside, of course. And Jane: she would fill her role by keeping the home fires burning – Upton, the family. But he wouldn't go burdening his Jane with self-pity.

Such were the thoughts of Jumbo Mainwaring as Searle drove him back to Eaton Square after the board meeting at which the merger documents were signed.

And the next month Jamie was to leave Eton, the fourth successive generation of Mainwarings to have been educated there. Jumbo had had it vaguely in mind for years to attend Jamie's last School Concert, and in spite of all he would not deny himself. He hadn't seen Jamie for some five weeks: the blinding peroxide would presumably have mostly grown out. Jumbo drove himself down from London – it was only fifty minutes from the flat – Eaton to Eton. He was on his own: Jane was at Upton. He just milled in with the rest of the boys and the masters and a scattering of parents, and sat in the packed hall. He had not warned Jamie he was coming.

Jamie was on stage as a member of the school orchestra. Jumbo saw him from the body of the hall, settling in with his friends in the brass section. Thank God the worst of the dye had gone. Jamie was no master of the trumpet, but his parts were simple enough. The main orchestral piece, as it happened, was for strings and woodwind only, the Precentor doubtless aware of the potential for havoc from brass or percussion whose ability to count rests was unpredictable. It was only during this enforced idleness that Jamie caught sight of his father amid the audience. The quick smile exchanged across those many heads and several yards was – was, ah, just like ancient times: a father and his lad. The surge of relief and love opened Jumbo's throat and lungs for the last, familiar Leavers' Song, in which the entire hall joined in the chorus and the entire orchestra, brass and all, let rip in swirling oom-pa-pa . . .

> Time ever flowing bids us be going
>> Dear Mother Eton, far from thee!
> Hearts growing older, love never colder.
>> Never forgotten shalt thou be!
> Eastward and westward, far divided
>> Northward and southward, go must we.

And then again.

> Hearts growing older, love never colder,
> Never forgotten shalt thou be!

Jumbo threw back his head, gave it all had had got, surrendered to its mastering banalities all the substance of life.

Life's duties call us; – whate'er befall us . . . a distinguished leaver, a member of Pop in brocaded waistcoat, was singing his solo verse. Jumbo had left the school at the nadir of the war, the bad time, early '42. Singapore had fallen that Lent Half. He was straining at the leash to get into uniform, confront the heathen, the hosts of Midian. Every Thursday night in chapel an Intercession Service was held – a few prayers, a hymn, and the names of the Old Boys reported killed that previous week were read out. Attendance was voluntary, and those who did attend *wanted* to be there, to offer their prayers, lift their

voices. The Intercession Services were the most moving communal experience of Jumbo's young life till
then . . . perhaps, even, all his life.

High lot or lowly,

sang the boy

weal or woe,
Brother with brother, thou our Mother,
In thee united we will go.
For home and kinsfolk, for old comrades,
For Queen and country, and for thee.

And now again, the packed hall, the open throats,
the open breasts, the trumpets and the cymbals

Hearts growing older, love never colder . . .

The next day Searle fetched Jamie from Eton for the
last time and ferried him in the Daimler with all his
school clobber in the boot to London, where he had
much to do, before going on to Upton. He ran into
his father in the flat that evening and Jumbo warmly
congratulated him on his school concert.

Jamie said, 'Saw you really letting rip with that last
song we did. Dear Mother Eton thingumme.'

Jumbo gave a grin.

'You knew it ?' asked Jamie.

'Of course I knew it,' Jumbo told him. 'Everyone knows it.'

'It was the first time we did it.'

Jumbo was nonplussed. 'What can you mean?'

'We revived it. It's not been sung for donkey's years. It's a great song.'

'What made you revive it?' his father asked him, the joy crippled.

'Oh – the nostalgia gig,' Jamie said, with a waggle of the head.

'What's that, Ginger?' said the weasel-faced man, stepping back from the heat of the furnace to where the big man stood in half-darkness manipulating the ladle.

'Said, we're gettin' no Nips 'ere,' the senior furnaceman told him.

'We don't want 'em.'

'We want 'em, Les. I'm saying, we want 'em.' The big furnaceman watched the molten slick ooze into the billet moulds like blazing honey. There was no purity in the world to equal it. 'They're going into the Bolton works. And Scunthorpe. But they're not coomin' in 'ere. Why?'

'We don't want 'em,' said Les.

'Don't be daft, Les,' Ginger said. 'We want 'em. They've left uz out of the agreement. *Why?*'

Leslie felt foolish. Ginger could see things. Ginger always asked the right questions.

A mere nine days after these events, three days after Chistmas Day, despite his having failed to attend the lunch with the man from Unicef, Jamie left for Africa. He was to be gone for eight months.

PART II

CHAPTER TEN

When Jamie had left for Africa Tibby hardly knew what to think. She had only seen him once since their St Andrew's Day adventure when she had allowed him to have that secret butterfly pricked for ever on to her skin as his 'seal against his return'. The only remaining *exeat* weekend from St Mary's fell when Jamie was doing his exams for Cambridge and he had of course kept her away. Then he had gone to Scotland with Anthony, and had sent her a photograph of him standing on some sort of turret looking out over a great open landscape with his hair blowing across his forehead. His face looked so strong. She told nobody at school about the butterfly because it was her most secret possession, known only to the two of them. And some of them at school were anyway so — so grown-up nasty-minded.

After her school broke up there was the rush of buying everything for Christmas. She and her parents were to stay with her grandmother in Lincolnshire. There was just the one party in London, a dance at a private house, to which she and Jamie had been separately invited. It was the first London dance she had ever attended and she had had to plead with her mother for permission to go. First she went to a grand dinner party where she was given beef with pastry rolled around it and a delicious pudding called raspberry Romanoff. She had put on make-up for the first time, and when she got to the house where the ball was and they took her school overcoat (it was all she had: she was not 'out' yet) and put it among hundreds of others, she felt quite strange and lost. She longed for Jamie to arrive and make her feel all right, but eleven o' clock came and then twelve and still he did not appear. She was to be collected at one o'clock by her father. She danced with a few young men she met through the handful of acquaintances present from her school (they were all older than she), but she failed to make any impression on anyone; mostly because, she supposed, she did not wish to. She felt much younger than everyone else. They all had some purpose of their own for being there which eluded Tibby. The young men who invited her to dance jiggled away at a distance, too far off to say anything (the disco was anyway too loud for talking), occasionally swinging her around so that they could jiggle away at the same distance facing in another direction. When the break in the music came, they handed her a glass of Buck's Fizz – sometimes not even that – and left her.

Her invitation to the party had come through some intervention by Jamie; she did not understand how Jamie could have failed to turn up himself. Then at half an hour after midnight he arrived, all among a group of others, young men and girls, the young men being mostly former Eton friends and all of them quite drunk. Tibby had just come down from the ladies' room for the sixth or seventh time and saw immediately that Jamie was also drunk.

She wanted to leave the party at once then, but there was still another twenty minutes at least before her father was due to come for her. Jamie caught sight of her from across the hall before she had been able to get down the last of the stairs through the couples sitting on the lower steps and disappear into the crowd. He gave her an oafish leer, and she could see his eyes had no meaning in them. He looked quite unlike the photograph of him she had received only a fortnight before, standing on the castle turret. She didn't know whether to smile back or pretend she hadn't seen him. She did smile but very quickly, and he went on leering in the same way.

Then Gus, standing just below her, who had arrived with this new group, spotted her and exclaimed 'Tibbikins!' and immediately dragged her away to dance. Gus, she felt, was one of those men to whom it was natural to be quite drunk. Even when he wasn't he pretended to be.

'Why've you only just arrived?' she succeeding in getting him to hear across the din of the amplifiers.

'We've been to another party.'

'Why?'

'*Why?*'

'Yes. Why?'

'They invited us.'

'Jamie too?'

'Of course, Tibbikins.'

She found Jamie in another room eating scrambled egg and sausages with three or four others, including girls. When he saw her, he put the plate aside and took her by the hand to a dark corner where there was a window seat. They sat there, half turned towards one another. He tilted his head towards hers until his sweaty brow rested on the side of her head. 'Little Tibby,' he muttered. That was all he said. She had had her hair waved for him.

Then her father was there to collect her. Jamie let her go without a word. On the way to her uncle's flat where they were to sleep the night her father asked her if she'd had a good time. She did not answer because she was crying. Her father didn't notice – he seldom noticed anything about her.

Earlier she had had the intention of seeing Jamie off for Africa, but her Christmastide visit to Lincolnshire put paid to that. She knew which day, the Sunday three days after Christmas, but that was all. He was to fly to Paris, and from there to a country called Mali where there had been a drought for ages and ages. All the vegetation had died and the people there were terribly hungry and the babies dying. She had seen pictures in the newspapers of places like that, and sometimes there were reports about it on television, although she had never heard anyone mention Mali, except Jamie. He had told her very little about it all – why he wanted to go there, what he was going to do. She had only noticed that he seemed happier when he had decided to go and especially when whoever the people were he was going to work with had told him definitely that he could join them. She knew when Jamie was happy because he was quieter. He was noisy when he was unhappy. She supposed that was the opposite to most people; otherwise, what about parties, which were surely meant to make people happy, where everyone went out of their way to make them as noisy as possible?

Then at a quarter past eight on the morning of Sunday the 28th he rang up from Heathrow airport, just before he was due to take off. Everyone was having a lie-in and her grandmother took the call in her bedroom. She came through to Tibby's little room to wake her, though she was scarcely asleep any more, and said she'd better take the telephone upstairs in her bedroom where the call came through. So Tibby had hurried through to her Granny's bedroom just as she was, in her nightie, and sat on the edge of Granny's bed where her Grandpa was lying in his pyjamas, all tousled and stubbly, and there was Jamie's voice saying 'I love you'. She could hear the airport noises in the background. He had never said that to her before – nobody had except Mummy and possibly Daddy – and she didn't know what to say herself. She heard him say 'Tibby?' as if he thought she might not have heard or had been disconnected or something, and she said 'Yes, Jamie'. He then said, 'I'm just off. I — ' and then the line did go: obviously the money had run out.

Tibby handed the receiver to her Granny who said, 'Finished already?' She put it to her ear and heard the dialling tone and put it back on the cradle. 'That wasn't much of a conversation,' she said, quite kindly. And her Grandpa murmured in a tousled way, 'Early birds, Tibby's friends,' and turned his head away into his pillow.

So Tibby did not really know what to think. Jamie was to be away until August or September, as long as Tibby could imagine. She had often admitted to herself that she loved Jamie, although she was not sure that she was old enough to have the right to say that about a boy, and sometimes she was certain she hated him. What puzzled her was that what she seemed to love most about him was the mystery of him. That seemed to her very contrary, for surely it was what you knew about someone that you could love (or not love), not what you didn't know. And in the mystery of him was a fear, too: fear or awe, at the secret power of him. It was as if something expected of her that she should leap out and across to him through a dark veil, trusting in the readiness and strength of his arms to catch her and hold her. (She did know of his strength, and his quickness too.)

She had never quite let him kiss her, not completely (no one else had, of course). Once recently

he had put his lips on hers and she had felt his
tongue trying to probe and snake between her lips. It
was remarkable how strong it was, but she would not
let it in – she didn't dare to. Just for a moment her
own tongue flickered against his – involuntarily, as a
kind of acknowledgement that she wasn't really, not
deep inside her, fighting him: that she'd received the
signal, as it were, and would let him know when the
time came that she might be ready for such a leap . . .
That was the most that had happened between them,
although sometimes she'd had to move his hand
from this place or that to somewhere safer.

Mummy had asked her once, recently, if she loved
Jamie, and she answered, Yes, she thought she did.
Her mother had then said, 'You're very young still,
darling.' She knew that Mummy approved of her seeing Jamie, though. They had got to know each other
quite soon after they had moved near Upton, when
she was only eleven and Jamie had just gone to Eton.
First they met at tennis at one house or another, and
then they used to see each other out hunting. Horses
were her passion then. Mummy had got to know
Lady Mainwaring quite well taking Tibby to or from
Upton, and liked her too; but Daddy hardly knew
Sir James at all and once she had heard him remark
that he doubted Jumbo Mainwaring wanted to spend
his time with insurance salesmen. She was surprised
at this because she knew her father was a successful
man – Mummy often said so – and that his work was
important and always came first. The Mainwarings

were a famous family, of course, because of all the factories, and their house was a lot grander than the Hoskynses', although the Hoskynses had a swimming pool in the garden while all that the Mainwarings had at Upton were the two ponds full of weed and frogs. Tibby didn't feel any real difference between them.

Mummy did approve, she knew, but she did also repeat that Jamie's going away to Africa was really rather a good thing because it would give Tibby the chance to get out and meet some more boys. Mummy had quite a store of wisdom about how things should be, and all that store was for the sake of Tibby, her only child.

CHAPTER ELEVEN

After the first few rather hurried, factual, unsatisfying letters and postcards with their strange stamps bearing the head of a black man in a very high military cap with a lot of gold on its peak, nobody heard much from Jamie. Jumbo got out the big, old *Times* atlas to look up the place, Bandiagara, which was to be Jamie's posting when he moved on from the capital. He saw it was well to the south of Timbuktu ('Timbuktoo', the atlas spelt it), which was the only place anybody had heard of in that country. Sometimes old friends asked him – in White's, for example – what young Jamie was up to these days. Jumbo would reply, as a kind of easy shorthand, that he was 'dishing out aid in Timbuktu', and they would respond 'Oh, great fun,' or 'Rather fun,' sometimes adding 'Good for young Jamie,' or 'I wish my young would do something useful like that,' with a grin which could suggest that they privately thought *their* young were on to something smarter.

Jumbo missed Jamie, not being able to picture at all clearly what his daily life consisted of, or what might be occupying his thoughts. It was the first time that he had felt thus deprived since Jamie had been born. And he knew he and Jamie had not recovered their trust, their old intimacy, since the hair-dyeing episode. Jamie had got himself attached to some food-dispensing organization for the Third World that was mostly funded from money raised by rock band concerts. He had fixed it all up himself, including his medical requirements, his work permit, long-stay visa, and so on. Jamie had evidently paid for his own air fare out of the allowance which for a year or two now Jumbo had arranged to be transferred monthly into his bank account. Jumbo wrote out the information he had gleaned from the Unicef man at their lunch for two, and handed the sheets of paper to Jamie when they were together at Upton for Christmas. It was a kind of summary of the aid-giving structure operating in the sub-Saharan region. Jamie thanked him courteously and said it would be 'really useful', leaving his father to wonder if perhaps he knew it all already.

Then on Christmas Eve itself had come word that Jamie had been accepted by King's, Cambridge, the 'family' college for whose famous Chapel their common Mainwaring ancestor had given the great west window and where Jamie, that next October, would be the fourth successive Mainwaring to go up. Jamie let it go at lunch as casually as he could – to his mother, in fact: 'Oh, I made it to King's.' Jumbo had half-heard it, and when the confirmation came (he could tell from the look he received from Jane across the table) he felt such a surge of joy and pride that his eye went moist, though he trusted not visibly so. He could not help reminding Jane and Vicky that getting into Cambridge nowadays was not at all the same as it was in his day, when the girls were excluded except at the two ladies' colleges and the 'grammar school contingent' was negligible. (He had gone up immediately after the War.) He had often made the same point lately, preparing himself for a disappointment. He didn't wish to let his own delight be such as to suggest that it was for his sake that Jamie had won his place, which was why he refrained from adding that this achievement confirmed Jamie's natural membership of those who would provide the leadership of the country in due time. One could say that Jamie's own muted satisfaction exemplified that very naturalness. Even so, at morning service at Upton church next day, Jumbo did give thanks to God for the sweetness of this blessing, amid those other matters which had the taste of gall.

As for the Group, the two Japanese at main board level settled in with a vigour and tact which won admiration and reduced with unexpected rapidity the sheer weight of Jumbo's day-to-day responsibilities. There was no change in Jumbo's title as Group Chairman but, as Sir Harry Fortescue put it cheerfully to Jumbo, there was 'nothing to be lost in letting Wishee and Washee get on and do all the work, now we've brought 'em in'. Harry Fortescue and

two other old colleagues of Jumbo's on the Group
board shortly retired, by rotation, and Ishikawa and
Iseki were soon joined by two more Japanese, as their
agreement anticipated. Jumbo chaired, but the tone
of the board gatherings had changed profoundly.
It was all he could do to deter several of the non-
executive members from deferring to the newcomers
over everything, to the manifest discomfiture of the
English executive directors promoted from within
the Group, not least Carstairs. It had to be said the
Japanese were careful not to overplay their hands:
they were trained accordingly, Jumbo could see. Even
so, at board meetings or policy discussions between
senior executives it always seemed that the English
did most of the talking in the tacit assumption that
the Japanese would have the final word. It was as if
they possessed some arcane Oriental secret, some
ultimate mystery that gave them a power in human
destiny denied to the blundering English. Yet who
was it, if not Mainwarings, who had produced the
world's first hot-water radiators? Or who first alloyed
the iron and titanium for pistons that lasted twice as
long as any previously?

It was Carstairs towards whom Jumbo felt most protective. Carstairs could scarcely bring himself to utter
the word 'Japanese'. He referred to them invariably
as 'our friends', or worse still as 'our good friends'.
Jumbo could see the way the Japs circled Carstairs
with a kind of silence, as if they were simply waiting
for him to demonstrate his own insufficiency in such

a way that nobody would resist his being replaced. Jumbo felt the injustice of it. Jeremy Carstairs had been his own choice – his own creation, one might say. His very merits were being turned against him: his caution, his respect for the traditional Mainwaring products and markets, in a manner of speaking his very loyalty to Jumbo himself. How dare the implication arise that he lacked imagination? It was not the role of a finance director to be imaginative. And simultaneously, as Jumbo was well aware, the Japs had put paid to Carstairs's other role in life.

The closing down of the Mainwaring Bolt Company was to become Jumbo's central preoccupation. It came up on him with distressing swiftness in those bleak winter weeks following Jamie's departure. He and Carstairs had to face it together, and it began to go wrong. This is what happened.

Having operated at a mounting trading loss four years in succession, the Bolt Company had become heavily indebted. The company's overdraft was secured by one hundred per cent of the privately owned shares, all of which were held by the Mainwaring family. The largest single block of shares were owned by Charlie Ryder – approximately forty per cent. A further small percentage belonged to Charlie's immediate relatives. The rest – about half the shares – had been inherited by Jumbo who in turn had made over a proportion of them to Jane and the children. Jumbo had obtained a written proxy from Jamie before he left for Africa in respect of Jamie's own shares. As a further precaution, the bank had obtained a personal guarantee from Charlie Ryder and Jumbo Mainwaring, who had conceded them a lien on his Group shares.

The bank had of course been comforted from the start by the fact that Mainwaring Group Holdings, plc, owned forty-nine per cent of the company. So long as that was the case, it was impossible to suppose that the Bolt Company could go bust and default on its creditors. The Group would bail it out. But Mainwaring Group Holdings no longer existed as such: it was Mainwaring-Nippon now, with a considerably expanded shareholding structure, much of it in Japan. And the new Group could no longer be seen as being under primarily Mainwaring family management. The bank began to look at its security. It was reasonable enough. What were shares in the Bolt Company worth?

At the time of the merger, that late November, it was agreed on both sides that no valuation should be put on the shares. The implication was that, once the 'mutual digestion' of the main merger had taken place, a way would be found to maximize the asset of the holding in the Bolt Company, perhaps by giving it some sub-contractual function in relation to the Group. The Japanese had not specifically ruled out such a possibility, and perhaps rather wishfully Jumbo had allowed the Group board to assume that such a development might occur. He knew that it was wishful, since the Japanese had never said anything to endorse that possibility. It was in any case of no particular concern to any of the Group directors apart from himself and Carstairs, and incidentally Harry Fortescue, who happened to be chairman of the bank which looked after the Bolt Company and much of the Group's business also. It was not until after Sir Harry's resignation from the Group's board in January that the bank began to look at its security.

It happened, however, with some immediacy: it transpired that that very same week (in January) the bank's manager in charge of the Bolt Company account wrote an identical letter to Charles Ryder, Esq, and Sir James Mainwaring, Bt, CBE, suggesting a meeting to discuss the Bolt Company's overdraft and the securities relating to it. This in turn provoked an anxious telephone call from Charlie Ryder to cousin Jumbo. In brief, it was soon to emerge that, apart from his house and a smallish piece of adjoining agricultural land, a string of racehorses in training and his shoot in Ayrshire, which did not amount to much, Charlie Ryder had no assets to back his personal guarantee, and no realizable assets at all, except perhaps the horses. Jumbo knew that as things stood their shares in the Bolt Company were worthless: it was not that the Japanese were adamantly refusing to throw a bone to the Bolt Company but that they had got themselves in an Oriental haze of puzzled incapacity to come up with any proposal concerning that factory. Events had called Jumbo's bluff. The Bolt Company had to go, and the alternative was either to carry virtually the entire outstanding debt himself, or put the company into receivership. The first could constitute nothing less than a financial calamity for the Mainwaring wing of the family, subject to the break-up value of the Bolt Company. The second . . . well, the ignominy of it, the betrayal of it not only to the various creditors who would have to wait months or years for their money (if they ever got it back at all) but to all that the Mainwaring industrial tradition signified – for the City; for the country; for himself and his family. For the employees.

In a matter of days the raw truth of the situation had come upon Jumbo with rising horror. He could not recall ever having experienced this horror before, except perhaps in nightmares as a child. It was like a nightmare seeping under the foundations of his very existence, so that nothing could be depended on any more, all that was presumed and familiar in his life, his bearing, his attitudes, views, convictions – all that comprised his estimation of himself – was revealed as invalid, irrelevant, absurd. One evening in his bed-room in the flat, being required to put on his alder-manic dress for a City function, as he drew on his gab-erdine breeches he felt nightmare lick up at him from the floor with such vividness, a black tongue into his groin, that he virtually toppled back on to the bed, and was obliged to sit there a full minute, getting a grip on himself. Bobby Neal. Bobby Neal would be there, ex-Lord Mayor of London, that quick-footed, social-climbing accountant, receiver extraordinary, receiver to the distinguished, distinguished extinguished. And he, Jumbo Mainwaring in his breeches and buckles and hose and jabot, a period puppet of wood and straw, was he to drift across to Bobby Neal and catch his ear? – 'I must drop by on you one of these days, Bobby. Have a chat. I've got a situation you're just the fellow for.' Was it about to come to that?

No one would have known of this private nightmare. He spent longer periods than customary on his own. He did not talk of it to Jane, or even describe the dreadful alternatives he was faced with: it was not his practice to discuss his business life with her. He had married Jane in the very year he had taken over from his father as Group chairman, when he was thirty-nine and she was twenty-five. He was already a considerable figure in the business world. Jane Wellesley's experience of business consisted of helping to run a small gallery specializing in twentieth-century lithographic prints in Mayfair opposite Claridges. He wished her to take an interest in his business only insofar as it affected their social life.

That is how Jane herself perceived her function. Thus she was able to fit all the many colleagues and business associates who entered Jumbo's social life into the broad structure of his affairs. She knew who were the Main Board members, she knew several of the subsidiary board members and Mainwaring senior managers; she knew various of his 'opposite numbers' in related industries, his bankers (like Harry Fortescue), the heads of certain associated companies abroad; she knew his own stockbroker, his agent at Lloyds, and those connected with his semi-public life in the Court of the Bank of England, the Confederation of British Industry, the Association of British Metal Manufacturers, and the Corporation of the City of London. Then there were the Church dignitaries that Jumbo encountered through Synod, and those he was involved with through the Country Landowners' Association. And, naturally enough, a variety of politicians, mostly those concerned with industry and trade, but also various Members of Parliament representing constituencies containing Mainwaring factories. She had taken on the ramifications of his life easily and gracefully, as they spread this way and that throughout her married life, playing her part as hostess and keeping herself well informed on the general trends of business and the main issues of the day. But she never attempted to enter the machinery of his business affairs beyond the broad outlines – the Ryder connexion, for instance, and the Japanese not allowing the Bolt Company into the merged Group.

Her first and chosen task had always been to look after Jumbo as wife and escort, bring up his children, and run the house and garden and Upton and the flat. That was quite career enough for any woman, though nowadays she gave two mornings a week to Mencap. She had no time for fashionable nostrums put about by the feminists. If she did not fill the roles she did, who would? No wonder there were so many broken homes, disturbed children, young people on drugs. Once in the drawing room in the flat an old friend had said, 'Why Mencap, Jane?' and she had instinctively replied (not intending a joke), it helps to keep me sane.' Jumbo looked up from across the room, and, caught out by the knowledge, however untraceable, that there was a certain truth to what she had replied, she felt a sudden, shameful betrayal of her husband.

For she did love Jumbo, with a quiet devotion, and respected him too. She had been loyal to him from the day they first declared their love, as she was sure that he had been loyal to her. She respected him for his unwavering principles, his sense of duty, the deft way he handled people, his natural leadership and the fortitude and unflappability that went with it. Sometimes she wished he would give more, reveal more of himself, but she supposed that was what was sacrificed in the making of an Englishman like Jumbo. In the old argument about courage – Can one count a man brave who doesn't feel fear? – Jumbo would get impatient. 'Of course everyone can be afraid if there's something to be afraid of. But if you admit fear you generate it. And that means generating it in yourself, too. So you don't.' Instead you were 'brave', by prior decision, as Nanny had urged over the grazed knee *before* the tears came: 'Be brave.'

Vulnerability didn't come into the manly formula. Boys don't cry. 'Be brave.' Brave at private school, brave at public school. So that when it came to fighting Japs in the jungle you could handle it, you got an MC at twenty-one . . . Jane's father was a regular: he had commanded a Gurkha battalion. She had grown up in the knowledge of it all, what it was to be an Englishman, an English man. It was much more than the school system – that was a mere manifestation of it. Within it and behind it was an entire ethos, a mystique of chivalry and honour and endurance and grace, a Christianity processed and tempered immemorially in the English weald. When she said Yes to Jumbo she said Yes to something she knew she understood.

Jumbo was not a cold man: Jane knew that. He cared deeply about things – about people, about people as deep commitments. Jane his wife. Jamie his son. Even Vicky his daughter (though Vicky induced in him an obscure impatience). He did truly care. Perhaps that was why he had been slow to marry – because he foresaw the totality of the commitment. (There had been one or two love affairs previously, but nothing that had come close to his making a proposal.) No, Jumbo was not cold. She knew him tender and gentle. He was no more egocentric than any others of the male sex she knew, including her son. He could be thoughtful of others. He did not suffer fools; he was often intolerant; he could seem arrogant; he could be ruthless with twerps; he despised the pretentious; he was outraged when inferior people imputed to him motives of their own inferior grade. But he was not hard or cold or insensitive. He

kept his anxieties and strains and sorrows to himself. She could read the consequences of them if not
always the cause; this was permitted her, tacitly, and
thus was a need fulfilled, she reading him and he,
nothing said, knowing she read him.

And now he was seeking his own company, taking
Dribble out for solitary walks, falling silent at meals,
withdrawing to the library at Upton but, if there was
a book there that drew him, not bringing it with
him into the rest of the house. She caught him at
moments looking quite haggard, an old man almost.
She'd never thought of him as 'old' despite the nearly
fifteen years that divided them.

She knew it was the Bolt Company, the company
that meant so much to Jumbo personally. Josiah
Mainwaring's original company, the 'first-born' as
Jumbo sometimes referred to it. '*Est 1862,*' it said on
the company writing paper. She knew there had been
a 'hell of a bust-up' with Charlie Ryder, because Jumbo
had told her that much, in those words, and she knew
that Charlie Ryder deserved little sympathy because
it was Charlie, all those years ago, when Jumbo took
the Group public, who had doggedly insisted that
the Bolt Company stayed out of it, or at least outside
Group control, thinking he was on to a better thing.
(She never thought very much of Charlie. Sometimes
Charlie resembled Jumbo, but Jumbo without the
substance.) 'If we don't go for receivership, it'll wipe
Charlie out,' Jumbo commented to her once, at this
time. It was the first occasion on which he had used

the word 'receivership' to her and she felt the pain of it for him, like a sharp pain in the chest.

Jeremy Carstairs, responding to a summons from Jumbo's secretary, entered Jumbo's office on the floor above his without knocking, because Ellen Spence had nodded as he passed her desk and the door was ajar. Jumbo was standing near the window but turned towards the blank wall right in front of him. Perhaps he had not heard him come in, so Carstairs cleared his throat.

Jumbo shifted his position so as to look out of the window. You could see part of the dome of St Paul's from there. Without turning round he said, 'I've spoken to Sir Robert Neal.'

There was a certain comfort in using Bobby Neal's title, however recently acquired. He needn't have turned to Neal – there were other partnerships in the same field. But Neal was known to be the most skilful and was probably now the most experienced: to go elsewhere would have been cowardice, and Jumbo was not a coward.

To give him his due, Neal was admirably business-like and made it all seem like a part of the regular course of life, which, for him, it was. He talked refreshingly of other 'Victorian companies' his partnership had handled which had 'outlived their usefulness'. It was as if it was a natural process of industrial or commerical renewal at work. He spoke of the role

of receivership being insufficiently understood in
the British business community. He wryly lamented
that British company law allowed for nothing quite
comparable to America's 'Chapter Eleven' by which
a court could allow a company to hold off all creditors 'for two or three years if necessary' and still
continue trading under its own management, subject to certain safeguards. Even so, receivership was
not necessarily the finality that was often supposed.
That was the first aspect to look at closely – whether
the Mainwaring Bolt Company could not be turned
around and headed for a profit again, or be sold off
as a going concern, albeit with its accumulated liabili-
ties. But Jumbo had done the thinking. There was no
question of 'turning it round' or finding a buyer for
the whole business. It was a matter of stemming the
haemorrhage of its losses as swiftly as possible, dis-
banding the work-force, and getting what price they
could for its separate assets to pay off the bank first,
of course, and then if there was anything left, the rest
of the creditors *pro rata.*

The timing and the speed then became the cru-
cial factors, and the secrecy. Until the moment – the
hour – the receiver was formally called in, no one
must know, except the bank which must approve the
choice of receiver. It did not demur. Yet despite their
attempt at strictest confidentiality, the writs began to
come. Someone must have caught the scent in the
air, like the scent of fear – a quarry betraying its own
knowledge that it was cornered. Several creditors had

been restive for some while, but none had hinted of writs. Now they came in. Noon on a Friday was a good time to call in a receiver, Neal had advised: it gave the work force a weekend to get over the shock, and it was too late for the creditors to get in touch with each other and issue concerted objectionable statements to the media. But on the previous Wednesday one writ was served on behalf of a creditor bent on getting his full claim met ahead of the rest, and by Friday morning more had come in. In each case the writ-servers tried to serve Sir James Mainwaring himself, as the most prominent director, whose name the company carried; and each time Ellen Spence, on Jumbo's instructions, sent the man downstairs to serve Jeremy Carstairs, representing the board.

One of the writs was from a marketing company owed commission, one was a Bradford accountant with a sub-contractual role, one was a Midlands caterer, and one a packager and printer. The sums owed varied, and none of them was a major creditor. None of the writs had been preceded by a final demand or a telephone call: the writ itself was the object – to get the bill paid before the collapse came. These were the alert, the assiduous, the 'good husbandmen' of whom Paul wrote to the apostle Timothy. Three of the five companies, Jumbo noticed, bore Jewish names, and he wondered now if this good husbandry was what he somehow lacked, he himself having grown grand and assured and lofty, and they never failing to tend their own vineyard – vine by vine – with their own fingers, through drought, through deluge. Was this not why they would survive and flourish, their sense of threat from non-Jews bred and burnt into their ancient history? Jumbo was as familiar as any with that history. Vulnerability was in their very souls. Every Sunday in Church Jumbo sang of the Jews being 'saved from our enemies' and 'delivered from the hands of them that hate us'. Such endemic fear had been no part of Jumbo Mainwaring. Musing there alone in his office in eerie inactivity during the two days to that Friday noon, he felt now, against the shame of those writs, a kinship with Jewry such as he would never have imagined of himself; and were it not for the folly of it he would have personally telephoned those who had issued them to say, You are right to have sought what is due to you, and had I not been born and reared without that fear which makes you the husbandmen you are, it would not be too late for the Mainwaring Bolt Company to pay you, we would not be going under.

They would have thought him touched in the head.

It was not so devastating. It was hateful that the company bore the Mainwaring name (Josiah's name to be precise) but as a private company with a majority of family shareholders it aroused only a moment's interest in the financial press and a couple of surprised and unvindictive paragraphs in the Lex column of the *Financial Times*. The worst part was the work force.

Some of the men had been with the company all their working lives: Jumbo knew many of their faces and several by name. He wanted to go down to Bradford and talk to them, but was dissuaded by Bobby Neal personally. He warned Jumbo that whatever his good intentions his visit would be exploited by the political trouble-makers who would engineer incidents, and so damage Bradford's chance of attracting a new industry to take over the Bolt Company premises with more or less the same work-force. The redundancy payments had been generous, at Jumbo's insistence (adding to his own personal financial exposure): it was best to leave it at that. Jumbo could have pressed the point, of course. But it was the Receiver's company now, the creditors the Receiver's responsibility, formally speaking.

Jumbo kept away from White's for the time being. He didn't want to hear any 'Bad lucks' at the bar. He wanted no sympathy. He was still chairman of the Mainwaring-Nippon Group, which had half as much capital again as Mainwaring before the merger. Nor did he want to run into Harry Fortescue. He was puzzled about Harry. In effect it was the bank who had put the boot in, not the Jewish writ-issuers, and the timing of the bank's intervention had been – he had to admit – suspicious. He had Searle stop by for him at the club now and then, very briefly, on the way back to the flat at six or so when no one much else was there, just for a ten-minute glass of sherry and a last glance at the tapes and the Wall Street prices.

CHAPTER TWELVE

He was relieved that Jamie was far away and wholly caught up with his own life during this period. They had not heard from Jamie for several weeks. They were not anxious: they would surely have heard if any mishap had occurred. Then in April came a long letter addressed to them both. Jamie sent it to the flat, and Jane was already reading it when Jumbo came into breakfast. She said, 'A letter from Jamie,' and continued reading.

Jumbo poured his coffee and started on his egg. He propped the *Financial Times* on the stand that the Bradford craftsmen had specially made and drew it towards him, but he could not get himself interested in anything in the paper that morning, not on the front page anyway. He was waiting to read Jamie's letter. It covered four or five sheets and Jumbo was mildly irritated that Jane did not choose to pass him one sheet at a time as she finished it. She heard Jumbo begin on his toast and marmalade and fleetingly wondered whether Jamie would make as much noise eating toast when he had turned sixty. (Jamie could make a dreadful racket with his cutlery on his plate but she had never been aware of him making any noise eating.) When she had evidently finished the letter, she re-read some of the earlier passages and only then did she pass it to Jumbo, saying nothing.

The letter was tightly written in – for Jamie – an unusually careful hand. It read:

BP 17, Bandiagara, Rép du Mali
14 April

Dear Ma and Pa

I have not written for quite a while because it has taken time to collect my thoughts and decide what I wanted to say. I have seen a fair amount of this country in these 4 months and I think I have enough experience now to make a fair assessment. I had nearly one month in the capital when I arrived and then moved out to this aid station at Bandiagara which is about 5 hours' drive north-east. I have been able to use this as a base to drive further north to Goundam and Timbuktu and east from there where the desert is encroaching all the time and where the real famine exists.

The first point is that this whole aid effort, whatever the original intention, finishes up 90 per cent politics and corruption and 10 per cent actually helping people.

The aid that comes from international bodies like the ODA and Unicef and WHO is window-dressing pure and simple. Nobody expects it to make any difference to any-one and it doesn't. It's bullshit. It allows the civilised world to pretend that it cares and is doing something, which is the civilised thing, and it gives tax free jobs at really phenomenal saleries [sic] to a bunch of fat international civil servants who spend most of their time giving each other pseudo-diplomatic parties and travelling first class in 747s to Rome and New York and Geneva and so on. If you think I'm sounding quite angry it's because I am as you will discover.

Most governments don't of course give most of their aid through those pantomine bodies. I'm beginning to understand why Mrs T and the Yanks quit Unesco, incidentally. Most give aid to specific projects either administered by the government of the recipient country or by special teams led by people from the donor country. If it's the first the money gets rapidly lost into the ministry in question and mostly in the minister's pocket. If the aid comes in food or medicines the minister or officials sell most of it on the black market and pocket it that way. (The 'government' of this country is of course a shambles. I was stopped by 14 police road blocks between the capital and my post here whose sole intention was to extort money or, failing that, cigarettes.) But it makes for 'closer ties' between whichever group happens to be in power here at the moment and the donor country, which is usually the US or us or France or Germany. The thing is it keeps the place in the 'Western' camp and buys a few votes in the General Assembly.

If it's the second method, the local politics come in. This is the sector I work in, as you probably realize. Donor government aid often goes into projects already being run by voluntary aid organisations like the one I work for and voluntarily subscribed money is sometimes used to beef up donor-run projects. You might have thought these schemes would be pretty well tamper-proof but I assure you they are not. *This is the really important point I want to make.* [Jamie had underlined that sentence.]

The fact is that we are being frustrated and cheated at all levels and people are dying. Babies and children are dying while, effectively, most of the money subscribed by ordinary people at home and all round the world, and I suppose money from taxpayers too, is going to waste. The money or the food are simply not getting to where it is needed and where it can really save lives, except in tiny quantities and then only for a brief moment probably. This is because we have to work through the ministries here and the local government. Either they don't like the consequences of their shambolic admin to be exposed; or the local (government appointed) headmen skilfully ensure that all the food goes to feed their supporters, irrespective of whether they are hungry, or, if we aren't on the spot, it is sold for their personal enrichment. In some areas the local officials are quite happy if the people starve, if they are the wrong tribe (e. g. Tuareg), provided of course the outside world never gets to know.

I've told you I've just been up north where there's real famine. What I haven't told you is that I'm back here because it was considered I was a 'trouble maker' and I was a 'trouble maker' because I was trying actually to save lives. My own boss (Project Head) ordered me back, by radio, on instructions which supposedly came from the Ministry in the capital. There are some really fine people out here and I do not necessarily except my Project Head. His job is to *stay* here of course, and heaven knows there are few enough of us out here in all. But he *is* weak, he should have protested against the order, gone to our ambassador, etc. He should have known me well enough by now to realize that I know what I'm doing and don't make trouble.

What really brought it to a head was a single family in the semi-desert beyond Timbuktu. They are Tuaregs of course (the Government is pretty well all Bambara). There was a mother and three children plus her baby of about six months. The father had gone off somewhere weeks before looking for work/money/food, etc and had not returned. They had *one camel* on whose milk they survived entirely, and this camel had almost nothing to graze on. When I and my driver came across them in my Toyota Landcruiser (with half the back loaded with grain, milk powder and so on) they were practically done for, the baby the worst of all. So I stopped, to do what I could. I was on a fact-gathering assignment but we couldn't just drive on and leave them to die. So I stopped and made camp, and tried to feed them. Most urgent was the baby. The mother's milk had run dry. I prepared a milk solution and began to feed the baby, using a thing like a penfiller. It was extremely hot and we stretched a piece of tent over the top of their hut which was letting in quite a lot of sun through the thatch. With the mother I looked after that baby for three days and three nights.

I had no sleep at all during that time, and most of it the baby was in my arms or I was right beside it with the mother. It took some of the food in the first two days. On the third day it didn't take much food. But the mother was strengthening and I was hoping that her own milk would come back. She had a good solid sleep on the third night. I stayed awake the whole night with the baby nestled against me. The dawn started coming and almost the moment the edge of the sun broke the horizon the mother woke up. She took up the baby and it was dead. It was the worst moment of my life.

I didn't know what to do at first. When I had pulled myself together I proposed to the mother that I drive her and the three children on to the next village, about 20 miles away, leading the camel behind the vehicle. That is what we did, after we buried the baby. It took an entire day. It was a wretched village, but I couldn't just leave them. I then reported by radio what had happened. Project hq didn't come back on the air until the following evening when they said that Bamako (the capital) had said I was disturbing the tribes in the area and was responsible for the death and that I must return to hq at Bandiagara at once. Of course it was utter nonsense what Bamako had said. They couldn't possibly have 'heard' anything except what our own hq had told them. They were just making it all up, to get me out of the area and save them embarrassment.

Now, Pa, this is what I want you to do. I want you to get one of your friends in Parliament, preferably someone involved with the ODA or the Third World, to *ask a series of questions* which effectively expose the scandal of the aid effort in all this part of Africa. (I've no reason to suppose it's much different in Burkina Fasso or Niger or Chad, etc.) Please show him or her this letter, if so inclined, or anyone else useful or interested. I'm going to stay on here for my promised period, however futile it may be. There are a few things I can do. But I do want to feel that I've got some support back in Westminster/Whitehall and that you can get some of the basic facts across.

I'm quite well other than a few persistent lice.

Love from

Jamie

It was a well-written letter, Jumbo thought. He was aware that quite a lot of what Jamie had written about the logistics of the Third World aid-giving was to be found, implicitly if not explicitly, in the notes he had passed to him as a result of his lunch with the official from Unicef which Jamie never attended. Here it was coming back as if the boy had discovered it for himself, in a way.

He found Jane regarding him. She smiled questioningly.

'He's obviously got himself quite worked up,' was Jumbo's comment as he put the letter aside at last.

Jane's smile faded. 'It's quite a letter,' she said quietly.

'Oh yes. It's quite an impressive letter.'

'What are you going to do?'

'Oh, well now. That's a different matter.'

'How – "different"?'

'Well,' Jumbo said a little warily, sensing an obscure but profound divergence. 'It's a question of what makes sense in the circumstances.'

'You're not going to do what he's asked?'

'The point is, would it achieve anything?' Jumbo looked straight ahead down the length of the table and paused. 'The only thing that would put right what he wants to put right is the return of the colonial empires, and Jamie wouldn't appove of that.'

Jane fixed him with a look of scorn.

'You knew all that before Jamie went out to Africa,' she said. 'What?'

'That his whole endeavour was futile.'

'Not as far as he is concerned. Not futile for Jamie.'

This halted her for a moment. She followed narrowly.

'So what do you intend to tell him?'

'He could write a letter to *The Times.*' Jumbo hesitated. 'When he's safely back home.'

'And what about the child?'

'What child?'

'The child. The child Jamie wrote about. The baby.'

Jumbo went silent.

'Jamie was quite concerned,' Jane said with a sarcastic edge. 'You don't seem to share that concern.'

'Of course I share his concern, Jane,' Jumbo retorted, riled at last. 'The fact that it died will probably have given the other ones a better chance. That's the sort of thing Jamie will have come to realize.' He nudged the *Financial Times* a fraction closer and touched his spectacles. He knew this was the wrong issue on which to have a row with Jane and he couldn't think just now how it could have come up, or what it was really about.

CHAPTER THIRTEEN

There were no immediate buyers for the Mainwaring Bolt Factory site at Bradford and by the spring the weeds were coming up in the forecourt – ragwort and chervil, and willowherb moving in; along the top of the wall too. The great chimney soared above as before, a monument to its own redundancy. The paint on the door headed WORKS ENTRANCE had begun to curl. Even the slogan on the latrines' brick wall, HONEYFORD OUT, had become difficult to read and seemed to belong to another epoch. Somebody had sprayed up a new slogan: COME IN NIPS ALL IS FOGIVEN. It was remarkable how quickly a place showed the symptoms of dereliction.

It was spotting with rain as a pale blue Ford Cortina paused outside the gates on the road which ran along the perimeter of the site. The gates were chained and padlocked. The meaty hands resting on the steering-wheel were those of the big man with red hair, the one-time foreman of the foundry whom Jamie had noticed on his visit six or seven months previously.

The skinny man with the weaselish face sitting alongside was his former workmate in the foundry. He said,

'Nobody's bought it, that's obvious.'

'There's nowt interest in it,' the big man said decisively. He flicked on his wipers, at *slow*. The car was almost brand new. He had bought it with part of his redundancy money.

'What'll they want to do with it, then, Ginger? Eh?'

'Boong it up Sir Jumbo's bum. For all I care.'

It was the only place Ginger had ever worked in, that factory. Thirty-three years. He had left school at fifteen and gone straight in.

He looked at the weeds pushing up along the edge of the brick walkway that led from the gate to the works entrance, where the tarmac had crumbled slightly along the outer line of bricks. The ragwort was already in dark yellow bloom. How many times, rain and shine, winter and summer, had he walked that brick path? (Nobody laid brick paths at factories these days.) Since that big pasty boy with the shock of carroty hair (which made him instantly recognizable to everyone) had first trodden it? The Bolt Company had been the flag-ship of the Group then, so they told him, whatever a flag-ship was. Thirty-three years. It had been a tidy sum, his redundancy. No surprise.

A dark-faced, hunched figure, heavily swathed against the rain, had emerged from between the factory and the latrines – a Paki of one sort or another, dark henna in his hair not so distant from Ginger's own natural copperiness of these days. There had been no takers among the white community for the watchman vacancies. The Paki stood looking across at the pale blue car beyond the chained gates like some troglodyte disturbed.

'Wah's 'e want?' the skinny man, Leslie, said.

Ginger made no reply. He had grown to kingship at this place, their Vulcan, keeper of the white fire that may never be extinguished for so long as this was a manufactory. Out of his quenched steel, his ingots and billets, his many and varied casts, had come all that the rest of the factory-hands for years had fettled and dressed and polished and packed for transportation. He could mix his virgin alloys, tap his furnace, ladle his molten metal into the moulds, harden it, temper it, mill it, roll it, drop-forge it, all by the function of his hands and arms and eyes. All that his man's life would ever be was beyond where the weeds now grew, beyond where the looped barbed wire now blocked intrusion by the zig-zagging fire-escapes, beyond where the henna-ed Paki skulked.

All at once Leslie noticed something strange – that Ginger's eyes were shut. Ginger was reading once again a sample of steel that he had spooned out, cooled and split, determining from indefinable clues of the frac-tured surface whether the molten steel in his furnace was ready for tapping or not. On this judgement, by this arcane skill exercised in silence and inwardness, half a lifetime in the acquisition, hung the quality and reputation of all that Mainwarings made. Not a score of men in Yorkshire could pass a sample as unerringly as he.

Ginger put the Cortina into gear and moved off slowly into the drizzle.

As they approached the pleasantly laid out council estate where both men lived, the first four electronically produced bars of 'Home, Sweet Home' reached their ears. The Candyman van was drawn up at the small roundabout where four 'avenues' of semi-detached pebble-and-dash houses converged. It was mid-to-late afternoon, after school, but the light rain had cleared the streets of youngsters. A few children were emerging at the sound of the Toni-bell.

'Wah's 'e trying to sell ices for, day like this?' Leslie said.

'Not only ices, Les,' said Ginger. 'Let's go to club.'

They drove on past.

Three or four small children were gathered at the Candyman van, the side of which had been lowered to form a counter. A young man with long feathery hair served from within. The van advertised Ices, Choc Bars, Mr Whippy, Soft Drinks, Confectionery, Hot Dogs, Home Made Sandwiches, Etcetera. The 'Candyman' himself had put a hot-dog on the counter in a paper napkin.

'One or two, sonny?'

'One,' said the small boy.

'One Yorkie,' said a little girl, smaller still, standing beside her brother.

'One Yorkie,' the small boy repeated.

'One Yorkie it is,' said the Candyman, addressing the little girl. His accent was different from the children's – a London accent, not Yorkshire. He had quick eyes and an air of slick confidence.

The small boy put the exact money on the counter.

When the young kids had moved away a bigger boy, about fourteen, came up on a bicycle.

'Afternoon, Colin,' the Candyman said. 'What's it to be?'

'You choose,' Colin replied.

'Vimto, Colin. How much you got there?'

'Fiver?' Colin responded with a query.

'Make it six,' the Candyman said. 'Suits me computer.'

Colin put his five pound note on the counter and added an extra pound coin. The Candyman turned to lift a can of Vimto out of his coolbox. He put it on the counter. Alongside was a screw of silver paper. Colin picked up both items.

'That's all then, Colin?'

'Thursday?' said the boy, who seemed to turn all his answers back into questions.

''Pends on the weather, don' it?' the Candyman said. 'Can't sell ices in the pouring rain, can we?'

Jumbo Mainwaring had dressed down. He wore his tweed cap, a light tweed jacket, grey flannels, and half-brogues. It was a bit countrified, but at least he didn't resemble a city gent, a corporation chairman. He followed the storeman's feet up the narrow spiral staircase. At the top the strip lights flickered on, casting a weak light on a low-ceilinged, labyrinthine storage place, or warehouse, containing row upon row of makeshift shelving laden yard by yard with ledgers, Trimlock files, cardboard boxes, batches of folders tied with string or faded ribbon, and so forth, all the detritus in written record of company upon company that had once known the light of day and had come to die. The ceiling was so low, and so cluttered with pipes and girders, that Jumbo had to duck frequently to protect his head as he followed the diminutive warehouseman in his white overall between the narrow rows, and very soon he settled for moving with his head permanently bent. Every few feet or so a projecting tab, carrying the name of a company handwritten in large capitals, indicated the end of one company's records and the start of another's.

It was an ossuary of human endeavour. Jumbo could see that the documents for each company were shelved in date order – from the first budding of the enterprise, the burgeoning hopes, the years, the decades, of flourishing activity, the confident illusion of perpetuity, and then the onset of decay and death. Many of the ledgers were firmly bound in red leather and carried their dates on the spine. The companies were evidently shelved by the date of their decease. The lives of some, he could see, had been quite brief. Others had survived for generations, from before the

First World War and earlier still, from King Edward's reign or Victoria's. Some of the names were familiar, as familiar to the average man once as Mainwaring. Here was all a Receiver needed to preserve year after year (so it seemed) to meet the last claim, the unexpected suit, the residual fag-end liability, share-out of pitiable asset . . . the Combined Registers, Registers of Members, Registers of Directors, Minute Books, Employee Registers, Purchase Invoices, Sales Returns. Buried here were the fading clues of that which had occupied the greater part of the lives of thousands upon thousands of individual men and women – so many *souls* as one used to say: clues of that which had filled their days, consumed their energies, ringed their loyalties, primed their hopes, spurred their ambitions, fed their families, that for which they had woken early, struggled out into the dark wintered streets, tramped back through snow and rain and blown leaves, stood in tram queues; where they had found their sweethearts, broken hearts, their own sweet hearts grown slow and old . . .

Why had Jumbo come here? Could he have said, precisely? He had given Searle the morning off: it was a free afternoon for Searle in any case. Not even Mrs Spence knew of his coming here. He had told her some days in advance to leave his diary open that morning. He had said nothing to Jane, either. He had dressed casually and come by underground, incognito. To Wapping. He had ascertained the telephone number and made the preparatory call himself. He

had exposed himself to no requirement to explain
to anyone, himself included. Si nemo ex me quaerat,
scio; si quaerenti explicari velim, nescio.* He used to
quote that fragment from Augustine to the children
sometimes when they came to him with the unanswer-
able; Jamie particularly, for instance that if all things
bright and beautiful are His creation, whose were the
other things? and who drew the line between them? –
Jamie at ten or twelve. And he, Jumbo, could only say
that you could not depend on words for the deepest
truths, and he cited music (Jamie was quite musical)
and asked him whether music did not often contain
a truth as valid as anything that could be expressed
by words. At a certain point you must be prepared to
let go of humdrum explicability and risk just *knowing*. If you wished to banish the idea of a loving God
because of the problem of pain, then what about the
problem of beauty? Try to resolve *that* without Him!

Walking from Wapping station to the receiver's
store he kept glimpsing the river, between the ware-
houses and go-downs by the water's edge. He realized what a beautiful May day it was. If beauty was to
require examples, Jumbo could always have spoken
up, all his long life: depending upon the listener,
whether it be one of his children or some friend or
another, or himself alone, he might have spoken of
Jane, or the sun setting across the Cotswolds from
Upton, or certain music that bore connotation with

If nobody asks me, I know it; if I am required by someone to
explain, I do not.

event or place, not least with church or chapel, the beauty of holiness. Where a river gave itself to the sea there was always beauty, he knew that.

He had never visited this part of London before, where the river began to spread into the estuary, even though Wapping was only a few stops on beyond the Bank or Monument, which of course he knew in every detail . . . .Yes, you could call it 'research' that he had come for, but that did not suggest an imperative factor. He was *obliged* to come because he had to see for himself what had become of it all. There had been quite a bit to endure lately – for a start, the Bolt Company and Bobby Neal's men moving in and taking over like a team of undertakers, with all the practised blandness and self-assured unobtrusiveness of a team of undertakers, the same unstated statutory condolence of undertakers. He remembered when his Mama had died at Upton, how the undertakers had worked to such an unerring routine, unhurried, acquainted with all the exigencies-distressed relatives, *rigor* having bequeathed an awkward shape, and so on: how they had handled the corpse so deftly, shrouding it for their special stretcher, and so strapping it that it could be carried down any manner of stairway however steep or narrow or twisting . . . though naturally at Upton the stairway was broad and dignified.

Yet it was not only the Bolt Company but the countless other consequences of the merger: the ever so subtle change in the bearing of the staff towards him at Lombard Street (as if in any interchange there was something left unsaid), the permeating obsequiousness of the Japanese at board meetings (was the deference he received genuine or staged?), the marked positiveness and long-term optimism that had begun to infect the Group's promotional literature (with its implications as to the recent past). He could never tell whether in the last resort the Japanese were obeisant towards the civilization of the West they had adopted with such deliberation or whether they did not harbour an ultimate presumption of *superiority*. It was not that he was not chairman: he was no less than chairman: yet there was much that he had had to put up with in silence.

Against all that, against Neal's persuasion not to go back to Bradford itself, he had to know what had become of it all, to see for himself, to see what visible remains . . .

With all the half-concealed protrusions along the ceiling of the ill-lit warehouse Jumbo was glad of his tweed cap. Perhaps Bobby Neal's people had taken on this particular elderly warehouseman on account of his short stature – he would never have to bend when moving around the labyrinth of shelving. Jumbo could see the unsightly lumps on the man's greasy skull under his scanty slicks of greyed hair. They had approached an area of open shelves, awaiting the next to be Received. The penultimate row of assembled documents was identified with a tab carefully written in blue felt pen capitals, MAINWARING BOLT co. It took up a good six or seven feet of shelf space.

'Main-waring,' the warehouseman said with proud satisfaction. 'It'll all be there. Whatever you want. Take your time, gentleman. I can't let you take nothink out, not without Receiver's written permission. You follow, gentleman? That's the regulations. Every-think in this warehouse is Receiver's property. None of my documents 'ere belong to the companies. Companies themselves, they're defunct.'

He left Jumbo there, disappearing into the gloom of his private catacombs, a charnel-keeper with his prescribed residual role. Jumbo noticed how he did not prefix the word Receiver with the definite article, as would also be the case with God.

Jumbo's hand went out to the ledger in front of him, at chest level. They were all finely bound in leather, and well preserved. He did not recall ever having laid eyes on them before. They belonged to the earlier period – he was standing opposite the start of the Mainwaring Bolt Company section. He saw from the dates on the spines that at some point in the 1890s they had moved to a different ledger supplier: the style of binding changed. He put on his reading glasses and drew from the shelf a ledger of the period – 1889 – and opened a page of entries, the names of employees long dead in immaculate Victorian copperplate penmanship. There were page upon page of names, hour upon hour of devoted work on high stools in poor light like this poor light he was reading by now. One surname, one Christian name, listed by alphabet, with the craft or trade alongside ('lathe hand', 'furnaceman', 'polisher', 'fettler', 'lad'), a date of first employment, Jumbo guessed, and the weekly wage, in shillings and pence. Never an abbreviation, almost never a crossing out or visible alteration. *Carruthers, Andrew. First hand. Carstairs, Amos. Engineer.* He wondered if he could be any relation. He knew nothing of Jeremy Carstairs's Victorian ancestors – nor, very likely, did Jeremy Carstairs.

He came across a fragment of blotting paper, crisscrossed by ancient unintelligible penmanship. There was such confidence here, in the regular hand, the assured legibility, the unhurried devotion. This was the springtime of the great enterprise. There came into his mind a curious incident at Upton a few days previously. The electrician from the nearby market-town had been called in to attend to some re-wiring in the library. Jumbo had known the man, Jones, for four years, since he had started coming to Upton to attend to its electrical requirements. He was white-haired – a gentle, courteous, rather diffident man of late middle age. All at once in the library, when he turned to Jumbo to explain something, apologizing for interrupting his reading, Jumbo saw the young man in Jones. It was extraordinarily vivid: he could see the quiet boyish charm of this man as he must have been in his early twenties, an innocence and Welshness and grace and promise, such as surely some girl perceived in him and fell for, blithely and perfectly, when he, Jones, had still been in his uniform of cornflower grey-blue as a radio mechanic in the RAF, such as Jumbo knew he had once been – fell for, and most likely married.

Now Jumbo saw with the same dreamlike vividness, with this ledger in his hands, the same promise and spring of his own heritage and family, his stock. And seeing it there, in the image of old Jones who was as in his youth, he thought of Jamie's letter, how as he read it that breakfast-time the other day he had come to smile inwardly and sadly at its urgency, its presumption that the world could be changed, that Jamie himself could put it to rights. And how, by some devilment in the exchange with Jane, that sad smile had swiftly taken on the characteristic of scorn. Yet did he deny the right to those who built the Mainwaring enterprise from nothing to change the world? Those whose names swum before his eyes in this ledger, and those who stood behind them, Josiah and his sons, had they not the right to suppose they might change the world for better? Were they not helping to bring radiated heat to half the houses and workplaces of England and Europe? The world *did* change; something brought about that change. Why should it not be Jamie: even if Jamie's was no more than one young man's yearning and dream among a hundred million, had he not the *right?* Did not a hundred million young hopes change the world? What better wisdom, what other right, had Jumbo now, past sixty, to declare in his heart, You will not change the world, my son?

He closed the ledger and returned it to the shelf.

What conceivable purpose could the Receiver have for such records? For some forgotten reversionary patent right? Jumbo shifted along the shelf. As the company's business grew more complex and it approached the modern era, its documentary records grew more varied. Ring binders appeared, and Annual Reports bound with plastic spines. He withdrew a ledger entitled Board Minutes and dating from the early 1960s. Were the portents to be discerned already? The book opened at where a typed page had been pasted in. Jumbo read

> . . . properties in the form required of which is attached, be granted by the Midland Bank Ltd by way of security for all present and future indebtedness and liabilities of the Company and THAT the affixing of the seal be and is hereby confirmed . . .

He shut the book and put it back and pulled out the latest box file, entitled Salaried Staff. It contained computer print-outs of names and addresses in the Bradford area.

Jumbo felt his head swimming, a suffocation or claustrophobia closing upon him in this narrow place. He heard a whistling sound. He looked around for a source – any source – of outside light. He moved breathlessly to a little window at the end of his tunnel of shelves. Bright sunlight beyond drew him towards it, hurrying. It was a tiny window, sealed and cobwebbed. Beyond it lay the Thames estuary, water and sky a brilliant, brilliant blue. Tugs were plying up and down the ancient rivermouth. Here civilization grew, that to which he belonged, which had spawned him, had taken his tithe.

The whistling had stopped. The warehouseman had come up alongside.

'Brought you a cuppa, gentleman.'

Jumbo brought his hand to his cheek. Was there a tear there?

'I sugared it,' the warehouseman said. 'On the off chance.'

Jumbo took the cup and saucer.

'Found what you're lookin' for, then?"

'Thank you,' Jumbo said.

He stirred his tea. The warehouseman regarded him, perplexed. He said,

'I do have my photo-copier, mind. You can make your own copies. Within reason. Receiver allows that.'

'Thank you,' Jumbo said. 'I don't think I'll need to take photocopies.'

He began to move back, to replace the Salaried Staff print-out on its shelf.

''Istory, right? You writin' a 'istory of the company? If I understood correctly.'

'Possibly,' Jumbo said.

'Research,' said the warehouseman. They had paused by the Bolt Company section. Jumbo was touching the ledgers with his fingertips. He said,

'Just to remind myself what material there is.'

'There's a 'istory of England in my store here,' the warehouseman told him. 'Some of the documents, they go back a 'undred years. More.'

He paused, and looked at Jumbo carefully.

'You connected in a personal way, then, with this company. Main-waring Bolts? Correct me if I'm wrong.'

Jumbo's hand dropped to his side. He drew himself up, as best he could, his head among the pipes.

'I have a connection with the Group,' he replied, 'It was one of the companies in the Group.'

'I didn't get your name exactly, did I, gentleman?'

'What?'

'Your name,' the warehouseman said.

'James.'

'James,' the man echoed reflectively.

Why did Jumbo feel so dizzy and weak? He must mention it to his doctor.

The little man led the way towards the office, Jumbo hunched and often ducking his head between the shelved reliquaries. The names on the tabs kept catching the corner of his eye, a little clamour of whispers and muffled pleas from the place of shades directed to him as one still of the world of the living . . . COLTEC DATA SYSTEMS . . . HANDLEY PAGE . . . BRITTAINS PAPER . . . Some of the names had a familiar sound so that in his mind he was whispering back, *Ah, I did not know that you were dead.*

The warehouseman's poky sanctuary of dusty glass and painted plywood occupied the corner at the innermost recess of the store, furthest from the fragment of window that looked across the river. There was a desk, a calendar, a ledger, a shelf of earlier registers, a telephone, that morning's tabloid newspaper folded open at Your Stars, and two chairs. One chair was round-backed and a grubby tablecloth of grey and pink had been folded on its seat to give it extra height; the other was square and very upright for any visitor from the world beyond. A Japanese photocopier stood on its own trestle, and alongside 011 a little deal table dusted with sugar granules, a gas-ring, and the whistling kettle on a biscuit tin lid. A Mainwaring factory still made gas-rings.

''Istory,' mused the warehouseman. He threw a brief, tender glance up at his tall visitor, still in his cap: Jumbo felt the tenderness and accepted the comfort. 'I needn't tell *you*, Mr James. All flesh is grass. I've been written off meself, you know. Once. Written off.'

Jumbo returned as he had come, by Underground. He still felt lightheaded and strange, as if not truly in command of his actions, or as if something might happen to him that he would not be able to control. He supposed it was because he had had no lunch, except for the cup of tea the warehouseman had brought him, and it was already early afternoon. He should have changed at Whitechapel to the District Line, which would have taken him all the way to Sloane Square. In error, he went on to Shoreditch, and after that it seemed sensible to transfer to the Central Line and change at Oxford Circus for Victoria. Victoria was good enough for Eaton Square.

At Oxford Circus the pedestrian tunnel connecting the two lines was long and at its far end bent away out of sight. From somewhere there came the sound of music. Jumbo felt drawn by the music's vibrancy just as soon as he entered the tunnel from the central concourse. London had already begun to draw to its heart student tourists in their pairs and threes and fours from all over the world. Jumbo felt how young this world was, here in this very artery or ventricle of ancient London, and this and the exaltation of the music ahead brought back to mind his earlier thoughts of Jamie in the Receiver's store. How right it was, youth's demand to hope in, and for, the world! How triumphant that right of youth! His own frame and heart were possessed by this conviction as he neared the source of the young busker's music (he knew it was of the young: all these tube musicians were young): the beat and glory of it grew around him, guitar, harmonica, percussion too, crescendoed by the acoustic of the tunnel. He felt in his pocket for a coin worthy of this transmitted conviction, a token of endorsement, youth's declaration of joy endorsed by age.

Following the bend of the tunnel, his own step sprung and lightened by the exultant sound, he came suddenly upon the musician. Filthy and unkempt, his untended hair straggling and falling about his unshaven face, the lank, lost pallor declaring his subjection to drugs, and strapped and harnessed into his instruments like some fearful creation of Masoch, the generator of that which had drawn Jumbo with heightening conviction as to the rights of youth was all that spelled to him depravity, a parasite upon society, kept alive by a system of vote-buying politics that mistook corruption for compassion. He was a young man who comprised all that Jumbo held in scorn and disgust. His hand that had found its coin froze in his pocket.

At the head of the descending stairway where this long tunnel now ended, Jumbo paused. Thus utterly rebuffed, he felt faint with fear that he might die there, trapped and unrecognized. It could so be: he felt so frail. Then he began on the steps, carefully, holding to the rail.

CHAPTER FOURTEEN

No one seemed to have heard much from Jamie for weeks. A postcard addressed to mother and father jointly told of his having moved to the capital, but he reported no change in his Boîte Postale number and they had begun to wonder if their letters were reaching him. Jane had taken a telephone call from some young Frenchman, a student by the sound of him, who had met Jamie out there, asking if he had returned to Britain yet. By the time of the July village cricket match at Upton (Upton vs. Chinnery), there was only a month remaining before his promised return, though certainty concerning it had faltered and the exact date was unknown. In Jamie's absence, the Mainwarings had seen little of the Hoskynses – Tibby and her parents – and it was privately in the hope of picking up some news of Jamie that Jane invited them over for the cricket match. Tibby was brought by her mother only, her father having declared himself 'no devotee' of cricket. Yet it was a sweet day for village cricket, and such peace here, on the edge of the village, the road – which led only to Chinnery – skirting the field like a curious enquirer.

Upton had gone in to bat, and Jumbo himself went to the crease at number 5, when the score was 37. He was still at the wicket ten minutes later. Vicky had brought Rowley down for the weekend and he was eagerly selected for the Upton team, with his reputation as a spin bowler. The gentle vicar (of both parishes, though he occupied the Upton vicarage), who had spoken so warmly of Jamie to Jumbo the previous year, was scorer. Upton's twelfth man (the Mainwarings' cowman's lad) was on the scoreboard. The Upton players already out or still to bat occupied the pavilion's veranda, and several supporters of both teams formed a horseshoe of spectators round the pavilion and the adjacent table where the orangeade was already set out and a light lunch would follow.

Jumbo had had little of the ball: his partner, Alan Barnes, the village shopkeeper (and also captain) would try to snatch a second run or take a quick single on the last ball of the over. When Jumbo got the bowling he looked stiff and orthodox and decidedly cautious, even letting the odd ball go through to the wicket-keeper without playing a stroke. He dealt so far in blocking singles, some of which came off the edge of the bat. Clearly he saw his role as one of staying put, coming in at 37 for 3. Now at last he was facing the bowling again, solid and determined in his rather tight white flannels.

He struck a strong four from the middle of the bat between extra cover and mid-off. There was an immediate spatter of applause, amplified by a gas-rattle brought by an Upton enthusiast. Vicky looked up from her magazine.

'He's on form all right,' Rowley said, from his deck chair. He had white calf-skin cricket boots and a silk stock carrying the colours of some club or another which Jumbo had not recognized and had not enquired about in case it turned out he'd never heard of it.

'And he complains he can't see the ball,' Jane replied, from her chair alongside.

Jumbo had completed his thorough survey of the field and was taking stance again carefully. Mrs Hoskyns said, 'It's a shame Jamie's not here to back him up.' She paused. 'We really don't know what he's doing with himself.' She paused again. 'Do we, Tibby?'

'What?'

Tibby, although immediately to one side, seemed not to have been following.

'Jamie,' her mother prompted her.

Jane Mainwaring said, 'Jamie's going through a patch of not keeping in touch.'

'A phase,' Vicky said.

'Tibby had a card,' Mrs Hoskyns was able to tell them. 'Where was that card from, Tibby?'

'What card?'

'Oh, Tibby.' Why did she choose now to be difficult? Jane Mainwaring was a dear friend. 'Jamie's card. Where was it from?'

'Mopwe.'

'Where?' her mother pressed her.

'Mopwe,' Tibby gave sulkily. 'A place called Mopwe.'

Jane asked, 'He didn't happen to say, Tibby dear, when he's coming home?'

'Not really.'

'Because he *is* meant to be starting Cambridge in the autumn and there's a whole heap of forms waiting to be filled in.' But though it was university she spoke of, she had no interest in the forms as such. 'We just hope he doesn't hang around out there.'

'He'll come home as soon as he runs out of money,' Rowley assured them.

Then there was more applause. Jumbo had been caught at cover point – a potty catch from a timidly defensive stroke.

Vicky said, 'Oh God, it's you, Rowley.'

Rowley tightened the top strap of his pad and reached for his gloves in a leisurely way. Jumbo was approaching the pavilion and the cluster of surrounding spectators, who indulged him with some desultory clapping which had all but died by the time he reached the pavilion steps.

'I knew I should have left that ball alone,' Jumbo told them all as soon as he was in easy earshot. 'Complete folly. I'm getting ga-ga.'

'You did very well, Dad,' Vicky said, and glanced up at the scoreboard. 'Fourteen!'

'Fourteen,' Jumbo repeated contemptuously.

When his pads were off, he came to sit with them outside the pavilion.

Tibby's had a postcard from Jamie,' Jane told him, and Jumbo at once turned towards Tibby.

'Not a postcard, as a matter of fact,' the girl said, in a voice in which an intruded-upon privacy might have been detected.

'A letter!' said Jumbo. 'You mean an actual letter?!' And Jane felt the sarcasm, though cheerfully made, was not justified. For although the last letter, as such, that they had received was the very full, frustrated, analytical letter of a good three months earlier, it was a remarkable and impressive document.

'He didn't say anything, I suppose?' Jumbo added.

'What?' Tibby said, implying 'Such as what?'. In the strong sunlight they could have hardly noticed her blush.

Jumbo did not press his question, and his face took on its firm, composed lines.

Tibby's recent long letter from Jamie came unexpectedly in her last week before leaving school for keeps. She had read it about twenty times and still did not know what to make of it. It was all about the purpose of life, and living in the accepted structure of Western society being 'a cliché', and something about death being the only 'purposeful and individual thing left to live for'. He wrote of the impossibility of 'reconciling freedom with all the rest of it', and 'not even the herb providing an adequate solution'. He quoted Camus and other people she'd never heard of, some German specially. She did wonder if he was terribly depressed, which is how he could get, she knew; yet what he wrote was often very funny and made her laugh, so she could say he was just 'depressed' – which was quite normal and people were allowed to be – not terribly so. But he told almost nothing about what he was really doing out there, or what his life was like, except that he had 'picked up crabs from a brush with innocence', and his project director had 'finally turned out to be really an anus with more than a little in common with old Rodney J' (which she took to be a reference to his Eton housemaster he used to gripe about). She could not imagine what he meant by the reference to crabs, and having spoken to one friend at school and looked up the word in at least two dictionaries, she was no wiser. Yet she knew Jamie was confiding in her in his troubled way, and she clung to the manner he had finished, 'Hold true, true-self, true-and-fast, fast-dye, stead-fast, my own little, un-Sloane little, Tibby darling – for Jamie.'

What a funny way to write. '*For* Jamie'. She did feel the same person she was all that time ago when he was still in England and he had rung at the very last minute to say 'three little words' (as Mummy had called them, to whom she revealed that secret). She was the same person inside even though now she had left school and was planning to take a course in London and Mummy and she had gone out and bought a whole lot of new clothes, some of which she had on now.

And she did sense the excitement of his impending return, and the certainty that he would be returning for her if not for anything else – excitement of a kind different to anything she had felt before, that touched her body as she thought of him in her tummy and at the points of her breasts. It affected the manner of her movement, walking, when her thoughts were on Jamie, and made her wonder, lately twisting round in privacy (about to step into her bath or drying herself) to glimpse the butterfly that had been his 'pledge', what there was to a woman's body that drew a man.

Rowley played a stylish shot.

Jumbo said, 'He's got a very good late cut, Rowley.' He had propped his floppy white hat over his forehead against the glare and the heat of the sun.

'I never really know what's going on,' Vicky complained.

But Jumbo was already elsewhere.

'If he's not home soon . . .'

Tibby got up to cross to the orangeade table. She wanted no further intrusion. Jumbo saw how prettily she was dressed in her long yellow shorts and loose calico shirt and all her grown-up bangles. How pretty and slim and natural the young girls looked round the table, where the paper plates were coming out. He himself had put on weight since last year. He hadn't realized it – at least, not how much – until he had come to step into his cricket trousers again. He could hardly do the top button up! That had never happened before, and he'd had those trousers for thirty years: they buttoned at the fly. He remembered when Jamie, at the age of eight, had discovered that his father was wearing a pair of trousers with fly *buttons,* he and a schoolfriend staying for that week thought it was the most hilarious thing they had ever heard of. Jane had called the trousers 'antediluvian' and the boys fell about in helpless laughter, this time at the word.

And now he must have put on a stone in a year!

It was important to be slim, Jumbo mused, looking about him at the young. Nothing emphasized, nothing overstated, everything awaiting discovery, in its own time. Was this not of the essence of youth, this slimness, this unselfconsciousness, this unblemishedness that was Upton and its kind? Then suddenly he thought of the pornography at Barnes's village shop, with a surge of outrage. The pornographic magazines had crept in during recent years, and now they were always there on the upper tier of the circular rack that carried the rest of the coloured journals. Who, possibly, could they sell to in Upton, that lewdity, that foul-fleshed travesty of the function of love? He had mentioned it once to Mrs Barnes who served in the shop more often that her husband – 'Soho's the place for that, surely, Mrs Barnes, not Upton'– and she had dismissed it with a laugh as if it was of no consequence. But it *was* of consequence, it was a symptom of the shattering of the ancient covenant, upon which the civilization had grown – the covenant with God, the church, the landscape of England, that which was uniquely *England:* the language and the literature, the literature and the music, the music and the beauty and the peace. The entire understanding of it. He could see now at once what terrible threat it was all under. He could see it on all sides. Was it not all but already gone, all that must be most precious to an Englishman? The inner language gone, the elfin meanings and echoes of all its symbols? 'We are the writing on the wall.' How many were left like him, Jumbo, who held to that understanding still – of the people and the place, the place and its history and the paramountcy of its continuity?

He looked beyond the green to the church and beyond the church to the line of trees and the line of hills. What did it mean to this generation? What was left of the covenant for the masses in all this? – what, save material for the advertising of foreign motor cars or margarine? Who now could read the headstones? Who could worship the English Jesus now in the ringing of His bells? What did they know of the culture, those who were spray-painting the walls of the urban churches? – the covenant of culture, *colere, cultum,* the tilling and cherishing of the soil for the holy purpose of germination of barley, wheat and rye, of growing, mulching, of shielding from all harm, of ripening and reaping, season upon season, generation upon generation? What did they know of it? The politicians might pay it lip service, the 'educationists' (what was an educationist?) might allow it into a syllabus. Jumbo was not fooled: it was cheap votes and tourists, England, this sceptred isle, fragments of the past for CSEs. Dare any English child today be moved by Shakespeare's John of Gaunt's anticipatory yearning for his island home? It was all gone under the hill. The holy covenant was broken, it was shattered and shards, and he, Jumbo Mainwaring, knew it so. He did not even notice the uproar when Rowley turned down Alan Barnes's call on a square cut, refused to run, and had his partner at the wicket run out. He did not notice and did not care.

'Mum said you need one of these,' Vicky broke in upon his thoughts and handed him a tumbler. It was a gin-and-tonic. She picked up his soft hat at the crown by her fingertips, kissed him on the apex of his fine forehead, and dropped his hat back on. Jumbo twisted round and saw Jane over by the trestle table. She caught his glance and holding it those few moments read the distress there, a certain sorrow, the cause of which he would not of course vouchsafe her.

Upton won the match by fourteen runs, exactly Jumbo's contribution. One and all seemed satisfied, and felt at least mildly exercised and bronzed and a little drunk by the end of the day. It was a cloudless evening; and the unseen cloud that had stood over Jumbo so black and dense for that short passage of the morning might seem to have passed utterly. It was not so, or it was dispelled only to the extent that he had countered it with the thought of his son Jamie's return. For he found that such reflection upon Jamie restored the equilibrium in him and recalled to him that he was not alone: his own blood, his own boy, his own inheritor was at hand, on the brink of adulthood, to follow on from him in this world grown half strange to him yet where there were still constants, Eton for one, King's at Cambridge for another, Upton in the Cotswolds for another, which in their antique authority and excellence could bind father with son, son with father. When Jane gave him Jamie, Jumbo knew nearly twenty years ago, she was giving him an earthly immortality. Come what may, there was the covenant of the blood. Out in the field that afternoon – where he took a good catch high, one-handed, to his own surprise – he recognized it was Jamie he had missed these past bad months.

Mrs Hoskyns and Tibby, being friends of the family, helped the Mainwarings clear up the refreshments and the beer mugs; and just as they were leaving for home Jumbo turned to Tibby and especially asked her to be sure, if by chance she picked up any news of Jamie's homecoming, just to give him a ring; and he would do likewise. Tibby promised, but was astonished, for it was the first time that she had ever known Jumbo speak to her in earnest like a real person with a real part to play.

Yet there were to be no such advance warnings. A month later, he just turned up at Upton, with his rucksack, direct from Heathrow. Jane found him on the lawn with Dribble.

CHAPTER FIFTEEN

There was a mystery to him: they were all prepared to admit that now – though Tibby only
to herself. (It was the mystery in him that had always
drawn her to him most.) He was still the same Jamie
they had always known; and it was not that they felt
there was any secret as such. But now there was also a
separateness that he had chosen for himself, a privacy
stockaded against intrusion, which his mother, in particular, guessed was at the centre of him. For instance,
she was aware of how little he had really told them
about Africa. The politics, yes, the administration (or
lack of it), the mechanisms of aid and diplomacy – all
that: and she marvelled a little at his sophistication.
But there was so little that he had given of his own
experience. He had already been back a fortnight.

She had entered his bedroom now with a pile of
the shirts and pants that she and Kate had washed
in the machine, and ironed and folded. He seemed
leaner than before – more sinewy, at any rate; so
very male. Old Kate had given the opinion that he
needed 'feeding up' and checking for 'them African

worms' that her brother had got in Egypt in the war. But Jane knew he was fit, and as he wished to be. His face seemed that much narrower, though that may have been the short haircut. His jaw was darker and the line of his chin firmer. He had had his earlobe pierced, and had come back with a small brass ring in it: when she mentioned to him, with a casualness that masked an urgency, that she hoped Dad wouldn't 'take it [the earring] wrong' she noted that he had removed it before Jumbo returned to Upton the following evening from London. It was a sign of maturing, she thought, that little gesture.

She set down the laundered clothes on the end of the bed to put them away, underclothes in one drawer, shirts in another. The mere aroma of the laundered shirts whispered a mother's love. How many hundreds of times had she done this. He had occupied this room since he was eight, ever since he had moved from the nursery wing. It was just the same as she had always known it – a clutter of his things, some in current use, some left over from past ages – books, magazines, records, a camera, passport, odd garments (what was this? – a headband); on the walls, framed school photographs, a rowing citation. There was the tea-towel he and she had pinned up together ten or eleven years previously, with its printed poem, 'A Father's advice':

> If a sportsman true you'd be
> Listen carefully to me.

> Never, never let your gun
> Pointed be at anyone.
> That it may unloaded be
> Matters not the least to me.
> When a hedge or fence you cross
> Though of time it cause a loss
> From your gun the cartridge take
> For the greater safety's sake . . .

How scrupulous he had been, as a small boy, in obeying the 'sportsman true' rules. And how proud of his four-ten shotgun that he used to take out with Jumbo on the late summer evenings looking for rabbits in the fields that bordered Badger Wood. The ages of youth came and went so fast.

Africa seemed to have made him no tidier. She paused by his desk – 'deep litter' as Jumbo would have called it. Here was a journal concerning Glasnost. She didn't know much about his political views, she realized, though they would have been coming upon him no less inexorably than his sexual energies. And here, as it happened, underneath a list of 'Fringe Events' at the forthcoming Edinburgh Festival, was a colour magazine opened at a page filled with a photograph of a young woman with her legs spread apart fingering her pudendum. Underneath that was another photograph, a black-and-white print of an African baby slung in a cloth across its mother's chest, baby and mother alike hollow-eyed and spindle-necked from extreme malnutrition. Presumably it was Jamie's own photograph: though he had shown them snaps of where he had lodged and the team he had worked with, he had never shown them this.

Through the open window framed by creeper she could hear the *whap* of ball on racket from the tennis court, and the occasional cries of the contestants, Tibby and Jamie. She could just see them at the bottom of the garden below the cedars over the top of the lime hedge. Tibby's game had come on fast: she was a natural athlete: but Jamie still gave her an extra first service, to even it up.

When Jane descended the stairs, Mrs Hoskyns had already arrived, come to gather up Tibby. The two mothers fell to talking in the drawing room. Ella Hoskyns agreed that Jamie had changed; she had seen it at once.

'He's not giving away very much,' Jane said.

'Gone into himself, rather,' Mrs Hoskyns offered, but Jane felt that the way she herself had put it was more accurate. It was not so different from his father, after all. Not an introspection so much as an English reticence. No one but she might have told, just the other day, the *joy* of Jumbo when he had come home to Upton to greet Jamie. *She* knew it was joy; and something as deep, no doubt, in Jamie too. Yet there were the two of them engaged in the laconic English ritual, making measured distances between one another, demonstrating a minimum of gesture of language – 'Oh, hi Pa'/ 'Well, m'boy, had a good time?'/'Yeah, not bad.'/'Had a decent bath?' and within a few seconds Jumbo complaining, and Jamie condoling, about the utter inability of the English selectors to pick a team capable of winning a Test Match. *Test Match!* 'They don't play much cricket in Mali?' Jumbo had eventually queried, lest it be thought he hadn't been aware where his son had spent the last nine months of his short life. It was half a joke, naturally; in the half that wasn't Jamie would have caught the inference, namely that his tribesmen would have been that much more worth saving from starvation if Mali had been a cricketing nation.

'He still seems devoted to Tibby,' Mrs Hoskyns said, I'm worried that he expects too much from her.'

'You mean . . .' Jane Mainwaring began.

'No, I don't mean that. Not primarily. Of course there is a physical thing between them. Tibby's very sensible, though. She's not yet seventeen. There's such a lot going on inside Jamie, wouldn't you say? He expects her to share it rather.'

It was a desultory game. The score was, they agreed, four-three and 40—love to Jamie when Tibby vigorously wooded a service return and the ball arched over the court's fence into the shrubbery below. Tibby scampered from the court to where she had seen the ball go while it was still in her mind's eye. Jamie followed in a leisurely way, summoning Dribble.

The ball had evidently landed where the garden met the fields, in the undergrowth along the ditch there. They hunted around in grass and ferns and docks, probing with their rackets.

'Find it, Dribble!' Tibby commanded, and Dribble descended into the ditch enjoying the joke of it, though the weather was no cooler than it need be and best for sleeping in the shade. Jamie followed the labrador. Tibby said,

'It didn't go so far, surely.'

'It went quite a way. It was a mighty swipe.'

'A big bish.'

The ditch, which carried a trickle of water, disappeared into a culvert under the gated pathway by which the garden could be reached from the fields.

'Let's give it up,' Tibby said, 'I'll bring you a ball next time I come. Let's finish the set.'

'I've forgotten the score,' Jamie said.

'Don't be so hopeless, Jamie. It's five-three.'

'I played enough tennis by the time I was fifteen,' Jamie told her. He stooped to peer into the culvert.

'I thought you liked tennis.'

'I pretend to. To please you. Ah – I think I see it.'

Tibby joined him, to peer into the glinting gloom of the culvert. The ball was lodged midway along the length of it.

She said, 'How on earth did it get there?' and ran round to the other end of the culvert.

'Nature abhors a vacuum,' Jamie informed her. He began to crawl into the culvert, on hands and knees. He could see her crouching at the other end, and now she too started to crawl in. Each of them had left their rackets in the grasses at either end.

'How am I supposed to see?' Jamie asked, it's slimy,' Tibby said.

Weed grew out of the brickwork each side of the tunnel, and the small trickle of water, just enough to have carried the ball, wet their knees.

Jamie's hand found the ball.

'Have you got it?' she demanded, i'm searching, aren't I?'

She crawled on to where he was. Then she uttered a playful squeal.

'I thought for a moment . . . ' Jamie began, very low.

'What?' she whispered.

'I thought I had the ball. It was too squadgy.'

They had begun to kiss, upside down.

Right against his mouth Tibby whispered, 'Can I ask you a question?'

'Try me.'

'Did you – do it with those African girls?'

'Which?'

'Mopte, wherever.'

'It can't matter to you.'

'Is that what you think?'

But they were kissing again, and now she was trying to turn round inside the culvert. It was a very awkward manoeuvre, and meant getting quite wet and her shirt and tennis slip soiled by the weed and algae of the culvert. But at last they were horizontal together in the darkness, and reconciled to the trickle of water they lay in; more than reconciled. The culvert's structure, being circular, rolled them together. His free hand began to move over her body without hindrance. They kissed; and so fully that Tibby had known no kissing like it.

'How do I know,' she said, freeing her mouth, 'you're not riddled with disease?'

He shifted over her, and she giggled. She was quite wet now, hair and all.

'I'm not going to let you,' she whispered.

But her head arched back, into the water, and she felt his kisses on her neck, her breasts . . .

'I can feel the ball,' she said sharply. 'It's in your hand.'

He tried to guide her hand to where he wished it, where it could amaze her, but she resisted.

Then they heard a distant cry. *'Tibby? Tibby?'*

It was her mother, from up by the house. It froze her, but only for a moment, but him not at all, perhaps even adding an urgency.

'I don't think you really love me,' she whispered.

'Is this not loving?' he cried.

He was greatly aflame.

'Sssh! . . . You just want one thing!'

And suddenly he stopped. She felt him recoiling from her.

'You'll hold back on love,' he accused her. 'Then one day you'll find yourself opening your legs to anyone who flatters you. If they've got enough money. Just like Vicky. You won't ever have known what loving is!'

Oh, such a speech – an entire speech of accusation! She felt the cruelty and the despair of him rush into their secret darkness and separate them utterly.

'How dare you!' she exclaimed, having no proper words, but blazing in her eyes.

'Sssh!'

They could hear her mother now, close by, most likely immediately above them, by the gate.

'Jamie? Tibby?'

The calls were terribly loud, right on top of them, curling up at each second syllable in bewilderment and frustration. Jamie could imagine the tendons standing out on Mrs Hoskyns' hen-like neck: there *was* something hennish in Mrs Hoskyns. How could she have failed to notice the rackets, one at each end of the culvert? Or Dribble, inanely wagging his tail down there in the ditch?

'T*i*bby!' This time the stress on the first syllable, in impatience. And then to herself (so she thought): 'Where *can* the girl have got to?'

A small smile had crept back into Tibby's face. A little pout invited a minor kiss. But she shifted her body away from him, which paltry movement dislodged the tennis ball.

The ball trickled with the tiny current out of the culvert and settled against the weed just below where Mrs Hoskyns' feet were planted. But the feet moved away. From further away they heard her voice calling 'Tibby?' and then, 'Jane, have you seen the children?'

Yet Jamie had turned aside from Tibby. Only his middle finger and thumb were lightly tracing the line of her jaw, and then the small divide of her nose that had still to be finally formed.

Tibby said, 'Where've you gone to, silly?'

What might he reply to her. Trapped? But he said nothing.

So Tibby had a suggestion of her own. 'Trapped?' she said.

CHAPTER SIXTEEN

There were still six weeks to pass before Jamie was to go up to Cambridge in October. Jumbo was fixed upon bringing Jamie with him to visit the old college, King's, before term began, to show him this and that – the Mainwaring window in the great chapel, which Jamie had never seen. But first Jamie intended to fulfil a promise to attend the Edinburgh Festival where two or three of his Eton contemporaries who had gone up to Oxford the previous autumn were putting on a performance, with others, at a 'fringe' theatre, of a play they had constructed themselves. Both of these events came to bear, however marginally, on what was to befall Jamie Mainwaring.

The play for the Edinburgh 'fringe' was a dramatic collage taking its title from T.S. Eliot's The Waste Land and drawn from that poem and other Eliotiana.* It had commended itself to its adapters,

---

* *The Waste Land* and *The Four Quartets,* from which the fragments below are taken, are in copyright *(Collected Poems 1909–1962)* and published by Faber.

players and a few reckless backers (its costs were all of £800) as stemming from seminal works of twentieth-century literature, after whose original publication nothing had been quite the same. Jamie was familiar with the poetry which contributed to the dramatic offering. It was to be given six performances in a playhouse converted from a Presbyterian church, and much time and energy had been expended in scattering the severe stone façades of various landmarks of the Scottish capital with posters and fiy-bills heralding this significant cultural event. Fully half the tickets had already been sold or handed out to special friends and relations of those involved, or otherwise allocated; but there was still a lot of drumming up to be done and Jamie, once his re-emergence from darkest Africa had become known of, was persuaded to arrive two days ahead of the first night for this purpose. It involved him, among other things, as one with a reputation for a cool nerve, in the perilous suspension of a cloth banner across the stonework above the broad but lofty arch which formed the entrance to the former house of worship, for the entrance looked down the whole length of the street to George IV Bridge.

It also enabled him to attend the final rehearsal.

This took place, under Gus's often rather frenetic direction, on the stage itself. Jamie was not unaware of having had his own private experience of fringe theatre at the altar end of a church. He made no reference to it on this occasion. If he had changed at all since these old friends had seen him last, they were

all too busy to notice it. Were not all of them changing so fast anyway, at this time of life? Yet they seemed
little changed to him, though he knew he was different from what he had been.

They were all still clutching their scripts. It
seemed to Jamie too late for that, for this penultimate
rehearsal. A student was reading, with a convincing
Greek accent,

> 'Asked me in demotic French
> To luncheon at the Cannon Street Hotel
> Followed by a weekend at the Metropole.'

This rendering of Mr Eugenides was cut short by
Gus, who urgently re-formed the group of three
young men and the girl.

'Okay, Henry, it's you.'

Henry moved forward, right of stage.

'Don't overdo, Henry. Just live it.'

Henry threw Gus a glance of exasperation. The
others had donned black top hats and lugubrious
expressions, forming a light funeral cortège.

Henry intoned:

> 'O dark dark dark. They all go into the dark,
> The vacant intersellar spaces, the vacant into the
> vacant. . .'

Gus stopped him. It was by any measure dreadfully
hammed. It would have the audience in giggles,

which was not the purpose. How had Henry ever come to be selected as narrator? Jamie had always known Henry couldn't act.

'Jamie – can we hear you?'

He wondered what Gus was up to, at such a point in the proceedings. He slipped on stage, borrowing Henry's script. He half-knew the lines already.

'O dark dark dark. They all go into the dark,/ The vacant interstellar spaces, the vacant into the vacant. . .'

'Good,' Gus said. 'Again. Stay with it.'

Jamie gave the lines again. He knew he made it sound as it should sound, and he knew he set the exact tone for the rest, as they joined him, Gus shunting Henry round to join the top-hatted group:

'The captains, merchant bankers, eminent men of letters. The generous patrons of art, the statesmen and the rulers, Distinguished civil servants, chairmen of many committees, Industrial lords and petty contractors, all go into the dark. . .'

Then Jamie on his own with 'And dark the Sun and Moon, and the Almanach de Gotha/And the Stock Exchange Gazette, the Directory of Directors,/And cold the sense and lost the motive of action . . .'

'Straight to the next tableau,' Gus said.

Two of them carried a table strewn with breakfast things to one side of the stage, and moved a settee to a chalk mark across from it. The girl in the tight skirt started clearing the breakfast things.

'Jamie, centre,' Gus instructed. Jamie glanced round at Henry, but Gus nullified the glance with an impatient gesture and Jamie did as he was bid. As the girl mimed, Jamie gave the lines:

> 'At the violet hour, the evening hour that strives Homeward, and brings the sailor home from sea, The typist home at teatime, clears her breakfast, lights Her stove, and lays out food in tins.'

Instinctively Jamie altered the pitch and mood of his voice.

> 'I Tiresias, old man with wrinkled dugs
> Perceived the scene, and foretold the rest —
> I too awaited the expected guest.'

A student, playing squat and perky, came on stage, acting out Jamie's continuing commentary as 'the young man carbuncular' who arrives, 'a small house agents's clerk, with the bold stare,/One of the low on whom assurance sits/As a silk hat on a Bradford millionaire.

'The time is now propitious,' continued Jamie, 'as he guesses,

> 'The meal is ended, she is bored and tired,
> Endeavours to engage her in caresses

Which still are unreproved, if undesired.
Flushed and decided, he assaults at once;
Exploring hands encounter no defence;
His vanity requires no response,
And makes a welcome of indifference.'

All this was played by the student couple, with poignant skill. Jamie noticed the boyish charm of the girl, with her Twenties bob. Then it was for Jamie to say:

'And I Tiresias have foresuffered all
Enacted on this same divan or bed;
I who have sat by Thebes below the wall
And walked among the lowest of the dead.'

Gus took him aside and there and then offered him the part. And he took it. His acquaintance with the poetry helped, but he sat up half that night learning the role – that of the commentator throughout the hour-long production. Henry, who had been unhappy in the part, joined in the group speeches with good grace. They were content to announce the change from the footlights rather than alter the programmes. Jamie stayed the week and played every performance.

It was judged a success, and on the last night Gus got drunk as a lord (which, when father died, he would become) and generously made Jamie hero of the show, declaring him to have a career ahead with the Cambridge Footlights. Jamie stayed sober, and later that night the girl, although she was attached to Gus, gave her body to Jamie. The next morning he caught the train south, leaving before most of them had woken.

His head, his soul (if he were to permit himself such a word, which he did not) were full of many things, jostling and eddying and refusing any resolution or clarity; though clarity is what he yearned for. It had been a short night: as it was, he had had little sleep all week, yet there was no restfulness in him, only turmoil. He felt contaminated by betrayal, mostly on his own part. Gus, for example: he had surely betrayed Gus with the girl. He had not even liked her much. She was attractive, but had proved to be extremely opinionated. There was nothing in the world on which she did not have an emphatic opinion, but the strength of her feelings seemed to be in inverse ratio to the importance of the issue. (What outraged her most just now was the Government's unspeakable immorality in countenancing a fifty pence entrance fee payable by those – except for the young, the old, the poor and the disabled – who wished to visit the country's museums.) She was bound to tell Gus, of course, because she could not hold anything back and had in fact talked all the time they were making love. And he could not but feel also a betrayal of little Tibby. It wasn't reasonable to expect to keep himself chaste for the sake of Tibby. Yet Tibby, he was imprecisely aware, comprised the innocence in him and was the only person so far with whom he had risked the word 'love'. It would confuse Tibby, he knew, what he had done and the manner of his doing it, 'enacted on that same divan or bed': it would destroy a little something in her, should she know, should she have stood witness – something most precious. It would rubbish her.

And had he not even betrayed his good friend Henry by usurping his part in the play? It wasn't he that had sought it. Oh, but he had acceded to Gus's request quite readily, and had given himself over to the role so fully.

Henry was a good man, better than he.

But was there not betrayal in the very enterprise he and his friends had been engaged upon? Betrayal of that which had forced the poetry out of the writer? His head was full of the Eliotiana he had committed to memory and given out nightly. He could fill the role because he, though not yet twenty years, could pull on the faded mantle of Tiresias. He did perceive, was certain of, the integrity of the poet writing half a century or more earlier – the integrity of his despair for man, modern man. That is why they had endured, those lines: on account of the mystic ring of their integrity. *Quant à la destinée humaine, je suis pessimiste,* as his revered Camus had put it. So also Eliot. Thus, presumably, had Gus and his friends chosen to perform it – had cobbled together the theatric bits and made a show of it. But to what end? To have *fun with it,* to get their spot on the fringe of the Festival. To get drunk on the last night.

Had that been Eliot's purpose for his work, half a century on?

Gus's father, Jamie knew, was a merchant banker, and Gus's intention was to follow in the same profession. Cazenove's, Schroeders, Morgan Grenfell – Gus knew his way amid the jungle of them. (The famous banks, Jamie knew, had taken to trawling for the academically most gifted of the Oxbridge young men. If Gus himself fell short of such an élite, the pulling of a parental string or two plus the right kind of suit and haircut for the interview should take the trick.) Yet there was Gus giving every evidence of going along with the quasi-revolutionary views on whatever topic was under discussion. Was he pretending, or just fooling himself? If ever there was a man destined for the vacant interstellar spaces by way of the Stock Exchange Gazette and the Directory of Directors, it was Gus. Eliot had written, and nothing had been learned.

Was nothing ever to be learned? *Quant à la destinée humaine, je suis pessimiste.*

Yet Eliot had finished up some sort of Christian, Jamie seemed to recall.

Gus had asked him, one night, 'What's been happening to your Dad's business?' As a student of 'PPE' (Politics, Philosophy and Economics) he had begun to attend to the financial pages of his newspapers. Before Jamie had a chance to reply, Gus added, 'Are you going to be working for the Nips?' When it came down to it, Gus didn't doubt he would go into

Mainwaring's, that is to say make a career of, devote his existence to, Mainwaring's. Apparently Gus hadn't noticed about the Bolt Company, and Jamie wasn't going out of his way to tell him – the couple of thousand or so out of work at Bradford, the end of the founding factory.

He knew little of the detail of it himself, beyond what his father had told him in a letter he had received in Mali – one of the three stiff, if affectionate, letters he had received from him there. The information had been half obliterated for him at the time because it was in the same letter that purported to be a response to his own long plea addressed to both parents, in which his father had proposed that 'you put down your ideas in a letter *to The Times* when you get home.' (After that he knew it worthless trying to share in that quarter any of his experiences that were significant.) Since his return home Pa had just mentioned the Bolt Company once or twice, but Jamie had caught the look Ma gave him that warned him not to pursue the topic.

Such were some of Jamie's thoughts as the train carried him south again to London. Where 'further' was their further education carrying them, those old school friends of his and their new university comrades? What more did they need to be taught in a seat of learning to fit them for life (unless they were to be doctors or lawyers or pedagogues themselves)? Yet of course it was expected of them all, the slightly cleverer ones. One must get the intellectual polish one needed. One must make friends. One must have a good time. One's parents had to 'make sacrifices' for one's allowance, but it pleased *them* too, they were proud of one . . . .

After three years at Cambridge, Jamie thought, after how many nubiles shafted, bottles drunk, books dipped into, arguments won or lost or abandoned, how much better will I play Tiresias? To what greater effect will I have delved the meaning of Eliot or whoever else?

And almost at once the second incident was upon him – the promised 'advance visit' with Jumbo to Cambridge. They were to drive over leaving Jamie to stay on a night with Anthony. The beginning of term was still a month away, but as a Choral Scholar and thus a member of his college, St John's, choir, Anthony was obliged to come up six weeks early.

Mercifully (Jamie thought) his father had dispensed with Searle for the day and drove the family Volvo himself. They reached Cambridge by mid-morning. Pa had the whole day planned out. They walked the Backs in the morning-it was a sunny autumn day – and called in at the University Library. They ate a good lunch at Midsummer House and afterwards visited two or three colleges (Trinity, Clare, Downing) which, for reasons Pa explained in some detail, had particular memories for him and which, besides King's itself, he thought of as particularly beautiful and the buildings 'quintessentially Cambridge'. His father seemed so specially happy, Jamie noticed, almost elated – 'lifted up', as Jamie thought of it. He frequently found it difficult to make his responses sound fitting to father's mood, but Pa didn't seem put out by his silent patches or even to notice them: he had been so swept up in his own coming up to King's in 1945, 'literally three weeks out of uniform' – how it came as 'a sort of miracle' (to him) that such a world as Cambridge had endured the war, he arriving more or less straight out of the jungle and the transit camp at Chittagong.

Father and son came out of the sunlight of King's Parade and under the archway of the gate-tower of King's itself at about three-fifteen. The great quadrangle spread before them, with the magnificent Gothic Chapel on their right and the ancient buildings of the College itself on the three remaining sides. They paused there – Jumbo paused and Jamie with him. The soft tilting sunlight bathed the stone façade and pinnacles of the gate-tower. Despite a difference of some forty years anyone might have guessed they were father and son.

In a moment they would see the window, the 'Mainwaring Bequest'. Something deep within Jamie compelled him to comment, out of the silence – though not absolute silence, for they could just hear chanting coming from the Chapel across the greensward: 'I don't really go in for the ecclesiastical stuff these days.'

214

'I dare say,' Jumbo replied at once. He was quite aware of Jamie's problems with the Christian religion. It grieved him, but he trusted that time and an open mind . . . He continued, 'You can hardly overlook the fact that your great-great-grandfather *gave* the great west window. When my grandfather came up here in 1880.'

'I know.' God, did he know! He had known it as long as he had known his own name.

'It's the biggest single scene in stained glass in Western Europe. Or it was, when they put it in.'

'I know. I know.' Jamie knew all right. The fif-teenth-century college hadn't the funds to fill the Chapel's west window with coloured glass before the Reformation put a stop to that sort of thing anyway. It wasn't till three centuries later in high Victorian Anglicanism that anyone got round to fulfilling the original intention.

'The Last Judgement,' Jumbo reminded him.

Jamie was spared further, for the moment, by the arrival of a bevy of Japanese tourists entering the court by the archway. Jumbo watched them.

The Japanese were all male, all indistinguish-able, all with cameras. Jumbo watched intently. They lined up in a tight, grinning group, for pho-tographs, with the gate-tower behind them. On each one's snapping, another popped out to follow suit, all done at the double with the precision of instinctive ritual. At the moment of each snapping, as at the moment of each execution in the prison camps, their chattering was suspended. Turning,

Jumbo muttered, 'They'd buy it if they could.' The son had no response, having not heard exactly or picked up his train of thought – that albeit in the few decades since he left Cambridge the yellow men's GNP had swelled to double that of England's from a mere sixth of it, yet there remained here that which was beyond violation: an immutability; a sanctum for such as him and his son, a *within* . . . within the island, Cambridge; within Cambridge, King's; within King's this green quadrangle that the Chapel flanked. Wherein a sweete Lorde.

As father and son now skirted the Chapel by the path which led to the north door, the chanting from within reached them more distinctly. It was Renaissance counterpoint, unaccompanied; Palestrina perhaps, yet somehow swerving, unsettled and unsettling: not so much Palestrina as Gesualdo. *Cui amore langueo.*

And as they entered the mighty Chapel the riven counterpoint burst upon their ears with the matching glow of tremendous light which the afternoon September sun poured through the west window in myriad colour. This whelming glow illuminated all of the nave and its exquisite fan-vaulting high above, as far as the rood-screen which divided nave from choir. That was where the singing flooded from: a choir practice was in train.

In the body of the Chapel there were no worshippers – only sightseers scattered along the nave and side-aisles. At a stall, the trippers were buying booklets and postcards. The familiar appeals for contributions for restoration were displayed on placards.

Jumbo was standing in awe. First he had gazed at the west window. Then he turned up the chapel. At the far end of the chancel, on the steps to the altar, beyond the rood-screen and the choir, he could just catch sight of the vivid crimson of Rubens' 'Adoration of the Magi'. He knew it was that picture since, although he had not been back here at King's for any alumnal function for several years, he had read of the Rubens having come to the Chapel on some sort of permanent loan, in the College Society's annual report.

Now he had turned again towards the sun-blazed window.

'The Mainwaring Bequest,' he said, almost to himself.

'I know, I know.'

Jamie's voice, uneasily, beside him.

The singing had stopped. Jumbo turned to the chapel notices, displayed beside the bookstall. He glanced at his watch. He said,

'They're starting Choral Evensong in five minutes. Let's go up.'

He meant, go up for the service itself, beyond the rood-screen.

Jamie did not answer. His attention appeared to be on the Japanese, who were taking notice of everything, guide books in hand, with futile enthusiasm. Jumbo said beside him,

'I know you're not a worshipper these days.'

He loved the boy so much, longed for him to share what he knew. 'It'll only be thirty-five minutes and beautifully sung.'

Jamie said, 'I don't think I can.'

Jamie hadn't moved, watching the Japanese . . . the bookstall. . . he wasn't watching anything. All at once he was moving towards the door and the daylight. But Jumbo had moved beside him, so very swiftly. He gripped the boy's arm. There was incredulity in him.

'For heaven's sake, Jamie. *Thirty-five minutes.*'

'No, Pa.'

Jamie was held there, quite still, not so much by his gripped arm as by the entire countervailing force – the entire cyclonic swirl of the building, the heritage, father-and-son, of which he was the eye, the still centre. And his father was pleading.

'You don't have to say the prayers! I'm not asking you to believe anything. Just for the beauty of it! The music! Look – it's two minutes to go.' He was beginning to pull at him. it's two minutes to go.'

But Jamie was not to be budged. The way he was standing now, he was looking at the west window.

'It's the family chapel,' Jumbo cried.

'Look!' said Jamie, with an involuntary smirk. 'No ladies!'

Jumbo glanced back at the window. Indeed it seemed no women were depicted. He had never noticed.

'Pull yourself together, Jamie,' he demanded.

Jamie said, quite airily, 'Let's go, Pa.'

'We're going to Choral Evensong.' He was angry now. He welcomed the anger.

'I *can't*. Don't you see? – I *cant't!*

Jumbo looked at him in shock of disbelief – as at one, for example, who in jesting play had killed.

But in the same instant Jamie seemed composed – distant, conscious of a wound inflicted, but firm and composed.

'You go,' he said, 'I'll wait outside.' And so he did turn to the great door, leaving his father where he was.

Thus it all occurred.

Outside on the edge of the grass, the chapel door behind him, Jamie stood alone in the direct glow of the western sun. It felt to him as if he had just broken to safety from the clutches of some monster, half-known, half-unknown; half-seen, half-unseeable. His heart pounded. He drew his breath with purpose and conscious regularity. He was quite stationary, having no will just now for any action, or any decision.

Within the Chapel, where Evensong was under way, the choir was already completing the first set of responses. It sang with an impenetrable perfection.

'As it was in the beginning, is now, and shall ever be; world without end. Amen.'

'Praise ye the Lord,' piped the priest. And the choir,

'The Lord's name be praised.'

What did it all mean? All meaning was extruded.

An undergraduate chorister, an alto, left the stall to read the Old Testament lesson. His short progress to the lectern was performed with a camp precision, making neat right-angles and including a little bob to the altar – or, more exactly, to Rubens' portrayal of the 'Adoration of the Magi'. The lesson was from the prophet Micah. 'Trust ye not in a friend,' read the young man, 'put ye not confidence in a guide; keep the doors of thy mouth from her that lieth in thy bosom. For the son dishonoureth the father, the daughter riseth up against . . .'

Besides the choir and the priest, there were three others in the stalls to listen to him who could be counted as congregation, all three of them from among the College's own ecclesial structure.

A little below the rood-screen, the motionless figure of a tallish, rather distinguished figure of late middle-age, standing on his own in the aisle. He looked neither up the chapel to the choir nor down the body of the building towards the window. He took no part in the act of worship, for he neither knelt when prayers were called, nor turned to the altar when the creed was intoned. It was impossible to tell what, if any, of the exquisitely schooled choral devotions reached him. He might be perceived by the closely observant to be a man riven with shock, incapable of action or decision.

He might be hearing (for he was well within earshot) the priest's narrow intoning, 'O Lloyd, show Thy mercy upon us,' and the choir's further importuning, 'And grant us they sal-va-shee-on,' and the priest's 'O Lloyd, sieve the Queegn.' Yet what he was really hearing was a cry of wild desperation: just that one cry, 'I *can't*. Don't you see? – I *can't*.'

CHAPTER SEVENTEEN

The principal change that Jamie noticed in his friend Anthony, his host that evening in college at St John's, was that he had become confirmed in his homosexuality. At Eton, Anthony's inclinations had seemed to Jamie an affectation – something that could be put aside at the appropriate time with a small effort of will and the arrival of a more regularly used shaving brush. But it hadn't turned out so. And now that the proclivity was confirmed, and was playing quite an important part in Anthony's life as well as touching his manner of speech and certain bodily gestures, it seemed to come between them. It surprised Jamie that it was so. Attempting to overlook this private factor made Jamie more aware of it; having Anthony expand upon it in open chatter produced the odd effect on him of conversing with his friend through a sheet of glass. This was so (he decided) because he could not help feeling that it was a misfortune for Anthony. He was aware of the illiberalism of this view, but he realized now that he had long held the suspicion that the homosexuals' choice of the word 'gay' for their kind was a rather sad one. In Anthony now he perceived what it was: that while all mankind had its share of vanity, the essence of Anthony's condition was a physical narcissism and by that unfortunate fact he was ever after precluded from the essential reciprocity and *mystery* of heterosexual love. Any passion, for Anthony, must end up as a vice shared; for the straight, there was in any love the ultimate possibility of the supreme purpose of self, namely the ecstatic melting away into a greater, an infinite, whole, the lover and the loved. Jamie would admit that he had yet to know such love. Yet even already, although tangled and troubled by his erratic half-steps into the territory of love (where Tibby might be found), by the unpredictable race of his blood, by the dead-ends and inconsequence of his own lustful encounters so far, he could have none the less struggled through to a definition of what his instinct told him concerning the goal of bodily love.

This division between them was nothing formidable; the perception of it by Jamie was merely a symptom of all else that had built up in him. And on Anthony's part, all he observed was that Jamie was rather subdued, a bit off form by his familiar reckless standards. Anthony did gather that Jumbo had been something of a trial during the day – Mainwaring *père* had already taken himself off home by tea-time when Jamie walked over to his rooms in St John's to join him. Jamie hadn't chosen to pass on the detail; and Anthony found that, however ready he was to assent that the very nature of parents was to be *tiresome,* it was not enough to crack the inwardness and reserve of his old Eton messmate.

Before he left Cambridge the next morning, Jamie borrowed a sheet of plain writing paper from Anthony, and an envelope. He wrote a brief, careful letter, then paused for a minute or more in thought before writing the envelope. The previous evening he had more or less decided to say nothing to Anthony, but at the last moment before sealing it up, aware of being later thought of as disloyal, he drew the letter from the envelope and showed it to his friend. Anthony, still in his pyjamas, read it in astonishment; before he could find words to utter, Jamie had whipped it from his fingers, sealed it into its envelope, and had set off down the stairs and out into the court and the weather.

Jamie walked through the gusting rain and put the letter in at the porter's lodge under the gatehouse at King's. He had debated whether to address it to the Provost or the Admissions Tutor, settling in the end for the latter since, at the lower level, there was less chance of instant collusion with his father. He did not want his father to suppose it to be an impetuous over-reaction to the crisis in the Chapel the day before, dreadful though it had been.

From the station he telephoned Tibby and told her. She didn't say much, although obviously she was excited by the grandeur of the secret. He told her to say nothing to anyone for the time being.

He felt better, having done that. He had got quite wet walking to the station, but it was a warm day and the rain had washed away the sensation of tackiness he had acquired in Anthony's cramped 'rooms' (there was only one of them). He had the whole world, he said to himself; the whole world was his.

It was in fact through Tibby that word got out. Of course it had to get out sooner or later, and very likely a leakage was better than an announcement and some sort of blistering confrontation. And in its way the machine got to work without delay.

Jamie's intention was to let his parents know when they came back from Scotland. Scotland was a standard pilgrimage at that time of year. Cousin Charlie had a shoot in Ayrshire and despite all the anguish over the Bolt Company (and the hole blown in the family finances), the invitation had been renewed. Jumbo had consequently gone north, taking Jane of course, to 'kill some grouse and mend the fences' as he remarked to her. Precisely how he should inform his parents Jamie had not decided. He was aware only of a single phrase in his mind on stand-by – it's my life, not yours!'

But his parents had been gone a week – it was a fortnight's ritual with the Ryders – when Jamie got to know the cat was out of the bag. Rowley had rung him and, asking him casually what he was up to (neither of them mentioning Cambridge where term would begin in three weeks), invited him out to dinner in London the next night. 'Dress up a bit. We'll go somewhere decent.'

It was just the three of them – Rowley, Vicky and Jamie, who put on his blue suit and had even brought the brown felt hat he wore occasionally at weekend house-parties and race meetings. Rowley had said in his languid way, 'Let's push the boat out.' They began the evening in the small house just off the King's Road that Rowley shared with Vicky, had a couple of extended side-cars there, and not much before ten p.m. went on in Rowley's Porsche to a well-known, if exclusive, dining and gambling establishment in Curzon Street.

It was a converted town house built originally for a Regency grandee, and had been magnificently, yet none the less tastefully, done up, no expense spared. It had the air of a club for those whose common factor was the achievement of success, the success in question being the acquisition of wealth as a direct and exclusive consequence of a desire to acquire wealth. Potentates apart, the membership included few who had come into wealth by long inheritance. It did number one or two who, while having not so much wealth as debts, found meaning in life only in the close company of those of assured wealth, and who possessed the not inconsiderable skill of scrounging meals and baccarat chips by an ability to hold any amount of drink, to be always witty, to know who had got into or out of bed with whom in St Moritz, Mustique, Cap Ferrat, Badminton and so on; and who occasionally pulled off a big win at backgammon, at which they were invariably very skilled. The membership also included certain of the mega-rich from far beyond the shores of Britain who were heirs to, or in one or two cases sat on, so-called thrones of territories where petroleum had been discovered, or the close enough relatives of the latter, or their arms-buyers, fixers, *et al.*

So diverse a membership maintained its cohesion with a kind of wary camaraderie which comprised no intimacy whatever, except for tiny cliques. Everyone knew more or less who everyone else was; most had a pretty shrewd notion of one another's financial status (subject to the well known proviso of a former Texan member who, incredibly, had since gone bust, that anybody who knows what he's worth ain't worth very much'). But only in rare instances would any member have known, or met, the *parents* of any other, and in virtually no cases, except among the scattering of Arabs, would the parents of one have any acquaintance with the parents of another.

The only guaranteed common allegiance was to the proprietor of the place, himself a figure of very considerable wealth, all made on the premises where he was to be found most nights. This celebrated proprietor constituted the junction-box for what passed as friendship among those who in the leisured expression of their wealth had made him their equal and their confidant. Rowley was proud to be a member of such an establishment. It proved that he had arrived. Where had be arrived? He had arrived here.

The establishment's male servants reminded Jamie of Searle. They were less lazy, very likely, and more highly paid; but they had a similar parasitical oiliness and, ultimately, ruthlessness by which, if required by those they served, they would perform anything, however utterly bestial.

Jamie however did not mind; indeed he was happy and carefree. The place had its own ersatz magic; it was shamelessly luxurious; several of those scattered around were celebrities (of the kind that avoided personal publicity). It fitted Rowley, whose company Jamie enjoyed and whom he despised. Rowley in turn fitted Vicky, of whom Jamie had no opinion whatever, being far too close to her. She had been unpleasant to him as a little girl. As she (and he) grew older she had been successively patronizing, stand-offish, confidential, and sugary-sweet. There had been moments when it almost seemed as if she was proud of him. She was a Sloane, of course, which was a condition he had heard described as proving the reverse of the adage that 'the whole is greater than the sum of its parts'. (Even so it was a condition to which several girls of his acquaintance happily aspired.) She was quite thick – Jamie could never understand why, unless it was the awful schools with saints' names his parents insisted on sending her to where, more or less admittedly, they taught her nothing, but where she would 'make a lot of friends' (i.e. identikit embryo Sloanes). She did what everybody else did, no more, no less, and the clothes she wore conformed (no more, no less)

to whatever was the current thing, like a shifting uniform. She appeared to have no other purpose in life
than to exist, drifting like weed on a Thames backwa-
ter Jamie knew just below Marlow, sharing bed and
board with this Rowley, to whom she brought a pre-
carious social status. All in all he was fond of Vicky,
who disgusted him.

The food and the wine were perfectly delicious
beneath the chandeliers in their damask-walled corner and the talk slid harmlessly from this to that. It was
only towards the very end of the meal that Cambridge
came up and Jamie realized at once that Rowley knew
he had decided he wasn't going to go up. By this time
Jamie was fairly drunk. He was unconcerned as to
how Rowley had found out. Indeed, he was quite glad
for the two of them to know about it. After all, Rowley
and Vicky were out in the big world and here was
he, Jamie, having just joined them in it, by virtue of
having written and delivered by hand one, decisive,
three-sentence letter a week or so previously.

By the time they were in the Porsche driving
back to Rowley's house, Jamie had begun to realize that the entire evening was a put-up job, with
the express intention of Rowley and Vicky finding
out what Jamie was playing at and doling out some
heavy advice. Yet even then Jamie didn't much
mind. Through the fog of alcohol it was apparent
to him that his parents had done the putting-up,
which meant they had given up hope of influencing
him directly themselves. They *knew*, and they hadn't

come roaring down from Scotland. In the second place, nothing that Rowley might have to advise was likely to make a blind bit of difference. Jamie had already agreed to stay the night at their place, and he wasn't going to go back on that out of funk, with them already on their way to the King's Road well after midnight and him wanting nothing more than to get his head down on the nearest possible pillow. Vicky was already half or more-than-half asleep, crunched up horizontal on the back seat.

'Of *course* my father won't understand,' Jamie was saying, alongside Rowley at the wheel.

'Because you don't want him to understand.'

The goldy bits on Rowley's hands and wrists glinted in other people's headlights, and the special cuffs on his sleeves made shadows.

'Who cares?' Jamie said, making a non-question.

'Your father sees the world in you, naturally,' Rowley said.

'What world?'

'"What world?"' came Vicky's voice from the back seat, mimicking her brother derisively.

'You won't want to alienate your old man, Jamie,' Rowley pursued. 'You're going to need him.'

'Really?'

'Obviously yes. You won't be out of the kindergarten until you've got your own capital base. Some serious money to work with. Most people aren't so lucky to have a papa who —'

'Work with?' Jamie cut in.

'Money makes money, Jamie,' Rowley said heavily. 'That's the name of the game. One must start with other people's.'

They had pulled up at the red light where Sloane Street joins Knightsbridge, by the Hyde Park Hotel. A meths-drinking wino, bearded and greasy, in a woollen cap, and wrapped up in a tattered greatcoat, crossed slowly in front of them, coming from the tube entrance towards the park beyond the hotel. Rowley switched his headlights full beam, and caught the witless grin on his face – by no means an old face.

The powerful headlights picked up every detail – the vigour and gloss of his beard, the fragment of grey in it and a strand of grass, the two useless remaining buttons on his greatcoat (the ones sewn there for symmetry, for which there were no button holes) and the white twine which held the coat around him. He was still crossing when the lights turned green; Rowley had to wait until the wino had shuffled on well clear, and he missed his chance to cut across the traffic leftwards into Sloane Street. It obliged him to make the circle rightwards under Bowater House. The Porsche leapt forward like a young stallion.

'I can't say I altogether disagree,' Rowley resumed. 'You could be wasting your time going up to Cambridge.' (Had they actually abandoned hope of a change of mind?) 'But you must see how upset your father would be – passing up a place at King's.'

He paused. They were at the lights again, alongside the hotel, facing south, having all but done the circle. There was the wino again, right beside them.

'I know some young fellows not more than a year or two older than you, Jamie, well on their way to their first half million.'

'Doing what?'

'Oh. Money-broking. Futures. Bonds.'

They were off again.

'And then?' Jamie said.

'Meaning?' Rowley frowned.

'After the first half million?'

A strained tolerance entered Rowley's face, of the recently experienced confronted by the still callow. He delayed his reply.

'You've got a lot going for you, Jamie. Family contacts. My God. Even without a university degree you could probably walk into a decent merchant bank. If you wanted a bit of capital to start on your own you could touch your daddy over breakfast.'

Jamie said nothing.

'I could put you on your way to earning a hundred grand a year in three or four years' time,' Rowley added.

They had done the whole of Sloane Street in about twenty seconds. Now they were coming out of Sloane Square into the King's Road. There was a group of young revellers right in front. Jamie wondered if he knew any of them. One young man stepped backwards off the pavement and the Porsche had to swerve to avoid him.

Vicky, out of sight in the back, whined,'Do you have to swoop so?'

'If you got knocked down by a careless driver,' Rowley resumed to his companion, 'have you any idea what your family could sue for? Supposing you were killed – have you any idea? The value of your life at this point in time?'

'I hadn't thought,' Jamie said.

'Five million. Six million. Now do you see?'

Jamie was making a genuine effort, on a small scale, to get the relevance of this – what it was he had to see. There was an unarguability here, he supposed, that any fool could grasp, if not too zonked. At length he said, 'Why are you telling me this?'

They had pulled up in Draycott Place, and Rowley was reversing into a space.

'Wakey-wakey,' he called over his shoulder.

'Why are you telling me this?' Jamie repeated.

Rowley had got out and was tilting his seat forward for Vicky. He said, 'Because you could be about to screw it all up.'

Vicky sat up suddenly on the back seat. 'About to screw what up?' she demanded.

'Jamie. His life,' Rowley said.

'Jamie? Course he will,' Vicky said. 'Come on Jamie, help me out.' She was extricating herself with difficulty. When her feet at last reached the pavement, she had a moment's problem getting her balance, 'I'm not in the least *pissée*,' she announced. 'Just flaked.'

When they went into the little front hall, with its eighteenth-century mirror and Rowley's slim briefcase on the console table, Jamie started it up again, although he knew it was against his better judgement. Whatever the case with his sister, he *was* rather pissed. He told Rowley, 'I thought you agreed I'd be wasting my time at Cambridge.'

'None of my business, Jamie old man.'

'Go on. Say what you think.'

Rowley turned, if you've passed up Cambridge to knuckle down and make some' – here he made the money sign with fingers and thumb of his right hand – 'we're talking the same lingo. If you're dropping out to smoke pot and find your soul, that's quite another deck of cards.'

Vicky came in at once. She was bound to. 'And please don't ask me to go to Daddy and plead your cause.' She had opened the door of the downstairs bedroom. 'You're in here. I'll find you a toothbrush.' Now she turned to face him. 'You're breaking his heart, that's all.'

'Do *you* care?' Jamie said nastily.

'What a silly thing to say, Jamie.'

He already knew it was.

And almost the identical response was made at the end of another, closely related interchange.

When Tibby had let slip to her mother about Jamie's last-minute decision not to take his place at Cambridge, Mrs Hoskyns had immediately been urged to secrecy on the subject. Whether or not she actually promised her daughter, her superior duty lay elsewhere.

By a not altogether roundabout route she ensured that Jane Mainwaring got to hear of it, despite the Mainwarings' absence in Scotland; and a day or so later she received a telephone call from Jane Mainwaring seeking to find out what she knew. One result of this was a further talk with Tibby, which took place while they were out exercising the horses. Trotting together along a farm track between Chinnery and Upton Ridge, Mrs Hoskyns pointed out to Tibby how important her role was with James, as 'the only one who can get through to him', at a time when he might be making a dreadfully wrong decision.

Tibby seemed sulky. They slowed to a walk, Tibby on Soldier-boy, Mrs Hoskyns on the big mare Bundle of Joy.

'I rather think his parents feel they can't reach him. He's gone into himself,' Mrs Hoskyns said.

'Have you been talking to them?'

'They're in Scotland,' Mrs Hoskyns said. 'What does he think he's going to do with himself?'

'Work somewhere.'

'What at?'

'Something really useful.'

'Such as, Tibby?' Her mother suspected she was holding back, and when Tibby heeled Soldier-boy into a trot she knew it. She kept pace with her.

'Abroad again?'

'I don't expect so.'

'Where then? Who with?'

'How am I expected to know, Mummy?'

But Mrs Hoskyns felt just as exasperated as her daughter. Jamie was a good match, provided . . .

'If he wants to go out and help those less fortunate than himself,' Mrs Hoskyns guessed, 'he's much best doing it from among his own kind.'

'What do you mean, his own kind?' Tibby demanded petulantly.

'Darling, what a silly thing to say,' said Mrs Hoskyns, then snatching a glance at Tibby's bunched little face . . . 'for someone so sensible.'

And as a result of hearing something of this, and other factors, before his parents returned from Scotland Jamie went to ground. He left them a letter about Cambridge (which he knew they knew already) and went into no explanations. And removed himself from the scene. Went to ground.

PART III

CHAPTER EIGHTEEN

J amie let himself out of a back-room office by a frosted glass doorway which carried the sign in clean black capitals, FREE ADVICE. PLEASE WAIT UNTIL CALLED. He switched off the light. The frosted door, which he shut behind him, led him into a rather larger office room. No one was there. He made his way past two or three cluttered desks with chairs on each side, a bench and two more chairs for anyone waiting to be attended to, and several wall posters reading IS THERE AN ALTERNATIVE TO UNEMPLOYMENT FOR YOU? YES. START YOUR OWN COOPERATIVE! And . . . UNEMPLOYED? THINKING OF MOVING OUT? And . . . SICK OR DISABLED BECAUSE OF INDUSTRIAL ACCIDENT OR DISEASE?

Reaching the main door, he let himself out into the lamplit street, shut the door and secured the place with both keys. Bradford's Community Welfare Shop, which was the sign written above the door and the display window, had twice been broken into in the past, presumably by a sample of the sort of people it was there to assist, in the same way as church Poor-Boxes are not infrequently prised open and emptied.

A year or so previously Jamie had driven through this bleak and unloved section of this bleak unloved north midlands city in his father's Daimler with two Japanese and Searle beside him at the wheel. It was then that his eye had fallen on the façade of the Community Welfare Shop. He had not especially remarked the place, but it had clung to the memory like the material for dreams so that when the moment came for its recall, it was there.

Across the street a former Congregational chapel stood with its windows like neglected sermons and now become a mosque. Its large unilluminated neon sign in Arabic lettering had been erected above the doorway in approximately the same position as the banner announcing *The Waste Land* suspended by Jamie above the Presbyterian entrance in Edinburgh.

Just as Jamie was moving away the neon sign flickered on, and immediately that part of the street was washed in a fierce chemical green light, including Jamie's own face and hair.

He had five hundred yards to walk to his lodgings.

When his friend Anthony had thought of Jamie's most familiar characteristic as recklessness, he was not unjust to him. For was this not at the core of Jamie's attraction to his friends – that in his defiance of the 'reck' by which humankind constrained itself, Jamie was in earnest, Jamie took the real risk? And so might discover what they might never quite dare to? Vicariously, for them all. The Dionysiac release, say – the unbearable truth about the human condition which, in the end, King Midas persuaded Dionysus's side-kick and protector, Silenus, to vouchsafe him, when he encountered him in the woods and which Sophocles too gives choric utterance to.* (Anthony was a classicist as well as a chorister; he was familiar with the mythology and what it enlightened.) Jamie acted upon impulse, not out of weakness, or licentiousness, but because he believed that without impulse there might be nothing. And in such a belief he would strip impulse naked.

Disdaining the common reck of the world brought its swift penalities: it always would. Jamie's landlady was waiting for him on his return at number 26 Alpine Road (any place less Alpine was difficult to conceive). As soon as she heard him enter she came out of her room at the bottom of the mean stairs. He saw the look on her face and the cheque in her hand at the same instant – his cheque, referred to drawer. After all his persuading that she should take a cheque instead of cash, he knew this was it. He attempted no argument. He went straight up to his dingy room, with its glass photo of William Ewart Gladstone and its Chinese

---

* μὴ φῦναι τὸν απαντα νικᾷ λόγον· τό δ᾽, ἐπεὶ φανῇ
βῆναι κεῖθεν ὅθεν περ ἥκει,
πολὺ δεύτερον, ὡς τάχιστα.

The best thing is not to have been born.
But once you have seen the light of day,
to go back whence you came as fast
as possible is by far the next best thing.

Oedipus Coloneus

jar on the shelf above the gas grate in the depths of which he had found a used French letter, and stuffed his things into his suitcase. He gave the landlady all the cash he had left, to meet the value of the cheque as near as he could, except for two pounds, and went out into the night with his bag. It was remarkable, he thought, the disgust and venom that had gathered to such intensity in the landlady's face and eyes. She had raised children, he knew, presumably with love, and treasured her grandchildren of whom she had shown him a photograph. Yet in throwing him out just now she would have gladly seen him smashed up and butchered. Did people have wells of hate to draw from instantly just as deep and full as any wells of love?

He was somewhat at a loss as to what to do. There were hostels – maybe one of them would settle for a couple of quid. He could, he supposed, doss down for the night in the office. He was hungry. He supposed that if he had something in his stomach he would be able to think. He headed in the direction of a café where he was known, a few doors along from his office at the Community Welfare Shop. The cash problem could be resolved, of course, but it needed thought.

Thirty yards short of the café the newsagent was still open: maybe the *Telegraph and Argus* would list the hostels. He paused opposite the window of the shop. Curried music seeped from within. Several handwritten cards were displayed advertising cheap accommodation in the neighbourhood. They were easily legible in the light of the street lamp from across the street, reinforced by the powerful glow from the mosque's neon Koranic exhortation. The hitch was that they would all demand a week's rent in advance. He could pledge his wristwatch, he supposed, until he got the money sorted out. But then again, it was rather late to start knocking on doors. He half regretted having surrendered so tamely to Mrs Chalmers at his last lodgings: very likely he could have pleaded her around to giving him a couple of days to bring her the cash. But a shaft of despair had gone into him as soon as he saw his bounced cheque – knowing *why* it had bounced; that and the hate in her face, so totally displacing her slightly flustered sweetness that his habitual chivalry and 'class' had evoked in her when he had moved in. That shaft had taken the fight out of him.

He put his suitcase down on the pavement beside him and drew his notebook from the pocket. He began noting the telephone numbers and weekly rates. He became aware of someone having paused alongside him, presumably also scrutinizing the window – fragments of the outline of him were reflected in the window. Jamie glanced down at his suitcase, which stood between them.

'Lookin' for something?'

Jamie turned to the speaker. He was a fellow of about twenty-five in a camelhair overcoat of the very short variety, more like an over-long jacket. He had extremely fine, pale feathery hair and an instant ingratiation in his cunning little eyes.

'I'm looking for digs,' Jamie told him.

'Digs? B and B?'

'Yes.'

'Just arrived?'

'I've been here a few weeks.' Jamie noticed an ice-cream van parked across the street, with a large multicoloured sign saying CANDYMAN.

'Really? Got a job?'

The young man's voice seemed to belong to the south-east of the country, not up here in Yorkshire.

'I work with the unemployed,' Jamie told him.

'Plenty o' them. *With* them, eh?'

'Welfare,' said Jamie.

'Oh. Welfare. Good works.' There was the merest whiff of contempt, and it made for a moment's silence.

Jamie asked, 'What about you?'

'I'm in business.' The young man jerked his head towards the Candyman van, to which they were half turned.

'Ice-cream,' Jamie said.

'And other lines.'

Jamie looked back at the advertisement for lodgings. The other scrutinized him. He said,

'What money?'

'Twenty, twenty-five a week.'

'I might have an idea,' the Candyman said. 'Time for a cuppa? A pint?'

'I've got to find somewhere to sleep,' Jamie told him. He glanced at his watch.

The Candyman said, 'Leave it to me.'

He stood back, putting out his hand to shake. 'Noel's the name. Noel.'

'James Bingham,' Jamie said, taking the hand.

'How d'you do, James.' Noel gave him a smile that showed no teeth but comprised the clenching of the muscles of the chin and underlip in a mixture of man-to-man mutual assessment and complicity.

Noel the Candyman's lodging consisted of a one-bedroom flat with a kitchenette off the living room. The lighting of the living room and vestibule was heavily shaded with red foil. With its Gauloise and ski posters it had an air of tawdry swank like a wine-bar in a plebeian neighbourhood.

Noel had laid the table for two on which already stood an open bottle of Tia Maria. Jamie, on the settee, held a glass engraved with frosted roses containing the black liqueur. On an empty stomach its sticky sweetness had brought on a mild nausea. The musical and philosophic achievements of Elton John were coming from a speaker in a dark corner.

Noel entered from the kitchenette in an apron and a straw boater he sometimes wore in his van. He carried a bottle of Mateus rosé and two more glasses and was singing along quietly with Elton John. He poured the sparkling pink wine, which had turned brown in the light. He raised one of the wine-glasses. 'Cheers again,' he said.

'Cheers,' Jamie returned.

'You like music? Can't manage without music. Elton. Tina.'

'I've got some tapes,' Jamie said.

He reached for his suitcase and opened it up in front of him on the floor. He felt around among the jumble of clothes and books and items of toiletry for the tapes. A minute or two later Noel came back to the table with a pan of risotto which he emptied on to two plates. He put the pan down to look at Jamie's tapes. 'Meteors,' he read approvingly. 'Police. The Damned. Klaus Nomi – don't know him. Looks good though. Meatloaf. Here, let's listen to that. Okay?'

Jamie had his washing kit in his hand, in a transparent bag.

'Toilet,' Noel said, and pointed to one of the two doors leading off the end of the room.

Jamie crossed the door to the bathroom. Noel heard him slip the bolt across. He leaned across and looked at the cassette player lying among Jamie's things in his open suitcase: there was another tape in it – something classical. Brahms. Then he saw the pair of ivory-backed hairbrushes. He picked up one of the brushes appraisingly. When Jamie came out of the bathroom he had it in his hand

'Nice brushes. "James Bingham".' He was looking at the initials. 'What's the M?'

'Nothing,' Jamie said. 'Belonged to some ancestor.'

Noel glanced at Jamie with mischievous complicity. 'They're in good nick, James.'

They sat down to their risotto and Mateus rosé, Meatloaf coming out of the amplifier.

'Where's home for you? I expect you'd have one?'

'Oh, we've moved around,' Jamie said. 'London mostly.'

'Feltham,' Noel said. 'Know Feltham at all?'

'I'm afraid not.'

'Your daddy, what's his line of business?'

'My pa? Oh, the City. I never know what he does, exactly. Futures, mostly.'

'That so? Pots of money?'

Jamie smiled. 'He's just stopped my allowance,' he said. 'He must be skint.'

'Allowance?'

'What he used to pay monthly into my bank account. The account's run dry, so it seems.'

'You must 'ave upset 'im, James. You'll 'ave to say sorry.' Jamie was silent. 'So why d'e pack you off up here? See the world? How the other half lives?'

'It was I decided.'

'Daddy doesn't approve. Correct? Most people go the other direction. The sensible ones. Just me and you come up north. Oop north, ludd.'

'I want to help the people out-of-work.'

'Sociology? You preparing a thesis?'

'Could be.'

'Don't take me wrong, James. I approve. They need all the help they can get, poor blighters. I *approve.*' He took a swig from his wine glass, 'I try to help them a bit meself, in my way. Lighten the load.'

'What brought you north?'

'I told you. Business. Gap in the market. Meeting a need. Narmean?'

Exactly which need Noel the Candyman was meeting was not yet clear to Jamie. However, he had met his own need.

After the meal Noel found a pair of clean sheets, a pillowcase which he put round a cushion, and a red blanket. (Red was his preferred colour.) These he put, neatly folded, on the end of the settee.

'I want you to feel at home, James. Why not push it up the corner. It's cosier.'

Together they moved the settee against the wall, under a Sid and Nancy poster, and a varnished boomerang manufactured for the tourist which Noel took down to show his guest. 'A beautiful thing,' he said, handing it across. 'Got it from an Australian mate of mine. A business colleague. I want you to feel at home, James, just like it was your place.'

And the prevailing part of Jamie acceded to that invitation, even if another part perceived its tawdriness and falsity. Tawdriness and falsity were all this Noel had to offer anyone, and that all, coupled with their common foreignness in this northern place, constituted a companionship the balm of which was almost physical.

Jumbo had not told Jane about cutting off Jamie's allowance, because he was not certain how she would take it. Readjusting his presumptions about

Jamie was hard enough without falling out with Jane over it.

On the whole he found it preferable not to discuss Jamie with Jane. There was either too little to say; or there was too much to say. There was too little to say because there was virtually nothing they could do. To call in the police was quite inappropriate and risked utterly unsatisfactory publicity. If they quizzed Jamie's former Eton friends it would at once get back to Jamie, should any of them be in contact – and could easily frustrate their purpose. There was too much to say because of the vastness of the question *why;* and that would have meant fruitless pain. So there was no call for a lot of talk with Jane. They had refused to over-react when they heard about Cambridge; they knew their son well enough for that. They had nothing to do but sit it out, he said to himself.

Within, Jumbo's mood shifted between anger, bewilderment and numbness. Grief was on stand-by. He got on with his life, and carried out his responsibilities briskly and punctiliously. He fended off enquiries after Jamie with a cavalier dismissiveness – 'don't ask *me* what the boy's up to!' He chose not to think about him, or rather, not to dwell on him. He had heard of ridiculous fathers declaring that such-and-such offspring 'is no longer a son/daughter of mine'. It was not in the least like that. He merely chose not to dwell on Jamie or discuss his behaviour with anybody.

Only in church at Upton, or wherever he was on a Sunday (for he would never miss), did he no longer keep up the embargo on what was innermost. Then, in that brief hour, he would lay it all before his God, not in so many words or defined thoughts but in a suspension of thoughts and words, a surrender and rendering up. The anger and bewilderment and numbness would float off from him like encrusted dirt; and even grief, standing by, would assume a certain glow which was also the glow of thanksgiving for the mercy of God. At such times every spoken line of divine service, every uttered supplication and response, every note of canticle or psalm or hymn, every episode of scripture, would seem minted anew like gold coin. Thus treasureladen at the close of worship, taking the vicar's hand at the church door as usual, he could feel as did the disciples when, on the lake of Gennasaret, at Jesus's bidding they let down their nets once more and caught such a draught of fishes that their boat began to sink and Simon Peter cried, 'Depart from me, for I am a sinful man, O Lord.'

The vicar never knew what his mattins had wrought in Jumbo, nor did anyone else.

He did however say something about Jamie to his doctor – about his 'going off on some scheme of his own without saying a word'. Being the family's doctor he was also Jamie's, insofar as he ever needed one. Jumbo's remark was only in response to a conversational enquiry from the doctor during

Jumbo's recent check-up (at which he advised Jumbo against taking violent exercise too suddenly). The doctor took a level-headed line, making much the same sort of comment as Jumbo used to make when he heard others running down the younger generation. But Jumbo had told neither the doctor nor anyone else that he and Jane didn't know where Jamie was. That was too much for anyone to need to be told.

To Carstairs, sitting across his desk in Lombard Street, he said, 'He's gone north.' He said it in a way as if it did not matter much precisely where.

'North?'

'He talked about it. Some time ago. Good works – I haven't liked to ask the detail. One doesn't want — '

He left the sentence unfinished. There was no purpose in compromising himself unnecessarily.

'Whereabouts exactly?' Carstairs said.

'He doesn't keep in touch very often.'

He could tell from the look in Carstairs's face that he suspected the truth.

'His mother had a telephone call,' Jumbo added.

'They have to find out on their own,' Carstairs said. Jumbo did not want Carstairs's condolings. 'Some sort of welfare, I suppose?'

'I wouldn't be at all surprised.'

He felt Carstairs probing, he was not quite sure for what motive. He didn't entirely trust, and certainly did not require, Jeremy Carstairs's concern.

It had the familiar taste of the prodigal's brother enquiring after the latest rumour about his sibling. He had fathered Carstairs in a way.

'He'll get lonely,' Carstairs said.

'What?'

'Lonely,' Carstairs repeated. And added, 'There'll be ways of reeling him in, that's for sure.'

Jumbo switched the discussion to the business in hand, which happened to concern an offer for the Bolt Company's machine tools. It was, however, Carstairs's remark about 'reeling him in' that triggered his writing to his bank to stop Jamie's allowance. The thought had previously occurred to him, but it had needed the hint from an outsider that he was being weak or supine. He did not know if Jamie had other resources besides the allowance.

Neither Jumbo nor Jane knew what Jamie was occupying himself with. The telephone call Jane received from Jamie a week previously was brief, moderately affectionate, and entirely uninformative. He was well, busy 'doing something which I hope is useful', and would 'not lose touch entirely'. He gave his mother almost no opportunity to say anything.

They both suspected that little Tibby Hoskyns knew where Jamie was and what he was doing. But she was not saying, and they were not going pleading to a young girl and displaying anxiety and something very like failure. A remark Tibby had let drop to her mother when it was first known he was not

taking up his place at Cambridge hinted at a northern intention. Beyond that and the 'useful work'
it was anybody's conjecture. But the consensus was
that his disillusionment in Africa had played its
part – that he might be fixed on catching the same
rainbow which so eluded him when he reached for
it that first time. Jane and Jumbo separately raked
their memories for clues that Jamie might have left
in remarks and conversations since his return from
Africa.

In citing Africa, they were near the mark.
Whatever had happened to Jamie in Africa had
touched the centre of him, and being the person he
was, nothing was quite the same for him thereafter.

Tibby held her secret tight. It was the most precious
thing she had ever been given. He had rung her four
times in as many weeks. She knew his number at work,
and the 'false' name he used. She knew exactly where
he was, and more or less what he was doing. She had
wanted to go to Bradford to work with him, but of
course he wouldn't allow that. Yet he had promised
that before long, if she could find some excuse to get
away, she could catch the early train from St Pancras
and help him out for a day when his own assistant
had her day off.

What Jamie was trying to do was, she felt, the noblest
thing she could imagine. It wasn't his father's fault
that the factory had closed down – Jamie didn't think
so either. But it was in a way an ancient Mainwaring

responsibility and he had recognized it and acted upon it irrespective of the sacrifice to himself. What she could not quite grasp was the need for such secrecy. She could see that up there, at Bradford, it was best if Jamie was not known as the son of the famous head of the company that was shut down – bearing the same name that everybody would know. But she couldn't understand why he could not have explained it all to his mother and father and gone up with their blessing. Sir James did seem a rather remote figure, always arriving and leaving with his chauffeur, but she thought he had a kind face. And Lady Mainwaring was really nice and friendly, and Mummy liked her a lot. She could imagine how lost they must feel not knowing where Jamie was or what he was doing, and part of her longed to tell them both what a wonderful task Jamie had taken up, quite unbidden and selflessly. But her first duty was to Jamie, and he had entrusted her with the secret with the utmost gravity.

When, in the second or third telephone call she had taken from Jamie (he knew which afternoons her mother was out at her bridge parties), she had taxed him with the worry he must be causing his parents, he replied very seriously, 'Listen, Tibby. I know what I'm doing. The time may come when they can know – when I've really got something going up here. If they knew at this stage it would be physically impossible for them to keep out. That would be the end of it for me. Can you see that?'

'Yes, Jamie, I do.' And for the time being she did.

'This is father's own back-yard. It's Mainwaring territory. He couldn't bear it. He'd think I was trying to do his job for him. He'd never understand why I'm really here. You've got to see that.'

So she had loyally clutched to her secret, but after a while wondering if she really did grasp that side of it, thinking of his poor parents, and thinking of all his other friends too. Jamie had cut himself off so completely and was missing so much of life. She herself was beginning to go to quite a lot of parties. There were one or two young men in London who seemed to be interested in her – brothers of school friends, mostly. They were quite different from Jamie, of course: they did all the normal things and were interested in what everybody else was interested in. But they did have fun. When she was out at a party where there was a good disco and people she knew, with all the young men in their smart dinner jackets and stick-up collars and some of the girls in really fabulous dresses, she would suddenly think of Jamie in what she visualized as the permanent grey gloom of Bradford and feel almost guilty at enjoying herself so. Jamie seemed to belong to a different species. Finer, nobler. She felt if he came into the room where people were dancing and drinking and having a good time, everything would stop and everybody would look at him. She would go up to him melting at the knees, and cling to him. And after he had acknowledged her, he would make some sort of signal with his hand and only then would the party resume.

Yet she also remembered that the only occasion – a year previously – at which both she and Jamie had been together at a brilliant party with a disco and a band and a lot of fashionable people, Jamie had been drunk.

CHAPTER NINETEEN

On the wall alongside the frosted glass door to Jamie's office which read FREE ADVICE was a slotted board with each different batch of leaflets printed in a different colour in each of the tiered slots. The leaflets carried such headings as Relocation Job Opportunities, or Child Benefit for People Entering Britain, or Occupational Deafness.

Three white men were seated on the bench provided for those awaiting admittance. Behind one of the three desks in the cluttered main office where the men were waiting – the Community Welfare Shop was converted from a real shop – sat a woman of about thirty with short, tightly curled hair listening to a wisp of a girl seated opposite carrying a tiny baby of racially mixed parentage which she jiggled inexpertly against her bony shoulder to ease its whimpering. The wisp of a girl was scarcely more than a child herself. She was evidently of locally born working-class origin, while the tightly curled woman behind the desk wore the authority of someone who had experienced some education over and above that provided by school alone, and when she came to speak – with a look of sympathetic resentment – her opening remarks were on a quite different plane from the practical hardship she had been hearing, but were about social injustice, chauvinist guilt, and Tory cuts. The wisp of a girl gave her counsellor a little smile of childlike pride at all that she and her fatherless baby were victims of.

On the bench the men smoked. Two read the *Sun* newspaper, and one read *Sunday Sport* which told how a woman in Batley, of whom there was a photograph, had been raped by a Martian.

''E's takin' 'is time,' said Charlie, the first in the queue, who was well turned out in creased trousers, a nylon tweed jacket, and crepe-soled shoes. At about forty-five he was the oldest of the three.

'Fookin' is,' the youngest confirmed, who was no more than nineteen. He turned on from the Martian rapist to the page of advertisements which offered a choice of telephone numbers to call, at 15p a minute, to hear one lady or another talk about spanking.

The street door opened and everyone looked up involuntarily. It was big Ginger, once the foundry's foreman. He did not come right in but asked from the door, 'Oo's 'e closeted with?'

'Oo?' said Charlie.

'Young Woodley – Master James Bingham.' Ginger pretended to tug his forelock.

'A wog,' Charlie told him.

'Trust a wog,' Ginger said.

'Would you mind closing the door,' the tight-curled community counsellor put in.

'I'm not staying, Tania,' Ginger told her.

'Fifteen minutes already,' Charlie said. The man next to him rolled his eyes at the clock on the wall. 'Twenty,' he corrected.

'And 'is girlfriend,' Charlie added.

'Oo's girlfriend?' Ginger needed to know.

The young lad's,' Charlie told him. 'Got the afternoon off from

Ascot Races.'

'You won't mind me saying, Charlie, you're wasting your time. So when you're through . . .' Ginger mimed a swig of beer.

Charlie nodded glumly and Ginger was on the point of withdrawing when Noel the Candyman brushed by.

Noel's entry induced a perceptible stiffening among most of those present. 'James in there?' he asked.

'Mister Bingham to you,' Ginger told him.

'He's busy on a wog,' Charlie said, and Ginger added,

'Wogs don't like ice-cream. Pigs' blubber. Against their religion.'

Ignoring them, Noel proceeded through the main office past the wisp of a girl with her baby and the bench with the waiting man.

''Ere, take your turn, lad,' Charlie said.

'I've jobs to *offer,* 'aven't I?' Noel countered, 'I'm not lookin' for work.' And he pushed open the frosted door, shutting it behind him.

Jamie looked up from behind his table, over the head of the Asian he was interviewing in the corner opposite the door. He said, i'm going to be tied up for another hour, Noel.' He turned to the young woman at the filing cabinet against the wall with her back to the man. 'When's your train?'

Tibby half turned to see if it was her he was speaking to.

'Four fifty-seven,' she replied.

'Forty-five minutes,' Jamie corrected to Noel, i'm taking Tibby to the station. This is Tibby,'he added by way of introduction. 'Tibby-Candyman. He sells choc-ices.'

'Hi,' said Noel, relaxed and familiar, as if he knew all he needed to know about her, looking her up and down with his hands in his pockets, and bringing the smallest of blushes to Tibby's neck. She had given so much thought as to how she should dress for this strange day's outing to Jamie's hideaway in Bradford. In the end she had settled for a Guernsey sweater, bangles and pale green denim trousers she had had made for her. She had felt really confident in this ensemble when she had set out, but ever since she had arrived she had never once felt quite at ease in it.

They seemed to be one chair short, so Noel the Candyman propped himself on the corner of the desk with the typwriter on it, where Tibby had been working. He treated the place as his own. She knew who he was: Jamie had told her.

'How're you getting there?' asked Noel.

'Taxi, maybe,' Jamie told him.

'I'll run you.'

Tibby had found what she thought was the correct c.v. form, and sat at the desk. She stared across to Jamie, willing him to look up. She didn't want the Candyman taking them to the station. She and Jamie had had virtually no time together since she had arrived at half past ten that morning. Going back to the station seemed to her the last chance they might get of being alone. But Jamie was busy talking to the Indian man.

'Meghanigal verk. Anny kind,' the man was saying. He wore a thin suit tightly buttoned across his pot belly and two days' growth of white beard dusted the dark skin of his face.

It was such a depressing little office, Tibby thought, so dingy, with its chipped paint and second- or third-hand office furniture. A large wall map of England headed 'Job Oportunities' had unintelligible coloured blobs on it. A poster read, 'We Have Need of Painters, Decorators, Gardeners, Handypersons'. She wished she was a handyperson, but she knew she wasn't. Back at the typewriter copying out the list Jamie had given her (which she had to check against the files) she had to be repeatedly back-spacing and white-ing out her mistakes. She felt the Candyman's eyes on her and with her fingers kept on driving back from her forehead the hair she had so carefully shampooed and 'conditioned' the evening before.

She was half way through her course in London and had promised Jamie she could do typing. So she could, she thought. But this machine . . .

'What's the matter?'

'It doesn't work properly.'

'What?'

She could clearly detect Jamie's irritation, it keeps going two spaces back instead of one.'

'You shouldn't need to back-space,' Jamie said.

'Most of these names are the same anyway.'

'Tibby, *please.*'

'Can I?' the Candyman said.

Tibby felt instantly on guard. But how could she refuse?

Noel had moved beside her, and now she stood up to give way to him. Jamie was looking back at the notes on the little table in front of him. He said,

'So there's yourself and three sons, Ali, Ahmed and Babar, all ex-Mainwaring employees. And four other dependants.'

'Five,' the man corrected. 'Dapandants, five.'

'I thought you said you had three children in the family plus their mother.'

'One more lady.'

Jamie resumed his note-taking. 'Who is she?' he asked.

'My brother's wife.'

'What about your brother?'

'He is dad. She is vidow-lady.'

'You are all ready to sell the house if you can and transfer the mortgage?'

Noel had settled at Tibby's typewriter and with a display of deftness had picked up copying the list where Tibby had left off. He caught her eye at the Bangladeshi's tally of dependants and winked. It was a wink of complicity, endorsing their common recognition of the futility of Jamie's endeavours. She wanted no complicity with this man. She felt alien to him. There was a slickness and deceit about him that frightened her. She knew he was unaware exactly who Jamie was – Jamie had told her so. Yet she could not understand how Jamie could consort with such a person. And they each had rings in their left earlobes which seemed just the same.

She felt lost and lonely. How could this be, in Jamie's presence? It had turned out so different from what she had imagined, this adventurous excursion to Bradford that she had had to take such elaborate precautions to keep secret. It had seemed so much in character – so aristocratic – what Jamie had done – turning wish into action by sheer confidence of vision. She had thought of him, Whatever he wants to do he will do. And here he was in a dingy back room with one part-time helper (it was her day off), bogged down in the minutiae of the lives of a whole lot of people, most of them immigrants if the names she had been typing were anything to go by, all of them quite unaware of the sacrifice that he was making on their behalf. For all she could tell, his endeavours might be utterly futile. He had worked all day, just as he did every day, she knew, five and a half days a week. He was living on money he had arranged to borrow from the bank against his shares in the family company. Where would it all lead?

She could not possibly tell, yet she could not keep out a terrible premonition. It was that somehow he would be carried away from them, he who was at the heart of her world, he who had invited her to love, who had spoken the name of love in a way that she supposed that none of her friends had ever heard it spoken. He would be *swept* away, round the bend and out of sight, as once she had helplessly watched a doll of hers swept away when it tumbled from the foot-bridge across the spating stream at Chinnery during the winter thaw.

In the mere half-hour they had taken for lunch, at the curry-house, he had asked so little about what they shared – about Upton, their families, their friends. She had told him this and that, of course – tried to tell him of what surely, surely he must be concerned about: the pitiable bewilderment of his stoic parents. She, holding her secret, knowing its value, had no need to be shown to whom pity was due, though she had been vividly reminded of it since Jamie's 'disappearance' twice – once when she had met his mother at a horse show and once coming across both his parents at the county Festival of Choirs. It was written across their faces, and she heard it in what they did not say. All Jamie wished to talk of was what he was trying to do, and more confusingly, why: that these people he had come to help lived and died under the control of forces they could not influence or even understand, 'and that therefore they could be said never to live at all. They dared not live, they dared not even suffer.' That's how he spoke.

Was he then a revolutionary? 'No,' he answered. 'Revolutions fail.' And so? 'I can discover what can be done, and in the meantime give a few of them a chance to hope.' Rattling on like this he had made her want to cry out, 'Wait for me, let me catch up, delve out what lies in you, or you will be gone beyond our reach before I am ready, before I am even ready to know what is meant by the word love in your mouth.'

He had made his speeches but she had made none of hers. and all she knew was that this place was wrong, her clothes were all wrong, she had let him down at the typewriter, and was close to tears.

In the saloon bar of the Swan in Lilycroft Lane round the corner, there were no Asians. A skinny barmaid in a short skirt had come up with four fresh pints on her beer-swilled tray to put down on to a table where four half-empty beermugs already stood. Her four customers at that table were talking of Jamie. Ginger's wife Edie, who was as straggled and grey as he was thick-fleshed and red, was telling him,

'I wouldn't stand in 'is way, Ginger. If 'e wants to move some of 'em out, that's all right by uz. Leave 'im to it, Ginger. Don't ob-struct 'im.' She was a woman who knew her mind.

Leslie was there too, and Charlie, who had given up queuing in the Community Shop. Leslie never liked to contradict Ginger. Bringing out his purse he said, 'There's ninety-six thousand of 'em, Edie. In this city alone. It's a drop out t'bucket.'

Ginger said, 'I'm 'andling this,' and did so at once with a five-pound note while Leslie was still fiddling with his coins. 'I'm not obstructing 'im. It's too late to be 'eated about Pakis, as Les so aptly says. Ninety-six thousand and a new one every four-and-half minutes. You can mourn for Yorkshire but you won't bring it back. Yorkshire was done for twenty years ago. You can't blame *them*. Guvvament let 'em in.' He eased himself with the remnant half pint, if you grew up in slums of Bangla Desh and someone offered a oneway ticket to a Welfare State, you'd 'ave took it same as they. Did you not see that programme on telly? They abandon their babies in the street for lack of food.'

'Hark at 'im,' Edie said. ''E'll be standing for bloody council next. So why *do* you ob-struct 'im, Ginger?'

'There's other things, Edie,' Charlie put in.

Ginger endorsed this darkly. 'Motivation,' he introduced. 'That's the puzzle. Young James Bingham's motivation.'

'The company 'e keeps,' Les added in. 'Personal 'abits.'

'After hours,' said Charlie.

Les had heard another thing. ''E 'ad 'is girl-friend oop from the gymkhana. Right, Charlie? "Ooh James dahling. Ay'm terribly terribly sor-reigh for all these poor people the Mainwaring Bolt Company es put on the doale. But Ay simply cahn't understand a word they say. How d'you spell redundant, James dahling?"'

Les was a real jester. They laughed across towards the public bar, beyond the bar lights and the Kung Fu machine, where they had seen Jamie coming for a pint or two lately.

Edie could follow a train of thought. 'What you driving at, then, Ginger?'

'First of all,' Ginger told her, 'there's precious little this young toffee-nose can do Labour Exchange can't. Second of all, what's in it for him? 'Oo does 'e work for? Is 'e trainee management? What's 'e going to learn that's any use, job like that? Nowt. On face of it, nowt, or I'll be blamed. On face of it.'

'Anyroad,' said Edie, ''e's not doing nobody 'arm. Not actively.'

'On face of it, Edie. I'll grant.' And the other two men looked at Ginger.

Ginger couldn't rid himself of the notion that he had seen James Bingham before, but he said nothing about it, it being so unlikely.

The subject of their discussion was sitting beside his girlfriend 'up from the gymkhana' on the broad front seat of the Candyman van in the forecourt of

Bradford's London station. Noel himself had crossed to have a chat with the man who managed the mobile snackbar beyond the clock, an acquaintance.

Tibby had tried to brighten up her face with a touch of make-up and she was trying, trying to banish the clot of despair she felt in her throat. 'It wasn't that at all, Jamie,' she was saying. 'It was only, whether what you say you've got to go through with will achieve what you expect.' She was fingering furiously the ring which held the cashmere scarf round her neck.

Jamie had a grim face on. She wished he would say something. They were a thousand miles apart, perched up here on the Lycra seat of the van under the forecourt lights and minutes running out. Dare she provoke him?

'If I said, what d'you really think you're doing here? – you'll snub me.'

'It's time for you to be off,' Jamie said.

He wasn't even looking at her. Nor were they touching, not anywhere. On the ten-minute run to the station with the Candyman at the wheel they had been bunched up and touching in several places (though he hadn't taken her hand). Now they were not quite touching anywhere. She was on the door side: she hadn't wanted to sit near Noel. She was quite cold and there was a funny smell.

She strained up at the clock under its pediment. 'Five minutes,' she said.

Then he moved to kiss her. But she put up her open hand between his face and hers, giving a little shake of her head. Then she turned her hand so that it shielded her eyes from his, to shield her eyes from the penetration of his or shield her distress from him – either. James drew back. He said,

'I'm doing *something*. I'm doing nine hours a day. Every day.'

'You could be doing great things. You could be.'

What was she betraying?

'Our world has run out of the kind of greatness you mean, Tibby.'

All at once she turned on him. 'You're running away. That's what I think.'

'What from?'

'Yourself.'

Oh, it had leapt out of her. And he was responding with a trace of a smirk. How she loathed that smirk, its unbearable superiority.

She looked at her watch now. 'Help!' she exclaimed.

She flung the door open and grabbed her bag.

Jamie followed her, half running across the forecourt past where Noel was standing chatting and into the station to the ticket barrier. She had her ticket in her hand.

'What d'you want me to be?' he said breathlessly. 'One of those barrow-boys in the City?'

The Asian inspector clipped the ticket.

'Rowley,' he continued, is that what you want? One of the City barrow-boys?'

'You must hurry,' the inspector said sharply.

'Who's talking about barrow-boys? What about –'
but the guard's warning whistle obliterated her
words.

'Barrier's closing, mem.'

She ducked under the barrier.

'Your ice-cream man,' she called back at him with
all her scorn; and she ran for the train against the
departing whistle.

'Okay — ' Jamie had begun, meaning to correct
her, that a barrow-boy acting as a barrow-boy was one
thing, but for those who had been reared to other
things than greed and fear . . . It was too late.

Ginger, Edie, Leslie and Charlie were still at their
table in the saloon bar of the Swan when Noel and
Jamie came into the public bar. A new round of
pints was arriving on the beer-wet tray – three only:
Edie had stayed out, this round.

Charlie reached for his money, 'It's me.'

'It's me,' said Leslie.

'It's Les,' Ginger decided for them.

Leslie paid. As he did so, looking up, he caught
sight of the two young men across the fairytale lights
of the bar. He gestured to the others with his eyes
and head.

'Speak of the devil,' Ginger said.

'And in 'e walks,' added Leslie.

Edie said, 'I don't take to that Candyman.'

'If it was only 'im.' James Bingham was the one
that troubled Ginger. Though quite why?

They could not have seen what Jamie and Noel were drinking or heard what they were saying. Jamie's was a Bloody Mary, Noel's a White Lady with something or other extra the barman seemed to know about. What they were saying was almost nothing, Jamie so sunk into lowering inwardness.

The Candyman would cheer up his friend. He pulled out his tobacco tin and from it produced a screw of silver foil.

'You're off it altogether?'

Jamie gave him a negative tremor of the head. He had told him: he had given it up.

Noel returned the silver paper to the tobacco tin. He rolled a cigarette for himself, lit up and drew.

Jamie made so tiny a gesture of the hand as to be no more than a signal between lovers; and it was responded to with the same instancy. The tin had moved from Noel's hand to Jamie's.

For a moment Jamie remained there, quite still on his bar stool. Then he slipped off the stool and made for the gents. There was a half smile on the Candyman's face.

Ginger had seen Jamie leaving for the gents, and he said to Leslie, 'Go and see, Les.'

Jumbo would not say how he found out. If it was Tibby it was not because Tibby had given anything away consciously. Maybe it was only a process of deduction. Jumbo was no fool. His mind would work on problems independently of his will.

Alison took the call in Jamie's office from her wheelchair. The chair Tibby had used was opposite her desk now. 'Community Welfare,' she said, relieved to have a call to take: there had been so few just lately. But it seemed that the caller was not making himself or herself clear, so Alison said again, 'Bradford Community Welfare Shop.' And then, 'We've a Mr James *Bingham.*'

Jamie looked up from his paper.

'I think it's for you,' Alison said, holding out the receiver.

It took Jamie a second or two to realize who it was. 'Oh, it's you. Hello.'

'Ma and I were wondering if you were taking a break in the spring,' Jumbo said.

'I hadn't really given it thought.'

Jamie had sat in the chair across from Alison. He felt a little weak. His cover was blown. More than that. Much more than that. It was his father.

'You want to give yourself two or three weeks,' his father was saying, 'I'd have thought.'

'There's a lot to be done up here.'

'You very busy, then?'

'Plenty.'

The interchange hesitated. Pa couldn't know that things had turned oddly slack. He couldn't know anything very much.

'It'd be nice to see you.'

Jamie said, 'Yes.'

'We'll have the hunter trials coming up. Be a lot of chums. You'll need a break.'

'I expect I might.' Hunter trials. Chums and hunter trials, the life he'd been bred for.

'How's things in Bradford?'

'So-so.'

'You finding some of them work?'

'If they're willing to move. But when they're buying their own council houses . . .'

'Of course,' his father said quickly.

'Most of the Yorkshiremen still expect the factory to reopen. They're looking to the next Government.'

'It won't happen.'

'What won't?'

'Even if the other lot get elected, it won't happen. Don't let them delude themselves, Jamie.'

'They know about delusion.'

There was a morsel of silence.

'You haven't asked after your mother.'

An Asian, gaunt and scraggy, with a glistening beard, had timidly entered the office. Jamie motioned him to a chair.

'How's Ma?'

Ma was all right, Jumbo supposed.

When Jumbo took Jane to lunch in the West End they went to the ladies' annexe of Boodle's: Jumbo kept on his membership of Boodle's, three or four doors down St James's from White's, for that very purpose. He had called Jamie from a telephone booth in the annexe. Jane had waited for him at the lunch table.

He came to the table a little pale and said, 'I spoke to him.'

Jane did not say anything immediately, just reading his face. In any case a club stewardess had come up to take their order. A frown passed across Jumbo's face at the interruption. Jane passed the menu card to him, but he knew what he wanted already. Jane took the Dover sole, grilled; and Jumbo the cod's roe and a minute steak.

'And?' Jane said when the stewardess was gone.

'He's not coming home.'

Jane was not looking at him now.

'I'm still not sure you should have called him.'

'How could one not?' Was that not as true as anything that could be said? He went on: 'He'll achieve nothing. He doesn't know what he's got himself into.'

'That's not the point.'

'You sound like Jamie.'

Jane coloured slightly. She said, 'It's his life.'

'And we've to sit by and watch him throw it away. That's our job?'

'He's very young.'

Jumbo looked at her. He wanted no dispute, nor did she, she knew. Yet it lay so deep, where his function was his duty.

'I mean,' Jane said, 'he's got time to make mistakes, take risks. When you were his age you were in Burma, commanding men, being shot at by Japanese. Taking risks.'

'We knew what we were doing. And why.'

'It was another age, darling. Another world.' She was looking back at him now, but not meeting him

– penetrating him. 'It was a great cause. There's nothing remotely as clear-cut for today's young. I've heard you say something of the kind yourself. They have to discover it all for themselves. In their own way.'

The wine steward had come up and Jumbo ordered: a bottle of Malvern water, and a glass of red burgundy for himself. There was a hint of humour in what he said next, the old robust Jumbo. 'So we encourage them to compound the bugger's muddle. Is that it?'

'That's it,' said Jane, gently closing the topic. Yet closing nothing more.

CHAPTER TWENTY

The bar-billiards room at the Hawthorne work-ingmen's club, catering for the suburban estate of Bradford where Ginger lived among many of his former workmates at the Mainwaring Bolt Company, was very different from the spacious Regency billiard rooms at White's or Boodle's. Its bar-billiards occupied one of the two small basement rooms that comprised the club's entire premises, and was so cramped that at either end of the bar-billiards table it was not possible to pass behind a player while he was cueing a shot. Charlie was currently engaged in a game with Benjy, a powerful, overblown man bursting out of his skin, with meaty hands in which a cue resembled a mere stick. A large spotted red handkerchief was stuffed into Benjy's jacket pocket, and in his glittering eyes and overwhelming physical presence there was a disconcertingly zealous cheer.

A wide opening gave upon a similarly cramped bar-room, one third of which was occupied by the vinyl-topped bar. Here, Leslie was filling the role of barman. Jujube-tinted lights above the booths and plastic flowers on the bar itself made this heart of the club immediately welcoming and homely. In addition there were posters up in full colour of Bradford City FC, the front row crouching round a brand new black-and-white soccer ball, Torremolinos with a beach girl, and Prince Charles and Princess Di. And a juke box and a couple of fruit machines. The club rules were stuck up framed behind glass. There was also a darts board on the wall opposite the bar, and several darts had penetrated the Torremolinos beach girl at the point where her legs met at her body. Being a full basement, the club had no windows, and air was circulated only by an electrically operated ventilator in the ceiling above the bar.

It was for men only, although the rules did not say so. And for white men only. The rules certainly did not say *that*. A narrow man called Terry sat by the door which led to the outside steps from above. There was an eye-level slit in the outer door, with a shutter across it.

In front of the bar was Jamie, who had just arrived with Ginger. It was Jamie's first visit. When Ginger, accompanied by Charlie and Les, had met him outside his office a couple of nights previously and made the invitation, Jamie was glad to accept, for this could be the start of his acceptance by the indigenous Yorkshire unemployed. Up to now, with just a few exceptions, they had treated him with such wariness, or indifference. And over the past several days things had gone inexplicably slack: those seeking his counselling and his widening range of knowledge of alternative employment, retraining, the financial mechanics of moving home, and so on, for which he had worked so hard, instead of expanding had seemed to fall away; he was stood up at appointments, and his telephone messages remained unresponded to. Ginger had collected him at work in his pale blue Cortina. He had never vouchsafed a surname.

Jamie made as if to buy his host a drink. Ginger restrained him at once.

'No, no. It's a club 'ere, James.' He indicated the notice over the bar: Members Only May be Served. 'The privilege is always ours.'

'Right there, Ginger,' said Les with just the same affability.

'What's it to be then, James – I needn't say Mr Bingham, need I? Basic tariff, mind.'

Jamie said a pint.

'Two pints it is, Les. Two Tetleys. We can't do them fancy drinks your Candyman friend goes for.'

Les had two beermugs on the bar in a jiffy and poured the beer from cans.

'You known 'im long, then?'

'A month or two.' Jamie knew it was Noel that Ginger referred to.

'Since you came oop 'ere from South, like, to 'elp uz out? Never knew 'im before? Cheers.'

Ginger raised his mug, and Jamie his. Jamie had seen Ginger about the place from soon after he arrived. He remembered him precisely from his first visit, with his father and the two Japanese. He had no doubt it was the same man, despite the helmet he wore in the foundry and the sweat smearing his face. The cold contempt of the man's eyes had struck him then – that and the monster hands. He read him differently now. It had not been contempt but defiance –he would be what he was, as he was, irrespective: irrespective (if it had to be) of history itself. Authority was natural in him, Jamie saw. He engendered his own brand of awe. There was a basic quality of hardihood to him, a rightful earthy might. The Mainwaring Bolt Company was dead and gone, yet it had had its day and what would it have ever been without such men?

Jamie felt confident he himself remained unrecognized. He would have got wind of it by now, otherwise. He told Ginger he had simply run across the Candyman since he'd arrived up here.

'Oh, oop 'ere. Oh. Course, couple of newcomers in a strange place, that'd bring two lads together. So 'ow's it working out, like, James?'

'The job?'

'Exactly that. Coming oop 'ere to 'elp pick oop pieces after the deebarkle.'

'The factory closing . . .'

'Exactly that.'

Jamie did feel the pity of a man such as this, on the heap in midlife. What meaning had he now without the foundry? – the great hands' authority redundant, the belly's muscle turning to otiose fat under its two tiers of coloured jumpers.

'I can sometimes give people courage to move to a different part of the country, where there's more work to be had.'

'I wouldn't say it's courage we're short of,' Ginger said. And Jamie thought, No, indeed: it's iron-smelting you're short of, the esoteric craft of infinite antiquity the Celts brought. Britain was just about finished as a site for smelting and smithing, in a world economy.

Terry had evidently pushed a button for a record on the juke box, and a chirpy Andy Williams was Sitting Right down to Write Himself a Ledder.

'Some of uz belong 'ere,' Ginger resumed.

'Until the wogs came, we did.'

'Wogs or no wogs, Les,' Ginger corrected, 'we were born and bred 'ere.'

Terry had unbolted the door to a newcomer, a sallow man of forty or so like the others, carrying a toolbag, which he put carefully on the floor under the dartboard. Both he and Terry now joined the trio at the bar.

'This is my mate Terry,' Ginger proceeded with the introductions. 'And my mate Keith. Keith, meet James Bingham. Works for Sir James Mainwaring, 'is namesake, otherwise Jumbo. Indirectly one might say.'

Jamie felt a shaft of uneasiness at the way Ginger had put it. But reviewing Ginger's words and blandness he decided he could only have meant by 'namesake' the common Christian name, and by 'working for Sir James Mainwaring' his assisting of ex-Mainwaring employees – though he had never restricted himself to Mainwaring men.

Keith took up his beermug. They were all standing, propping the bar. Ginger said, 'I was putting it to young James, soom of uz won't be relocated so lightly. Soom parts of the body aren't suitable for transplantation.'

'The knackers,' said Les.

Ginger ignored him. 'What d'you say to that, James?'

'I can't blame anyone for wanting to stay put. It's a sad business when an industry crumbles and puts a large part of a city on the dole.'

'If industry 'as to crumble,' Les said.

'You'll belong somewhere, James, if I'm not mistaken. The Bingham family.'

'My great-great grandfather came from the Midlands. Possibly Yorkshire.'

'That would be a while ago,' Ginger said. 'Nowadays, we mean, James. A place you y'self belong.'

Big Benjy and Charlie drifted in from the bar-billiards, Jamie the centre of them all.

'Evenin' Keith,' Benjy beamed. 'Not empty-'anded, I trust?'

'Young James 'ere,' Ginger was proceeding, 'who's come to mop oop after t'deebarkle, is honouring uz with a little visit. We were just chatting about belonging. You know. A sense of community. Allegiance, like. You don't get much of that in London, I don't suppose.'

There was an unrelentingness to Ginger. Jamie supposed that it was part of his social stock-in-trade. He had still not quite recovered his composure after Ginger's reference to his 'namesake', and he would have preferred not to have been so exclusively the focus of attention among these half dozen men. He said something about the average household in the south-east moving every four-and-a-half years.

'We're a different species 'ere,' Ginger told him.

'Very protective of the community, in these parts,' Benjy affirmed. 'Very protective.'

Benjy rewarded himself with a good draft of his ale and looked at the others over the rim of his mug.

Jamie said, 'It's the Yorkshire personality.'

'They told you about that, did they?' Ginger said. 'They were right. Mind, there's nobody doesn't 'ave to look after themselves these days. You wouldn't quarrel with that.'

'Uz, for instance,' Leslie offered.

'Uz, right,' Ginger endorsed. 'Your lot-the Mainwaring Group. It's just the same.'

There it was again. Was there an edge to it, a mocking? Should he deny any involvement with the Mainwaring Group, or could that lead to deep water? He was aware of questions they might have asked him and hadn't. He told Ginger,

'When it's a matter of survival.'

'Exactly that. I mean, if someone's giving trouble, aggravating as they say, breaking the law like, oopsetting community, one looks after oneself, doesn't one? You'd do the same, James.'

'Course 'e would,' Benjy came in. But Ginger wasn't finished.

'You can't depend on the law these days. You get on with it yourself, right? Tell the police, "Coom back in 'arf-an-hour." Right, James?'

He began to sense it now: a menace. The low-ceilinged room, dug out of the earth, the bunched men. Yet there could surely be no menace . . .

'You all right for beer, James? Another Tetley's for our guest, Les. Ever heard of vigilantes?'

'Certainly.'

'That's uz on this estate. Hawthorne. Uz 'arf dozen in our little club right now.'

'What are you mostly on guard against?'

This set off a little collective merriment. Jamie found himself grinning too, though he knew not what at.

'You touched a spot there, James. He touched a spot, didn't 'e?'

Benjy was beaming. 'He touched a spot, Ginger.'

Jamie felt the beating of his heart. His glance flickered to the door.

'We're all on our own-io, here. All quiet and secluded.' They all seemed to wait on Ginger. 'As to your question, that was a good one.'

'A very good one,' said the weasely Leslie from behind the bar.

'We could put it to you, James.' Ginger turned to the others. 'We'd be favoured to know what young James thinks, wouldn't we. On account of 'im 'aving gone to t'trouble to accept our invitation.'

The sarcasm was thick and obvious now. But Jamie had no choices. 'We get a lot of petty theft in London.' He did not trust his voice. 'I found a burglar trying to get into our flat a year or so back.'

'Did you now! We don't get quite so much of that 'ere.'

'They wouldn't dare,' Benjy said.

'Try again, James.'

There was a nasty pause.

'Give 'im a clue,' Leslie proposed.

'I'll give 'im a clue,' Ginger followed. 'We've all got youngsters.'

Jamie knew he was pale now, betraying fear. All the faces were smiling, with varying derision, except for one, Keith: his face got along without the smile.

'Corrupting our youngters,' Ginger said. 'We wouldn't stand for that, would we? You wouldn't expect uz.'

'I wouldn't,' Jamie said.

Charlie spoke. 'Tell 'im Ginger. Go on.'

'No. Let 'im tell uz.' Ginger looked squarely at their victim. 'You wouldn't like to say, would you? You and your Candyman.'

Benjy did a quick triple mime, sniffing, smoking, injecting a vein.

'Dope,' Ginger said, and the smiles all quit their faces – except for Keith who at last achieved one. 'We wanted to 'ave a bit of a chat with you, James. You'll not be comfortable, standing, not for a good chat.'

Benjy moved an upright chair to the middle of the floor. ''Ere, James. Try this.'

Jamie was truly afraid now. He looked at each of the faces.

'What is it you're driving at?'

The strength of his own voice pulled him together, just for that moment.

Ginger said, 'Sit yourself down and be comfortable.'

They stood back from him a little to make way. They were going to do something to him, he knew. He could not tell what it was, or exactly why. He did not think they would kill him. He had no precedent for this. They would hurt him, he could not doubt that. He couldn't think beyond what was going to happen.

He sat on the chair in a daze and they formed an uneven circle around him, like some ritual.

'Our kiddies are being sold dope,' Ginger said. ''Appen you know 'ow. They buy the filthy stuff off Candyman, Candyman gets it from you.'

'It's not true.'

Leslie said, 'You wouldn't accuse Ginger of fibbing. It wouldn't be sense.'

'It's rubbish.'

Ginger said, 'Police picked oop your friend Candyman this dinnertime, and 'e's confessed already – di'n' waste no time. Gets the filthy stuff from you.'

'Filthy stuff.'

'Our kids.'

The voices came at him from this direction and that.

'When we've done,' Ginger explained, 'police'll 'ave you too. They wouldn't want to interrupt uz, I'll vouch. They approve of uz.'

'Neighbour'ood Watch.'

'Tha's right, Les. Neighbour'ood Watch. We've a right to protect ourselves.'

Jamie felt the clammy sweat on him. He said, 'You've got the wrong man.' But they had arrived with their anger, an accumulation of anger that could only be vented, not dissolved.

'We've got you,' Ginger answered. 'That'll do to be getting on with. Benjy, would you like to be making him snug?'

And a grinning Benjy moved behind Jamie, and, delicately from behind, took each of his wrists between fingers and thumb. Then Jamie resisted, and instantly Benjy snatched the wrists, making him gasp.

'Aw, lad.'

Benjy deftly tied Jamie's hands to the chair-back with strips of cloth.

Nobody spoke. Ginger gave a nod to Benjy, drawing the red spotted bandana from his pocket, and folding it carefully, made a tight blindfold across Jamie's eyes.

'Some music, Ginger?'

'No music yet, Terry.'

Jamie's imagination could not encompass the hatred of his tormentors. He could not credit it – six men, random neighbours, fathers, husbands, thus engaged. He was young. He had not known this was mankind, his own kind. English. All that he had presumed of *English*. Fair play. Lovingkindness — somewhere, in a crevice, in the last resort. Fear was mounting with the speed and toweringness of waves. He fought to control it, but what could he do against such curling towers of black seas poised to crash upon him?

'I want you to look at it from our point of view, James.'

Jamie shook his dropped head, awaiting blows,

'I never supplied drugs to anybody.'

'We don't like causing unwarranted damage. Unwarranted. You'll be some mother's son yourself. Maybe we'll be doing you a good turn. *Bot*,' Ginger landed heavily on the qualification, 'fair and square, we've to protect our own kind. We're all Yorkshiremen born and bred. Our fathers fought t'last war. Our grandads t'previous. For England, naturally. For their 'omes and their families. If they'd neglected that we wouldn't be 'ere.' He paused. 'Likewise uz. The Guvvament 'as flooded us with wogs, and t'capitalists in London chucked away t'industry on which we depended. *Bot'* – it came again like a drumbeat – 'we belong 'ere, nowt finishes uz. We'll protect our own,

the future generations, as our forefathers did. You
follow me, James?'

'You are making a mistake. Why do you suppose —'

'You follow me, James?'

'Are any of you prepared to listen? Why should I
have come to Bradford?'

'Let's get on with it, Ginger.'

'If the lad's got something to tell uz . . .'

'You don't know who I am.'

'Oh, do we not, James Bingham?' Ginger said.

'Dirty little dope merchant.' 'Let's get on with it.'
The voices came at him faster now, like darts.

'If you do anything to me, my father — '

'Come on, Ginger.'

'Oh, your father?' Ginger's voice once more, is 'e
in dope racket too?'

'I don't deal in dope!' Jamie shouted at the pitch
of his lungs. He was in panic. He thought, 'They can
kill me.' They could kill him; they could blind him;
they could castrate him; they could abandon him
here for ever in blackness.

'Spot of music, then,' Ginger said.

Someone pressed a button on the juke box.

'No mallet?'

'There wasn't one.'

'Lucy in the Sky with Diamonds' began and up
went the volume to maximum.

'I didn't have to come here,' Jamie was shouting,
'I came to help you!'

But they had proceeded beyond any plea, any recall. One was gripping one leg by the ankle and another (Benjy, he knew, with a wrapped hammer) struck the kneecap so violent a blow that all present heard the cracking of the bone. And immediately thereafter a similar devastation of the other kneecap.

The sound that emerged from Jamie came via his throat from his stomach. He was pure pain, comprised of pain, his pain rolling in an ocean of pain. It had drowned out fear, outrage, all other experience.

They were still talking as they dragged and bundled him out. 'Now why would you want to 'elp uz?' 'What are we to you, eh?' 'What were you oop to – saving your bloody soul?' Laughter. Now they had broken him they wanted to render him nothing, to prove to themselves his worthlessness. But the voices and their words could not reach him across the infinite bounds of his pain.

They humped him out and up the stairs and into a motorcar. They drove for ten minutes and dumped him in a lay-by off a main road. They had none of them known who he was.

CHAPTER TWENTY-ONE

So Jamie Mainwaring began his coming of age, if by that is meant what must be endured, and how, and also why, in the pilgrimage to find oneself.

The trial took place two and a half months later at the Crown Court at Bradford. Noel Cunnington and James Mainwaring were accused jointly of possessing (Section 5 of the Act) and supplying (Section 4) 'controlled drugs'. Both pleaded Not Guilty to supplying and Guilty to possessing. The two accused were kept separate when held on remand. Each intended to blame the other in his evidence and was separately represented in court. Jumbo and Jane had visited Jamie together, soon after he had entered hospital when the police had picked him up in the lay-by, and Jane had paid him a second visit on her own. Even so it came as a shock when their son made his appearance.

In court there was the usual complement of legal persons for a trial of two defendants. And the jury, of course. Those in the public gallery formed two uneasy groups. There were those drawn to the court by their curiosity or prurience or because they had nothing better to do. This group was quite numerous, since the case (due to the Mainwarings' prominence) had caused a moderate degree of publicity in the national press and more extended coverage in the local press. These may or may not have included some connected with the men who had taken part in the maiming of Jamie: it was impossible to tell. The other group was smaller and more cohesive, being bound by a common concern for one of the two accused, Jamie. If Noel the Candyman had drawn any friend or relative to the court, he or she was not immediately identifiable.

On the first day, the group assembled on behalf of Jamie comprised only his father and his mother (whom the press photographed hurrying up the steps of the court), his sister Vicky, his friend Anthony, who had obtained leave from both his Tutor and the Precentor at St John's College, Cambridge, and Jamie's (and also Anthony's) former housemaster at Eton, Rodney Jarvis, a shy, enthusiastic bachelor who offset his inability to secure an easy companionship with his charges by a scrupulous concern for their happiness and success. He was that same housemaster whom Jamie had so disparagingly likened to his project director in Mali, in his long letter to Tibby. These five sat in the front row.

The two non-family members had come spontaneously and without warning. The Mainwaring parents were, of course, touched by their loyalty. Being accustomed to attendance at certain gatherings where sombreness was appropriate, the Mainwarings mastered the reflexive instincts at the renewal of acquaintanceship to greet with grins and vapid chatter. Even so such brief talk as was exchanged before proceedings began was not, typically, upon Jamie or the case in hand, but on things Etonian or at Cambridge.

Tibby was not expected. She had paid one visit to Jamie in hospital, weeping quite a lot in the presence of the prison officer in plain clothes assigned to keep watch on Jamie. She had been dissuaded from going to see him during his weeks in prison on remand (at Wakefield) or from interrupting her course further still for what could be the drawn-out duration of the trial.

Candyman was first to appear in the dock, in his jeans and overtailored jacket. He settled into his seat alongside his guard, and glanced first at the jury, then up at the gallery. He gave no sign of searching for anyone. He was a loner, they knew by now, even if the court was presumed as yet to be in ignorance. He had grown up in approved schools since he was eleven, the eldest of four children fathered by a father who quit that role early when he was put away for however many years it took to break the plywood structure of such a family.

'Put up James Bingham Mainwaring,' cried the court's clerk.

There is an entrance, as a rule, below the dock of any Crown Court by which the prisoner ascends to the

level of a courtroom from that region below, which
contains the cells for those awaiting trial. It is usually
reached by a long stone or brick stairway built wide
enough for a prisoner and, should the man be violent or a potential escaper, for a prison warder handcuffed to him. Most courts in Britain were built long
ago, and the cells beneath them, being occupied only
briefly, have generally been overlooked in the short-
lived endeavours at modernization of places of incarceration that have occurred erratically over the past
century and a half. Thus it is that the prisoner, emerging into court for the first time for a trial which very
often he has been awaiting several months in prison
elsewhere, has so vivid an impression of rising from
one realm of existence and scale of time to another.
It is somewhat as if making the passage from Hades to
the land of the living. The impression is sharpened by
the peculiar poignancy of the all-but-undemarcated
divisions inside the courtroom. There, as he enters,
if he looks around at all, or raises his eyes to one side
or over his shoulder a little – there, separated by no
more than a space of a few yards or feet and a rail
or balustrade of mere wood, are his friends, those he
has loved or still loves, who have brought him into
the world or borne his offspring: free people, gazing
down or across at him, the broad light of the day quite
likely shining behind them or upon them.

Thus it may be assumed to have been for Jamie.

For some of those awaiting him in court a painful
prolongation ensued between the summons of the

clerk, with his strange command, *put up*, and the prisoner's appearance. This was not due to any requirement for handcuffing, but to a factor immediately apparent upon his arrival. He entered on crutches, with which he must have ascended the stairway. And not only was he clearly unpractised at handling them, but also he was still unable to put more than momentary weight on either leg. His attention was so concentrated on his movement that only when settled in the dock, adjacent but not close to Noel the Candyman, did he turn to glance at the public gallery. There he saw the five pairs of eyes that had waited for him, and the frightened smile of one of them, Vicky's.

He was dressed in the blue suit he had rarely and reluctantly worn previously (that same suit he had so frantically started to change into until he saw the wheels of his father's Daimler carrying him away to lunch at White's with the man from Unicef). His mother had brought the suit down from London to the remand prison especially so that he could wear it at the trial, to make a favourable impression. However, by some mischance, or possibly a rule forbidding access to anything that might be used as means of suicide, he had become separated from his tie. The top button of his white shirt was done up, but without the tie: it would have been better left open. Also his hair was excessively long – not all that long by the fashion of the day for young men but somehow too long for the suit. It was washed clean but it tumbled and flopped over his collar. And moreover, he still wore a ring in his left earlobe, just as the other defendant did.

All these things were noticed by Jumbo, and hung around in his mind to bother him. If only he could reach the boy, somehow to put these little things right. But of course he could not. The poignant separation was experienced on both sides. It was as if his son was sealed in an invisible capsule.

It was anyway too late now. Even if Jumbo might reach Jamie during the trial through his defence counsel, with whom he was already acquainted and in whose selection he had been instrumental, the first impression would already have left its mark on judge and jury.

The trial, although of two men, progressed with greater alacrity than they had feared it might. Noel Cunnington was the first defendant to enter the witness box. He gave an impression of brittle cocksureness. When his falsehoods were challenged, first by the prosecuting counsel then by Jamie's counsel, he reacted with a little-boy-lost innocent bewilderment which shifted swiftly, under sharper challenge, through indignation to wounded resentment. His chosen line was that of the victim – victim of others' superior evil, victim of the lawyers' hostility, victim – in sum – of the injustice of his life. If there was anyone present to feel for him, he might have been seen as a pathetic figure. Once the youth Colin had been called, and it was clear he had bargained for freedom from prosecution by grassing to the police, he abandoned any attempt to deny that, now and then, pressed by others, he had sold smack from his Candyman van. But he had been put up to it by Jamie and others unknown. Those unknown people in London from whom he had first obtained cannabis resin for personal use had sent Jamie to him to open up the business and push harder. He had been all against it.

Jamie was called to the witness box by mid-afternoon. His progress to the stand was protracted and evidently painful: it required the full focusing of mind and body. Once he was propped up in the box, the clerk of the court asked him if he wished to take the oath or to affirm.

'Affirm,' Jamie told him.

'Say after me: "I solemnly and sincerely declare and affirm"' – Jamie repeated the phrase and continued likewise — '"that the evidence that I shall give shall be the truth, the whole truth, and nothing but the truth."'

Jumbo knew that an oath upon a text acknowledged as sacred must carry more weight with any jury.

'You may sit, if you wish,' the judge said.

Jamie sat.

His own counsel rose. 'Are you James Bingham Mainwaring of 51A Eaton Square, London South West One?'

'I am.'

'You are twenty-one years old?'

'Yes.'

'Mr Mainwaring, would you describe to the court in your own words the full nature and extent of your relationship with Noel Cunnington, otherwise known as the Candyman?'

Jamie began on a description of their first encounter, his temporary lodgement with him, and their companionship, such as it was. He sat facing the jury. He had only to raise his glance ever so slightly to the right to see those who had come to be as near to him as was possible at this moment. Every now and then his eyes did rest on them briefly. Nothing was transmitted from him to them. Likewise his father's eyes carried no discernible expression. From time to time his father removed his glasses, polished them, and replaced them. Jumbo, concentrating intently, found himself transported to a world quite strange to him. Nothing changed in his face when, in response to a question from counsel, his son explained why he had been thrown out of his previous lodgings and found himself with virtually no money. Jamie's mother's gaze held a steady tenderness. In Vicky there was some sort of ardent appeal on his behalf. His housemaster was, as usual, shy, and also very alert. Into Anthony's eyes had crept an affectionate humour.

The Candyman, in the dock, looked straight ahead.

'And so you freely admit,' his counsel was saying, 'to the possession of a small quantity of cannabis resin for personal use only but you insist that the heroin derivative known as smack which police have testified they found in a drawer in your office desk was put there by other persons in order to incriminate you.'

'Yes, that's so. To get me on a charge of supplying.'

'Do you have anyone in mind who would wish to incriminate you?'

'The other defendant in this case.'

'Please explain.'

'He has falsely declared me to be his supplier.'

'Why?'

'Presumably in order to provide cover for his true supplier.' Jamie had expected nothing better of Noel Cunnington: he knew that perfectly well from the start. Quite open-eyed and perverse, he had defied his own better judgement. He had been playing at life as a child does to fill a void, playing Let's Pretend, as if by imputing true comradeship to the other he could make it real.

Counsel said, 'The drug smack was found in the flat you occupied with Noel Cunnington.' it did not belong to me.'

'Have you ever used smack?'

'Yes.'

'On how many occasions?'

'One.'

'Why?'

'I was interested to know what goes on in the world.'

'That is an attitude of mind, I think you will agree, that can be taken too far, where the law of the land is involved.'

This contained a reprimand, on behalf of judge and jury, who could have heard in Jamie's answer an aristocratic superiority to the curbs and prohibitions of a legality designed for the common run of humanity. Counsel waited for an assenting response from his client, but got nothing. He hurried on.

'Anyone else who might wish to incriminate you?'

But the sense of dislocation had taken hold. And here was a question for which Jamie seemed unprepared, his unpreparedness communicating itself instantly to the court, and to those in the gallery also. Jamie looked up and around as if out of a miasma of despair. He said,

'Such as?'

'Would you like to tell the court how you received injuries to your knees?'

Jamie glanced at counsel, then at the judge, then back at counsel. Jumbo looked away.

'Some people,' he began hesitantly, 'were misled into supposing I was involved in selling smack to their children. They took it upon themselves. . .' Here he faltered. He was foundering-so Jumbo felt – upon a fathomless grief at what men supposed to be the true nature of their species, that it was vile.

'Yes?'

'They broke my kneecaps.'

'Are you intending to bring charges against these people?'

'No.'

'Why is that, if I may ask?'

'If I believed what they believed it's possible I would have . . . it's possible I would have felt as strongly as they did.'

There was a stir in court, and Jumbo's alarm was that, in the generosity of this admission, the simple minds of those present might have read a presumption of guilt.

'Really?'

'There was more to it than that. Perhaps . . .'

Counsel now looked surprised. 'More to it?'

'They had a – fund of anger in them' (he had come close to the word foundry). 'At the way life had turned out for them. They had found something – someone – on which they could vent it.'

His eyes flickered, in distress, on those of his father, which however betrayed nothing.

'A final question.'

The court had stilled, though with what taint or influence from the preceding interchange none could be sure.

'When you were working in the Bradford area, what name did you use?'

'James Bingham.'

'This is not of course your full name. It was a form of disguise.'

'Yes.'

'Why did you wish to hide your true identity?'

This time his glance did not stray to his father. Yet there was still a hesitance.

'I only wished to hide my identity in one respect.'

'And what was that?'

'As my father's son,' Jamie's reply came, but indistinctly.

The judge intervened. 'Will you please speak up?'

'As my father's son.'

'For what reason?' counsel followed.

'My family name is well known in this city. My forbears helped to . . . bring it into existence. The group of companies which my father heads was obliged to shut down the factory here, or rather, let it die on its own, and nearly eighteen hundred men lost their jobs. I didn't want what I was trying to do to look like an exercise in public relations.'

'It was your decision, was it not, to take on this job as a way of exercising your sense of social responsibility towards those who had fallen victim to the changing industrial fortunes of this country?'

'I wanted to help them.'

'It was entirely your idea to do so?'

A smile's shadows passed across Jamie's face.

'Entirely.'

His counsel sat.

Next morning all the national press carried reports of the trial, at differing extensiveness and prominence. Jamie was variously referred to in headlines as 'Mainwaring Heir' or, in the tabloids – Mainwaring containing an excessive quantity of letters – as 'Tycoon's Son'. (Jumbo had never thought of himself as a 'tycoon', although such an appellation had occurred before now.) It seemed possible that it would all be over by that second day, but the extended cross-examination of the boy Colin and the calling as witness for Jamie of his crippled assistant Alison delayed the judge's summing up until the third day, when the verdict was to be expected. Colin's evidence introduced an unsettling doubt. The defence were looking to him to corroborate that Noel Cunnington alone had been engaged in selling smack. Indeed he did so, from his description of how the drug was passed out. The boy had been promised immunity from prosecution in exchange for his evidence; but the manner in which he chose to give it was one of sulky hostility towards all involved in the trial – police, barristers, and both defendants. His very involvement in the case served to confirm his unexpungible contamination by the adult world. A question from Noel Cunnington's counsel as to whether he had seen Jamie on the housing estate in the Candyman's company produced an answer that he 'thought he might have'. When further questioning hardened a casual possibility to a sour probability, the fact emerged – at this ill-timed juncture – that on two or three occasions Jamie had indeed accepted a lift in Cunnington's van to the city's estates to visit the unemployed. Such was the unwarranted doubt that Jamie's counsel strove to eliminate in his closing speech.

Jumbo and Jane had travelled by car daily across the country from Jane's widowed mother's home in

North Lancashire. They did not wish, for obvious reasons, to stay at a Bradford hotel, and they declined the thoughtful invitation of old friends whose home was a well-known Palladian West Yorkshire country house to be their guests while the trial continued: it was privacy they sought. Each night, they knew, Jamie was carried back in a sealed van to Wakefield prison, to an existence infinitely remote from them as if he had been transported to another planet. There, in Wakefield, Jamie himself knew that the trial had presented an account of events so different from what really happened. None of the facts that emerged (apart from Noel's lies) were erroneous as such, but the picture they presented was of a life devoid of meaning, devoid of hope – squalid, mean and futile.

Meanwhile Rodney Jarvis had had to return to Eton. Vicky had gone back to London, declaring that to hear the verdict in court would be more than she could possibly take.

Assembling for the third day, they were surprised to find Tibby among them.

Tibby had arrived off her train much too early and reached the court building before it had even opened. The cleaners let her in and put her in the visitors' waiting room where there was nothing to look at except notices saying what you were not allowed to take into the courtroom. She had sat there hunched up in her anorak over her tweed jacket for over an hour. It had been entirely her own decision to come and she reached it the night before when she read in the Evening Standard that the verdict was expected the following day. She could not bear to stay away any more, whatever anybody would say. The only person she told was one friend on her course the night before, and this friend was to fib for her and explain that she wasn't well and wouldn't be attending the course that day. She had never been in a court of law before and what surprised her, as the place began to fill up, was how casually and normally everybody behaved, the barristers sharing jokes as they hung about the broad corridors and other people even in the visitors' and juries' waiting rooms doing the crosswords in the papers and quite unconcerned about the to-ing and fro-ing around them: while right here, in this very place, terrible tragedies were being exposed and enacted, human lives were being irrevocably changed by the pronouncement of a few words or even a single word, and people marked for ever.

She was the very first person to be admitted when they opened the door to the public gallery, and she sat unobtrusively at the back as it slowly filled up around her. When Sir James and Lady Mainwaring arrived and settled further forward, they failed to notice Tibby, though she of course saw them. It was Anthony who caught sight of her first. When Jumbo and Jane realized she was there they naturally insisted she should come and sit with them, although in truth she would rather have remained entirely on her own, unrecognized except perhaps by Jamie when he was brought in, and perhaps not even by him.

She saw the Candyman in the dock first. She hated him with all the force of her being. When Jamie entered from beneath propped with crutches she felt such a rush of pity and horror and fury that she could have cried out; but as it was she turned a deep red. She just hoped Jamie would not look round and see her so red and think she was ashamed at seeing him a prisoner with a policeman sitting behind him. He did not look. When the judge came in everybody stood up, and it was only when Jamie was settling back on to his bench that he turned his head and, glancing up at the gallery, saw. She knew that he would assume she had come by arrangement with his parents, perhaps even at their suggestion; but that couldn't be helped.

Tibby was correct in her supposition. Yet Jamie, when he caught sight of her, did immediately realize that he had missed her presence until that moment. After her brief and tearful visit to him in hospital, he too had urged her not to come to the trial: perhaps he was the first to do so. Now that she was here, he was glad – glad that she should be here to experience with him, in whatever measure might be possible, whatever was to happen.

The judge's summing up of the trial could not be faulted for its accuracy. Yet he was perhaps over-scrupulous in his refraining from guiding the jury as to whether James Mainwaring had had smack in his possession or was in any way involved in its supply. That was for them to decide. When the judge had concluded his summing up all stood again. The judge withdrew; the jury retired to consider their verdict, and the usher cleared the court. Anthony took Tibby by the hand (she knew it must feel clammy): they stood in the marble corridor together. Someone had said a long retirement was not expected. Jumbo was speaking well of counsel, and his commendation was actually interrupted by the arrival of the barrister himself in his gown and fitted wig. The summing up had been equitable, he said, and he considered Jamie had made a favourable impression. He said something to the effect of a 'suspended sentence' being in order -presumably on the charge of possessing to which Jamie had pleaded guilty; yet there was also just now, as they were aware, a popular and political retributive mood in the matter of drug offences. And there was no foretelling, he added, briskly polishing his spectacles, the quirks and prejudices of juries. Tibby knew that a suspended sentence did not mean prison. After the barrister was gone Jane Mainwaring said it was rather like talking to the surgeon after he had come out from an operation before anyone had any idea whether the patient was going to come round. Jumbo had a good laugh at that. Tibby saw the court reporters chatting.

They were all called back into the court after no more than forty minutes. When everyone else was assembled, except the judge, the jury filed in. Tibby noticed there were two Indians among them and more than half the rest were women – she thought that ought to be a good thing. One man seemed scarcely older than Jamie himself.

When the judge came in they all stood up again and only sat down when he did. She could see the back of Jamie's head and one ear, the one without the ring in it. Jamie was sitting very still but the Candyman was looking all round the court.

The judge said, 'Members of the jury, have you reached verdicts on which all of you are agreed?'

A man who looked like a butcher at the end of the front row of the jury stood up and, looking at the judge, said, 'We have, my lord.'

The clerk said,

'Noel John Cunnington is charged with supplying or offering to supply controlled drugs contrary to the Misuse of Drugs Act, 1971, or possessing them with the intention of supplying. Do you find him guilty or not guilty?'

'Guilty, my lord,' said the jury foreman.

'James Bingham Mainwaring is charged with supplying or offering to supply controlled drugs contrary to the Misuse of Drugs Act, 1971, or possessing them with the intention of supplying. Do you find him guilty or not guilty?'

'Guilty, my lord.'

An audible gasp broke from those present and Jamie's counsel's head came up sharply. Jumbo's eyes had very slightly narrowed; a film of moisture obscured Jane's gaze. Tibby's hand, clammy or not, had found Anthony's and when Anthony, sorrowing for his friend, turned to her he saw her eyes grown very large and wild and staring, as if she were in inner battle with deep forces, which were in fact the stemming of tears of outrage and pity. There followed without any pause whatever a recital of Noel Cunnington's previous convictions, which proved to be three – two of obtaining property by deception and one of making off without payment. Then each counsel made a brief plea of mitigation upon predictable lines, invoking his client's supposedly abject contrition and, in Jamie's case, the physical assault already endured.

All that was left was for the judge to pass sentence.

'Noel John Cunnington' (he was prodded to his feet by his warder), 'you have been found guilty of the charge before the court. You are sentenced to serve a term in prison of two years and six months.'

As many an offender does at such a moment, knowing his guilt but knowing also much more – that his life is thus because it has been thus and his fate is thus because it was thus, and will always be thus — Noel the Candyman smiled at the judge a victim's sarcastic thanks.

But the judge was looking directly at Jamie, who was now standing.

'James Bingham Mainwaring, the court has found you guilty of the charge before them. You are a young man whom it is reasonable to expect should set an example to the community. You have chosen not to do so. You are to serve a term in prison of eighteen months.'

The murmur washed over the court like a returning wave. Counsel for James Bingham Mainwaring now drew back his head stiffly and straightened his papers, prior to gathering them up.

Jamie, whose life was thus because he had thus reached out for it, whose fate was thus because his staff had turned to a serpent, did not look any more at the judge. As he turned from the dock to descend to that other world from which he had been briefly borrowed, he looked up at the gallery, found his parents there and Tibby and Anthony, and stared at their white faces as if they were all unknown to him.

CHAPTER TWENTY-TWO

I t may be said that the shock of annihilation normally experienced by those arrested and imprisoned for the first time did not occur in Jamie's instance – not at least with its customary suddenness
and force . . . In the first place, when the police, on
information received, picked him up in the roadside
lay-by he was considerably injured, and, although under arrest and charged and subject to remand conditions, remained in an ordinary hospital (under
guard) for several weeks. Then, when he joined the
prison community on remand in Wakefield gaol he
was, like the others, allowed to wear his own clothes,
receive food and books from outside, and see visitors
when he chose. This does not mean that the new re-
gime was easy. But it did mean that the transference
to Wandsworth prison in London after the sentence
came to him more as an intensification of the treatment he had already known than as a difference in
kind. Prison clothing was now obligatory, no gifts
from outside were permitted, access to books was restricted to the most inadequate prison library, only

one outgoing letter was allowed weekly and a limit was placed on letters received. As for visitors from outside, these were restricted to one a month.

The experience of shock had truly occurred even before he was arrested and charged – in the basement workingmen's club of the Hawthorne estate at Bradford. There was the shock of extreme fear and extreme pain. There was also, as he came to perceive, something else which took place in that basement: the shattering not just of his knees but of a presumption he did not know he had, so rooted was it in him from his earliest infancy. In the end, man did not conduct himself on a basis of morality or justice or mercy, but on a basis that was amoral, oblivious of justice, and infinitely merciless. That this might just be true of a single person, or of men engaged in some fearful contest, or of distant races living in the darkness of savagery, had perhaps been allowed for in his inner mind. But it had not been so allowed for his own kind, speaking his own language, randomly gathered, not so far from the heart of what could be taken as civilized Christendom.

He, who denied the existence of God – should he have been so shocked to have his denial endorsed? Yet since that was so, and shock remained in him, what should be concluded from it? For he had, in that same moment of fear of the imminence of death (his own), perceived as a truth more sharply, painfully, indelibly defined than he had till then perceived, the sacredness of life.

Jamie was given a prison number and put in a cell on the ground floor landing of B wing. He had become 220618 Mainwaring J B237 – 2 in the latter figure being the landing (the basement was 1), and 37 the cell, which was thirteen feet long and six feet wide, and contained two metal beds with grey blankets, one corner cupboard, a corner washstand, a plastic washing bowl, two wooden chairs, a two-by-two foot wooden table, two enamelled plates and plastic utensils and mug, a waste bin, a plastic jug and a plastic bucket, with a lid, should he require to relieve himself at other times besides the three periods when the cells on his landing were briefly unlocked. The small barred window aperture was three feet above eye level, but he could look out if he stood on a chair, which was against Prison Regulations. The steel door contained a peephole, with a flap on the other side, by which the screws (warders) could peer into the cell. He could not recall it having been mentioned that Mainwarings ever made steel cell doors but it seemed perfectly possible that when these doors were put in, a century or more ago, they did.

For two days he was on his own. He came out of his cell at 7.30 and 12 noon to fetch the meals (the last meal of the day was brought to the cells), but not at 3 p. m. for exercise like the rest because of the condition of his legs. He was noticed, of course, and he soon realized it was generally known on the wing who he was and why he was there. They had seen something of the case in their newspapers.

He felt inwardly numbed; in suspension; unable to focus properly on his situation, plan the conduct of his existence, or construct his thoughts. It had been so from the moment of the unjust verdict and his consequent sentence, persisting throughout the (very brief) visit he had been allowed from his parents in the cells below the courtroom, and the inexplicably prolonged journey – seven hours – in the prison van coming south from Bradford, during which he had been able to watch through the slot only the tops of trees and the telephone wires going by like someone, it occurred to him, who had suffered a certain form of brain damage. During that interminable ride he had begun to feel car-sick. He had not felt car-sick since he was a small boy.

Now he was also excessively bored. Four of the six books he had brought with him were taken from him at Reception for storage with his 'property', as was his transistor radio – disallowed in this prison on account of having a VHF waveband. He felt no inclination to read the two books he had more or less randomly selected for retention. He had been brought in on a Saturday morning: 'library' was not until Wednesday. A big man in a grey uniform whose glittering cheer reminded him of his torturer Benjy let himself into his cell and asked him whether, despite his having written 'none' against Religion on his reception form, he would not like to have a holy bible. Jamie accepted the bible to please the man: it was called The Good News Bible and appeared to have been re-written for American fundamentalists.

He did not read that book either. A man in the next-door cell, encountered momentarily on the landing, passed him a partly filled-in crossword book, and he did what was left of that, thus occupying forty-five minutes. He lay on his grey blanket in his prison denims and coarse striped shirt staring at the vaulted ceiling of thickly painted brick and listening to the perpetual bangs, cries, clatterings and cell bells from near and far. The cell bells would be ignored by the screws for half an hour or longer: he could discern this from the direction and distance of the sounds reaching him and the characteristic patterns of who-ever might be pushing the bells. Prisons, he knew by now, all must possess the same perpetual muffled clamour like the clamour of souls drowned at sea.

For two nights that first week he had the com-pany of a man about to be allocated to a prison on the Isle of Wight. This man's feet smelt worse than any Jamie had ever known. The man had tried every-thing he could think of to eradicate the smell, but nothing succeeded. Each night he stuffed his socks and his shoes up among the bars of the cell's window aperture in an attempt to air them. He was resigned to living with the appalling smell for the remaining two years of his sentence. As a result of this affliction he had become a pariah.

Then Jamie moved cells.

In the sanctity of St Paul's Cathedral a glorious out-flow of Thomas Walmisley's setting of Psalm 19, com-bining the choir and great organ in aerial and mighty praise, flooded the body of the entire edifice and poured upon the ears of the packed congregation.

'The heavens declare the glory of God: and the firmament sheweth his handiwork.

'One day telleth another: one night certifieth another.

'There is neither speech nor language: but their voices are heard among them.

'Their sound is gone out into all the land: and their words unto the end of the earth.'

A short distance up the chancel, behind the decani half of the choir, the Archbishop of Canterbury occupied the predicator's stall, since he would be preaching. Further up towards the high altar beneath its wondrous canopy kept aloft by gilt angels, the prelates' stalls were filled by the dean and his canons, the sacrist, and then the Bishop of London himself, whose cathedral this was. All were in their finest copes and stoles of embroidered gold and silver thread. Across from them, in his own stall, was the latest Lord Mayor in his ermine and deep red velvet cape. None of them was actually singing: the choir was doing that for them.

From a side aisle there now appeared a verger in a gown of deep green and black trimmed with silver, bearing across his body his silver verge, or rod. As the psalm's Gloria faded this verger had reached the centre of the top of the nave's aisle, just below the chancel steps. He turned down the aisle, and proceeded past the Queen of England and her Consort, sitting back now in their special chairs before their prie-dieu, to a point level with the first full row of worshippers behind the Monarch, which contained a royal cousin, various equerries, ladies-in-waiting and detectives in morning dress like the rest. Seated behind royalty were the Prime Minister and her husband, her bodyguard, and several other ministers and wives, notably from the Exchequer, Trade and Industry, Energy, and Food (including Agriculture and Fisheries); and just behind members of the present Government, the Leader of Her Majesty's Opposition (who, like Jamie, denied the existence of God) and selected members of his 'shadow cabinet'. Then certain senior Civil Servants . . .

But the verger turned to his right, inclined his head and tilted his silver verge (topped with a wrought acorn) to the figure in the seat nearest the aisle, who rose and stepped from his place. This was Sir James Mainwaring in the scarlet gown of an Alderman of the City of London, with his baronet's badge on its neck ribbon and his several decorations. The entire pew from which he had stepped was occupied by his fellow Aldermen in scarlet gowns plus the City Marshal. These gentlemen's wives, who included Jane Mainwaring, occupied the row behind.

Jumbo processed behind the splay-footed verger to the foot of the lectern steps, where the verger inclined his head once more and left the reader to mount the seven steps alone to the great bible upon its brazen eagle as vast as the living bird.

Jumbo glanced briefly over the top of his glasses at the sea of royalty and politicians and servants of the Crown, and City Aldermen and members of the Confederation of British Industry, the governors of Banks, chairmen of corporations, Presidents of Chambers of Commerce, guildmasters, major contractors and business dignitaries from every part of the land, each with their lady wives, assembled for this Service of Thanksgiving and Intercession for Industry and Commerce. A good deal of pleasure and pride had been engendered among most of those chosen to participate in this worship, not least the wives and especially those who (at the cost of some invidiousness among those omitted) were selected for invitation by a somewhat narrow margin. Not one of the two thousand or so present, being reminded of the name by their printed service sheets, would have been unaware that the previous week the son of Sir James Mainwaring had been sent to prison for some offence connected with drugs; for they, like the inmates of Her Majesty's Prison, Wandsworth, read their newspapers. Those who knew Sir James personally, and whose eyesight was good enough at that distance, might say that he had aged.

'Here beginneth,' Jumbo said, his voice carrying by means of the system of amplifiers switched
on today for one hundred per cent coverage of the
cathedral, 'the tenth verse of the third chapter of the
first epistle of St Paul to the Corinthians.'

In this passage St Paul was making use of the idea
of building and workmanship to illustrate how the
gospel of Christ should be assiduously spread. For
those members of the congregation who were actually listening to the passage it could have relevance in
the context of the act of worship only if the apostle's
intention was reversed, and if what he really meant
to do was use the gospel of Christ to illustrate how
manufacturing and building industries could be
most assiduously developed. Such attentive ones
were therefore left in a mental fog. Jumbo, though
reading with apparent conviction, was one of these;
and his concentration was ever so slightly ruffled by
realizing, too late, that since the translation he was
reading from was The New English Bible he should
not have said 'beginneth' but 'begins'. He did like to
get things exactly right.

Most of the congregation, however, were not really
listening and received the impression that something
there in holy writ was saying that the doing of business et cetera was in some obscure way holy; and this
was gratifying.

This impression was, happily, to receive an
appropriately up-to-date endorsement. After various further canticles, intoned prayers (including for

our Sovereign Lady, Queen Elizabeth, right there where they could check that she was indeed okay), responses, and rolling hymns, the Archbishop himself climbed into the high pulpit, and after removing his mitre and invoking the name of the Father, the Son, and the Holy Ghost, waded in directly in his rather penetrating, sharp-edged, nasal voice:

'We are called to this great place of worship today – the heart of our capital city, which above all others exemplifies the gift of human enterprise – to seek God's blessing on British Industry Year.

'The divine resonance in the concept of human industry was surely there at the start of our era in the sound of mallet and chisel in that very carpenter's workshop on which Our Saviour's earthly life was centred as a child . . .'

The collective sense of gratification was in no way dimmed by such an opening, and the congregation gazed up at their eminent preacher in the virtual certainty, given the loftiness of his office and the height of the dome above him, that he could not be wrong. To hold him in view those in the forward pews immediately below the pulpit, such as jumbo and his fellow aldermen, had to strain upwards, which here and there had the effect of parting the lips or even jaws, as if to absorb these truths not only by the ears but by the mouth also.

St Paul's was indeed sited in London's heartland and could reasonably be counted as being within the boundaries of what is popularly known as the Square

Mile. Despite the current popularity of the concept of the 'workshop', however, the Square Mile contained nothing in any way approximating to the carpenter's workshop in Nazareth at the beginning of 'our era'. No working area could, perhaps, be devised in more vivid contrast to Joseph's family joinery than the dealing room of Grimston and Pilbeam, traders in commodity futures – one of the most distinguished in that industry – of Four Quays, lower Hill, EC2, less than a thousand yards east of the dome of St Paul's. Here Rowley, a partner in the business and one of its most successful executives, was earning his living. He operated both as a trader or broker on behalf of outside clients, and separately, on his own account. At the moment he was engaged in the latter, using the services of a junior trader, a fellow not much older than Jamie, behind whose swivel chair he was standing.

Trading in commodity futures is a knife-edge operation. Those with a taste for it, and the skills, can see their fortunes expanding, or diminishing, by tens of thousands of pounds, or – among the bigger fry – hundreds of thousands, within a matter of minutes. Rowley would not yet count himself among the big fry, but he was not far from that category. His specialities were sugar and cocoa, though sometimes he dropped into currencies pure and simple. Today it was sugar.

From time to time Rowley's junior trader half swivelled round to glance up at him interrogatively, inviting his order to sell. Rowley's eyes held to the little green figures illuminated on the computer screen immediately in front of where the trader sat. The entire room was comprised of rows of such computer screens, each of which was manned by young traders who, with a telephone to the ear, were simultaneously in contact with both client and the Market 'floor' at Commodity Quay along the way. On this occasion Rowley's trader was of course receiving his instructions direct, as the market moved on his screen. To him, Rowley was something of a hero: an example, anyway – so very cool, damn well turned out, with one or two semilegendary coups behind him, and patently still on top of the game.

Rowley, however, was holding back, not selling yet, relishing the gamble, watching the price continue to edge upwards. They had come in at 173.8 (dollars per tonne). It had climbed quickly to 179, then broke the 180 barrier. Now it was 181.9 . . . and hovering. Rowley's eyes, slimming a little, made no other sign.

Then the figures began to fall back in rapid steps to 176.2.

The young trader frowned. He said, 'It's crapping out.'

'Stay in.'

Rowley was watching the screen with an intensity in his face akin to, in appearance, that of a man of religious fervour in the midst of supplicatory prayer. The wordless supplication in this instance was of course that the price which fellow commodity gamblers all over the world estimated as the possible price of sugar per tonne in six months' time would turn upwards. Whether or not by the exercise of prayer, it did. With nervous swiftness it rose in steps to touch 189.

'Sell!'

It was spoken quietly, however decisively.

'Sell twenty lots September at 189 or better,' the youthful trader instantly instructed the 'floor' on his telephone, simultaneously entering the sale on his transaction form. He gave a deep nod — a nod of gratification – towards the screen before turning to Rowley to signal congratulation. Oh, this Rowley had nerve all right; a manly nerve; and an extraordinary instinct for anticipating the global community's instinct. His hero's well cared-for hand was already moving to the pocket calculator on his trader's desk to tot up the profit thus secured.

Rowley now glanced at his clock on the far wall, one of the six which gave the time in Tokyo, Hong Kong, Frankfurt/Paris, London, New York and Los Angeles. The service, he calculated, would not be over for another twenty-five minutes, and it would take a few minutes more for the Royals and the PM and so on to get out of the place and into their official cars.

As it was, the sermon, though quite brief and compactly written by one of the faceless and worthy exponents of tact and the felicitous phrase employed by the Archbishop to write his texts, was still in train. 'What Britain makes,' he was saying, 'makes Britain.' Neatly turned, his attentive congregation silently acknowledged.

'Our wellbeing as a nation depends upon the achievements of our industry. Like Bunyan's Christian on his journey to the Celestial City, we cannot turn back. Thus it is that this Service of Thanksgiving and Intercession for Industry and Commerce is a declaration of the moral and spiritual heart of our enterprise as a people.'

What more could they ask for? The swell and roar of the mighty organ's Voluntary in D by Hubert Parry was still audible to the several hundred members of the congregation even after they had welled out into the open space outside St Paul's great west doors. Her Majesty and the Prime Minister had already been borne away before a clutch of onlookers across Ludgate Hill. A number of chauffeured limousines had now clustered along the curved pavement's edge to gather up their VIPs and their ladies.

Jumbo, amid the mill of folk, many of whom were known to him, held himself bland and courteous. There was a detectable isolation to him. He seldom pursued a greeting beyond the acknowledgement. And to Jane, beside him, dignified in dress and comportment and beautiful in the cut of her face and depth of eye, a guardianship of him might have been ascribed.

'Ow-dee, Sir James.'

'Good morning to you, Scrimgeour.'

The Mainwarings might have bargained for the presence here of Albert Scrimgeour MP, Opposition spokesperson on Industry. Neither of them had seen him since the banquet in the Guildhall a good eighteen months or more previously.

Jumbo made to press ahead, looking out for his car.

'Did you find a buyer, then? For that site?' (Jumbo pushed on.) '"Our" site, one could say.'

Scrimgeour was impossible to ignore: Jumbo reluctantly turned.

'Which do you refer to?'

'The Mainwaring Bolt Company.'

Scrimgeour's accent was such as to suggest that if ever he set foot outside the Bradford constituency he represented in Parliament he did so under duress.

'Nothing that I would call a serious bid,' Jumbo told him.

'Soom of the men 'ave been discussing a co-operative. You'll know that.'

'Good luck to them.'

Jumbo had become visibly distant.

'By the bye, I was oopset to 'ear about your lad.'

'Thank you, Scrimgeour.'

'Life 'as its oops and downs.'

Jumbo gave him a courteous smile. What eyebrows the fellow had cultivated. Was it for the sake of cartoonists? He was just beginning to become known nationally. Jumbo pushed on through the mill of people to escape him . . . Suddenly he found himself wondering if he was being unfair to Scrimgeour. It struck him that Scrimgeour had only accosted him and put that question about selling the Bolt Company site so that he could express his sympathy about Jamie. And why should he have inwardly taken exception to Scrimgeour referring to it as 'our' site? It was 'their' site: it was Scrimgeour's home town, he would have grown up among many of the men who were out of work. It was . . . it was Scrimgeour's and his supporters' site just as much as Jumbo's, or Mainwarings'. By the same token Scrimgeour might have been truly sad for him on account of Jamie, not crowing at all.

Jumbo wanted to turn back through the throng and find him, take him by the hands and thank him. But it was too late now. He and Jane had been borne on among the flow of people towards the edge of the pavement; and Jane had now seen Rowley's Porsche drawing up.

Among all the other sedate saloons, Rowley's car did seem to Jumbo incongruously low and sportive with its horizontal fin out the back of it like a surfboard. A voice within him said it was a mistake to have taken up Rowley's proposal that he pick them up after the service to go on to their luncheon engagement. But it was a small voice. As he stood aside to let Jane clamber into the back seat (the Porsche only having two doors), the bigger voice told him it was of no account what sort of motorcar picked them up after the service. Even the service itself might be of no account. What was of account? His son was of account. Something had been not right about the service: all that fine music, all that panoply and assembled devotion – it had not reached him. It was more than the misplaced 'beginneth'; it was deeper than that. He could find no place for Jamie there: that was it.

When Jumbo had threaded himself into the front seat, Rowley gave him a light, supportive pat on the knee. He wasn't sure he really appreciated the gesture – but that was of no account either.

CHAPTER TWENTY-THREE

On each double landing of three out of the five spider wings of Wandsworth Prison, two of the cells were built to contain four inmates, instead of the usual one-man cells. In practice, because the prison was overcrowded, most of the one-man cells contained two, and the four-man cells often contained five. The Wing Officers generally selected for the 'four-up' cells bodies (as they termed the inmates) from among those least likely to cause trouble, especially collective trouble; but they would not move a man into a communal cell against his will. Jamie had no objection when he was moved into such a cell – first on the second landing (the ground level), and later, after a few weeks, when his knees were fast improving and he no longer required his crutches, on the fourth, or top, landing. The disadvantages of the communal cell, as he saw it, were in the virtually certain racket of one, or more than one, of his cellmates' radios and the all-but-total elimination of privacy. The advantage was a greater space to move about in and a wider variety of men to get to know and, possibly, befriend.

Comradeships in prisons, he had been quick to learn, could be dangerous, leading a man willy-nilly into factional hostilities he had no control over, or into obligations to break regulations (such as the circulation of drugs) which, if discovered, could mean a knock-back of weeks or months or at best a spell in solitary 'down the block' – which is to say, the punishment cells. On the other hand, to be quite friendless was a liability. Extortion by means of threats or actual violence was commonplace, mostly in connection with tobacco, which was consumed by everybody and was replenished weekly by the 117 pence canteen allowance. Tobacco was thus established as a kind of currency among them. Not infrequently a wing had its convict 'baron' who by long, recurring experience of prison and by the assertion of his own style of power through physical strength, arrogance, and intimate knowledge of the system drew to him his toadies, exacted his tribute, and exercised a sway which often extended to the warders themselves. Such a baron, on B wing, was 'Spike' Evans, now in the fourth year of his current bird, to whom the opportunities to exercise power through bodily intimidation, which constituted life's profoundest satisfaction, were greater inside prison than outside.

A few friendships, therefore, however fleeting, provided a measure of insurance against victimization. A few friendships, however fleeting, however

fragmentary, hung tiny bridges across the nothing-
ness of time and let drops fall into the loneliness.
For Jamie also, as indeed for any other whose heart
was not yet stone, there might be found a friend
for no other motive than that he was a friend.
Jamie had about a year to serve, given the statutory
remission on sentence and the subtraction of time
spent in custody awaiting trial. He would not be
out until early the following calendar year, and that
was subject, of course, to the loss of remission for
any misdemeanour occurring during the imprison-
ment. Any captive swiftly discovers the intolerabil-
ity of allowing the mind to focus on the prospect
of release. The world beyond the prison wall is
another world. There is a time for freedom, and a
time for captivity.

A year or so to a free man can seem a fleeting eva-
nescence; but to a man inside, a period not in itself
contemplatable, least of all a man whose life had so
far comprised a mere twenty other years. From no cell
window at Wandsworth was it possible to look beyond
the prison walls, save only to the sky. It was best that
way, Jamie knew. When an early cellmate, discussing
the dutiful but vain attempts of the prison chaplain
to 'humanize', however marginally, the atmosphere
of the place, referred to the decorated Christmas tree
seasonally placed at the centre point of the spider-
wings as 'a wind-up', Jamie did not need to ask the
man what he meant. You close off the options, or you
do not keep your mind. You settle into prison life:

that is the requirement; and for Jamie – he could perceive this quite clearly – he would not match the outer bars with inner ones any more than he had to, even though many a sad man did.

So he accepted transference to a communal cell sanguinely. There would be several cell companions, because of the turnover of men from time to time, and the purely thuggish would probably be excluded. Most of his new cellmates proved to have been convicted of offences, like himself, connected to drugs, often with bizarre complications but not involving the extended criminality of drug racketeering.

Thus 'banged up' (as prison jargon describes the act of locking in) together with those with the drug habit – albeit Jamie himself had no such habit – it was not long before he made an unexpeced discovery. On Landing One, the basement level, was the man whom Jamie had personally captured some two years previously after his attempt to enter his parents' flat in Eaton Square. The suspicion that it was he struck Jamie when he first saw him in the exercise yard: the stubby, over-fleshed figure, short in the legs, with a wary geniality, habitually a little short of breath. When Jamie privately established from his name, Raymond Green, that he was the same man, he realized he must be back inside serving a new sentence, since the sixth months' 'bird' for the Mainwaring flat offence would have been completed long ago. Now what should Jamie do about this?

His immediate instinct was to do nothing – keep quiet and hope not to be recognized: they were, after all, separated by three landings, and it might well be that the fellow was soon due for release. He was just coming to regard this as cowardly, though still at a loss as to what to do, when the matter was taken out of his hands. Passing by the man in the exercise yard three or four afternoons after the dicovery of his identity, Jamie heard him mutter,

'I know you.'

'I know you.'

After a split second of alarm, Jamie found himself relieved. He smiled. Ray Green returned a quick grin.

'One 23,' Ray said.

'Four 18.'

'Four-up?'

'Yes.'

Ray Green knew his Wandsworth geography.

The next day they walked round the exercise yard (forty-five minutes) together. A week or so later, Ray said, "Ow about I join you?'

'On the Fours?'

'Yeah.'

'There's no space.'

'Leave itta me. Okay?'

'Okay,' said Jamie.

'Leave itta me.'

When the first vacancy occurred in Four 18, 493822 Green R moved in.

Part of the wall of Four 18 was hung with a hand-lettered poster, in several colours. It was more of a dramatically displayed diagram than a poster, and the letters proved to be a collage of cut-outs, razored from sheets of paper of various colours, rather than painted on to the poster direct. It was stuck up in a central position for all occupants of the cell to mark and comprehend. Its words were laid out so as to form the approximate shape of the Christian cross (like that on the dome of St Paul's for example). The uppermost vertical of the cross was written in black capitals. This section comprised the words LION and SEED. The transom of the cross, in red, carried the words ZION FOR 1. the lower shaft of the cross comprised the actual words describing the very colour of which each word was formed, namely BLUE, GREEN, and SILVER. At the foot of the cross appeared a heart, cut out in black, and beneath that, also in black, the words BLACK MAN.

The black man who had created this cabbalistic masterpiece left off pressing the bell alongside the door of his cell declaring,

'Ah don' wait for these bastards. Man, Ah don'.'

He was attired in shirt and socks only – that and his dreadlocks which reached his shoulders. At the corner washstand he now poured a little water from his jug into his basin. He carried the basin over to his bedspace, pulled a grey blanket off his bed, put it over his head like a tent, and taking off the lid squatted down on the plastic bucket to relieve his stricken bowels.

The noise of the brief explosive evacuation was not much muffled by the sound of the reggae from the transistor beside him on his chair.

On the other wall above his bed several coloured snapshots adhered to the wall. These showed a black girl of about nine in a white party frock, with white shoes and socks, and a white bow in her hair whose tight crinkles had been unfurled to make it stand out as far as possible from her little skull. Another snap was of a black manikin of about six in a made-to-measure suit complete. Another was of the two children with a big black woman with a gleaming skin and magnificient teeth. It seemed a shame that a family otherwise so healthy and happy should be deprived of its father, who must surely be devoted to them.

Further along the same wall was a snapshot of a white girl on a large horse. This was Tibby and the horse was her mother's mare, Bundle of Joy. Below this snap, Jamie, on his bed, propped himself on one elbow and reached for his tobacco tin. It was almost empty. With the remaining fragments he rolled a very thin cigarette. Then he took one of the three matches in his possession, and with a needle divided it skillfully into four. This quarter-match he struck on his match-box with his forefinger-and thumb-nail right against its head, and lit up.

There was a rattle of a key in the lock outside. The door swung open, and Jamie, reaching for his plastic mug, made to stand. But, from the other bed in the cell, Ray intervened.

'Allow me, James.'

Ray went to the door with his mug and Jamie's, to be poured a cup of tea from the tea-jerry carried by a white-jacketed con. This inmate was accompanied on the landing by two uniformed warders. Behind Ray was Joe, the fourth occupant of the cell, also with a mug in each hand.

From beneath the tented blanket the voice of the black man with dreadlocks was heard calling.

'Don' you never answer no bell? Ah been pressin' that bell twenty-five minutes. Mah bowels in deep trouble, man.'

This protest to the 'screws' beyond the door was, however, wasted. Ray was returning to Jamie with his mug of heavily sugared, weak, lukewarm tea.

'I want 'em to see us, lovin' one another,' Ray explained in a halfwhisper. Jamie took the mug. They expect us to be tearing each other limb from limb – don't you officer?' Ray added out loud, turning to the warder who had put his head round the door to make the count.

This too was apparently wasted on the warder in question; yet not so, according to Ray. it bothers 'em,' said Ray. 'They can't fathom it. Ommmmm.'

Ray was an enthusiastic, if backsliding, Buddhist and thus a self-proclaimed exemplar of toleration.

He had made sure the entire wing knew of his and Jamie's original encounter, and took delight in their fellowship. Far from his capture by Jamie being a cause of resentment, it was counted a unique, even mystical, bond. It helped, no doubt, that Jamie was a fellow prisoner, but Jamie had a feeling that Ray might have insisted on the bond in whatever circumstances they met again. Jamie's ferocious and intimate grip on him after he had brought him down in the street with the rugger tackle endorsed it, especially when Jamie told him that this was the grip the ancient Hebrews used to swear an oath one to another and found the passage in Genesis 24 of The Good News Bible to prove it. (Jamie also remembered the intimacy of Ray's bodily smell, but he chose not to mention that.) Ray related to Jamie the terrible beating he had got at the instigation of Spike on the very first morning after entering Wandsworth on that bird. He had been carried off to hospital and still bore scars on his head from what they did. Since one of the warders had been involved in the original, probably deliberate misinformation that had provoked the beating, no one had been punished, apart from Spike and the two other cleaners spending three days 'down the block'. Nobody wanted an enquiry when that sort of provocation might come out, and for the victim it was too late anyway.

Ray had served two sentences since then, each one the result of a casual attempt at petty theft to feed his appetite for cannabis. So it had been for years now, ever since he left his 'funny school'. He told Jamie his story and in turn listened, absorbed, to Jamie's. When it came to Jamie turning down his place at Cambridge, Ray had approved gravely. He too had no time for Cambridge either – 'loads of Constable clouds covering up the sodding sun.' Jamie was surprised that Ray knew Cambridge: 'Constable' surprised him too — but he did the art class on Mondays. It turned out that Ray had spent six months in Stradishall gaol near Newmarket; so it was Cambridgeshire skies he knew.

And now he repeated, as he settled back at the table to his Scrabble game with Joe, 'You and me, Jamie, we have the screws worried.'

'Bastards,' said their Rastafarian cellmate at last emerging from under his blanket. 'Scum of the earth!'

The Rasta washed his hand in his basin and tipped the water into the plastic bucket, replacing the lid.

Joe said, 'You are totally wrong, Rasta. We are the scum' – scorn, in his musical Irish – 'we are the scorn of the earth. They are the chosen of God – God's elect, I mean – to whom all the benefits of creation shall ac – what's the word I'm lookin' for, Jamie?'

'Crap,' said the Rasta.

'Accrue,' Jamie told him, but this answer was unheard as Joe retorted to the Rasta, 'Don't crap me.' Then to Jamie: 'What's that again?'

'Accrue.'

Joe was in his mid-thirties, a small man with curly hair cropped short and a saintlike face. He was an Irish tinker by stock. He said,

'How're you spellin' that, now?'

Jamie spelt Accrue.

Joe picked up his pencil and began laboriously to add the word to a list he had been compiling.

Ray said, it's still your fuckin' turn, Joe.'

Suddenly the Rasta was standing over Joe with eyes blazing. He had a razor-blade in his fingers a mere six inches from Joe's throat. Joe raised his neck in ready sacrifice.

'I am not scum!' fumed the black man.

Joe kept his chin up and his throat exposed.i do not retaliate!' he declared. 'Didn't I swear it? I shall not hit 'im! I shall not even kick 'im! Mind you —'

'I am not scum!'

'Well,' Joe said, 'that's a question we must discuss. I was —'

'Fuckin' shut up, Joe,' Ray told him. 'Calm down, Rasta. Give it to Uncle Raymond.' He held out his hand. 'Joe's just got you your tea.'

The Rasta appeared unmoved.

'Say I am not scum.'

Ray said, 'Course you're not scum, Rasta. You're a man of God. That's obvious. C'mon, give it to me.'

At last the Rasta lowered his hand.

'R-E-U,' Joe said as he completed his pencil-work.

'R-U-E,' Jamie corrected.

Joe said, 'At any rate, I am scum.'

As Ray told Joe once more to fuckin' keep off it, Jamie was saying, 'Rasta, I want you to explain that chart. I want to learn.'

Jamie had got to his feet.

'What chart, man?'

Jamie indicated the cross-shaped diagram.

'That's an altar, man.'

'Altar then.'

The Rasta had been distracted; yet Joe was off again, 'What put me back in here?' (Joe will talk himself to death one day, Jamie thought.) indecent assault on a woman aged sixty-three and burglary and bein' high on dope all in one. An' 1 have terrible thoughts. Terrible tormentin' thoughts. That's scom. Which of us is better than that? Let him throw the first stone.'

'Make a fuckin' word, Joe,' Ray urged him.

'There's no such word as the only one that I can make,' Joe insisted irishly.

'Show me your letters.'

'Certainly not. I'll show them to James. He'll decide. Here, James.'

But Jamie was deep in conversation with the Rasta about the poster-diagram.

'Lion?' he was saying.

'Lion of Judah, man.'

'And seed?'

'Seed of David.'

'Ah,' said Jamie, the etymology dawning on him. 'Ras-tafari. Head of David's line. Descendant of the Queen of Sheba and King David.'

'Right, man.' The Rasta was mollified.

'And "Zion for I"?' Jamie continued, reading the cross-beam.

'Zion for I,' the Rasta said, supposedly in explanation.

'Zion for I?'

'Right, man.'

Jamie remained puzzled.

'Zion for I,' said the Rasta, opening his fingers against his own chest.

'Ah – for you. Paradise for you!'

Joe was impatiently pulling at Jamie to attend to his Scrabble letters.

'Look, that's the word I want, an' who's to say it doesn't exist if I put it down? You can't let words diminish you.'

Jamie reordered Joe's letters. 'Try that,' he said, pointing to the board to show where the word fitted, but only to find that he had released in Joe a stream of philosophical reminiscences.

'What is right and what is wrong is not to be decoded from outside. You know that, James.'

Nonetheless, Jamie personally set out a word for Joe on the board, so that at last Ray could proceed with his turn.

'I knew that as a fact from my earliest days as an infant child,' Joe continued without a pause, I'll tell you where it was, James. I was in St Joseph's Orphanage in Killarney about three years of age and little Joseph Griffin, he and Paddy Hanrahan were my friends. Now Joe Griffin, he was one year older than me. He wore calipers on one leg, and this nun' – non – 'was forcin' him to sit on the pot, like, but on account of his stiff leg he couldn't get down on it proper: it was too low. The pot was slippin' around all over the place and this non was beltin' him mercilessly with the leather that hung from her waist. She black-an'-blued him. From that time on I could not surrender to moulding from outside – it was impossible. You know what I mean, James?'

'James is not interested,' Ray said. 'Are you, James? It's your turn again.'

But Joe had seen the interest in Jamie's eyes.

'That was exactly when I became a criminal,' Joe resumed at once. 'I saw through that non as if she was a ghost. She was drunk, like, with sadism. The other boys were standin' around with their hands in their mouths. There was some sort of line – know what I mean? I came out to the front -1 didn't do anything: I just stared. She was in a trance.

'I pitied her. I actually saw her wakin' up. Of course, we all had a fuckin' Hail Mary after it, as a formal punishment for bein' there at all, for havin' excited her into all that strappin' and hittin'. "Kneel down. 'Hail Mary, full of grace . .

For Joe McNally the business of writing was fraught with anxiety (he had never mastered the distinction between capital letters and small letters.) But with the spoken word he was Eden-free and profligate. And he collected new words like a jewel-thief.

It was Joe who, in time, grew closest to Jamie. Joe would weave his stories and his 'philosophy' around Jamie and himself together in a web of miraculous intricacy. It was not a web of fantasy. It was a world, an existence, of its own, but no less real, no less vivid, Jamie realized, than the world of any other man.

CHAPTER TWENTY-FOUR

T hey came to see Jamie in prison just as one would expect. Like everyone else he was allowed one visit a month, by one person, unless it were parents in which case both could come together, or children, in which case a wife was permitted to bring up to two. The inmates had to fill out the Visitor's Order which was initialled by an Assistant Governor and mailed to the prospective visitor or visitors. Visits could take place on any afternoon except Sundays between three and four. One hour was the theoretical maximum. Three-quarters of an hour was the actual maximum allowing for the time taken for visitors to be checked in and out of the prison, and the inmates to be brought under escort to the Visiting Room.

Jumbo and Jane came together the first time. They found the circumstances so strange, not to say shocking and even intimidating, and Jamie so remote and uncommunicative, although seemingly not deliberately so, that little passed between them. Jamie had receded into shadow: they could not make him out with any precision. Each in their own way, they had become acquainted with the blurring of the identity of their son over recent months – ever since his return from Africa. Maybe it had begun long before that, with the intrusion of puberty. But then the precision was always to hand, that etched image of him who had been theirs since infancy . . . for Jane, since birth itself. That etching had constantly been reworked, but the instinctual precision that derived from the blood and from the intimacy of the family was always there. Even when the blurring crept in, the precision was surely recoverable, in any of the myriad contexts of their common life: the Jamie they knew, severally and separately, as only a mother or a father can know her and his own offspring. Neither had doubted that precision to be recoverable, given the favour of certain circumstances, during the period of his remand right up to his conviction. Yet now he seemed to them in such deep shadow each was unsure of it, for the first time in their lives.

Jamie himself was aware of this. To render the 'son they knew' recoverable by them had appeared to him as a temptation to which he could have yielded. This temptation had come upon him most sharply when he was lying in the hospital bed, under guard and on remand at Wakefield, after the battery on his knees. There were moments when he supposed that he had surrendered: that when his mother next visited him, with her hand touching his on the lip of the taut white bedclothes, his eyes would meet hers and grow round, and thus drowning his plea would be

given utterance, 'Get me out of this. Get me out of
this and take me back.' For he had already recalled
that at the instant of the shattering of his kneecaps,
somewhere amid the infinitely searing cacophony
of his mind was a sight of those same mother's eyes
above him in piteous alarm as when, six years old,
hurtling down the tilted stable yard at Upton, he had
come a cropper and torn open his knees in the loose
gravel. Yet when she actually came to him in hospital, the temptation seemed to have receded. And it
was not because of the presence of the prison warder
more or less within earshot on the other side of the
bedspace reading his comic books. It was for some
cause that was positive, not negative. There was that
which he required more strongly than rescue: not
rescue, but discovery . . . though discovery of what he
could not have told, and could not still tell.

Indeed, there could be no discovery yet. But if it
were ever to occur it would only be by way of this dissolution, this blurring, this retreat into deep shadow
that he himself could not have penetrated from without, that is to say from that position upon the stage of
life that he had occupied until now as Jamie-son and
Jamie-boy-becoming-man. He would not now step out
of that shadow to regale his folk with stories of prison
life, as if he were one of them looking in upon himself
through the bars: not possibly as he had spoken after
his capture of the would-be intruder into their flat. If
he spoke to them of his fellow prisoners it was in fragments vouchsafed of what they could not comprehend,

nor had any right to comprehend. He had gathered up nothing for their visit. He would not reassert his 'old' identity for them. He knew himself to be husked. He would not reintroduce the former grain in facsimile. If grain were in course of time to enter the husk that he had become, it would be new grain. There was a time for freedom and a time for captivity; there was a time for grain and a time for husk.

Perception of this came upon him fleetingly in those very first weeks of his sentence. What surprisingly triggered it was an event of apparent inconsequentiality – the departure of an elderly convict in an adjacent cell. This man, Jerry, in his late fifties, had been in and out of prison constantly for over thirty years. He was a fully qualified member of the underworld, and proud of it; he scorned that majority of misérables who were there not because they had taken calculated risks (some won, some lost) but because they could not handle their lives, and he was outraged by the nonces (who brought the entire criminal profession into disrepute). Outside he had a home, a wife, two sons and a daughter. Both his sons, Terence John, and Francis Edward, twenty-one and twenty respectively (the daughter was only thirteen) were already initiated into many of the skills and dodges of the family business, namely stealing from and securing the market for the produce of every sort of factory.

Yet it was obvious to Jamie that, for Jerry, life in prison generated a validity of its own – a validity different from, but no less than, life outside. Prison was demonstrably a norm of existence: he had spent at least as many of his adult years inside as out. He was a remarkably spruce, energetic and well-ordered man, and his gait along the concrete walkways brisk and erect. He had the whole place taped. He played the system with unerring deftness, the exercise of which he relished. He could precisely gauge the strengths and weaknesses of the warders and the relationship among themselves and between them and the prison's management at 'governor level'. Despite long hours of confinement his daily life was filled with activity, extracting privileges, entering complaints, dishing out advice and, where appropriate, warnings, drafting appeals for Parole, and so on. From the depths of the hat which virtually everyone else was quite certain must be empty, jerry unfailingly produced his kicking rabbit.

When Jerry disappeared off the wing unexpectedly to enter hospital (for tests, prior to his donation of one of his kidneys to a cousin in dialysis whom he had met only twice in the past ten years) Jamie experienced a sharp sensation of loss. He and Jerry had formed no discernible comradeship. But at the old lag's sudden departure Jamie at once perceived the source of balm that this man had unwittingly represented: balm to the deprivation in Jamie of the very premise on which, despite all, his faith in life had rested up to the point of his crippling, framing, arrest, conviction and incarceration.

Up to that point – and it was, in its effect, all one, and came to be seen by Jamie as the split second of the first hammer-blow to his knee, since that was the symbolic snatching away of the efficiency and overt purpose of his body – up to that point the premise of his 'faith in life' had remained in its essence intact. His will to engage in the business of life, his right to hope, his zest, his conviction, even his sorrow and his mercy, were premised upon his power to act wherever his will directed him. He might fail or falter; his will might weaken; yet it was there for the summoning and permitted him all those rights. Such will had carried him to Bradford, and there, futilely or not, he would intervene, de haut en bas, out of the eminence of his personal will into the base of a mute inchoate destiny. He saw all that now: he saw beyond what he supposed his parents could see, and beyond what he wished them to see. Here he could intervene not at all, he could initiate nothing. He might react to whatever happened to him within the severe confinements of penitentiary life. But of what had borne him forward, as all Mainwarings were borne forward, there was now nothing. He could not be otherwise than nothing to them because he had become nothing to himself. The meaning of the parable he had glimpsed in his sense of loss at the departure of old Jerry was that in that nothing some quite other premise might exist upon which as yet he had no hold. As yet it allowed no more than to suppose that the mere fact of life indeed contained the sacredness which, out of the midst of its horrific amorality, had flashed upon him so vividly in the split-second of his threatened extinction.

The month after that first barren visit there was an all-too-common confusion over the Visitor's Order. Jamie had addressed it to Anthony, but Anthony's choral duties at St John's made it impossible for him to come, and by the time he had returned the VO for reissue its validity had expired. The next month, Vicky came.

Vicky arrived in high 'Sloane' gear. The other visitors lined up outside the prison gates had almost all taken trouble with their appearance, being wives or sweethearts, or sometimes brothers or sisters or parents – all of them wishing to make as much as they could of their respectability, in the particular circumstances of their afternoon outing. Even so Vicky stood out. She wore a velvet jacket and a tartan skirt, in which green and black predominated. Under the jacket she had on a cashmere pullover, and beneath that a white blouse with a frilly collar. She carried a largish Gucci handbag and wore high-heeled shoes from Bromley's (just along Bond Street from Gucci's). She had not made any special effort: she was dressed perfectly normally for visiting anybody. The effort had been in finding the place in her A to Z.

Once she was through the postern gate (which was let into the massive, studded, arched doors), her

Gucci bag was most thoroughly searched. In fact, it was turned upside down and the entire contents were spilled out on to the slab.

As soon as she had settled down at the vinyl-topped table in the Visiting Room she had her cigarettes out, and was for ever shifting her hair – which was blow-dried and cut, unwaved, to collar length – from one side to the other, either by tilting her head and shaking it or by running her fingers through it from her forehead.

'But you must be going absolutely insane,' she said. 'Twenty-three hours a day. With that lot.'

'Not an option, Vicky,' Jamie said.

'You know what I mean.'

'I'm not sure I do.'

'I mean, your blackamoor's radio going non-stop, and the Irishman telling you his life story. And the other one – who was he, you say?'

'Ray.'

Her voice did cut through rather – not like a knife exactly: but Jamie did notice some of the other pairs of visitors and inmates from two or three tables away occasionally looking round to see who it was speaking. And one of the screws over where the tea or confectionery could be bought seemed amused by something.

'Who was he, you say?'

'Ray,' Jamie reminded her.

'That's right. That's wacky. That's too unbelievable!' She was feeling for her Rothmans again, found them, and selected one. 'I mean, the *same man*! It's amazing.'

'He asked to join my cell.'

She remembered Jamie and offered him a cigarette, which he took.

'I mean, what can you think about all day?'

'Them mostly.'

Jamie's hand trembled slightly as he lit his sister's cigarette. He was irritated by that trembling: a sort of betrayal by the body. He did not want her to suppose he was under strain, for that was not the case.

'But they must be the absolute dregs,' Vicky said. 'What are they in for? I mean, we know about the one who raided Mummy's and Daddy's flat, but the others?'

'Much the same as me. Mostly.'

'What do you mean?'

'Drugs, or drugs-related offences. Joe's doing time for indecent assault as well. There's some sort of firearms conviction against Ray, but that could be the Old Bill fitting him up. They're the salt of the earth.'

Vicky was momentarily shocked. 'Oh, come on, Jamie!' But he must be joking. She looked at him more closely. Now she was shocked. 'Oh my God, you do mean it!'

They were naturally waiting for Vicky to report. The two siblings together.

It was spring at Upton already, and the croquet hoops were out again with the daffodils on the lawn below the south face of the manor, whose Virginia creeper shone with virid density in May sunlight. Her mother and Tibby and Mrs Hoskyns were there to hear, though croquet, and later tea, were the given pretext.

'I do think he could be going potty,' Vicky said, as Jane Mainwaring completed her shot.

Mrs Hoskyns, whose turn it was, had this to say. it must be a dreadful ordeal. I've often thought Jamie to be much more sensitive than he's ever let on.'

Vicky said, 'He's got this enormous black man with him, with dreadlocks, who seems to spend most of his time at night doing you know what.'

'What?' said Tibby.

'It keeps Jamie awake.'

It was Vicky's turn again already. How could she concentrate?

'He said he spends most of his time thinking about his cellmates. One's an Irish tinker – Joe something. He's the one he talked about.' She struck the ball and missed with it. 'There! What d'you expect?' She went on, 'One sounds out of his tree – a Buddhist. That's the one who broke into your flat, Mummy. Or nearly. Jamie says they're great friends.' She shook her head, 'I mean, it's what I said. It is the strangest.'

Jane Mainwaring said, 'Tibby – has he written to you? If you don't mind my asking.'

'Once.' Tibby seemed confused and tight-faced.

'He must be writing to somebody.'

'Why should he?' Tibby demanded unexpectedly.

A slight frown had crossed Jane's face.

'Ella,' she said, turning to Mrs Hoskyns, 'would you ever allow Tibby to visit him, if he sent her one of those Visitor's Orders?'

Tibby's mama seemed a little dubious.

'If we felt it'd do any good. I wouldn't stand in her way. Provided of course she was prepared to.'

It was three, separated, jerky little statements. But they were all three looking at Tibby, in the sun which kept disappearing.

'Only if he really wanted me to,' Tibby said.

Then there was a silence. Each knew that none of them knew what Jamie might really want. None wished to say so, least of all as far as Tibby was concerned.

Jane spoke first.

'He could be just sparing your feelings, Tibby dear. It isn't a nice place, not at all. It's not easy to' – she groped for her word – 'communicate, you know. On a visit like that. I mean, his father – it's a funny thing to say – he feels he can't reach him at all.' She had turned to Mrs Hoskyns personally. 'Of course, he doesn't say anything, but Jumbo's at his wit's end. Jamie's never out of his mind.'

The whole game had faltered.

Vicky said, like a reprimand for parental stupidity, 'He's not inside forever, Mummy.'

'I'm quite aware, Vicky. But Daddy can't help seeing it as a sort of life sentence.'

'Oh Mummy,' Vicky said, protesting the idiocy of age. She turned to Tibby for solidarity, if you go, you better talk to me first.'

The Rasta's tendency to threaten violent solutions to his emotional crises, albeit never carried through, resulted in his being moved out of the communal cell. The actual pretext for the expulsion was when the prison officers, who 'spun' every cell on the wing for drugs, found the razor-blade.

His replacement was Billy-Boy. 743131 Burr W was slightly built, pale-skinned and vacant, with psoriasis and bad teeth. He was a child to look at, but was – as Jamie soon discovered – twenty-four, the youngest of four brothers and two sisters. It was difficult to visualize any imprisonable crimes that Billy-Boy might have committed. A measure of criminality, however, was in the family, like a communicable disease. All his brothers had done time for this or that and Billy, despite his patent inadequacy for the contest of life, had succeeded in not being left out. Yet none of them came to see him in prison. Now that he was inside he suffered grievously whenever in the course of communal prison life it became necessary to expose his skinny, puny, discoloured body.

Tormented by sexuality like the rest of them, Billy-Boy carried an additional torment, known only to himself: his poor body had never known a woman's in consenting union, and he had come to suppose that it never would.

He sat on his bed, staring into space. Stuck up on the wall behind him was a coloured picture of Padre Pio, of whom Billy-Boy was a devotee, Padre Pio having been all but rejected as being unworthy of the priesthood before revealing – much later – the stigmata of Christ and becoming a source of miracles. Ray was watching Billy-Boy from across the cell. At the table, where Jamie and Joe were engaged at Scrabble, Joe was hopelessly, yet furiously, searching for words that did not exist in a small dog-eared dictionary. All at once Ray said,

''Ere, Billy-Boy!' and Billy-Boy looked up. 'If you sit there one minute longer doing nothing, I'm telling you – you're goin' to do my fuckin' 'ead in. One minute longer.'

A pause ensued – a suspension of all activity.

'What will happen then?' Joe said.

'I won't be responsible for my actions,' said Ray.

Suddenly Billy leapt into action. He danced round the cell like a boxer, throwing out lethal straight lefts and straight rights into thin air, and a murderous expression clamped on his childish features.

Just as suddenly he stopped, turned to his three cellmates, and grinned inanely with his discoloured, retreating teeth, one of which was missing.

Jamie said, 'That was very good, Billy-Boy. You ought to do it more often.'

'He frightens us all to death, don' 'e?' said Ray. 'If you get your teeth fixed, Jamie'll get 'is girlfriend to write you letters. Won't you, Jamie?'

'You want to look nice, Billy-Boy, in case you get your parole interview,' Jamie told him.

Joe put in, 'Padre Pio didn't get the marks on his hands by sittin' on 'is bunk starin' into space. He was wrestlin' with God day and night, like, wasn't he, Ray?'

Ray, who had begun to sing 'Day and night, night and day', to the tune of 'Begin and Beguine', broke off his performance for an announcement. 'Billy-Boy,' he said, ''as got as much chance of gettin' parole as puttin' 'alf a pound of butter up a porcupine's bum with a red-'ot poker.'

Billy-Boy was not listening. His eyes had gone to the window; and they all saw.

''E's got a visitor,' said Ray.

Billy-Boy now needed no stimulus to action. He snatched a remnant of bread which was waiting ready on his own bed, and jumped to his feet.

'Careful – you'll frighten him,' Jamie cautioned.

Billy-Boy climbed on to the end of his bed to bring his head level with the window where a pigeon had settled on the outer sill beyond the bars. Ray remarked to the others, 'The only visitor that poor basket 'as 'ad in two years! Enough to make Padre Pio bleed all over.'

Joe asked, 'How are you spellin' that, James?'

'What?'

'You know. Those marks. Like Padro Pio's.'

'Stigmata,' said Jamie.

'Okay. But how're you spellin' 'em?'

'S-T-I-G-M-A-T-A.'

'It's no good,' said Joe, 'it's eight letters.'

'There's an S on the board,' Jamie suggested.

'I know that. But Oi've none of the other letters.'

Billy-Boy had got down from the window to fetch more bread. Ray asked him,

'How's Long John Silver?'

'She's hungry.'

'Oh, it's a she, is it? Since when? You short of female company? You can't change people's sex just to suit your fancy.'

Billy-Boy glared at Ray.

'She's better than that shark,' he retorted, referring to the close-up magazine photograph of some monster of the deep stuck up by Ray above his bed.

'It's not a shark. It's a whale-shark.'

'Why stick up a thing like that?'

'It's for the screws, stupid. It makes 'em wonder. Ha!'

But Billy-Boy was up on his own bed again, feeding the pigeon. They knew that particular pigeon: it was a frequent visitor. So far as Billy-Boy had been able to discover, it had only one foot. Sometimes he prayed to Padre Pio for it.

They all heard a key in the lock, and the cell door swung open instantly. Billy-Boy jumped down.

A warder had entered, backed up by another warder – that same porcine Wing Officer whose misinformation had provoked the assault on Ray. The first warder demanded,

'What've you got up there, Burr?'

'A pigeon,' Billy-Boy told him.

'Sir.'

'Sir,' repeated Billy-Boy.

'Fetch it down.'

Billy-Boy hesitated at this. Meanwhile the porcine warder had come right into the cell.

Jamie said, it's only a pigeon, officer.'

'Nobody asked you to speak,' the porcine warder told him.

'Fetch it down,' ordered the first screw.

'I wouldn't be able to get it through the bars, sir.' There was a note of panic in Billy-Boy's voice.

'Fetch it down, Burr.'

Ray, from behind the two warders, was making urgent pushing signals at Billy-Boy.

'I want that pigeon here, or you'll be on the report again for disobedience.'

Billy-Boy climbed back on to his bed with extreme reluctance. He slid a weedy arm through the bars. The pigeon appeared to trust him utterly. Very carefully he drew it between the bars into the cell, and descended with it, holding it tenderly in two sore-covered hands. The others had watched in incredulous dismay.

'Let's have it,' said the first warder.

Jamie said hurriedly, 'That bird is Burr's best friend.'

The porcine warder turned to Jamie instantly,

'I'm warning you. I'm not telling you again.'

The first warder took the pigeon quite gently. It was accustomed to the touch of human hands. He passed it to the porcine warder. Ray said,

'It's only got one leg, that pigeon. It's a collector's piece.'

With his fat hands the porcine warder wrung the pigeon's neck and threw it into the bin.

'Inmates are not permitted pets in the cells. Prison Regulations,' the first warder quoted, and the two of them turned to go.

Billy-Boy was standing motionless – pale and utterly motionless. As the cell door banged shut Jamie moved across and rested his hands on his shoulders.

The whiteness of Billy-Boy's face became mottled, his child's eyes wet, and his jaw drooped open in a silent scream.

He twisted away from Jamie, dropped to his knees, and began to beat the concrete floor with his knuckles beside the bin.

CHAPTER TWENTY-FIVE

P rison changes a man. There is the dismantling,
already observed; there is its corollary, the bringing of him so close to himself – if it is prison for the
first time, close as never before.

Jamie was perhaps already less a stranger to himself than many of his age and class. Yet there were
discoveries to be made, and endured; and if not
always to be made as such, to be confirmed. One
such was the infinite value of life, every human life.
He had first glimpsed that inexpressible value when
the Tuareg baby died in his arms in the hutment east
of Timbuktu. Perhaps already by then he had been
directed by such an awareness, and perhaps from that
moment it had entered him more deeply and had
carried him to Bradford and into Bradford's grievous
rebuff. By now he did know it to state it: this supreme
value of life, this utter, unchallengeable sacredness.

The nature of this knowledge was such that if it
applied to himself and those close to him, it must be
applied by him to all others. Yet he wondered if some
lives might have become irredeemable – like Rowley's,

say, or the brutalized Spike's on B1. It seemed to him that lives became irredeemable mostly on account of the sheer accretion of form – men and women (but men particularly) conducting themselves entirely (even in their privatest thoughts) according to what was expected of them, by class or status or education or training or uniform, like these screws. It was above all form that denied people redemption, that made them, in certain circumstances – many circumstances – utterly indifferent to, or oblivious of, the livingness of others: other groups, other classes, other races . . . It could make them utterly cruel, utterly unfeeling, utterly contemptuous. It was right here in the prison, of course. The mere donning of a uniform about the body of a human, a living man, made one man a screw and another a con. If a con died in a cell (as one did the other night) and the uniformed screws on duty had none the less fulfilled their duties as laid down, they needn't-and didn't-expend a moment's sorrow or concern. It occurred to Jamie that next day to ask himself, if the Wing Officer on duty that night had, by some odd chance, mislaid his uniform and come to work in ordinary clothes such as he might be wearing as a father or a husband, whether he might then have allowed himself to care when he found the man so ingeniously self-hanged?

Yet the screws, despite their role, were probably more readily redeemable than many others. So, even, Jamie supposed, was Spike. It was the established, the well-set-up, the secure, the powerful, the always healthy, that were least redeemable. Somebody had once remarked – was it old Rodney Jarvis? – that the truest wisdom belonged to cripples. Was this now turning out to be Jamie's own discovery? Was this conceivably what was meant by the odd bit in the bible about 'rich men' finding it harder to get into the kingdom of heaven than a camel through the eye of a needle – men 'rich' in form, in what they took themselves to be?

For Jamie had discovered who were the truly redeemable. He had the discovery rammed at him. The truly redeemable, those whose lives had been refined to all but utter purity, were those who had nothing, who had become irreducible as human creatures: these very people with whom he shared his life, now – Joe, Ray, Billy-Boy. Such as these. In them did life persist at its purest, its most sacred. The paradox of this came to burn in Jamie day and night with a quiet, perfect flame.

When his mother had remarked at Upton, for all of them, that Jamie must be writing to somebody, she was wrong. He had virtually stopped writing letters to anyone. Early on he had tried to tell Anthony something of his life in prison – what it comprised, what it might mean. But he found it difficult, and not only because he was restricted by regulations to four sides of (regulation) lined paper or because he knew that

everything he wrote was read by the prison's correspondence censor. It was also because of the difficulty
he found in relating what he was discovering to anything in Anthony's own experience, with which Jamie
was naturally well acquainted. And Anthony's dutiful
but usually rather mannered letters to him, crowded
with literary references, seemed to reinforce this barrier of experience. The correspondence quite soon
waned.

Tibby had had two or three brief, funny letters
from Jamie, and she wrote at least once a month
with all her doings. But by now – by the time Tibby's
Visitor's Order arrived in the late summer – Jamie
was virtually writing to no one.

Tibby did feel dreadfully shy and awkward. She
found the prison parking area for visitors and left her
own new Metro there, with several other cars, to walk
round the high wall to where the gates were. When the
front of the prison came in view it hit her, wump: a lowering mediaeval fortress of a frontage. She kept going,
clutching her fluttering white VO and wondering if
there was any place inside where she could have a pee.
There were other visitors – mostly women – closing in
on the postern gate let into the great studded doors,
and among these she stepped over the postern's ledge.
She heard the postern gate slam behind her with a
resounding bang; and from then on – through the various checkings and hangings about (always in spaces
locked up at every exit and entrance) – what she was
mostly aware of were bangs and booms and shouts and

slammings, and the pervasive tang of institutional cabbage and male urine.

Now she was sitting alone at one of many vinyltopped tables in quite a large bleak room with strip lights above and on its walls weird and garish paintings of ships at sunset and impossible mountains that prisoners must have done. At one end she saw a mini-canteen where a lady volunteer was selling cups of tea and KitKats. There were two warders in dark blue heavy uniforms at each of the doors, with their keys dangling. She and the other visitors had come in by one door and the prisoners were coming in by the other, in dribs and drabs, in their blue trousers and narrow-striped shirts. A number of prisoners were there already, paired off with their visitors. Some prisoners already seemed to have got themselves into a condition of rather anguished erotic yearning, which rather amazed her, given how raddled and old some of the women visitors were.

One fattish ugly prisoner at a nearby table, being visited by a man, was studying her roguishly as if he knew who she was. This, though she was not to know it, was Ray who (more or less with jamie's consent) had arranged for his brother's visit to take place on the same day as Tibby's. She carefully avoided his eye.

Then she saw Jamie – standing in the doorway, looking around. It was a shock. She had tried to prepare herself, but it was still a shock. He was different. It wasn't only the short haircut up the sides. He was different: he was one of them.

She half-stood at his approach, which was still a little stiff-legged; then they both sat. There was just that moment's hesitance, but they did not kiss. For Jamie too had been taken aback somewhat: Tibby had changed. Predictably, he supposed, but he was not ready for it – unmistakably the Sloane uniform for Tibby's age group; the high-collared frilly white blouse, the round-necked Guernsey pullover, the ironed jeans, the leather pumps. She had even added a standard string of pearls. A little hand had gone out to Jamie, but he had failed to take it. And immediately the hand was needed to adjust the fall of hair, by that required finger-combing movement.

Her Jamie sat there, remote, defensively amused, borrowed from another world. She could see the edge of the family crest tattoo on his forearm. He said,

'Cup of tea? Coke?'

'Coke?'

'Okay.'

Neither moved.

'You have to buy it,' he said. 'I can't. You got money?'

She collected herself, clutching her bag. She went up to the lady serving. It seemed to take an age; but even so, when she got back, she wasn't ready with the right thing to say to him.

She put a certain shine in her eyes, is it awful?' she asked, 'I don't think that's the word. It's . . . another world.'

She was still too flustered to take any cue, though what he had said was just as she thought of it.

'Vicky said you had in your cell the one who broke into your flat. And an awful black man.'

'I never said awful. He's moved out anyway.' He lifted his Coke can. 'I've got some very good men.'

'Good men?'

'One of them has no visitors, no letters. I wondered if you'd write to him.'

'Me?' It was an alarming notion.

'He'd like to get a letter every now and then. They call out the names of those with letters.'

'What could I say?'

'Anything. He's twenty-four, Cockney. Catholic of a sort. He had a pet pigeon the screws – the warders – killed. He's got psoriasis. He's rather beautiful.'

Tibby knew she was out of her depth already, 'I don't know him.'

'Of course you don't. You won't ever. He's got four or five more years to do.'

'What happens when he's released and comes . . . He'll have to have our address.'

'For him it's just the fact of having someone to write to.'

'What's he in for, Jamie?' It was the first time she had said his name.

'The truth is, it was attempted rape. But he pretends it was plain assault.'

She had gone very white and far away.

'He did know the girl,' Jamie continued, hastening now, in an attempt to retrieve the suggestion. 'He thought she was his but it turned out she fancied someone else.'

He could see his attempt had failed.

After an anxious pause she said, 'Tell me about the others.'

'There are sixteen hundred of us here.'

'In your cell . . .'

'Well,' said Jamie, easing back with a smile. 'There's Joe. He's my best mate. He's an Irish tinker and grew up in orphanages in Ireland and was molested by the Christian Brothers. He was bantam weight boxing champion for Killarney when he was seventeen, so he says. He's got a wife who was a prostitute and she's had four children by him. The first three are in care and the fourth is a daughter who's still with her mum. Joe isn't absolutely sure that she's his daughter but he loves her more than anything on earth and he lives for the day when he can be with her and her mother again. He comes out just about the same time as me.'

This made a bright frown pass across Tibby's forehead.

'Does she visit him – his wife?'

'She's in Liverpool.'

'Is he really your friend?'

Jamie's smile was partly in recognition of her straining to comprehend him. Yet he might also have acknowledged another part of him that did not want her to comprehend him, because he believed it impossible for her; she had not earned the right to. He said, 'I teach him words, and he tells me how he searched Ireland for his father to kill him — '

'Kill him?'

'For abandoning him to the nuns and the Christian Brothers.'

'Did he find his father?'

'In the end.'

'Did he kill him?'

'He planted turnips for him.'

'Turnips?' Her young brow was crumpled puzzlement. 'What about the first three children?'

'He went to look for them too, after he came out of prison last time round. And found them. I love Joe,' he added.

Now Tibby did not know what to say, or what to think. What was Jamie speaking about? What had happened to him? She knew it would be all rather strange – Vicky had warned her – but nothing had prepared her for this.

There must be a bridge she could cross to him by. She pushed her hair the other way, and put the shine in her eyes again, as she had learned to do lately with young men. She said, 'What about the other one?'

Jamie nodded covertly towards where Ray was sitting. 'Over there. Don't look. He takes drugs every now and then. He makes me laugh.'

Now she furrowed at him tenderly, as if it was his mind that was all mixed, not hers. But she tried to keep her eyes coy and shiny, to draw him.

'Oh, Jamie,' she said. 'You know what's happening in the New Year? Bundle of Joy . . . yes, she's in foal! Our own beautiful Bundle! Her first foal! And what d'you think! – Mrs Pierce is expecting her next baby exactly the same week! It's a sort of race. We thought we'd make a link between the name of Bundle's foal and whatever Piercy calls her baby.'

'Good idea.'

'I've got lots and lots of messages from every-body. You know Lorna's engaged? You'll never guess who to.' Jamie seemed to have difficulty filling the little pause she was leaving. 'Jimmy Sargent-Smythe. You know Jimmy . . . Isn't it really-really strange! I mean, exactly my age. Can you imagine? One of my really-really good friends. Engaged\ Oh – and Lorna sent her love. She said why don't you write your memoirs: you'd probably make a fortune. Have you begun to think . . .'

But Jamie had not begun to think what he was going to do when he came out. He was hardly think-ing about what Tibby was saying at all. Instead he was wondering who this girl was, of all the girls in the kingdom, who was the one to whom it seemed appropriate to send his Visitor's Order, and who had come to see him devotedly at his merest beckon. What composed her? How had she come to choose these clothes? On whom had she been practising the strange new mannerism of lighting up her eyes as if someone behind them, on the command, was striking matches?

But what now? Had she detected his thoughts?

'I can't understand how you can say that Irishman – what was his name? Joe? I mean, how can he love his little daughter so much, and his wife, if he's done those awful things. I just don't understand.'

'Yet it's so.'

'When he comes out, won't he go back to his old ways? I mean, in real life.'

'Real life,' Jamie echoed, and did not proceed.

'Yes,' she said, with something close to bitterness. 'Real life.' Why should he make that simple phrase a point to get stuck at? He must know quite well what it meant, if he wanted to.

Was this waywardness in him not in part deliberate? There was a fairytale she knew as a child of a Hebridean lass who discovered her true love became a seal by night and so might never be counted wholly hers. Yet by an act of will . . .

'I don't know,' he said. 'Perhaps not this time.'

It was her turn not to be listening. She said, 'Have you forgotten how to love me?'

She was looking at him softly now, with no one striking any matches behind her eyes. Jamie's eyes flickered momentarily away — away to a prinked moll of a woman, someone so needed, she and her forty-year-old lover-con in adoring, lusting goo, speechless at their vinyl table, lost in each other's imperfect eyes. And from them to a screw, watching they didn't overstep, and the same screw glancing at the clock which read 3.57.

'Where are you?'

His eyes came back to her with no answer in them at all.

'Your Ma says she and your Pa can't get through to you,' she told him.

Jamie screwed his face up. She could almost have hit it. Yet what she said was another plea from her little quiver.

'Your Pa's really lost without you.'

'Yes.' He himself could hear its flatness.

'D'you ever think about me?'

She began to trace the outline of the family crest tattoo with her fingernail, nudging his shirtsleeve up to reach the design's upper contour.

'What d'you suppose?'

That could be taken any way. Her fingernail stayed against his multicoloured skin. Amor et fiducia.

'You know what you always wanted,' she began so bold and shy, 'and I wouldn't let you?' Her fingernail drifted across his skin by fractions of an inch, and that is what her eyes followed, 'I mean, go all the way?'

She wasn't sure if he said anything.

'I've decided' – and here shyness rose against the boldness – 'that is, if you still want to – when you come out . . .'

His eyes had slid from any part of them, away to the table and even the floor; and any light there was in them had quite gone. He said,

'What made you decide?'

'I just decided,' she told him very softly, 'I imagined you'd be pleased.'

He did not believe her. It had a smell of Vicky, and behind Vicky of Rowley.

Her hand had drawn away. And when he seemed to have no more to say she turned her eyes full on him, a little fear in them – meeting his.

He said, 'Was it your idea? Who've you been talking to?'

She was colouring violently.

'Visiting over!' came the loud call from the senior warder present. 'Visitors please return cups and saucers to the tea counter. Tins and papers in the bin!'

At once there was a general stirring and clattering of cups and saucers, and farewells were rapidly exchanged. The door by which the inmates had entered had been unlocked and flung open, reasserting the actuality of incarceration against the brief illusion of its abeyance.

Jamie too had stood, and Tibby involuntarily beside him. She did not know what to do with her treacherous face. She sought his hand, found it, and almost at once had turned and was gone. From across the room Jamie saw Ray throw him an ostentatious wink.

''Urry along,' the warder urged. ''Urry along.' Warders wasted no Pleases.

Tibby was hardly aware of leaving the prison. When she reached the car park she wanted to run the last few yards, although she did not. Why should it be she that felt such blame? She got into her Metro and pulled the door shut and locked it from the inside, and cried, and cried, and cried, and cried.

Jamie returned to his cell in dejection. They could all see that at once, except perhaps Billy-Boy who was up on the end of his bed trying to attract pigeons with bread pellets and little noises of his own invention. Ray made a face across the cell to Joe, and Joe took it upon himself.

'Listen to this!' he demanded of Ray, and with Jamie's poetry book in hand moved to the door to block any prying warders from seeing Billy-Boy at the window. 'Listen to this!' He held the book high. '''She dwelt amid the un-trod-den''' (he had some difficulty there) '''ways/Besoide the springs of Dove/A Maid whom there were none to praise/And very few to love.'''

Joe was putting his all into the declamation. But Jamie, prone and black-faced on his bed, was not to be so easily moved.

Joe picked up again at once.

'"She lived alone, and few could know/When Lucy ceased to be;/ Bot she is in her grave, and oh,/ The difference to me!'" He paused. 'Isn't that amazing? Isn't that mind-blowing? A mazing?'

'Amazing,' Ray agreed, from his bed.

'"A voilet by a mossy stone"', Joe resumed, transported, '"Half hidden from the eye" . . . That'd be like Jamie's girlfriend, most like.'

Jamie remained unmoved. Ray looked at him sadly. But Billy-Boy had been reached.

'Ain't you got one about birds?' he demanded.

'Birds! Birds!' Joe riffled through the anthology in mock frenzy. 'Sure to God there'll be one about birds. Wait!'

He continued his search, frowning fiercely when, in the effort of making out various first lines, he discovered one poem after another was not about birds.

Jamie spoke at last. 'Give it to me,' he said, and found a poem about birds, a masterpiece at that, knowing of a grievous injustice done to Tibby whether by him or some form of destiny outside his control he could not determine, yet knowing also his own driven loneliness on account of it.

CHAPTER TWENTY-SIX

It did not take them long to become aware that Tibby's visit had in some way failed.

Failed in what? And which 'them'? For there was no conspiracy as such. It is true that Vicky had talked in private to Tibby before her visit, young woman to young woman. Vicky was no master of psychology, but she did suppose she knew her brother, and in a great measure that was so; and she knew something – a lot more than little Tibby, an only child, much protected – of the bodily imperatives of the male. It was indeed Vicky who on learning something of the detail of Tibby's and Jamie's friendship persuaded her to make the proposition she did. And what else could Tibby do but give heed to Vicky – seven years her senior, with her own live-in lover off the King's Road, and she a Mainwaring, Jamie's very sister? How was Tibby to know of the deceptiveness of siblings' similarity? – how the very same genetic ingredients can produce two of a kind in so much: in bone and flesh and skin and hair, in voice and gesture, scent and glance, in humour

and style and the wiring and speed and dodges of
the mind, in a million and more of clues and tastes
and common instincts, and yet in the truest occu-
pations of the soul a difference so profound as to
exist in utter strangerhood one to another? Tibby
knew of course of Jamie's quarrelsome childhood
with Vicky, not long behind him, and knew how he
would chaff her to her face and disparage her in
her absence. But to Tibby brotherhood and sister-
hood had always stood for a mystery of ultimate
companionship of which fate had for ever deprived
and disadvantaged her; and when, while she was
still only a very small girl, her mother had vouchsafed after her latest miscarriage that she and
Daddy weren't to try any longer to have another
baby she knew it was a source of irreparable regret
to herself too.

Nevertheless, something within Tibby had warned
her against carrying through with the proposition that
had emanated from Vicky; and even when she had
entered the prison she was still uncertain whether she
would, or should, make it. When in the end she did,
it was only done (she thought later) when everything
else at their meeting had proved so hopeless and she
felt she could not bear that he should be parted from
her so remote, so sealed away from her, without the
last arrow in her little quiver loosed.

For that was all their common purpose: somehow to draw him back to them, keep him with them
(some portion of him at least), to share him and love

him and be with him in a world they were all familiar with, the only world they really knew. It was not reprehensible, it was not 'selfish' – a ridiculous word, since where is any experience without the Self? It was only in their common cause: common to them and Jamie himself. But it had failed, a specific, granite failure in the midst of all the inchoate failure; and failed, ironically, because of that very sibling instinct by which Jamie had read the root of it.

No one knew exactly what had happened but Tibby, and she was not going to tell. Not Vicky, certainly. In her loneliness she could have confessed to Mummy, but there were secret things to be kept even from Mummy. No, there was only Jamie himself she could tell, must try to tell, through the inadequacy of written words. Mrs Hoskyns, for her part, did not pry, but knew what must be done – sweep Tibby up in the stream and gaiety of life.

Jumbo had no involvement in any collusion over Tibby's visit. It was Jane and, in her way, Vicky who saw in Tibby an agency for the restoration of Jamie to their midst. Jane had spoken of Tibby to Jumbo, and Jumbo respected Jane's judgement in many matters, especially concerning the children. But as to him and Jamie, his love for Jamie, he looked to no other now for any stratagem: it was between him and Jamie alone.

There were moments when Jumbo was aware of the divestment that had taken place. It was he and Jamie, Jamie and he, father and son, single now, and all but lost to one another. He did not know what

Jamie might feel: he was not even sure what it was appropriate for a son to feel for a father when a grown man, twenty years of age. Was a son then to 'love' a father? Yet not as a child would. Not at twenty, with all the autonomy of bodily maturity. A fellow had the vote at eighteen these days. He had heard Harry Fortescue remark the other day in White's that once his offspring had left school he reckoned he had given them ninety-five per cent of what he would ever have to give to them – and he didn't mean property. There was a truth in that which jumbo couldn't deny. But was that to suggest that love was reduced to a five per cent left to give, and a five per cent still expected? He did know that was not so, could not be so, that there was something wrong with such a method of calculation. He knew for instance that he would give what was left of his life for Jamie — that is to say, his life as it was now, all of it, not five per cent of it or of anything. As for Jamie in respect of himself, he could not assess the matter. He was not nothing to Jamie, of that he was certain. There was virtually no visible link between them, no palpable communication. He had not altogether lost hope of 'finding' him on a visit to Wandsworth, but he did not pretend to himself that their exchanges were anything better than stilted, dutiful, statutory, whether face to face or in their rare letters. He must go back to see him at least once more before his release: he would not give up. He did know still that in some manner he was fundamental in Jamie, partly perhaps in the way that all fathers are fundamental in all sons, but partly in some other respect: that all that had taken place in Jamie in this past tumultuous year or so, in the catastrophe of it as they would see it here in White's (though they were admirably gentle and tactful about it), in some way stemmed from him, from the sonship of this particular son to this particular father. To whom the son had always meant so much.

Meant so much . . . not now, as it also used to be, represented so much. Here was the divestiture he had discovered to have taken place. The caparisoning had seemed to have fallen away – just become unloosed and dropped off on its own, all but unnoticed. He did not know what might be left of it. Jamie had been for him Jamie, but also Eton, and Cambridge, and the heirship of Upton; and the name too, Mainwaring, Josiah's blood, his own immortality, Jumbo and his seed for ever as the Old Testament patriarchs would have craved their immortality. When he looked through the Candidates' Book here at White's to see whose election he might support with his signature, he often came across the names of sons of members. It was a familiar exercise of father-and-sonhood—family friends, naturally, proposing and seconding, not the father himself. Sometimes the names went down in the book very young (there was a waiting list of several years); for there was a space for Age, just as there was for Profession—'landowner' or, less grandly, 'farmer', 'wine merchant', 'member of Lloyd's', sometimes no more than 'undergraduate'.

If Jamie's name were to be there, what should be the entry for Profession? inmate of HMP Wandsworth'? 'Convict'?

It made Jumbo smile; and in catching his own smile he made his discovery of the divestiture. His love was all but naked now. No Eton hung upon it. No King's, Cambridge. No Mainwaring Group. Nothing of the social weave of friends' offspring, in professional and marriage stakes. Even no Upton . . . though here he could not quite tell. Upton had been Jamie's home always, all of his twenty-one years, and happy enough, and full, surely. And he, Jumbo, was not a young man. A home cannot be readily eradicable, as could a son's love. Ah...eradicable. Was love so? The boy had loved him once: he was sure of that. He loved him and looked up to him with love and had taken from him all through his childhood. He had seen it, and remembered it now – long deep talks together, walking, out rabbiting at Badger Wood, riding, fishing, shooting with friends; and on holidays together ski-ing, sailing. Driving him to school, visiting him there, attending plays he was in, concerts, the Bumping Races on the river . . . He knew how to make the boy laugh, could double him up laughing sometimes when he, Jumbo, played the fool, and he could take the boy's teasing, even his most daring impudence. Could he believe it eradicable? When the Prodigal was in that 'far country', when he had wasted his substance and would fain have filled his belly with the husks that the swine did eat, to where and to whom was it supposed that he could alone return but to his home, and his father, however finally it might seem he had turned his back on him?

Thus our Saviour's hearers took for granted two thousand years ago. No one cavilled at that presumption, not even now, in these days when it seemed the only morality lay in challenging every presumption. Maybe some fool would raise it in Synod, which had come round again, where once again they were discussing the ordination of women and where Jumbo, knowing that the proposal was grievously mistaken, had sat through debate after debate, himself one of a diminishing minority yet always unable to find expressible reasons for his conviction.

It was, indirectly, Tibby's attempt to make expressible, in her letter to Jamie, the reasons for the agony of her visit to him, that led to the break-up of the contented foursome in Jamie's communal cell. The cause was not in anything Tibby wrote, but in the physical actuality of the letter. What she wrote was still not what she truly wanted to write. She knew that to be so, even though she had written and rewritten the letter several times. (The cause of that failure was that Tibby was only seventeen; her education – however expensive – was weak and not least in the putting of her thoughts on paper; and all that she needed to explain was of itself greatly complex.)

Inmates' incoming mail was handed out in the respective wings when the men were released from their cells to collect their midday meal. This was done, as a rule, landing by landing. In the frequent moving of prisoners from one cell to another within any wing, the wing 'baron' Spike had for a few weeks now been occupying a cell on B4, and had already come to use any opportunity he could find to be objectionable to Jamie, who by the very factor of his class was in some way less subject to Spike's authority than the rest. In the pervading tension of life in any prison, the 'winding up' of a man, as the jargon had it, was seldom difficult and frequently engaged in – by the 'cons' among themselves and of course by the warders also.

As the prisoners stood in line with their enamel plates to collect their two-course meal dished out by other inmates from large containers at the end of B4 landing, the mail clerk (also an inmate) with his handful of letters and cards was moving up and down the queue calling out the number (the last three digits) and name of each recipient.

'618 Mainwaring!'

Jamie, near the head of the meal queue, indicated his presence. He stepped from the line, took the letter, frowned at the envelope (it had already, as usual, been opened and its contents read by the prison authorities), and put it in the pocket of his denim jacket.

Spike at this moment was coming by with his empty plate to take his place at the tail of the queue. He stopped opposite Jamie.

'Aoh!' he began in the mocking drawl he invariably adopted with Jamie. 'How's Mummie? How's Daddie?'

Jamie attempted to ignore this, though it was spoken straight at his face; and the queue shuffled forward bringing him to one place away from where the meal was being doled out. Spike moved with him.

'I heah we have acquired evah such a delightful little lady! Right out of the top drawer, what!' (Spike had not much creative originality.) 'Fancy 'aving a poxy prick like yours up 'er pussy!' he added for all the queue to hear, in his normal manner of speech. 'Got the family crest on that too, 'ave we?'

Jamie attempted to ignore all this also, and by now was at the head of the queue. But Spike had publicly put to the test his power to wind his victim up. As Jamie held out his plate for the shepherd's pie to be ladled on to it, Spike jogged his arm. The dollop of pie fell to the floor. (The man behind Jamie at once moved forward to receive his helping.)

'Aoh, pardon me, I'm sure. Nao offence!'

Jamie bent down with plate and spoon to retrieve what he could of the fallen food. Spike put his foot in it. In straightening up Jamie butted Spike in the stomach. It was poorly executed and ineffectual, and Spike instantly kneed Jamie in the face. All this, taking place low down, was not readily observable to the warder stationed three or four paces behind the food-servers.

Jamie's temper, however, had ignited. He launched himself at the brute-faced Spike who leapt back, throwing his arms wide, an enamel plate in each hand, glancing in outraged innocence and quite easily escaping the force of Jamie's unpractised attempts at blows.

But now Joe burst from the queue several places behind Jamie. He, the smaller man, flung himself at Spike with a rain of ferocious and skilled lefts and rights.

'Break it up!' came the warder's command like a rifle shot, and in a moment first two, then three warders had moved in on the combatants, with a fourth running up.

'Everyone stand still!'

One screw had Jamie in a neck-hold, another had Joe. Spike had dodged down the other side of the landing to take his place innocently at the end of the queue via the gangway that crossed the landing. But as Jamie and Joe were dragged away, backwards, with maximum force, their feet bumping down the open metal stairway, a warder beckoned Spike out of the queue.

'And you!'

'Me?' Spike's outrage was gigantic. 'Why me?' He looked down the rest of the queue, some smirking, in astonishment at such an affront to purity. 'Wot's all this?'

'I don't want to 'ave to 'urt you,' the warder said.

There was no need to drag Spike: his purpose was served: the penalty already calculated.

'Wot's all this?' he mock-frowned as he preceded the warder down the metal steps after the manhandled Jamie and Joe. 'Wot'm I s'pose to 'ave done? Bloke's a fuckin' menace. A ravin' maniac.'

The high window apertures of the basement punishment cells were bolted over with metal plates with holes drilled in them: these holes, about the size of a 2p piece, provided the sole access of light and air from without. 'Furniture' consisted of a thin mattress on the concrete floor, a chair made of stiffened corrugated paper, thickly painted, a plastic bucket, jug of water, and mug. Jamie and Joe had been dragged into adjacent cells. They had taken away his shoes and his wristwatch.

· Jamie had cleaned up his nose, which had bled either as a result of Spike's knee or the assault of the screw, in water from the jug. Down here, with the panel across the window, the familiar cacophony of shouts, curses and unexplained sudden noises was muted. It was not possible to hear any of the bells. Jamie had nothing to read – nor would be allowed anything here – except for Tibby's letter in his pocket. She had no skills of expression on paper, little Tibby. He had read the letter word by word, but only once. She hadn't been able to say what she meant, yet Jamie knew what it was she would have written if she could; and already he found himself experiencing, though scarcely past twenty, like Tiresias who had 'foresuffered all', the remote despair of so much pre-cocious wisdom.

After a while he heard noises, seemingly coming from beyond the window plate – loud whisper noises. He climbed on to his corrugated-paper chair and put his ear to one of the holes in the steel plate. It was of course – what else, for was there a trick in the place he didn't know? – Joe, perched likewise, whispering urgently through an air-hole in his own plated-over window.

'Hullo.'

'Holy Mary fock are you stone deaf?'

'I'm listening.'

'Ring your fockin' bell and keep ringin'. They can't deprive us of our dinner entoirely. If we keep ringin' the both of us they'll have to com. D'you hear me Jamie?'

The stratagem worked. In due course they got a sort of meal each.

The cells in the punishment block, being for men in solitary only and where nothing could go wrong, except perhaps madness which was nobody's responsi-bility, were poorly supervised by the warders. This had the advantage of allowing for extended conversation between the two friends, perched on their respective paper chairs by means of the holes in the plates and the three or four feet of open air, without much fear of detection. (It was of course against Regulations.) Conversation, or rather, narration, was that art-form which the Maker of Joe, to whom He had denied so much, had bequeathed upon him, and Joe was never to be accused of having left his talent to waste in the buried ground.

In this hard-earned fashion, Jamie learned a lot more detail yet of Joe's earlier, chaotic life with the wife who commanded his devotion, and his separations from her while he served his countless sentences and of their one remaining beloved daughter, now aged five or six.

'Kathleen' (Jamie's ear picked up) 'was going wid a bla'fla during that bird [prison sentence] . . .'

'Bla'fla?'

'Tha's roight.

'I don't get it. Bla'fla?'

'Black feller, Jamie, Crissake. Bleck felloo.'

'Okay.'

'Kathleen was goin' wid this black feller. She said, "I love him." And I was thinkin', what will this do for my little Esmerelda? My little Esmerelda admired that feller. My mind went blank. Totally and utterly blanked out. I said to Kathleen, "You go with him. But just as soon as he raises a hand against you, I will come over and kill 'im. If he lays a finger on you, I will kill 'im. Because I love you." 'You would not believe it,' Joe continued, and Jamie knew that this was referring not to what had just been said but to what was to come, for Jamie was well familiar with Joe's style of narration.

'You-would – not – believe – IT,' Joe repeated with his maximum emphasis. 'Kathleen said to me, "If you were to come out of the nick however many years from now, and wanted to go with someone else, I would find a place to live as near to you as I could so as I could just glimpse you from toime to toime—" Hold it!'

Something had evidently interrupted Joe. Jamie too skipped down from his chair, in the same motion whipping it away from the window; and almost immediately there was a key in the lock and his cell door swung up. The food roster was bringing round the late tea and bread slice. Absorbed in their talk, the friends had misjudged the time. Jamie moved to the door with his mug, and there was Joe with his door opened, out on the landing with his mug.

One of the warders said, 'Can I piss in your tea, McNally?' dangling his keys above the mug.

'Oh, Mr Lawrence,' said Joe, 'with all your wisdom, what might you not have said to raise me from my level of degradation? And all you can talk of is piss!'

The screw moved on with his fingers in his ears, and the other one locked him in.

CHAPTER TWENTY-SEVEN

The first time Jumbo had visited Wandsworth gaol he had gone there in the mood that was necessary at the time, namely a certain defiance, and had had Searle drive him there in the Daimler and wait. But that mood, and surely the need for it, had passed. Jumbo was at the wheel now, with Jane beside him, in the family Volvo, up on a Saturday from Upton, a bit muddy on the paintwork behind the forward doors and the dog barrier visible behind the back seat. They were both in country clothes – Jumbo in one of his tweed jackets and twill trousers and brogues, and his brown felt hat; and Jane too in soft tweeds. It was getting colder: the frosts had started.

She had his arm in hers, nuzzling him ever so slightly, as they rounded the corner and the vast forbidding façade of the prison, which they knew now, came suddenly into view.

They knew all the drill, such as it was.

In the Visiting Room Jumbo got up for the three teas almost as soon as Jamie joined them at their table. In Jumbo's absence, Jane had her hand cupped over her son's on the table-top. There were crumbs and sugar granules all over it from the day before: one would have thought someone could have brushed the place down. Jane did try to search out her son's eyes, but found not much more than the guarded self-sufficiency she had grown used to in him here. And before Jumbo had returned with the third cup, Jamie had slid his hand away from under hers.

'Dear Tibby said you were refusing to allow yourself to be got down by it all,' she was saying, regarding him with a quizzical pride now. 'She said he was even managing to enjoy some of it, didn't she, Jumbo? Your interesting cellmates.' She was to and fro between them, 'I think that's one up to Jamie, don't you darling?'

'I don't suppose it's much of a ball,' said Jumbo with a chuckle. Jamie smiled and stirred his tea. He'd taken to putting sugar in his tea, they saw.

'It's not so horribly long now,' Jane said. 'Only four weeks after the New Year.'

'Five weeks,' Jamie said, and Jumbo frowned.

'I thought only four weeks into next year.' 'I lost a week's remission.'

'How was that?'

'A spot of trouble. It's sometimes unavoidable.'

His mother was searching for marks on his face,

'It's all right, ma. Nothing to show.'

'Don't lose any more, though, will you?' Jumbo said.

'Nobody enjoys being knocked back.'

And Jumbo followed: 'What about your friend, Joe?'

'He got knocked back too. He came to my aid. He says he's pleased. He and I had the same release date. We're still the same. He said he didn't want to come out ahead of me.'

'What'll he be up to when he comes out?' asked Jumbo.

'He's got a wife, somewhere. And a daughter.'

'You find plenty to talk to him about?'

'Joe?' Jamie smiled. 'I tell him about Africa.'

'Ah.'

'He's forgoing half his weekly money allowance. He's told the chaplain he wants to contribute to an African relief fund. I tell him it's useless, but he's still saving it up.'

'Half of how much?'

'A hundred and seventeen p.'

'Is that all you get to spend?'

'That's right.'

'He sounds like a good Christian!' Jumbo chuckled.

'Christian?' Jamie echoed. 'Joe?' He would give away half his tobacco and suffer for it sharply for days. He knew about Christianity. Saint Joseph's Orphanage. Saint Somebody's School. Christian Brothers. Joe knew the church of Christ as bestial and he might reach his Christ, which he often did, only after cutting his way through memories of all the terrible things that had been done to him in the name

of Christ like a man hacking his path through tan-
gling, clutching undergrowth, in a way,' Jamie added.

They all drank their teas. And then his mother
said,

'He means a lot to you, then. . . ?'

'Joe McNally. Yes.'

They heard the certainty in him.

'Why specially?'

'He's a real person, Ma.'

Somehow it jarred, that answer: as if somehow
they had failed him all these years by their unreality.
It took a moment or two before Jumbo could follow
on.

'You'll want to catch up with your old friends.'

'Such as I have.'

'I doubt you'll have lost any. If you have, you'll
have learned what they're worth. It takes a spot of bad
luck to sort the sheep from the goats.' Jane's hand
had found Jumbo's under the table: just to touch it.
Jumbo added, incongruously. 'You should never have
been sent to prison anyway.'

Jamie could see how his father had aged. The first
time he had ever actually remarked the fact of ageing
in Pa was when he got back from Africa. Now he was
noticing it again.

'The Hoskynses are all going to the sun for
Christmas,' Jane said brightly.

'Tibby told me.'

'She's absolutely determined to learn to water-ski.
She's such a gutsy little thing.'

Jumbo said, 'I expect you'll gain a lot from all this.'

'More than a Christmas on water-skis?'

'I rather fancy the joys of life elude one if one has never known the pains,' Jumbo declared. 'At least, that's my experience – I'm in my sixty-fourth year, Jamie. I've known a lot of the joys. . . and enough of the pain to value them.'

And his mother wished to endorse that. 'We've known a lot of joy together, your Pa and I. The sort of joy we'd wish on you and Vicky.' She glanced up at Jumbo with a look of almost girlish tenderness. 'Haven't we, Pa?' Jamie knew her hand still touched his father's under the table.

Their joy, his joy.

'Have you, Ma?' Jamie said. 'He's never given you an orgasm, so far as Vicky and I can work out.'

The gabble of voices from the rest of the room made a ring round their dreadful silence. Jumbo had gone quite white and his jaw was clenched.

Jane said, 'You don't know what you're talking about, Jamie.' Her hand had come out from under the table and was doing something with her cup. 'Sometimes you make remarks to shock like a little boy.'

'I'm sorry.'

'I should think so,' Jumbo got out.

He was sorry. In the next silence he asked himself, up to a point, why he had said what he had. It had happened involuntarily.

They were thankful for their tea.

'We've come a long way to come to see you today,' jumbo reminded him. 'Your mother and I.'

'I know. I'm sorry.' He had made a prison in a prison, a cage for the three of them. 'How's Upton? How's Dribble?'

'He's getting lumps on his head. Mr Fellowes says it doesn't matter. It's just old age.'

Jumbo could think of nothing to say. Jamie's glance flickered on his Pa when he was not looking. It was in the eye itself that age crept in, not the skin and the hair as people supposed. A child came back into the eye, a vulnerable child.

'We are getting through the tea today,' his mother said. She began poking at her purse for coins, i'll do it this time, darling. . .Pa's able to spend a bit more time at Upton these days,' she pursued, giving them a cue for when she went for the next round of tea. She had the strength of two men, or twenty. 'He's taken to going for walks with Dribble before breakfast.'

'It's a good time of day,' Jumbo told them.

It was because he was waking so early these days that he was getting up in the near dark and setting off across the fields with Dribble. He liked the world then, he found, in its moistness and freshness, born anew. He noticed things he never noticed before – this very morning the grey dawn light making a dark red glow through a calf s ear like a stage lantern. Being elderly, Dribble kept close to him. It was a trustful world at that time of day, before it was bleared and smeared.

Sometimes now when he woke in London, in the flat, and he listened to the low roar of the city swelling inexorably, he was afraid: he sensed the power of it – that it was too much for him. But in the country he would be up at dawn now almost by choice. He hadn't got up so early since the war, since Burma days in the jungle, when he was Jamie's age.

'What time of day do they get you up here?' he asked.

Only now that Jumbo was chatting again did Jane dare to go for more tea.

For these days Jumbo was being relieved of at least some of the weight and range of his responsibilities. He had betrayed no symptoms of protest. Indeed it was he who, with the decisiveness and briskness that he had made the hallmark of his conduct of affairs, initiated much of the delegation of accountability from his own desk. He still held the chairmanship of the Mainwaring Group: no review of his contract was due for three years: if there were any murmurs or manoeuvres for his replacement he was not aware of them. The major decisions were still made, or at the very least confirmed, in his own office or at the Main Board meetings which he of course presided over. Ultimately the Japanese had the authority through their voting power. But Jumbo had not waited for them to exert it: he himself had been seen to press for the Japanese and the new men coming up on the English side to be given their heads.

It was strange at first, this leaving to others the follow-through of policies and decisions. It was like a nakedness, a leap of faith. Already these new men had taken parts of the Group into quite unexpected products and co-ventures he knew little of the detail of, and into areas of the world he was unfamiliar with, such as Brazil and the Special Economic Zones of communist China. These new men all thought globally, and of England as little more than a piece of Europe – an inefficient piece at that. His loss of personal control, of his own acquaintance with so much of what lay within his nominal command, troubled him at first – where it might lead, into what confusion and liability. Watching the share price, he found himself coming to depend on the judgement of the young City analysts, knowing how cold their vigilance was. The share price after the split had kept up well: but what a pretty pass to have reached, he reflected, to depend on others' assessment of his own Group's health, as if he were some outside investor!

Lately, other feelings had entered. The Group was no longer a family company. Of course, it hadn't been so for years – not since very soon after his father's retirement he himself had taken the Group public. But he realized that he had never till now truly shed his presumption of the Group being the Mainwarings' business. It was by that same token that he had always assumed Jamie would go into it . . .

Perhaps it was the demise of the Bolt Company that had brought the truth home. The Edwardian panelled grandeur of the boardroom unsettled him for a while: the boardroom itself could not but remind him of the Group's origin in the Bolt Company. He, and he alone, was aware of who it was who hung there framed on the oaken wall, of exactly what it was that Josiah had founded. He, and he alone, never passed under the lintel of the boardroom door without reading the individual letters of the elaborate monogram carved out of the central oaken scroll: MBC.

He perceived these causes of his discomposure, and dismissed them. He perceived the dilution of his power. He observed, since the Japanese came in, various of the new co-ventures overseas not even incorporating the Mainwaring name. He drew himself up. He would not have these things trouble him. He would not fret and rail into his dotage as others might – like the superannuated Anstruther, for instance, whom his pity had brushed at the Guildhall. Like some abdicated Lear. There was that within him which strengthened him not to: that which in some strange manner was rooted in his son, though he could not have delved how nor whether it came out of the darkness thereof, or the light.

Jumbo reckoned he had had to part with not less than a fifth of his capital to pay off the bank on the Bolt Company guarantee (Charlie Ryder was a good third the poorer). There was the further paper loss, which his wife and son had had to suffer with him, of whatever value their Bolt Company shares might be deemed to have been worth before the collapse. But the truth was that the Group shares he had sold to meet the bill had mounted in value since the merger, and although proportionately Group shareholding was much diminished, in paper terms it meant he wasn't much worse off. The rest of the Bolt Company creditors, coming behind the bank, would have to wait a bit longer for their money; but Carstairs and the receiver were struggling away with the sale of the assets, and the creditors had a fair chance of getting it all back, or ninety pence or so in the pound . . . There would not be much left for Jeremy Carstairs to do once all that was complete. Jumbo could see now Jeremy's limitations, and he looked back with surprise to the period when he had thought of him as a possible successor to himself as Group chairman. He was competent and earnest, certainly, but he had no imagination and no daring at all.

Sometimes nowadays he speculated whether he had allowed Jeremy Carstairs to hold him back over the years. The gift of life did in return demand daring. (His son had daring all right – like Josiah!) He would see to it that Jeremy got a good handshake.

Jumbo still served on the Council of the CBI, and usefully so, he believed. But he would not stay on the Court of the Bank of England beyond that year. He would have some more time for other things – for Upton, for Synod. He was concerned about Synod.

Far from giving the Church new direction and meaning in the modern age it seemed bent on making it more rudderless still. All these zealous churchmen, gathered together in their expensive new conference centre, thrived on their intellectual modernity. Proud as punch of it, they were. They thrived and the Church sickened. Knowing themselves to be, as believing churchgoers, such a minority in the community, they assumed the right to promote (often with quite unChristian animosity and even venom) every species of solution to the Church's contemporary 'dilemma'. And no one reined them in. The Archbishop had proved disastrous. That was unexpected. The fellow had had a good War, in Europe, as a young man. But now he had reached the top in the Church he had led his men, as one of the newspapers said about him, like the Duke of Plazatoro – from the rear.

The other day it had come to Jumbo where the error concerning the opening of the priesthood to women was located. It lay somewhere in the fact that in the division of the genders as ordained by God lay the seeds of religion. It was from that yearning for completion through union with the opposite sex that the notion of yearning for union with God was generated. That is to say, the yearning love of God by mankind, and of mankind by God, was mirrored by love between man and woman, in the presumption of fullness of union: and that presumption did not exclude passion.

It was no chance that the same words served. Love; passion; mystery; beauty. All were there in personal love, physical love even. He could think of Jane, her sustaining beauty, such as was never truly possessable but was the agent of mutual dissolution of the polarity of gender. Men doing, women being. Oh they could giggle and sneer, these modernists, these know-all iconoclasts, who supposed the human race had quite changed last Tuesday week. But they had lost touch with the instinct of man, which was buried so deep in man's enduring institutions that the fools could no longer feel it. They could not perceive any more that while to the male adhered one function in the worship of God and of His Son Christ Jesus, another function not one whit less adhered to the female. To the male the requirement to define, to articulate, to cerebralize, to construct, to ritualize; to the female to experience purely, to submit, to surrender. To do and to be. To the male the priesthood, to the female that for which there was no term to define it since to be beyond definability was the very essence of the role: it was Mary's role and all her Saints', known and unknown. And thus, by means of this dichotomy, a clarity and a power, which the Church by divine instinct – the working of the Holy Spirit – had allowed for in its evolution. For it was an intimation of the ultimate structure of the soul.

Could what he was now aware of be turned into a speech to Synod? Phrases came to him: 'Would Mother Teresa fulfil Christ's gospel better if we wrapped her in hieratic purple? Alternatively, could a *man* have ever meant to us what she means?'

Oh, but would those garrulous diocesan delegates, those busy bees, with their meretricious point-scoring, be brought to see the wood for the trees? And by him? – the 'old' guard? He doubted so. He could pray. He could ask God. He could ask God now in the quietness of his heart without the edifice of His Church. Sometimes these days, in the very Abbey of Westminister itself, when the three houses of Synod – bishops, clergy and laity – were gathered there for worship, he would be overcome with a sudden sense of the delusiveness of the ritual and the panoply: that it did not lead to God at all but misled . . . And it was not merely worthless but worse than worthless, that its forms of worship did not preserve the clarity and depth of the faith but enshrined density and obscurity. These were unsettling moments: he sensed a loss of inner control, like that muscular tic that had come to afflict his eyelid some months previously. But this was graver. His first experience of it had occurred at that 'industrial' service at St Paul's. Now, when it returned, it could seem for a moment to nullify all, even the music and the poetry, the beauty itself – all, instead, in a grotesque charade, tawdry, so much fading cloth and tacky wood. And from this masque of illusion in which all that he had grown to honour could seem caught up, his mind would take flight in search of refuge – flee to Upton church where all his long life he had given praise and thanksgiving, where he would be buried. There, on that site hallowed by so many hearts, he would recover his own heart to pray within, in open presence of God a Father and a churchless Son, and banish thus imagined fears.

Jumbo admitted age now, to himself. The beginning of a closing in. From time to time lately he had been experiencing a certain physical weakening – it was something near to fainting, he supposed; and if it came on him, as it characteristically did, when alone (in the library, say, at Upton) he would find himself glancing across to the nearest telephone wondering if he could get to it 'in time'. It was no more than that: an onset of frailty, an incipient dizziness. It seemed to him as much of the mind as of the body: a doubt as to his powers, an imminent *inability*. And things unfinished, he would think, with a tremor of alarm. Jamie unfinished.

He said nothing to Jane; but he did mention it to his doctor who listened to his chest and gave him something to take when he felt its approach.

CHAPTER TWENTY-EIGHT

T he wailing racket of eerie pop from Tibby's bedroom was audible all over the house even though she had her door shut. She had it on loud to enjoy the full effect of it in the bathroom that led off her bedroom as she wallowed in her bath. It really was too much – too much for her mother, at any rate, who came up to tell her to turn it down.

'Tibby?' she called, entering the deserted bedroom. 'Tibby!' (louder) 'you're not out of the bath yet and the Etheridges'll be here any moment. I can't hear myself think.'

'Coming, Mum.' From Tibby beyond, with irritation.

'You must turn it down.'

'You turn it down if you have to.'

The dials on the complex mechanism were confusing to Mrs Hoskyns, and the tape really was dreadful – a male falsetto yowling with a vibrating booming underneath. However, she found a knob to dim it. She called through,

'I'm staying to help you get dressed.'

402

'I'll be all right, Mum.' it's just what you won't be.'

She began to take a dress out of Tibby's wardrobe. Her daughter emerged from the bathroom in a towel with another towel round her head to keep her hair out of the water. Tibby moved across to turn up the volume, though not as high as it was.

'Oh Tibby, really! It's so decadent.'

'How come "decadent"?' But she did reduce it a little. Then she saw the frock her mother had selected. 'Oh no, Mum. Not that. It's pukey.'

Tibby crossed commandingly to the wardrobe and reached up for an alternative garment. In her so doing, the towel slipped. She brought down her choice of clothing for the Etheridges' visit. Pulling the towel round her she crossed to the bed on which she dropped the dress.

'What's that you've got on your back?' her mother demanded. 'On my back? Nothing.'

'Yes you have. Down by your b. t. m.'

Tibby was getting into her panties now.

'Oh that. It's nothing.'

'Let me see.'

'Oh Mum! Really!'

'Turn round and let me see.'

'It's a butterfly,' Tibby said sulkily, 'that's all. It's been there ages.'

'What butterfly? I'm going to see.'

'Oh *Mum.*'

Tibby turned reluctantly, clutching her arms across her young breasts, which were not for her mother to see either. She felt her mother drawing down the elastic hem of her panties an inch or two and knew what she would find. She flicked her bottom out impudently and twisted away, snatching up her bra to resume dressing.

'You've had it tattooed, Tibby!' It was shocking, it'll be there for ever!'

'So what?'

'I mean to *say*. . .!'

'Who *cares*, Mum?'

'When did you have that done, young lady?'

'Oh, ages ago.' Tibby had slipped her dress on now. 'Me and Jamie went to this tattoo parlour . . .'

'Tibby, I can't bear it.' Her mother was showing signs of a crisis. 'What *did* you and Jamie get up to together?'

'I've never done anything with Jamie. I've told you so hundreds of times.' Crises were infectious, taking their various forms.

'But those tattooists' places are *horrible*. You get every sort of disease. Aids, easily. It's dreadful. And right down there on your bottom! You'll have to be tested.'

'Mum, don't be *ridiculous*.' Tibby had to shout at her.

'Ridiculous? Me? And turn off that *awful* music.'

Tibby sat on the bed. Suddenly she was lost and altogether despondent. Her mother said,

'I don't know how you can do this to me, Tibby.'

Mrs Hoskyns in her bewilderment had absently picked up the container for the cassette still playing.

It carried the portrait of a near transvestite with Cupid's-bow lips and two horned bobs of hair in a post-Beardsleyan image of degeneracy. The performer's name was something German.

Tibby was struggling with some button or clasp on the dress which seemed purposely contrary. At last the tape came to its eerie finish. Mrs Hoskyns altered her tone.

'I'm not going to have Jamie pulling you down any more. I know how loyal you have been to him, but you don't understand. He'll drag you down with him. It's a terrible thing to have to say, but that's the truth of it.'

Tibby's face had become a bunched mix of fury, exasperation and despair. But her mother had more.

'Your father's seen it all, longer than I have. The Mainwarings say he wasn't really involved in that drugs thing. Well, naturally they would. But your father says there's never smoke without fire. You're not going to see any more of Jamie Mainwaring, and that's that.'

Tibby was flushed now, and watery-eyed. She turned hopelessly from the mirror to confront her mother.

'I love Jamie!'

Shouting again.

'Love? Love, my girl? How can you know about *love?* You're a child. You're seventeen years of age, You don't understand what you're talking about.'

Once again Mrs Hoskyns switched her mood and her tack. Her two hands went out to invite Tibby towards her.

'Tibby, my little baby. How can you possibly know, my darling?' She saw Tibby hesitating.

'Come, darling.'

Mrs Hoskyns got up from the bed to draw Tibby to her, to settle beside her on the bed. And she came; she complied. Her little face was all confused and crumpled. In a twinkling Tibby knew herself to have become the lost-in-the-woods child Mummy would have her be when she was at hand to find her; yet she was also hating herself, heaving inside with self-disgust for this surrender. She had begun to blub.

'Who is there to love except Jamie?'

'Who else?' Her mother had her arms about her, rocking her, together on the edge the bed. 'You haven't met *anybody* yet. A pretty little person like you – why, you can pick anyone you choose. But you're still too *young,* my poppet. You must give yourself time to grow up.' They rocked awhile. 'That butterfly – those things can be taken away, you know.'

Tibby's knuckles had turned white, clinging to her mother's taffeta. It held him to her, the little butterfly. It was the most treasured thing she'd ever had. It confirmed that she was *somebody.*

'D'you want to stay here darling? – have your supper in bed? I can easily tell the Etheridges you're not feeling well.'

Mrs Hoskyns' eye was moist too, understandably, as they rocked.

❧ ❧ ❧

Jamie and Joe were doubled up now, like most of the
rest of the inmates, in a single cell. They had been
moved together after their couple of nights (that is
all it was) in solitary down on the punishment block.
Prison policy was not to divide men deliberately, if
they were friends – although one never knew (no one
knew) what a Wing Officer might do out of spite.

On the wall above the bed Joe had coloured snaps
of his Kathleen and their little Esmerelda. But Jamie
had not put up Tibby's picture again since they had
moved out of the communal four-up. Beside Jamie's
bed were a number of letters addressed to him –
three or four at least – still in their envelopes, but slit
open along the top if only by the prison censor. The
top letter had the words 'Excess mail' stamped across
it in purple. A man was officially allowed to receive
only one letter a week, but sometimes they were
lenient until the warnings proved to be neglected.
The envelopes were all in the same careful girl's tea-
cup handwriting, with the number as usual before
the name.

Joe, the former bantam champ of wherever it was
in Ireland, was engaged in press-ups on the floor, for
which Jamie had to move right up to the end of his
bed under the window aperture.

'The curfew tells –' Joe began again.

'Tolls,' corrected Jamie.

'The curfew tolls the knell of partin' day. The –'

Joe collapsed on to his chest. He was doing his
press-ups in rhythm to the verse (on his fingertips),

but he could not stop himself reciting too fast for his arms and legs to keep up.

'The lowing herd . . .' Jamie assisted.

'All right. All right. All right. The curfew tolls the knell o' partin' day.' This was given very quickly, to occupy a single press-up only, but finding that worthless as a rhythmic stimulus he suddenly slowed the recitation rate to one press-up per stress. '*The lowing herd winds slowly o'er the lea/The ploughman homeward plods his weary way/And leaves the world to darkness and to me.*'

'Now fades . . .'

'I'm exhausted, Jamie.'

'Now fades,' Jamie proceeded on his own; but no sooner had he begun than he found Joe joining in with him, now lying on his back on the cell floor: 'the glimmering landscape on the sight/And all the air a solemn stillness holds/Save where the beetle wheels his droning flight/And drowsy tinklings lull the distant folds.'

Joe said, 'Jesus Christ, it's beautiful stuff.'

Both men had grown grey-pale, their skin etiolated like plants left long in dark places. For like the rest of the inmates, the sun's rays never touched them, month upon month; and since they must lie or sit in their narrow space twenty-three hours in twenty-four and there were no demands upon their limbs from one day, week, month to the next but to shuffle in a circle in a yard entirely enclosed by high, faceless, grimed brick, their bodies like their minds and souls grew devoid of function, save to eat, crap and onanize. And better thus to become.

Jamie got up, stepped carefully over Joe and with some rearrangement of buckets made a space by the iron door to get down on the concrete for his own press-ups.

The two men resumed, exercising in rhythm.

'Beneath those rugged elms, that yew tree's shade . . .'

Any such deliberate exercising was a novel thing for them, harbingering an Outside. An efficient body presumed a function for it – a task, a woman. Better as a rule to live without this presumption; here Inside were no tasks, no women. Woman was reduced to an orifice, a dank opening, such as was represented in full colour, testing the printer's art, hundreds upon hundreds of times on cell walls throughout the place. To desire was to exist: the necessary proof: but desire the absolute minimum, that was the requirement- desire not any woman, any person, but a hole. Women existed beyond, perhaps like the delectable, impos- sible mountains the inmates painted and which were hung up on the walls of the Visiting Room like imagi- nary windows. To desire *a* woman as an object of love, to summon sexuality in the cause of love, was a threat to reason. Jamie did know of such a possibility in the matter of love: he had explored it in the imagination of his heart and in what he had read of – the possibility of a love such as entailed an otherness to which there

was no limit, which thus embraced his own limitless-
ness: a love which revealed the ultimate function of
the self to be in its melting away. He did not know
whether such love was attainable between a man and
a woman or whether love that could happen between
persons was the intimation of a further Love that had
no name. Grown so old so young amid such enforced
inactivity he was sharply aware of the boundaries of his
experience. In this he was remarkable.

'You're ravin' mad, of course,' Joe broke in almost
immediately. 'Not even readin' the girl's letters. I
mean, you're stark ravin' mad, Jamie. I've a good mind
to write to her myself and tell her to believe nothin'
you don't say.' He paused here, on his tummy now,
to shake his head. 'A lovely young woman like that,
savin' every inch of herself for you. The pity of it!'

Joe's protest hung there for a minute or so. They
lay still on the cell floor.

'Nothing can be the same, Joe, when I get out
of here. I can't ever pretend it will be so. The old
mould. I can't. I've told you so.'

'But the girl,' Joe expostulated.

There was a silence that not even Joe would fill
for him.

'I don't blame her: she can't help herself. But she
has to be contaminated. I could see —'

'Contaminated! Mary's child, Jamie, what is it
you'll ever find that's pure enough for you?'

'There's a purity here . . . '

'Now I know you're ravin' mad.' Instantly Joe resumed the recitation. 'Beneath the ragged elms, that yew tree's shade —'

'Rugged.'

'Ragged is better. A lot better. If he'd thought of ragged he'd o' put that. It's a churchyard, for Pete's sake. You don't believe in God, Jamie, but I'm different. I do and I don't. I know how he likes his churchyards. Can't you see that?'

'What?'

'Well, God knows it's all passin', nothin' permanent. That's the way he's fixed it. And that's what he's remindin' the rest of us in his churchyards. So not rugged but ragged. You can see it in the rest of the poem. If you read it properly. That's just about exactly the point the feller's tryin' to make. In fact, it precisely is IT,' he added, giving mystic relevance to the smallest possible word.

'And what do you think he intends by all of that?'

'That's just what I was waitin' for you to tell me, Jamie, with your education and all the rest of it. What if he put that girl there for you and takes all that trouble and it's your only chance because everything passes away and you pass it UP?'

The night before Jamie had been listening to his radio after lights were out. Brahms's violin concerto had come on. He remembered a comment from Rodney Jarvis once about violin concertos. He said it was a remarkable thing how so many of the great composers wrote only one concerto for the violin. He said he guessed that was because violin concertos, almost always, were written as acts of love and that each man ever loved only one other wholly in all his life. So he could only write the one concerto for the violin; the fiddle being the instrument it was. Music meant a lot to old Rodney (it was he who had pushed Anthony into his choral scholarship). It was difficult to think of Rodney ever having loved anyone totally like that: perhaps it was some boy. Yet last night Jamie had come to see there might be some truth in it. And at the same time he thought, listening to the Brahms: if I had written this, could it have been for Tibby? Or would it have to be for someone quite else, whom I'm not even ready yet to meet?

He said, 'I think there is a sacredness to life.'

'Exactly that, Jamie. The gift of it. Even if you do terrible degradin' things with it. It got itself given. And not by just the act o' fockin'. Because, who or what got us fockin' in the first place? That's what he's remindin' us. . . Beneath those ragged elms, that yew tree's shade/Each in his narrow cell for ever laid' (Jamie had joined in) 'The rude forefathers of the hamlet sleep. . .'

'His narrow cell for ever laid! Mother of God!'

CHAPTER TWENTY-NINE

C hristmas was approaching and allowed no exceptions. Jumbo, although in tweed overcoat
and felt hat, had reverted to Searle on this particular
visit, and the company's Daimler. Searle had parked
unobtrusively, out of sight of the designated car park
and all the other visitors assembling at the prison
that mid-December evening. Even the warders, so
it seemed to Jumbo as amid the general gathering
he was conducted by unfamiliar routes to a different
part of the penitentiary's complex, had a touch of the
seasonal good cheer.

The stream of visitors was directed up the stairway at the back of the chapel and into the tiered pews
which surmounted the raised altar area from behind.
Thus the visiting congregation faced down upon the
body of the bleak Victorian multi-denominational
place of worship. More and more poured in, making
quite a crush. The prisoners were already assembled
beneath. They were dressed as usual in their denim
jackets over their striped shirts. A great hum of unre-
strained conversation rose from this packed assembly

of inmates, an indistinguishable mush of sound rising from an indistinguishable mush of mankind. Up in the visitors' tiered gallery, however, there was a quite a reverential or, at least, anticipatory hush. Jumbo found himself placed several tiers from the front, and somewhat to one side. They had all been doled out printed carol sheets by warders at the entrance. The lighting up there in the gallery was none too good, but one could manage.

In the centre of the raised stage stood the altar, which was a plain table with a cloth on it and a simple large wooden cross (nothing in a prison was of metal if it could be made of anything else). To one side stood an illuminated Christmas tree, and over on the other side a coloured stable of plastic or painted wood, and some straw and presumably – though Jumbo could not see them from where he was-the usual figurines of dumb beasts and the Holy Family with their crib. There were no less than four to officiate: the Church of England chaplain, a Roman Catholic priest, a Methodist minister, and a large man in a grey Church Army uniform, with eyes a-glitter with joy – that same man who on bringing Jamie *The Good News Bible* on his first weekend inside reminded him of Benjy who had broken his knees with a hammer.

Also on the platform was a harmonium organ, with a woman from outside to play it, and also a cornettist and a euphonium player, who were both inmates.

All began together to sing of Shepherds Watching Their Flocks by Night. It was not a notably musical sound, but it got everybody going and conviction seemed to swell as it went along until the final 'Goodwill henceforth from heaven to men/Bee-gin and never cease' might have had one believing that it had indeed begun, never to cease, but for the sound reasons immediately to hand for supposing otherwise.

Then everybody sat for the first reading. This was given by an inmate of middle age whom Jumbo could only just see by the back and top of his bald head. The man gave his reading in a flat expressionless monotone.

'When all fings began, the Word already was. The Word dwelt wiv God and what God was, the Word was.'

Jumbo took the opportunity to search for Jamie among the sea of faces below. He was almost certain to be there, Jumbo felt, because it was Jamie who had mentioned this Carol Service in a letter (he was rather touched that he should have done so); and although he had not specifically said that he would attend himself, it was a very reasonable presumption.

'The Word, then, was wiv God at the beginning, and frough Him all fings came to be; no single fing was created wivout im.'

Jumbo took off his bi-focals and gave them a good polish.

'All that came to be alive was alive wiv his life, an that life was the light of man. The light shines on in the dark, an the darkness as never quenched it.'

By this point Jumbo's eyes had settled on an inmate who must surely be Jamie. The build, the age, the colouring were right. He just hoped he would look up and they might make some small signal of recognition.

But by now they must all attend to their carol sheets for another good sing. It was the choruses that gave the opportunity to look up from the print.

> 'Nowell, Nowell, Nowell, Nowell
> Born is the King of I-hi-his-ray-el.'

Jumbo willed his Jamie to glance up towards him. They all settled back for a second reading, and another con, with an effeminate manner of speech and a touch of prepared ecstasy, was exhorting them from *The Good News Bible:*

'"Don't be afraid! I am here with good news for you which will bring great joy to all the people. This very day in David's town your Saviour was born – Christ the Lord! And this is what will prove it to you: you will find a baby wrapped in strips of cloth and lying in a manger." Suddenly a great array of heaven's angels appeared with the angel, singing praises to God: "Glory to God in the highest heaven, and peace on earth to those with whom he is pleased!"'

All Jumbo's willing was in vain. Then, just as the reader closed the book, the chosen face looked up, and in the exchange of glances Jumbo's expression lit up. The other looked away. From time to time during the next carol the object of Jumbo's attention looked back again at Jumbo, always to find Jumbo's gaze upon him. During the next and the final reading Jumbo could not reasonably restrain himself: when the eyes met again he made a little salute with his hand. The young man responded to Jumbo's quite surreptitious gesture much more boldly with two fingers raised in lewd dismissal of the old gent's uncalled for advances. Only then did the dismayed Jumbo realize his error. He felt the heat of humiliation rising to his face.

Thereafter, during the final carol, not only did he not resume his search – he dared not – but he also became convinced that Jamie was not after all present. He withdrew into himself; and knew that Jamie's absence from that service, because of the way he had discovered it, had left him not only confused but very sad.

Yet Jamie was present all the while, and had seen Jumbo, and puzzled that he never looked his way. He had even pointed him out to Joe beside him.

There was only a month to go.

And then there was only one night.

In the darkness they could see the night sky, the steep bevelling below the barred window assisting in their view of their allotted stars. Apart from the stars there was the indirect glow of the arclights shining down from the top of both sides of the perimeter wall. And in the cell the tiny but sharp red glow of their thin rolled fags, their very last, every now and then brightening to illuminate one face or the other, the lean dark searching interiority of the one and the passionate, humorous, combative saintliness of the other. The latter gassing. The usual.

'The worst beatin' I ever got – that was when I'd wet the bed in the middle of the night. I got up an' took off the wet blanket -1 was about eight or nine at the time. It was dark, naturally, and all the other fellers were fast asleep. Did you not ever defile your bed Jamie?'

'Not that I remember.'

'Well this was a special problem I had. So then, I worked that wet blanket right up onder the blanket of the boy sleepin' in the bed next to me. My idea was: to draw, very very carefully, that's to say, peel away onderneath itself, the actual blanket on which the boy was lyin' – the dry one. And put that on me own bed.

'I'd got it down about half way when I felt that somethin' was wrong. I couldn't rightly say what told me somethin' was wrong. But I stopped still a moment. Then I turned around and there, right beside me, starin' down on top of me, was the biggest of the Christian Brothers, the very worst of them all with the strap. Did you never experience that sort of trouble, Jamie?'

'In a way, yes,' Jamie replied after a pause.

'Where would that be?'

'When I was much much older. The other day. In that club in Bradford. When I realized they were out to get me.'

'But you'd done nothin' wrong!' protested Joe.

'Nor had you.'

'It's true I couldn't help meself.'

'Nor could I.'

Joe paused, to think about this.

'For you, Jamie, this place will come to seem like that place was for me – that orphanage. A long long nightmare. Tomorrow you'll be back in your own bed in your great house an' already you'll begin to believe it never happened to you at all.'

'Is that what's going to happen, Joe?'

'Of course it is. An' that very very lovely girl with the beautiful' – and here he left his own blank out of sheer good taste – 'all eager for you an' maybe desperate. Whose letters pourin' from her little heart you don't even read because you're crazy MAD. You'll go ahead an' become a millionaire like your old father an' reside in a great house, a mansion to be precise, an' have many many children. You won't be able to help yourself. All your children will gather aroun' climbin' all over your knees like that feller wrote about in his poem, an' you'll be tellin' 'em, "You know, children, I had a terrible dream once. I was locked up in a terrible prison. An' there was this feller there called Joe McSomethin'-or-other an' he was in there for unspeakable an' abominable crimes, an' I used to teach him poetry to rescue him from the pit of hell. An' sometimes, children, I'd wake up thinkin' 'Holy Mary, Mother of God, it really happened – it really did.'" Have you got any more tobacco, Jamie, at all, by any chance?'

'I've just used my last.'

Joe stifled the last butt-ember of his four-year sentence and watched the stars.

'Well, Jamie, tomorrow the both of us, we'll be able just to stroll into any shop at all and say, "By the way, I think I'll have twenty Piccadilly please – no no my dear, I'll take twenty Rothmans . . . I think I prefer the Rothmans, don't you?"'

'And what about you, Joe? You'll be back with Kathleen and your little Esmerelda. You'll be getting your rail voucher—'

Joe broke in on him. 'Oh for the love of God, Jamie, don't go believin' all that stuff. I'll not be seein' Kathleen, she's on the game somewhere or other, I've no idea where. Liverpool, maybe. I loved her more than any creature in the whole of God's creation, but that was all finished and done with long ago and little Esmerelda, she's in care too, Lord only knows where: I never truly believed she was my child though Kathleen used to swear she was and as God in heaven knows I did love her like my own child. You've got to hold on to somethin',

Jamie, even if it's just in the mind, in the imagination like. Out there I've got nothin' at all waitin'.
— NO — THING — AT — ALL.'

Joe had talked himself into a rare silence, in which they both hung. Jamie in turn crushed his last butt. At length Joe said,

'You've got everythin', Jamie, and I've got nothin', an' we're both in here together an' both goin' out tomorrow. That's the joke of it.'

On that wakeful night they had nothing whatever to gaze at but what lay beyond the bars and glass of their slanted square, their permitted stars of the winter's sky. The barred night sky, the silence bruised and broken by bangs and booms and curses of any prison towards midnight. Neither spoke any more. 'A *major convulsion is taking place in the Milky Way. It involves hundreds, perhaps thousands of stars.*' A voice – his own – in Jamie's ancient recollection. '*The whole constellation of Sagittarius could disappear.*' / '*Rowley's Sagittarius.*' / '*Do you know what it means to be a black hole?*' / '*Oh Jamie, do go away*' . . . and he had gone away. 'Out there I've got nothing at all. No – thing – at – all.' Nothing at all between his friend's head, the fragile sentient orb, the being's bony vessel, at rest there on its harsh pillow, in its capuce of cropped hair, iconic, a saint on a panel, and the convulsions of the Milky Way involving hundreds, perhaps thousands of stars. Millions upon millions, and their indecipherable artificer.

If a man is to endure a prison sentence, unless it be a very short one, he will have learned that he must live his life inside the penitentiary as if there is no other life to be lived but that of a prisoner. The truth of this fact was understood almost as well by Jamie as by Joe: perhaps even better understood by Jamie, since a man undergoing his first sentence, capable of marking what is happening to him, will observe the rivets and bolts of such a requirement being driven into place one by one. However false such a presumption – of prison life being the only possible life – may be recognized as being, there is the corollary at the imminence of release: the fear that the meaningfulness of life outside may indeed after all be proved illusory; or, if not illusory, in some manner forfeited, as for example a man who knows he has long sinned may suppose upon the point of death that he has forfeited the ancient promise of immortality.

It is therefore a moment of vertigo, and in this vertigo of impending freedom Jamie learned that sleep does not come easy.

CHAPTER THIRTY

Coming by the dining room Jumbo noticed Jane had laid for six. He went in. She must have prepared it the previous night, before she had come to bed. He knew young Tibby would wish to be there for breakfast. Vicky had proposed herself, he knew, and Rowley said he would run her over – it was only five or six minutes to Eaton Square from Draycott Place. So that made six. Jane did have a skill at making a table look welcoming . . . She had even drawn back the curtains. It was still black night beyond the windows.

Jane came in and found him there, he ready to leave in his dark green Raglan overcoat, she in her pale crepe-de-chine wrap over her nightgown.

'Don't you want something before you go?'

'No.'

'Not a quick coffee even?'

'No, I'm all right. I can wait. What time do you make it?'

She looked at her watch. 'A quarter to.'

'I'll go now.'

He went into the hall of the flat and gathered up also his brown tweed overcoat and the scarf he had set aside. He put his tweed cap on.

'You're really sure it's not better to call a mini-cab?' she said.

'Yes.'

He had already told her what he intended: that he would not take a car – but not exactly why. 'I'd rather a taxi,' he said now.

'What's the difference, darling?'

He was curiously stubborn, 'I'll take a taxi to somewhere near and walk from there. I shan't keep it waiting. There's no exact time.' (Half past seven, give or take half an hour, is what Jamie had said.)

'You won't find a taxi out there to bring you back,' she had pointed out.

'We can come back by underground,' he replied, 'I'd prefer that.'

'Is there a station?'

'Tooting Bee.'

It seemed to Jane it could take them ages. She didn't fully understand, but he was not willing to say any more, she could see that.

She made a tiny, checked movement in lifting her face, and he caught in her eyes the fear and the love – fear for him, for them both together in the unity of their love and their parenthood. He took off his cap and drew her towards him, and letting go the other garments over his arm, embraced her, he in his greatcoat and she in her nightie and crêpe-de-chine wrap and all the softness of her familiar femininity melting against him. Thus they held one another, with nothing said nor needing to be said, cheek upon cheek.

After that, he replaced his cap and gathering up the other coat and scarf, let himself out.

Jumbo walked for three or four hundred yards through the dark and empty streets. He walked past the church which had been daubed with the graffiti; it was still just possible to make out 'We are the writing on the wall', although they had attempted to erase it. Soon after he picked up a taxi.

It was near enough spot-on 7.15, quite dark still, the high glaring arclights blazing, when five of them came out more or less in a group, stepping singly over the raised base of the little postern gate opening out of the great arched doors. Wives were already waiting for two of the men: they and a third man moved off beyond the arclights into the darkness, leaving only the two of them hesitant. It was sharply cold. They looked strange to one another, Joe in his leather jacket and fancy flowered shirt, Jamie in the same blue suit he had worn in court. It seemed to Jamie that Joe was hanging back, in the deep shadow of the prison entrance's overhang made by the arclights. All he could see of him was his breath on the frosty air where the arclight caught it.

'C'mon, Joe.'

It was a deserted world. The prison faced no street of houses but an empty road and parking lot for warders' cars, and then scrubby wintered ground with a few allotment huts with some distant thoroughfare beyond. The habitations of domestic man shrink back from a prison's gates. There was no one about except for a single warder and a leashed alsatian on perimeter patrol. The light of the high arclamps was entirely white, and thus greatly cold, like the cold of a universe of unchallengeable indifference.

'Come along Joe,' Jamie repeated, 'or they'll find an excuse to pull you back inside.'

'I'm just breathin' air.'

'You've not told me yet how I find —'

'That's easier asked than answered, Jamie,' Joe broke in, moving forward at last under the high white light. 'The critical decisions of a man's life, such *as* – the forst pint o' bitter beer after four-and-a-half-. years, arise of their very own accord out of the situation at the exact moment in question.'

Because of the focused glare of the vertical lights neither man had seen the approach of Jumbo. All at once he was there, a few feet away, in his cap and Raglan coat, with things draped over his arm.

'Am I late?' he said. 'Here, put this on.' And came closer with the extra overcoat.

Jamie said, 'Nice of you to come, Pa,' quite jarred for an instant, though it was no surprise he had come.

'Slip it on. Ma insisted.'

Jamie glanced at Joe, a pace or two away under the full glare of the light; but Joe shook his head to decline the implied offer of the coat Jamie's father brought.

'This is Joe,' Jamie said. 'Joe, this is my father.'

Jumbo gave a smile, nodding to him courteously. 'I've heard of you.'

Jamie now took the scarf from his father's arm and wound it round Joe's neck. He said, 'Pity it won't reach your ballocks.'

Such a comment made Joe glance guiltily at Jumbo. He was so big and fine an elderly gentleman in his enveloping coat, compared to his bantam self.

Joe said, 'I'll not decline, *provided* . . . you do as your good father says and slip on that overcoat.'

Jumbo began to help Jamie into the overcoat he had brought, the brown tweed one. He knew his father's greatcoats of old: they lasted for years. Perhaps they were inherited like the family furniture. In pulling his first arm into the sleeve, Jamie's face came close to his father's under the hard light and he could not help seeing how haggard he was and red-eyed.

That done, Jamie said, 'Come along, Joe,' and at the same time knew his father had thrown a glance at him. They set off down the lamplit street. Jumbo said:

'I didn't bring the motorcar. I didn't want to seem . . .' He left the remark there, and Jamie said, Thanks, Pa.'

They continued in silence, and were soon among houses. But there were no taxis to be seen; indeed, virtually no vehicles or other people were about at all, it being still so early, until after a few hundred yards they were on a main street and the lights of a tube station became visible some little way ahead. Jumbo and Jamie were alongside one another, falling into step, being the same length of leg. Joe was to one side. There was not the vigour in his father's gait, such as Jamie had been accustomed to all his life.

It was Jumbo who broke the silence.

'You're coming this way too, Joe?'

He spoke it with a studied courtesy, and inflected it hopefully, as if to have added, That's a bit of luck for us. it's as good as any, sor,' said Joe.

Now they had just passed by a bus stop. An early bus was approaching from behind them, lit within, almost empty. And here Joe had dropped back a fraction, scarcely more than a single pace.

All at once Jamie realized that Joe had jumped aboard the bus just as it drew away from the stop. As the bus accelerated past, he glimpsed Joe through the steamy windows settling into a seat. For a moment, alarm crossed Jamie's face.

Jumbo had seen him too. He said, 'Was that your friend?'

He was puzzled. He heard a grunt from Jamie, confirming it.

'Where has he gone to?'

'Nowhere,' Jamie said, seeming quite casual. 'Anywhere.'

'He never said goodbye.'

'No.'

'You know where to find him?'

'No.'

Jumbo said nothing for a few paces.

'Has he got money?'

'Twenty-seven pounds,' Jamie answered.

Then they reached the tube station. It was a down-at-heel place, littered, a disregarded quarter. They both looked for their money.

'I've got change,' Jumbo said, and he was first to find it and put two one-pound coins down, receiving two tickets to that value.

As he handed Jamie the ticket there was an interrogative look in the father's face. Jumbo did not wish to seem to have presumed anything – did not wish to presume anything now. But Jamie took the ticket from his hand with a little smile.

The branch line's West End junction – for Sloane Square, for instance, or Victoria, the stations for Eaton Square – was Embankment. Three tube lines met there: the Northern, the Bakerloo, and the District and Circle.

By the time they had reached there, the early morning rush hour was already under way. It was remarkable how swiftly the gathering of folk built up, like hill tributaries in spate all swelling the river together;

but this river and its courses ran underground. From the central concourse, deeply below the city, passengers dispersed along three tunnels; two escalators also descended to that point, and one ascended.

In this central concourse, which was growing busier by the minute with its traffic of office workers, there they were, in the green overcoat and the brown: the one in the cap – the old one; the young man bareheaded. It appeared their progress had faltered among the mêlée, and had now actually come to a halt. Yet nothing, or next to nothing, seemed to be spoken between them – only some sort of interchange in progress. It would not be clear to an onlooker (not that anyone was stopping to look) whether the older man – and he did give the impression of being an *old* man, quite all-in – was pausing so as to recover his strength, or to enable the two of them to settle which direction each was taking.

But now something was happening. The older man appeared to forestall an intended speech by the young man by taking off his tweed cap and offering it to the younger one. With the cap off, despite the very marked difference in age – a good forty years – it would have been unmistakable to anyone regarding them that this was father and son.

The father was proffering the cap humorously, and the son accepting it in the same good humour. He put it on: it was a shade too big, and he pulled it down comically low. The cap had left a pink line along the father's forehead. He was making some comment.

'You can always pop it.'

'What?' Jamie queried, with a confused grin. There was all the noise of feet and passing chatter.

'I said,' Jumbo repeated, 'you can always pop it. If you get hungry.'

Jumbo gave him a comradely thrust in his middle with his thumb. It was a little stagey.

With that they parted.

Jumbo made for the tunnel leading to the District and Circle line trains: Jamie in his cap – more than Jumbo himself, now, an odd one out amid the current of office workers, but slower than the current itself – along one of the other tunnels.

In Jumbo's face could be read the ravage of this moment. But, as he was Jumbo Mainwaring, this was not a time for his courage to falter. He set off down his tunnel, finding – predictably so – the great bulk of early travellers flooding the other way, bearing down on him as it were. So he kept to the side of his tunnel.

There was no faltering of the courage, but of the body. He had taken, oh, not more than fifteen or twenty paces when it became necessary to pause. He felt himself trembling in the legs. It was needful not only to pause but to rest, to lean against the concave wall of the tunnel. He did not trust his legs at all, or his heart – either or both. And down they came upon him from the other direction, all these hastening people. How might he go on? There he leans.

Now he turns, and keeping to the side – touching it with his hand quite often – begins to go back the way he has come, towards the concourse. And even to accelerate, to hurry himself, quite markedly, clumsily, urgently.

As to Jamie, there was no comparable urgency. He moved with the tide, yet at his own lesser pace, through the labyrinth, to whichever platform, whichever train. Fragments of unfamiliar liberty caught at him – a young couple, office-bound, nuzzling as they descended the stairway; a young City fellow (a younger Rowley) frowning at the print of his tightly folded *Financial Times* as he went; advertisements promising the company of women; no one in uniform; an obliviousness of fear.

Then he had reached a platform. A crammed train drew in, doors opened, a few got out. Jamie squeezed aboard. There was that sigh a tube train gives as the doors are about to close, and at this point he ducked out, puzzling for a second whoever he had been squashed up against. The platform was all but empty now.

He began to return by the way he had come, against the stream of people. At first he moved quite easily, even without real purpose. Then a conviction emerged and grew, and then swelled to an urgency. He had begun to hasten now.

When he reached the central concourse it was busier than when he had left it – even in that couple of minutes. He did not pause there, but set off hurrying along the tunnel he knew his father would have taken for his home train. Now there was much urgency in him. He got right down to the end of that tunnel and on to the westward-train platform. There were a few people on it – some sitting down in grouped seats against the wall, suggesting there had been no train within the past few minutes. His father was not to be seen.

For Jumbo was not near there. Where Jumbo had wished to go, when he had turned, was by the tunnel Jamie might have taken when he left him in the central concourse. He had no means of knowing which of the two tunnels that might have been. He was not seeking Jamie to call him back, to call him home. Not that at all. It was that he felt himself going – dying, that is – and he wanted his boy Jamie to be with him when it happened. That is all that he wished: his boy Jamie to be with him.

He chose the wrong tunnel. Wrong or right, he could not in any case get very far along it. He soon had to stop, and knew his legs would betray him any moment. He leaned against the wall and saw that some young man was also there, scarcely five feet away from him, a long-haired scraggy youth who had turned to regard him suddenly with a look of animal ferocity. The young man had an instrument-case open at his feet and was assembling some member of the woodwind family – could it be an oboe? But this was as far as Jumbo could go. He slid down there against the wall, the concavity of it nestling him there into the angle with the tunnel's floor, his heavy green coat bundled and bunched around him. Though he did look untidy, he knew, and his feet sticking out.

And in a minute the young man had begun to play. It was indeed an oboe. He started one piece, then stopped, turned to frown fiercely again at Jumbo down there so close by, and started another piece, some sort of chaconne. Seventeenth century. He had a music stand there. The feet of many people hurried by.

There it was that Jamie found him. He came up to his father quietly. Jumbo recognized his boy by his trouser-ends, because when he had provided him with the suit a couple of years previously the boy had insisted on taking the trousers to a jobbing tailor to have the ends narrowed, that being the youthful trend just then.

Jamie crouched beside him. When Jumbo looked up at him it was with a fragment of the old good-fellow, man-to-man humour the boy knew him for.

Jamie slipped right down beside him, so that the two were slumped there, one right by the other, both pairs of feet sticking out.

'The old ticker, Pa?'

'I've got a thing of pills somewhere,' Jumbo said.

Jamie began to search in the tumult of the great-coat and found a little plastic box in some pocket. Jumbo swallowed a tablet with difficulty. Jamie read the box: it said 'one tablet when required.'

From time to time the feet of passers-by paused, turned or half-turned towards them. It was as if the old man and the young man were an act together. Penny-for-the-Guy. It was the wrong season. The feet did not pause long.

Jamie said, 'Where were you off to?'

'Looking for you.'

'I was looking for *you,*' Jamie told him.

Now there was a pair of fancy shoes, Italian probably, and sharp-creased trousers, an umbrella too, halted before their eyes; though Jumbo, moved by certain emotions, could not see with precision.

'Good morning. May I assist, please?'

The voice was clearly that of a foreigner. In any case it was unheeded. Jamie was looking at the father, scrutinizing and searching, as with love. His fingers were touching his father's sleeve. They were engaged in their own dialogue, without any words.

'Good morning. Thank you.' The note of chivalry rebuffed was perceptible despite the formality of diction. The neat feet moved on with all the others.

And the chaconne came round to its repeat.

'Take you home, Pa,' Jamie said.

'No, no. I'll be all right. A couple of minutes.'

'I'll take you home.'

Jumbo shook his head. A different, undefiant strength had slid across his face. He said,

'They're all there, waiting for you. A reception committee.' He paused. His breathing was fine now.

'Ma will be disappointed.' He could see the breakfast table. 'Come and see us when you're good and ready. I'll explain. Ma understands anyway . . . Better than I, most likely,' he added with a twinkle. He felt quite peaceful there.

'It's nothing serious,' he added. 'I'm all right now in any case. Come with me to the escalator. I'll go up and get a taxi.'

He put out his two hands in front of him. Jamie stood, and planting himself opposite his father took his hands and helped him to his feet.

'You see,' Jumbo said with a grin, 'I couldn't have managed without you.'

For all of twenty years.

Now Jumbo drew himself up like a soldier, filling his chest out, turned decisively in his chosen direction, and offered his arm to Jamie. Thus they set off into the main concourse, towards the escalators.

There at the centre Jumbo paused and said, 'When you went off just now, it wasn't – I expect – to anywhere in particular, was it?'

'No,' said Jamie, smiling.

'Searching for the truth,' Jumbo said, and then set off on his own the last few paces to the foot of the escalator.

Jamie watched the figure of his father being carried away from him. The oboe was audible even here.

He watched him right to the top, and saw him step off confidently, until he was visible no more. Then he turned, and let the stream of people carry him along the tunnel he had chosen first.

1836-1900	Josiah Mainwaring
1861-1934	his son, the first baronet
1895-1966	his son
b. 1924	Sir James ('Jumbo') Mainwaring
b. 1967	Jamie Mainwaring

Made in the USA
San Bernardino, CA
31 March 2017